Co f Cats

By

Bev Harris

Happy Reading

Bev Harris

x

This is a work of fiction. Names, characters, places, and incidents either are the product of the author's imagination or are used fictitiously. Any resemblance to actual persons, living or dead, events, or locales is entirely coincidental.

ISBN - 9781068514906
Ebook ISBN - 9781068514913

First paperback edition August 2021
First Published in the UK by Olympia 2021
Reissued by Bev Harris Books (B. C. Harris) in 2024

www.bcharrisauthor.com

Cover from an original work 'The White House' by artist Vanessa Reynolds. Reproduced here with her kind permission.
www.Vreynoldsart.com

About the Author

Bev Harris is a Scot who, at the time of writing, had just finished renovating a farmhouse in France. A labour of love that began from first sight back in 2016. No sooner had the final length of flooring been laid and the last paintbrush dried, than disaster struck in the form of pandemic. France went into a strict lockdown and, with time to do more than simply daydream about writing books, a new project began to take shape.

Writing began as an escape from the fear and isolation that was soon affecting us all, and quickly flourished to become 'Conspiracy of Cats'. The global pandemic seems to be receding now, but the passion for writing has taken root. Find out more about Bev Harris online.

X: @BCHarris64
Instagram: @beverleycharrisauthor
Facebook: @AuthorBCHarris
Threads : beverleycharrisauthor

'… builds to a tense, sometimes frantic but satisfying conclusion…'
LoveReading Ambassador

'A remarkably original story written in a vivid and lively style…'
Penny Haw, Author of *The Wilderness Between Us*, *The invincible Miss Cust and The Woman at the Wheel.*

'… don't miss this fantastic feline work of fiction…'
Laura Lyndhurst, Author of *You Know What You Did,* the *Criminal Conversation trilogy* and other works

'… magical!'
Author, Lis McDermott

'… a first class debut novel.'
Tom Boles, Author of *Dark Energy, Shades of White* and *Murder comes by Limo*.

Also by Bev Harris

Making Sacrifices

To the world she is Vida.

To Isaac Saddler she epitomises only fear, the stuff of his nightmares, willed into existence through art and writing.

Transformed from victim to warrior, she became Vida, Queen of the Vidian Empire.

But Vida doesn't just exist between the pages of a book.

High on Exmoor archaeologists think they've found ancient remains, but the body proves to be evidence of a modern murder. A facial reconstruction publicised by the police quickly goes viral.

Now Isaac must find out why the woman of his nightmares ended up in a bog pool close to his childhood home.

A lifetime of secrets that threaten to undermine his entire existence.

Coming soon…

A Murder of Crows

Dedication

This book is primarily dedicated to every single reader… without you there wouldn't be any point. So, thank you for choosing to read this book.
To make me love you even more, dear reader, please consider leaving me an honest review. I will be forever in your debt.

*

I also dedicate this book to my husband. A wonderful man, who loves me and believes in me.

*

Last, but never least, I dedicate this book to my daughter. This is how I get to leave something of myself behind. For you.

Acknowledgements

Thank you, Africa, for the sights, the sunsets, the colours and the inspiration.
I shall return.

CHAPTER ONE

Jos Ferguson was twenty-four, five foot ten, with a cloud of thick, wavy, red hair. She was Scottish, so her skin tone was pale bordering on translucent, with a generous helping of freckles. She was on the plain side of pretty but did scrub up well when she could be bothered. Or maybe that should be when she absolutely had to be bothered, because Jos wasn't really one for choosing to socialise. At that moment she was disembarking from the flight that had brought her to Tanzania. This was going to be a wonderful holiday, an adventure, a chance to see the house her uncle built before she was born. It could as easily be a nightmare, and Jos wondered for the millionth time if she was doing the right thing.

Had Jos known that she was about to play a leading role in a story that had begun with murder and was destined to end the same way, she'd have fled Kilimanjaro International Airport and run all the way back to Edinburgh.

But she didn't, so Jos carried on putting one foot in front of the other and carried on smiling as if she was having the best time. Just her, that encouraging veneer, and a big old Fendi bag salvaged from a pile of unwanted possessions Auntie Jude had recently earmarked for the local charity shop.

The bag was stuffed with all the distractions Jos imagined she'd need when packing for her journey, two books… a crime thriller by Richard Montanari, and a book on Tanzania so she could swat up on the country of her hosts. She had lipstick, hairbrush, hair bands and clips, tissues, all her cash, debit cards, travel documents and tickets, camera, mobile, a summer top, sunnies and a pair of comfy flats. Nothing sharp and nothing flammable. She'd hardly touched any of it, except the summer top, which she changed into shortly before landing, because flying first class was a distraction in itself. A first for Jos, who hadn't ever travelled much beyond Scotland.

The lovely flight attendants had taken care of her every need throughout the nine-hour, overnight journey. There had been too much champagne, luxury chocolates, a fully reclining seat and a

17" TV. There was a lavender infused pillow, fluffy blanket, comfy slippers and cotton PJs. A selection of colourful canapes, served on white bone China. A fantastic five course dinner served when Jos felt like it. Drinks arrived in glasses, with ice and a side dish of warm, mixed nuts. There was also a Bo Mallory goodie bag stuffed with an array of useful and luxurious items. There were noise cancelling earplugs and a black velvet eye mask. Cotton socks. Luxurious lip balm, hand lotion, cleanser, eye serum and moisturiser. A small bottle of the latest perfume. Not a tiny tester with a plastic stopper, but a small and perfectly formed glass bottle of eau de toilette. Well rested after a decent four-hour sleep, (it could have been longer if only there hadn't been so many distractions) Jos had polished off a delicious three course breakfast, shortly before freshening up in the roomy and well stocked ladies' toilet. How the other half fly!

Jos had found herself in that other half thanks to resources left behind by Uncle Peter. There was the money that Jude lived on, as well as the house he'd built for them. The white house… both Jude and her old, Tanzanian friend, Beola Nyerere, referred to it as such, was supposed to have been their forever home. But their African adventure had ended in tragedy fourteen years previously when Peter died suddenly. Jude had flown back to England with his body and, once the funeral formalities were over in his native Wiltshire, had retreated to her home town of Edinburgh where she remained to that day. Jude had declined the invitation to join Jos on this trip, citing an unwillingness to be overwhelmed once more by a loss she was yet to get over.

Jos had allowed herself to be talked into making the trip alone by Beola, Peter and Jude's one-time housekeeper who was still keeping house after all these years. The thought terrified Jos; she never went anywhere more challenging than the local shops alone. She rarely went out at all. But Jos was also fed-up living like that. She was an adult, and it was about time she started behaving like one.

Jude hadn't voiced an opinion either way, at least not directly. 'It's entirely up to you, toots', she would say, in a dismissive tone that clearly suggested she would rather Jos did no such thing. But then Judy always got moody whenever the subject of her past life came up. Over the years Jos had learned to avoid the combined subjects of Peter and Africa, because it nearly always ended badly.

Avoiding talking about Africa proved increasingly impossible as departure day loomed and living with Jude had become somewhat challenging.

There was flouncing in and out of rooms, doors slammed, days when Jude rarely emerged from her bedroom, days of stilted conversation, meals eaten in silence, and at least one meal ruined because Jude abandoned it half way through cooking. She'd then taken up position, perched on a stool at the island, with a bottle of wine and a large glass, glowering, sulking, and generally making it very uncomfortable for Jos to be in the kitchen too. All because Jos had just answered the door to the courier who'd brought her a first-class ticket to Africa, and she'd come to share this exciting news with Jude. It went down like a lead balloon, and Jos ended up having a pizza delivered which she ate in her room. Nearly every day, Jos ended up feeling miserable, guilty, or both, because Jude reacted badly to some little thing, unintentionally said or done. By the time travel day finally arrived, she was glad to be leaving.

Having disembarked along with the rest of the group of just fourteen privileged people, Jos was guided from plane to passport control by Richard Isherwood, an elderly gentleman, also travelling alone, who had been her closest neighbour during the flight. Just as well, as Jos really didn't have a clue what was expected of her, never mind where she should go. It wasn't a huge airport like Heathrow, and the signage was all in English, but, under her smiling exterior, Jos was a nervous wreck. Again… what was she thinking? Strange country, strange culture, strange food, strange people, strange house.

The white house had a beautiful guest room with its own bathroom as well as garden, according to Beola. Jos would have all the privacy she needed. Beola's son, Ben, ran a small safari business, so she could travel into the bush whenever she liked knowing that he would be there to watch over her. Ben would pick her up from the airport too. There was no need to worry about anything.

Beola would organise everything.

Beola's voice was like rich velvety chocolate, smooth and sweet and irresistible. 'Come to Africa, Jos. Come and visit with us. We will take good care of you. Peter was more than just my boss. He was my very good friend. He was like my brother. We are all family here.'

*

Jos was rather family challenged as far as blood relatives went. A freak accident in a roadside café had killed both her parents. It was February in the Scottish Borders and less than five minutes' drive from their home. It had been snowing. The sky was dark and brooding with the promise of more to come. Car radio travel bulletins all warned of ice on the roads, so Julia Ferguson had driven with extra care and attention. They'd stopped at a favourite café on the way home from the weekly shopping trip. They had window seats, guzzling milk shakes and scoffing burgers, bouncing in time to the rock n roll music the owners always played a little too loud. Mike Ferguson had one side of the booth all to himself. He'd slipped on the iced over backdoor steps three weeks previously, landed badly and broke his left leg in three places. He was plastered from toes to thigh so, even though he was sitting in the middle of the two-seater, his foot still stuck out into the aisle. Their waitress had provided a 'caution wet floor' sign to help other customers navigate around this errant foot.

Julia, sitting opposite next to Jos, was closest to the steamy window. They were all laughing, singing along between mouthfuls, when Julia saw the truck out of the corner of her eye. She noticed it because its headlights were shining right at her.

They shouldn't have been.

The jauntily painted yellow and blue truck had half crashed through, half bounced over the low wall separating the café car parking from the narrow road. It had hit ice, skidded, and, no matter what the driver did, it was by then out of his control. He had not been speeding, but neither had he been driving with the extra care and attention the weather conditions demanded. He'd taken the nearby bend far too fast and now the truck was heading straight for the front of the café, with nothing but an old beat-up

Ford Escort and a plate glass window between it and the diners. The brakes had locked, the steering too. It wasn't a big truck, but it was carrying a fullsized skip containing over five tonnes of builder's rubble. The driver didn't understand physics, but he did know that, even if the truck was forced to stop, the load would carry on moving forward at the same speed the truck had been going before stopping. Lights out Vienna.

Julia feared the worst. Without hesitation she shoved her daughter hard to the side, sending Jos flying out of the booth and onto the floor, where she sat, stunned, covered in chocolate milkshake. Julia didn't stop to see that, because she was too busy launching herself across the table, hoping her momentum would be enough to do the same to her as well as her beloved husband, who was looking at her like she'd gone mad.

With his life flashing before his eyes, the driver gripped that steering wheel and twisted rightward for all he was worth. His voice roared with the effort, tyres screeched, skidding over the loose surface, which was more hardcore, than hard top. Just as the truck was about to hit the car, it turned enough to point the cab away from the café. As predicted the skip's momentum carried it onward, or rather sideward now, as it was still trying to follow the original trajectory. The nearside main arm and jackleg began to bend inward with an ear-splitting whine. The truck stalled in position as the now shrieking engine battled with the sideward motion of the sliding skip as it crashed into the far side arm and jackleg. The driver then felt his truck beginning to tip sideways and knew the skip was winning. Stalled for no more than a second by the other half of the lifting gear, it was just too heavy, and the metal arm buckled and folded. The skip swung out into space, almost gracefully, forward and downward. One chain snapped, and it became a skip shaped wrecking ball, slamming into the Escort and batting it through the plate glass like it was a car shaped ping pong ball.

The skip then landed roughly where the car had been, stopping the truck from tipping all the way over.

Julia only succeeded in tipping Mike to the side, as his plastered leg rigidly refused to budge. Her momentum gave out against the right side of his chest, so she just scrambled over the table, grabbed onto him and held on, her face buried into his neck.

He was still wondering what the hell his wife was up to when the Ford Escort smashed through the window. He barely had time to register what was happening, or the huge shards of glass exploding outward all around him, before the car landed half on their table and half on top of their still embraced bodies. They both died instantly.

Jos was still sitting on the floor when the car crashed into her little world and crushed both her parents. The bulk of the back-to-back booth seating shielded her from shrapnel. She only staved a wrist, but that was because she'd landed on it after her mother saved her life. She had nightmares for many years afterwards.

The truck driver walked away with minor cuts and abrasions. He also suffered from nightmares.

*

That was the day Jude Sinclair became Jos Ferguson's only living relative.

Jude rarely answered the phone but, for some reason, she'd picked it up that day. A phone call from a senior police officer who delivered the dreadful news about her sister and brother-in-law. There were a few moments of silent shock, followed by a few more moments of hushed indecision, and then Jude agreed to take responsibility for her niece. By the time she'd driven down to Melrose where Jos was being looked after at the police station, she'd composed herself. Julia and Mike were both dead, and their fifteen-year-old daughter needed Jude more than she needed to live inside the reclusive shell constructed since the death of her husband. So, Jude swept in and took control.

First, she took Jos home to collect enough of her belongings to be getting on with. The girl was understandably traumatised and wouldn't enter the house, so Jude just grabbed what seemed appropriate, packed it into one case, locked everything up and headed back to Edinburgh. Funeral arrangements, pension and insurance claims. Jude dealt with it all. When the legalities needed to be attended to, Jude contacted Peter's lawyers and they sent one of their minions up to Edinburgh to ensure she got full custody of Jos. When the time came, several years later, Jude also handled the sale of the Ferguson home.

Jude was Julia's older sister. Julia was the sensible one and Jude the wild one… although Jos hadn't ever seen any evidence of that. The Jude she knew was sensible to the point of being boring, though very astute when it came to finance. Jude had seen to it that all the various payments made to Jos upon the death of her parents, and later on the proceeds from the house sale, were invested on her behalf. When Jos was in her thirties these investments would begin maturing and, as long as she was careful, she shouldn't have to worry about money again. Until then she could continue living with Jude, a woman met only twice prior to the day fate joined them together.

The first time they met was soon after Jos was born. Jude and Peter had flown in from Africa. They stayed for a number of weeks and, when they flew off again, they left an album crammed with the happy and vibrant family photographs which were Jos' only recollection of the event.

The second time Jos met Jude was years later, and after Peter died. Jude had recently returned to Edinburgh where she bought a big old house in The Grange. She kept in touch with her little sister initially with the odd phone call. But Jude stopped calling and eventually stopped answering too. After a few months Julia insisted on a trip up to Edinburgh because she was worried.

That Jude was withdrawn, the life sucked out of her. The vivacious energy portrayed in those earlier photographs was gone. Even her bright orange hair seemed dulled by her loss. She wasn't really pleased to see her sister, so the visit was uncomfortable. Jude just kept insisting she wanted to be left alone, she needed time. But Jude remained distant no matter how much time passed. Years of never visiting or seeking visitors, rarely even answering her phone. She shut herself up inside her big old house and allowed the mature trees surrounding it to shield her from life.

The death of Jos' parents punched a hole in that shell, and that big old house had become her home too. She'd found it as easy to withdraw inside the safety and seclusion of its walls. Just her, Jude, and a small colony of cats, all living in their own little world.

Until that evening, not so long ago, when Beola burst the bubble.

*

Jude Sinclair never rattled, but she did float around in her late Victorian, stone built, detached villa in an exclusive and leafy district in Edinburgh's south side. Eight bedrooms… four small ones up in the gods and four ginormous ones on the first floor. There were two dressing rooms, three reception rooms, two kitchens, five bathrooms, a conservatory, a utility room, a boot room and an enormous walled garden. Much too big for the single woman who'd moved in, but it cost very close to the upper limit of the budget she was assigned from Peter's estate.

At the time that had mattered a lot.

This lovely old house was also home to a small collection of otherwise wayward cats; they died, they went missing, they may or may not be replaced depending upon the new cats that wandered in and hung around for more than a passing saucer of kibbles. If they chose to stay the night then Jude would whisk them off to the vet the following morning, get them checked, get them done, get them deloused and microchipped and take earnest responsibility for them. Most of them were literally stunned into submission by the rapid onslaught of medical interventions and Jude's obvious adoration. They were all named after dictators or dictators' wives.

Eva and Joseph, Augusto and Elena to name but four.

Imelda was the perceived oldest, the very first stray to stay, and the reason for Jude's absence when Africa called.

'Vet thinks Imelda was hit by a car,' Jude announced as she came in the front door toting said cat inside a pink plastic carrier, heels tap tapping across the tiled floor of the entrance hall. Her skirts swayed in layers of black crepe topped off with a floral chiffon blouse. Her once frizzy red hair was tamer these days, struck through with blonde and silver, piled up haphazardly and held in place with crystal encrusted combs and clips. Her make-up was immaculate as usual. A very attractive fifty something. 'Common injury apparently. Cat runs in front of a moving car, car clips the back end, sending the cat face first into the kerb.'

Placing the carrier on the floor, she released Imelda who immediately fled past Jos on her way upstairs. 'She's lucky her jaw wasn't broken, but she has lost a few teeth.

I've to feed her by hand for a few days and see how we go.' No response from Jos.

Glancing at her obviously distracted niece, sitting on the stairs next to the phone, Jude wondered, 'Anything happen while I was gone?'

'Beola called.'

On her way to the under the stairs cupboard to replace the cat carrier with several others stored in there, Jude stopped dead. 'Beola Nyerere?' As if there were lots of Beola's out there just dying to call. Mostly Jude was wondering how the hell Beola had gotten her number.

'She was looking for you.'

Jude opened the cupboard door and stashed the carrier. 'I doubt that.'

Jos frowned, 'Why would you say that?'

There was a time when any mention of Beola Nyerere would have inspired raging and ranting from Jude, but she kept a tight leash on those demons these days. At least on the outside. 'Me and Beola never really gelled…' she said. 'I didn't make much effort to keep in touch and neither did she. Seeing as Peter's already dead perhaps she called to let me know Kissi died?'

'Jude!' Jos was open mouthed with shocked. 'What a thing to say!'

Then she wondered, 'Who's Kissi?'

'Beola's husband. He was a ranger back then… maybe he still is. Maybe something ate him,' Jude winked to counter her niece's renewed shock. 'Being a ranger is a dangerous job, Jos. What did you and Beola really talk about?'

'The white house.' The idea of it had stuck, and Jos was becoming increasingly sure she was going to go through with the crazy plan. 'She asked if we would like to go for a visit.'

Jude sighed loudly. 'I loved that house.'

'So why leave it?'

'Because Peter left it to Beola.' Jude stood in the hallway outside the now closed cupboard, her gaze travelling upward until she was looking at twilight through the glass cupola high above. The sky was moving through deep red and violet into a blue, almost purple darkness. There really was nowhere else on Earth that delivered the long, drawn out sunsets regularly seen in Edinburgh. Except perhaps for Norway. Peter's mother was Norwegian. Beautiful, blonde, statuesque Astrid, and her painfully handsome son. Jude had loved him so much and couldn't believe that he'd fell for her as hard. But he had, and they were married within a few months of meeting. He was her Viking; her rich, educated, ambitious warrior. Peter had transformed Jude's existence, had altered her all the way down to her very soul.

Standing there in her wide hallway looking up at the sky reminded Jude of being in the white house. Her face went slack, her gaze drifted inward. Briefly taken back in time to the hours and days immediately after her husband's death. The shock of it all. The upheaval. The feelings of betrayal and loss. Forced to accompany his body back to Wiltshire because the terms of his will demanded it. Forced to wait there alone until legal matters were finalised and money released so she could buy this house and retreat to Edinburgh to lick her wounds. Why now, she wondered? Why had Beola reached out after all this time?

Coming back to herself, Jude took in a long breath and sighed it out slowly. Looking at her niece she said, 'Edinburgh is my town, Jos. When there was nothing left for me beyond it, I came home.' Heading towards the kitchen, she wondered, 'Hungry?'

*

Immigration was handled quickly and efficiently, and then Richard Isherwood took Jos to baggage reclaim and helped her to haul lift dump her supersized suitcase onto the floor. With a 35kg weight allowance Jos had packed just about her entire sunshine wardrobe along with ten different types of footwear. She'd even packed her yoga mat. Fortunately, the case had wheels so was then easily guided through customs and into the arrivals area.

After scanning the assembled friends, relatives and drivers awaiting passengers off the same plane and not seeing anyone holding onto her name,

Richard asked, 'Would you like me to wait here with you, Jos?' Yes.

'No,' she said with her biggest smile. 'I'll be fine.'

Richard was a retired teacher, widowed years previously. He now spent his life climbing up and down Kilimanjaro raising money for various charities. This trip was his ninth. He had become something of a local celebrity in Hampshire and was on track to break through the one million pounds raised barrier thanks to TV and radio interest in his more recent endeavours. The airline was also aware of his celebrity and had upgraded him from economy. He and Jos had become acquainted due to all those little distractions. He had the masculine version of the illustrious goodie bag, so there had been a brief show and tell while giggling like idiots. Blame the champagne. They'd each tanked around half a bottle before the plane even got off the ground. But he knew a shrinking violet when he met one.

Despite the early fun, Jos had soon quieted down. Richard could tell she was nervous, not much of a talker, so he'd spoken about himself, kept his questions to a minimum, and left her alone with her thoughts whenever her attention wavered. A real hero Jos thought, and, over breakfast, she'd pledged fifty quid to his latest fund. They'd exchanged mobile numbers, so she'd be among the first to know of his latest triumph.

Spontaneously hugging her new friend, Jos added, 'I'm sure Ben will arrive any second. Go climb that mountain.'

'If you're sure.' Richard guided Jos through the assembled meeters and greeters into the open space beyond and then took her to one side. He held onto both her hands for a few moments, seeing right through her green-eyed optimism. She was a rabbit caught in the headlights of life. But she was also brave travelling alone and he needed to just let her get on with it. 'Okay.' Letting go her hands, he gripped the handle of his suitcase, and tipped her his beloved and battered straw hat. 'Take care fair, Jos,' he smiled. 'I'll call you when I'm done with the climb, we'll meet in Moshi for a celebratory round.'

And with that Richard turned and headed for the exits with one final wave.

'See you,' Jos whispered. Sighing, she then looked around again for Ben Nyerere.

Ben and Jos had met briefly online earlier in the week. He looked a lot like Dwayne Johnson she thought, only darker skinned. She'd only really seen his head and shoulders, but he had massive shoulders and a powerful looking neck, so she was pretty sure Ben was built like The Rock too. Easy to spot in a crowd surely.

'Taxi, lady?' More than one man had appeared by her side and was asking her this.

'No,' she told them all politely but firmly. 'I'm waiting for a friend.'

Eager to retreat farther from this new threat of flocking taxi drivers, Jos moved sideways and stationed herself by the plate glass windows overlooking the front of the airport building. She put her supersized suitcase in front of her to ward off all comers, then surveyed the world outside. It looked so beautiful. Blue sky, bright sunshine, manicured lawns and neatly trimmed bushes between beds of fantastical, colourful, exotic flowers which lined both sides of the wide pathway linking the building with the car parking areas beyond. People were moving to and fro. Hopefully, Ben was among them.

In an effort to appear busy Jos began rooting around in her bag. Placing it on top of her case, she stowed her passport safely, checked she still had her purse, then removed her sunnies, put them on and then slid them up and back over her head. She then remembered her mobile. Perhaps Ben had been delayed? He wouldn't be able to let her know that until she switched the phone back on.

Activating that mobile triggered a small chain reaction.

Initially the newly powered phone beeped to let Jos know she had a message. As she was trying to access that, the phone began to tinkle. Beola was calling. Jos slung her bag over one shoulder, turned back towards the windows with one hand on her suitcase, and answered.

A man heading her way saw Jos lift the mobile to one ear and picked up his pace.

Wearing a tight navy-blue T-shirt with a red logo across one prominent pectoral, matching cargo shorts and flip flops, he was almost running by then. But people kept getting in the way. Ben Nyerere knew Jos on sight. She wasn't the only white woman in arrivals, but she was the only one with a mass of red hair. He also knew the call Jos was in the process of answering would be from his mama. He was late, Beola would find out and there would be hell to pay. Flip flops were not the best form of running shoe, but he was making great progress.

Just as he was within vocal reach, a woman set her bag down on the floor directly in Ben's path. He tried to jump over it, but flip flops were even less appropriate for leaping. His feet simply succeeded in getting caught up in the bag, and his entire eighteen stone mass pitched forward, head first. He probably would have smacked hard down onto the floor then, but someone else pushed a fully loaded luggage trolley into his flight path.

The resulting collision got Jos' attention.

She'd just finished telling Beola that, yes, she had landed safely, was through customs and was by then looking for Ben, when crash bang wallop, the supersized suitcase bumped into Jos hard enough to send her two steps forward and into the glass. Her sunnies as well as her phone clattered to the floor. 'What the hell…' Turning, she managed to shove her case far enough to one side so she could bend down to retrieve her things. Jos was also able to see why she had a sore forehead.

Three large cases and six smaller cabin bags lay scattered on the floor around a luggage trolley. Two adults and two teenagers were standing, open mouthed in shock, all looking down at a large black man who was splayed, face down upon the only suitcase that had stayed put upon the trolley.

When her eyes met his, Ben smiled up at her. 'Hey, Jos.'

Scrambling then to his now bare feet, he apologised profusely to the family and began to gather up their baggage, ignoring the woman whose bag he'd tripped over in the first place as she tossed a flip flop in his general direction. The dad of the family helped with the cases, apologising in turn as he'd not seen Ben coming and was just as much to blame.

Jos phone began to tinkle again, and she realised it must have cut Beola off in the fall. Before she could say anything, Beola demanded to know, 'What has happened? Is everything all right?'

'Everything is fine,' Jos assured. 'I tripped and dropped my phone; I think I must've cut you…'

‘It is better to trip with your toe than with your tongue, Jos.’ Introducing proverbs into general conversation was a thing in Tanzania, and Beola wasn’t one for wasting an opportunity. ‘But tell me, can you see my son?’ she wanted to know. ‘He should be there. He’d better be there.’

‘He’s right here.’ Jos was trying very hard not to laugh at Ben who was now looking somewhat alarmed.

‘Let me speak to him.’

‘He’s helping someone with their bags.’ Jos made herself useful and retrieved both of Ben’s flip flops.

‘Well, as long as he is there. Let me see… what time is it now…’ Beola wondered on her end. ‘Just after nine o’clock. I will expect you before eleven. Tell my son. Otherwise, he and Wendell can sing for their lunch!’

Jos barely had time to wonder who Wendell was, because it was time to meet Ben properly.

As soon as the baggage was safely on its way, and his flip flops were back on his feet, Ben drew in a deep breath, exhaled, smiled his best smile, reached out his right hand, and said, ‘Welcome to Tanzania, Jos… and thank you for covering for me.’

Jos matched his easy grin, shaking hands and feeling much more relaxed. Not only had her saviour arrived, but he’d also broken the ice. Ben wasn’t quite as tall as Dwayne Johnson, but he definitely shared the physique. Nobody would be messing with this man. She felt safe and ready for the next step and, once he had taken control of her case, was happy to hook her arm through Ben’s and walk with him out into the sunshine.

That was when Jos realised, she’d been air-conditioned into a false sense of security.

Sliding her sunnies down over her eyes, she asked, ‘Is it always this hot, this early?’

‘This is what passes for cool around here,’ Ben said. ‘I imagine it isn’t quite as cool as Scotland though.’

CHAPTER TWO

Wendell Cooper had been despatched along with Ben to meet the guest.

They were friends as well as business partners, escorting small groups of tourists, and the occasional scientist, on bush safaris and tailored trips within both Kilimanjaro and Arusha National Parks. Ben did the talking and Wendell the driving. Today there were to be no tours, no trips of any kind. Usually they had Wednesday's off, but had scheduled Tuesday off this week to be at Beola's disposal. They were working for her today and had been left in no uncertain terms that being late was not an option. No one failed to carry out the wishes of Beola Nyerere and the two men would have been at the airport well before the plane landed, if they hadn't needed to stop for a tyre change.

Punctures were common enough in their line of work, so they'd had plenty practice changing tyres. It hadn't taken long, but long enough to make them a little late. 'No worries though…' Wendell suggested in his Australian drawl. 'She'll be ages getting through control.'

'She's first class,' Ben pointed out. 'They get everything fast.'

So, instead of parking up and letting Ben hoof it over to the terminal, Wendell broke the rules and drove through the taxi only lane to drop him off as close to the entrance as possible. He'd then went looking for a parking space.

While he waited, Wendell cleaned out the dusty old Land Rover; awash with the detritus left behind by their own most recent batch of tourists. Empty juice cans, boxes and plastic bottles, soiled wet wipes, banana and orange peel, sweet wrappers, camera film containers… also empty, used gum… 'Aaaaow gimme a break!' he exclaimed, making a face while picking up the offending lump using one of the used wet wipes. Having gathered an extensive collection onto two of the rear seats in the open sided vehicle, he jumped down and transported the litter to an appropriate bin. It took two trips.

Wendell was born and raised in Australia by his Balinese mother; a maid-cum-waitress in a small outback hotel where she'd met her son's aboriginal father. Being a nomad was in Billy Cooper's soul, so Wendell hadn't seen much of him growing up. But he'd discovered a touch of wanderlust of his own and had started travelling as soon as he was old enough. He'd been to New Zealand, Thailand, Bali… to meet the maternals, and Japan by the time he turned twenty. From there he headed for Europe and had spent some time in Manchester as well as Carcassonne and Madrid. From Spain he'd crossed the Strait of Gibraltar to Tangier and had worked his way south and east on the African continent. He spoke to his mother as often as he could but hadn't been home to Oz for years. She was cool with it, and as soon as he could afford it, he would fly his mum over to Tanzy for a visit.

Wendell was very cool with life in Tanzania. Sure, there was a lot of poverty. The roads outside the main highways were shit, drainage worse, phone connections were poor at the best of times, and decent internet was mostly the preserve of the rich and famous. But there was a lot of good stuff too. The people, the diversity of local cultures, the landscape, the climate, the scenery and of course the wildlife all came together to create the perfect place to put down a few roots. There were a number of great education and medical projects being run by the locals. Many of the more remote communities had wells and windmills, and some even had solar panels. Lots of people grew their own veggies, with local groups pulling their resources so everyone ate. There was a real sense of community about the place, and Wendell loved being part of it.

He'd arrived in Moshi, flying by the seat of his pants, to take up a job as ground assistant to a hot air balloon rides business. Setting up, following, taking down, maintenance. That sort of thing. Needless to say, he'd totally lied about his capability for succeeding in such a role. He was seen through almost immediately of course, but he and Ola Mulambia made the best of it until Ola could find a proper assistant which, as luck would have it, took over four months. By then Wendell knew Ben Nyerere, and knew he wanted a career change. They began talking about setting up a small enterprise of their own. One thing led to another, and Red Earth Tours was born. That was three years ago.

Initially they took out a loan to buy a second hand, open sided Landy, seating up to nine passengers. Wendell did the driving and Ben, a licensed ranger like his old man, sat out front and acted as spotter as well as armed protector and general guide. They had livery put onto the Landy as well as their shirts and had managed to get a fair share of the lower end of the market within their first year. Students, volunteers, charity climbers looking to do something else with their time after they were done with the mountain. The margins weren't great, but they didn't care. They ate, they drank, and they paid their taxes and had paid off their loan by the end of the second year. They had since managed to trade in the old Landy for a slight upgrade, which they were using as a taxi today. Thanks to their relative success, they'd also been able to employ a part time member of staff to look after their office, which was at Ben's folk's place… two actually, because the first one quit within weeks, declaring she'd been attacked by evil spirits.

This was news to Wendell who had practically lived in the white house himself a couple of years back, when he was between homes. He'd shacked up in the lodge with Ben, but they ate all their meals at the Nyerere family table. One time, while he was walking along the fence line, looking at the bee hives from a safe distance, he'd spotted a big blonde bloke up on the roof looking out across the view. But then the sun must have got into Wendell's eyes, because the bloke seemed to vanish. He mentioned it to Ben a little later, but his friend said it was just someone repairing the irrigation system up there, and maybe he'd just ducked down behind the parapet. Only problem with that explanation was the fact that repair men usually come in vans, and there'd been no van parked outside that day. Disappearing repair man, or evil spirit? Wendell only knew for sure that the white house was always a nice place to be in his own experience.

Thankfully, the latest member of the team, Nightingale Sumari, seemed to agree. She'd stuck around despite the rotten wages and restricted hours and got on with Beola like a house on fire. Red Earth Tours could only afford to employ her three days a week, because they were saving hard for a much newer, closed sided land cruiser with a pop-up lid for viewing, as well as air con. It would be much comfier for the tourists which could lead to longer trips to Ngorongoro Conservation Area, and maybe even Maswa Game Reserve and Serengeti National Park! They would, of course, be raising their prices and aiming for a more upmarket clientele.

Business was business.

On his way back to the Landy after the final trip to the litter bin, Wendell spotted Ben escorting the V.I.G.B… that was Very Important Guest of Beola, across the car park. 'Pale,' he observed to no one in particular. 'Interesting,' he added, while wiping his hands clean on some of the wet wipes he kept in the door pocket. She was tall and slim with loads of red hair wafting around in the breeze. He couldn't really see much of her face behind her oversized shades. A big, black leather bag was slung over a shoulder. She wore a long dark green skirt and a strappy black top. High heeled black sandals were as strappy as the top. A silver bangle adorned one wrist, and a silver torque rested around her throat. It wasn't often Ben's mama got worked up about a visitor… worked up about anything! But she was sure worked up lately, and pretty much everyone who knew Beola was hoping this white woman's arrival would restore the balance.

Beola had been snappy, critical, demanding. Shift yourself from under my feet! Why haven't you completed the thousand and one jobs I allotted to you five minutes ago? Come with me into town, I have marketing to do and there is no way I can manage it all by myself. There had been extreme cleaning outside as well as in, manicure standard gardening, and a host of small repairs identified and carried out.

A week ago, Ben's old man had dodged his own bullets by volunteering to relocate a young rhino to Zambia. The risk of being bushwhacked by poachers was obviously Kissi's safer option! He wasn't due back until tomorrow night at the earliest.

Wendell was glad he'd found a place to rent pre V.I.G.B.

When they reached the dusty old Land Rover, Ben handled the introductions, 'Jos… this is Wendell Cooper, my very good friend and awful business partner.'

'G'day, Jos,' Wendell smiled, shaking her offered hand.

A tall dark Australian… almost as tall and wide as Ben, with long, plaited and beaded hair tied back in a loose ponytail. He was dressed in the same blue shorts and tee. The red logo read 'Red Earth Tours' under a little red giraffe. He wore sturdy walking boots on his own feet however, and was smiling amiably, his almond shaped eyes twinkling in the sunshine. Very good looking. 'You're a long way from home,' Jos observed.

'Reckon that makes us even,' Wendell winked, opening the front passenger door. 'Hop in.'

Ignoring Ben who was waiting for a hand lifting the enormous case into the back, he skipped around to the driver's side and got in. Keying the ignition, he added, 'Whenever you're ready, Ben.'

*

They soon left the airport behind and turned east onto a hardtop highway linking Moshi in the east and Arusha in the west. The road was awash with drifting red dust swept around on the warm breeze, as if the landscape were trying to disguise the intrusion of mankind. The earth was a vivid terracotta colour, red indeed, against which the greenery showed up in a beautiful contrast. Various umbrella shaped species of acacia rose elegantly into view, some standing alone, others in distant groups like static herd animals. Dry looking grasses and flowering succulents lined the roadway. The mountain was on their left by then, crowned in thick white cloud. Imposing and impressive.

Traffic was by no means heavy, but steady enough. Vehicles ranged from top of the range modern to the near derelict cars held together by gaffer tape. Big beast four-by-fours, and brightly coloured mini buses were packed with tourists. Dilapidated old trucks were loaded with people, produce or both. Here and there they passed pedestrians carrying their own loads either on their backs or on top of their heads. Horns were tooted and hands waved.

They passed through the many residential areas of colourful little houses which, like the cars, ranged from modern looking dwellings to run down old shacks to half-built projects that may or may not have been abandoned. There were small lodges and hotels. Billboards advertised more of the same as well as the local attractions, Kikuletwa Hot Springs, Lake Chala, Materuni Waterfalls. Bars, restaurants and even Red Earth Tours were all advertising by the roadside in an effort to entice the tourists. They passed lots of road side stalls, fruit and veg, hair beading, eggs, cold beers and hot patties. Children laughed and cried out, running alongside passing cars and buses as fast as they could, for as long as they could.

Wendell called back to them in what Jos imagined must be Swahili. After a time being entertained by all the scenery, she asked, 'Tell me about

Red Earth Tours… what does it involve?'

'Game drives mostly,' Wendell told her.

'Everyone loves to see the wildlife,' declared Ben. 'And after they are done lookin' at Wendell, we take them to one of the nearby national parks to take pictures of the animals.'

Wendell rolled his eyes at Jos.

'Sounds like a great way to make a living,' she laughed.

'What about you, Jos?" Wendell asked. 'What do you do when you're

not in Tanzy?'

She had walked right into that one!

At twenty-four Jos Ferguson had no career, no job, she couldn't drive, couldn't speak a foreign language beyond a few useless phrases of German retained from school. She had no skills, no talents, no boyfriend. No life! Nine years ago, she was a chatterbox fifteen-year-old with loads of friends and loads of options, because she was clever and confident. Now she was a rubbish human being with zero confidence, no real friends and nothing much of interest to say. Losing both parents in a tragic accident had not simply interrupted her life, it had completely derailed it. She had spent the years since failing to properly get over it, and it hadn't helped that Jude was a part time recluse failing to properly get over her own loss. Between the two of them they were failing miserably at everything the rest of the world seemed to take for granted.

So, she lied.

'Oh, I've tried my hand at a number of things,' Jos said vaguely. 'Discovered I'm best sticking to pulling pints or making cappuccinos. Maybe I'm still to find my niche.'

'Maybe you've just been waiting…' Ben spoke seriously, '… for that niche to find you.'

Something in his tone made Jos feel that perhaps Ben knew something she did not. She looked at him, expectantly.

Ben was well aware that he knew more than Jos about certain goings on, certain people. Peter Sinclair for example. The crazy white man had been a big part of Ben's life until he was seventeen. That loss affected him deeply because Peter had always been a part of his life. Ben had grown up with him and Jude, they'd played together, did homework together, went on outings together. Peter was always full of energy, full of mischief. Larger than life and larger than heaven too if Ben's mama was to be believed; Beola was adamant that Peter was still around, still influencing his legacies, still out there pulling strings. Scaring Red Earth Tours staff too if their first assistant was to be believed. Even level-headed, two feet firmly on the ground Benjamin Nyerere also believed there was something else living in the white house apart from his family. Night time disturbances had become the norm and, though Ben hadn't ever seen him, Peter had been known to make the odd personal appearance.

Ben moved out within a year of moving in, simply because he slept better at the lodge.

But there was no need to tell Jos any of that. No need to scare her away so soon after arriving. So, Ben simply said, 'I was twenty-eight before me and Wendell set up in business. Before that I was a ranger, not because that was what I wanted to do, but because that was what my father did, and he made it easy for me to do it too. I like what I do now a whole lot more.'

Wendell picked it up there, 'I bummed around for over a decade before Tanzy found me, Jos. I worked bars, washed dishes, cleaned floors. I did whatever I could to get the money not just to live but to keep moving. When I came here, I stopped wanting to move and that was when life started to take on a little shape for me. Africa is a pretty life changing experience wherever on the continent you happen to be, but here…' he indicated to the passing scenery. 'Life is a little bit special here. You are gonna love it.'

The conversation then naturally meandered back around to Red Earth Tours services, which included multi-day trips to the coast, dawn and dusk hot air balloon flights, hot springs, hidden pools, waterfall climbs, and the open invitation to join them in any available seats they had from that day until whenever Jos left. Ben would keep her up to date on what where and when, and if there was anywhere specific she wanted to go, Jos was to let them know and they would make it happen.

*

When they reached the next junction, just before the outskirts of Moshi Urban, they turned south onto a hard packed dirt track which snaked between a scattering of colourful abodes, and out the other side. Soon there was only the African bush as far as Jos could see in every direction. The track grew rougher the farther south they travelled, the Land Rover and its occupants bouncing around in their seats. They were heading towards a long ridge which cut across the landscape to the east and west. A great wrinkle in the fabric of the planet which grew and grew until it dominated the view ahead. The track met the ridge head on, before making a hairpin turn and beginning its steep ascent. A second hairpin around halfway up, and another steep climb took the vehicle to the top.

The Land Rover bounced as it crested the ridge, skidding slightly, spraying grit and red dust in its wake. Jos was hanging on by then. She had been hanging on since that second hairpin bend where she found herself on the outside, feeling like the vehicle and everyone in it were moments away from certain death. It was all she could do not to cling on to Wendell. But her terror was immediately replaced by wonder as soon as she noticed the next view.

From the top of the ridge, the land sloped sedately downward, becoming a gentle and undulating geography. It was greener on this side thanks to both recent rainfall and the rivers running through it. The earth was rich and fertile. An abundance of plant life attracted a wealth of species. An unofficial game reserve, there were predators as well as prey living there, but the rangers who watched over this patch of Tanzania monitored closely and would capture and relocate any animal deemed a danger to human beings. Mostly, the animals were left alone to live their lives as nature dictated, and it was rare for any animal to be removed.

*

'Oh my god!' Jos was seeing her very first free giraffe.

Its head literally popped up from behind a tree top very close to the road. Tall like a lighthouse; its great head and eyes watched curiously as the Land Rover passed on by.

Wendell slowed down so she could enjoy the sight for a bit longer. 'The giraffe is Tanzy's national animal symbol,' he informed. 'They're protected here.'

'Their long necks embody their visionary skills…' Ben added. 'They can see the past as well as the present. They remind us Tanzanians that we need to view life from every angle, and to use strength and flexibility to align the physical, the mental and the spiritual aspects.'

Jos was soon seeing a lot more of the local wildlife. Antelopes and gazelle grazed in loose knit herds among the trees and shrubs, unconcerned by the proximity of humans. Zebras were crowded together in the distance, their distinctive stripes shimmering in the heat. Suddenly, five little warthogs burst out from some thick bush at the side of the road ahead. They took fright at the sight of the Land Rover bearing down, turned tail and were soon racing down the middle of the track. Once again, Wendell slowed right down, keeping pace a few meters behind. On they all trotted at speed, bums to the humans, tails up straight in the air, their little feet doing nine to the dozen. Upon catching up with an adult a little farther on, all five veered off the road again and hid behind their parent.

Numerous birds, both colourful and huge, flitted between trees, or sat impassively on roadside branches. When a little river came close to the road, Colobus monkeys could be seen among the overhanging branches of trees along the opposite bank. Mostly black, with long white, fringing on their backs and tails. Their faces were bearded with the same white, under little black hats. Adorable. They all stopped grooming, snacking and arguing, to watch the Land Rover pass on by.

'Are there any lions around here?' Jos wondered.

'We tend to get leopards and cheetahs mostly,' Ben said. 'They're solitary and so easier to manage. And they steer well clear of any people.' 'I don't see many people,' Jos observed.

'That's because this land belongs to the house,' Ben told her.

CHAPTER THREE

THE WHITE HOUSE

The white house keeps three secrets.

The house, the lodge and all perimeter buildings, are sited within eight thousand acres of unspoilt and protected land and surrounded by a rich array of mature trees and plants, so the house itself is completely hidden from all but the birds passing overhead. The estate has only natural boundaries; the escarpment to the north, a highway to the east and rivers to the south and west, yet the wildlife within rarely breach those frontiers. A tributary of the western river meets the track where it comes down off the ridge, meanders along close by until, eventually, diving underground to pass through the low hill the house sits upon. There is a small cave system within that hill, where water has collected over millennia. A well was drilled down into it, to supply the house with all its water needs.

Near the top of the hill, the track passes between two tall and slender cypress trees and gradually becomes a gravel driveway sloping gently upward between white flowering magnolia, pink powder puff flowering monkey pod trees, and trees known as flamboyant trees thanks to their large fiery red flowers. The gravel drive then emerges into the sunlight before encircling a perfect oval of green lawn directly in front of the house. In the centre of the oval stands a life-sized bronze sculpture of a muscular lioness, lying half on her back, half on her side, one massive fore paw in the air, her tail hanging down one side of her hollow stone plinth.

Brilliant white in the sunshine, the house is built from Portland stone shipped at enormous expense from the UK. It was originally meant to be built using coralline rock from Zanzibar, but this erodes very easily, and Peter Sinclair was building for keeps. His house was conjured in the style of Victorian Greek revival, using blood sweat and tears of frustration. Peter had declared at the time that he was possibly having more trouble constructing this house than the ancient Egyptians had when building the pyramids at Giza. He didn't build without specialist help of course, but he did design it, had laid the cornerstone and contributed to the construction whenever and however he could.

The 'U' shaped design is oriented so the empty space faces south with a patio area tucked in against the house and kitchen garden filling most of the rest. The outside facade is north facing, fronted by a porch with a centralised flight of shallow steps before the double front doors. Eight Doric columns support the porch roof end to end. The east arm of the 'U' is single story, topped off with decorative crenulations. At roof level these walls are doubled up, with earth filled space between to form long continuous planters bursting with a colourful array of plants and flowers. The delicate pink and purple flowers of the African akebia compete with gaudy bougainvillea in bright reds, oranges and pinks as they all spill over to hang down the sides of that wing of the house. Drainage holes set at regular intervals are hidden by all the trailing foliage. Succulents, coral hibiscus, impatiens, flowering cactus, staghorn ferns as well as fuchsia, hang down into the flat roof space. Huge central planters and mosaic pathways create a beautiful roof top garden, and there is a flight of steps leading from the far end down to the patio.

Double front doors lead into a vestibule area. Double glass doors open from there into the marble floored foyer, which is large, cool and airy. The ceiling here forms part of the floor of the master bedroom above, stopped short of the centrally sited staircase which heads towards the back of the house before splitting east and west beneath a high, arched window, and travelling on up to their respective galleries. High above that the large cupola lets in the light. At ground level more stairs lead down and around either side of the main stairs, meeting behind where the marble floor continues towards two sets of French doors leading out on the patio. Tucked in under the main stairs is a door to a less grand flight of stairs which lead down into the cellar. The cellar, in turn, allows access to a stepped passageway down into the cave system beneath the house.

Hallways travel east and west from the main foyer. To the west lies the living room, games room, TV room, a small library, the drawing room which is now home to the Red Earth Tour's office, and a family bathroom. To the east lies the formal dining room, the breakfast room, a small kitchen, main kitchen/dinette, numerous pantries and storage spaces, a large utility room, the freezer room and two walk-in cupboards. Inside one of the walkin cupboards a locked gun cabinet is affixed to the wall. Inside there is space for a hand gun as well as a high-powered rifle. It would be stupid, as well as irresponsible, to live in such splendid isolation, surrounded by the wild African savannah, and not be prepared to take direct action should a predator come calling.

Taking the stairs up to either side of the 'U' shaped gallery, the east arm gives access to the largest guest room with en-suite bathroom and doors out onto the roof garden. The west arm gives access to the hallway serving three more large bedrooms and a family bathroom. The master bedroom is in the middle and had its own en-suite bathroom, as well as a dressing room.

Behind the house, beyond the rear lawns, there is a small solar field with additional wind turbine to power everything. In a clearing next to the solar field there are seven bee hives and a large shed for all the equipment needed to maintain the hives and harvest the honey. Outbuildings include a triple garage block to the west; the well housing and pumping station is incorporated into it, and the lodge sits beyond that; a cabin style bungalow which Jude and Peter shared while the house was being built.

The white house stands radiantly upon its hill, untouched by the years that have passed by since the death of its architect. It is a beautiful and tranquil place, a sanctuary for more than simply the people who live within its walls.

Waiting to reveal its secrets.

CHAPTER FOUR

When Beola Nyerere became housekeeper to Jude and Peter Sinclair she found herself blessed. Her employers were kind and friendly people who welcomed her into their lives as a valuable asset instead of merely the woman who cleaned up. She, Kissi and two-year-old Ben moved into the lodge, which was comfortably furnished and had all the modern conveniences. She was able to take Ben to work with her right up until he went to school, and her pay was nearly as good as her husband earned as a senior ranger working for the National Parks Authority.

Kissi and Peter were already great friends by then, having met at a wildlife rehabilitation centre where Kissi was employed to protect some of the animals from poachers. Peter and Jude also stayed there for a long time, working as volunteers, so they could watch over a little lion cub they rescued when her mother was shot. Lulu the lion was the reason the Sinclair's settled in Tanzania. The centre was owned and ran by Henk de Vries, a Dutchman who was another friend and a regular visitor to the white house.

There was always something going on there, always people coming and going.

Peter and Jude threw parties and barbeques, they knew a lot of people… a lot of the local politicians and officials that they entertained regularly, keeping them all sweet so they would gain permits and permissions for ventures Peter set up all over the region. The Maasai people were another group of regulars, and it wasn't unknown for an entire village to set up camp on the front lawn for days at a time when there was negotiating to be done between the tribes and the politicians.

They all had a very nice life, relaxed and free with very little in the way of worries, so it was a huge shock when Peter died suddenly.

Beola's husband and Ben, who was seventeen by then, were off tracking poachers through the park that day, and she had no idea when they would return. Jude had been out marketing most of the morning and, soon after she came home, had begun hauling the contents out of every cupboard in the kitchen so she could scrub and wipe shelves and doors that were already clean. This was familiar behaviour by then because Jude cleaned when she was angry. She'd been angry then, because she'd been planning a trip to Europe, which Peter kept postponing. Beola couldn't help knowing these things because Sinclair and Nyerere lives overlapped constantly. She'd offered to help in the kitchen, but Jude asked her to strip and change the bed in the master bedroom instead, and she was still up there when the terrible news arrived.

Beola watched through the window as Jude went out to meet the police officers. When she then heard Jude's wretched wails of pain, her heart stopped. She stood there, clutching onto the laundry, frozen in fear. It was only when Jude collapsed onto the ground, that the spell was broken. Beola tossed the laundry aside, ran downstairs and out the front door to comfort her. The two of them kneeling on the ground, clinging to one another, both of them weeping for the loss of a man they both loved. Little by little, Jude calmed and, when the officers bade her return to town with them, she refused Beola's offer of company, asking instead that she telephone Peter's best friend, Gary Preston, to let him know what had happened. Jude also refused the offer of a ride and, after grabbing her bag and keys, followed the police car in her own jeep.

Since then, Beola had had a lot of time to ponder the events leading up to Peter's death. How he'd been spending more time with the Maasai than with his wife by then, days and even entire weeks living the nomadic lifestyle of his tribal friends. At home he'd seemed withdrawn and uncommunicative, spending most of his time either in the library or up in the roof garden. In all the years Beola had known her friend, Peter had never been quiet, never miserable. His relationship with Jude had also changed and because she knew their lives and their habits inside out by then, Beola knew that he and Jude were no longer sharing a bed.

Jude seemed unconcerned and told Beola she was imagining it. Peter was simply busy as usual, planning more of his projects. They should just leave him be. He needed a holiday. They needed a holiday. She would take him to Europe and, when they returned, her husband would be back to his old energetic self.

The single time Beola asked Peter outright if anything was wrong, he'd told her, 'There is, Bee… but it will be all right in the end.' He'd held her tightly then, kissing her forehead tenderly. 'Have faith in me to overcome.' Looking back, it was as if Peter had known that he was going to die.

It was as if all of them had known, because the Maasai came prepared for their ritual even though their little brother died only a few hours before they arrived. It was the largest group of Maasai Beola had ever encountered at the white house. At least fifty men, most of them warriors, all carrying their weapons and their shields. Their chests and faces and arms painted as if they were going into battle. She watched them from the master bedroom window, just as she'd watched the police arrive, having gone back up to finish changing the bed so it would be clean and ready when Jude returned. They arrived on foot just before sunset, and it would have taken all day to walk from their village on the western side of Mount Kilimanjaro all the way to the white house.

Some of the warriors carried armfuls of wood, and immediately began building a large fire in the middle of the lawn. The elders, including their bearded laibon, sat down on the porch steps to rest and, when Beola went out to meet them, they asked only for water. When she offered food they politely refused. When Beola moved to go back inside to fetch the water, a young warrior stopped her. 'We must leave the white house in peace, little sister,' he told her, and then he and several of his fellow warriors guided her towards the lodge where they fetched enough water for all. When that was done, the young warrior told her, 'Word has been sent into the park so your husband and your son will come home soon. When they do, you must be ready to leave.'

'But why?'

'The laibon wishes to cleanse the white house of sorrow.'

Beola knew better than to argue with the wishes of a laibon, and so she nodded, resigned. 'How long must we stay away?'

'Moon die and come back again, man die and stay away. Come back with the new moon, sister.'

Back inside the lodge Beola began to pack, without any clear idea of where her family would go or who they would stay with. By then it was full dark, and the fire was burning so brightly she could see its orange glow above the garage blocking her direct view. Kissi and Ben arrived while she was still packing, in shock at both the death of their friend and the large gathering on the white house lawn. The evening breeze was becoming a wind by then, and the stars were obscured by gathering clouds. The warriors had begun to sing a sorrowful sounding song, their beautiful voices competing with the mounting voice of the wind.

By the time the Nyerere's were readying to leave, a storm was in full flow.

The perimeter of trees bent and swayed in the wind that had initially made their leaves whisper. That wind was howling and shrilling by then, a tempest that thrashed and whipped the leaves and branches. Storm clouds had gathered so close, they were piled on top of one another, grumbling, rumbling, crashing with thunder directly overhead. Lightening split the night over and over. Up on the roof garden, a solitary figure braved the onslaught. The old laibon was yelling into the night, his spells snatched away by the wind that seemed, in turns, to want to blow him away and push him down. Rain pelted down upon him, it blinded his eyes, dripped from his beard, soaked his shuka and chilled his bones. He fought against it, at the same time as he embraced it, arms stretched wide and high. Calling out, over and over, to the spirit of his friend.

As the Nyerere's were loading up their jeep, another vehicle arrived, lights sweeping across the scene as it circled the lawn. Beola thought that it must be Jude, but it was Henk de Vries, pulling up in his flatbed truck. She assumed he'd heard the news and had come to pay his respects. She ran towards him, but half a dozen warriors barred Beola's way. They told her to go, to never speak of this night to anyone. Beola struggled against them, and called out to Henk in some distress, but either the wind stole her voice, or the Dutchman chose to ignore her. Kissi was next to her by then and had to impel his wife bodily into the back of his Land Rover as Ben sat quietly weeping in the front. He then got in himself and set off for his father's home in Arusha, having called ahead to stay there were sanitation issues at their home, so they needed a place to say for a while. As they were moving around the lawn towards the drive, Beola watched Henk lower the tail gate of his truck and saw two warriors lift and carry something towards the fire.

Meat for the funeral feast, he told her much later.

When Kissi's Land Rover reached the foot of the hill, he turned north towards the main road that would take them to Arusha. They left the storm behind almost immediately. When they reached the top of the escarpment, he stopped and got out. Ben and Beola joined him. Together they stood atop the ridge, watching a small storm rage over the white house.

*

It was nearly two weeks later that the new moon saw the return of the Nyerere's.

Gary Preston had made two trips to Tanzania by then. The first began in the hours after Beola had called with the terrible news. He had collected Jude, Peter's coffin and closed up the white house before flying back to London. From there he'd flown to Norway to collect Astrid, telling her that her son was dead, only once he was there with her. He'd travelled with Astrid back to Wiltshire and together they'd arranged Peter's funeral. As soon as it was over Astrid returned to Norway, Jude headed north to Edinburgh, and Gary made his second trip to Tanzania along with Peter's last will and testament.

He was exhausted by then, seated on the porch and nodding off when the Nyerere's Land Rover drove out into the open beyond the tree line. Rousing himself from his chair, he went down the steps to greet them as they pulled up close to the house. Gary skipped the traditional handshakes in favour of bear hugs as he always had. But these hugs were packed with all the emotion of that moment, and all of the memories of the past twelve years, because that was how long they had all known one another.

Gary, Beola, Kissi and Ben united for a few short moments in terrible loss.

Beola was first to break away from the group. She'd expected the lawn to show the scars of the fire still, but the earth was freshly raked, seeded, new grass already beginning to grow, and, in the centre of the bare patch, someone had built a low, hollow rectangular structure from white stone. She moved towards it.

'Before he died, Peter commissioned a bronze Lulu.' Gary guided Kissi and Ben towards it too, until they all stood looking down at the structure the statue was destined to sit upon. Inside there was nothing to see but bare earth. 'These stones were left over from the build,' Gary's voice broke, fighting back tears. 'Lulu should arrive any day.'

That day Beola and Kissi Nyerere discovered the white house was theirs' until their deaths.

They'd arrived not knowing what the future held in store for them, but never in their wildest dreams had they imagined they would inherit the white house. Gary was executor of Peter's will and had all the necessary documentation, all properly signed and witnessed by Beola and Kissi less than six months previously. But they had no idea at that time they would benefit from it. They simply witnessed Peter signing his will and added their signatures as confirmation of that. Now the white house was their exclusive home. They would also receive an annual allowance as custodians, and support whenever needed.

'But what about Jude?' Beola wondered.

'Jude isn't coming back,' Gary told her. 'This is your home now. It's what Peter wanted.'

Gary stayed on until Lulu arrived, supervising the entire process as the heavy bronze statue was lifted off the flat bed transport truck using the boom crane. Kissi and Ben also helped, and together they lowered Lulu down slowly, until the single nipple on the underside of the white marble slab she lazed upon, was slotted into the recess a mason had expertly carved into one of the stones making up the side wall.

'Shouldn't there be more?' Ben wondered.

Clever boy.

'One should be plenty,' Gary told him. 'It's so heavy it probably doesn't even need that one to hold it in place.' That night they christened Lulu with a shot of tequila; Peter's favourite tipple, and then ended the rest of the bottle between them. The following day, Gary flew back to London with his hangover to begin his new career as manager of Peter's estate, which had been run as a business since Peter's father, Johnny Sinclair, set it up that way, for tax as well as succession reasons.

*

Initially, Beola insisted on staying in the lodge.

It just didn't feel right to be moving into her friends' home, especially under such tragic circumstances, but really Beola was wary of the magic performed there in the hours after Peter's death. Instead, she visited every single day. She cleaned and cared for it; she kept the house company. She tended the gardens, cared for the flowers and planted and harvested from the fruit and vegetables. She even looked after the bees. But she was a little afraid. The empty white house became a moody place, prone to bad behaviour.

It began with matches.

There was always a dish of matches in the kitchen, next to the hob which was powered by bottled gas. At first, she'd find the matches scattered around the dish as if spilled. Then there would just be a single match lying some distance from the dish as if placed there. Soon it was two or three or four matches, laid perhaps end to end, or making a triangle or a square. Finally, she found a pattern of matches that might have been a star or perhaps a flower. When the matches stopped jumping out of the dish, books started jumping off shelves.

Beola quickly lost track of the times she'd arrive in the mornings to find books pulled from library shelves, or maybe records scattered on the floor around the stereo. Sometimes, when she was busy downstairs, she would hear footsteps on the floor above, a door opening, closing. One morning she discovered every single cupboard door in the kitchen wide open and a set of playing cards mid game of solitaire on the dinette table.

Needless to say, Kissi thought it was all in her head and so Beola started having him come over to check the house over in the evenings. They would then spend the rest of their evening and night in the lodge and, as soon as they got up in the morning, they would go back into the white house to see if anything was amiss. The white house never disappointed.

Maybe someone is getting in during the night?' Kissi suggested. 'Maybe someone is playing tricks on us?'

'No one is getting in,' Beola told him. 'And the only one playing tricks is Peter!' She was absolutely convinced by then that Peter was haunting the white house so, when she encountered him for the first time, she wasn't completely surprised.

But that didn't stop her from running, screaming from the house!

*

Though the Nyerere's had moved into the white house eventually, the master bedroom had remained unoccupied. All Peter's personal belongings, as well as everything Jude abandoned, had been carefully boxed and stored down in the cellar. Beola and Kissi chose one of the other bedrooms for their own however, unwilling to make use of this room out of respect for their benefactor.

It was mostly a white room. As white as the exterior. White walls, white drapes, white bedding and white rugs. Even the furnishings were made from bleached, blonde wood. But there were framed colourful photographs and art all over the walls, so it was also a lively and vibrant space. The room was cleaned regularly, and Beola even changed the linens every so often to keep things fresh. She would bring in vases of flowers, and she would open windows. This is where she was when Ben and Wendell arrived with their guest.

Beola liked it in there because it was a quiet and peaceful place. It took her back often to the events of the day Peter died but being there had helped her come to terms with that as well as everything since. Maybe it was because it remained completely unchanged? Maybe it was the mountain? There was a big comfortable chair set at an angle before the windows. Sitting there she had a view out across the porch roof, across the lawn, beyond the statue of Lulu and out across the tree tops all the way to Kilimanjaro.

A beautiful and privileged view that Peter had built his white house around.

After their initial encounter up in the roof garden, Beola could count on one hand the number of times Peter had appeared to her over the subsequent years. She'd been tending to the plants that first time, drifting off into a strange dreamlike daze for a time before Peter appeared right next to her and sent her screaming back to the lodge. It drained him, he said. It was difficult to gather himself up into something visible. So, it was much easier to communicate from his distance, and so Beola had promised to pay attention. Even so, it took her a while to get a feel for the rhythms of his other communications.

Books proved to be a useful tool. All those books discovered out of their shelves in the library. A book on bee keeping lying nonchalantly on a side table close to the door. When Beola picked it up and carried it back to its place on the shelf, she was reminded she needed to inspect the hives. Another morning, another book. A book entitled Drilled Wells, which lay open at pages concerned with the importance of regularly maintaining and servicing the pump as well as the filtration system.

Beola was soon calling Gary Preston, who was their go to man for anything and everything as it concerned the white house. Gary arranged for an engineer to visit to service their own pump and filtration system.

Books on caring for flowers and plants. Books for fruit and vegetable growers. More recently a photograph album made an appearance in the kitchen, open to display a set of four images, Jude and her sister with a baby, Jude and Peter with the same baby, Peter and the baby, the baby. Feeling curious but uninspired Beola had simply replaced the album inside the drawer in the armoire in the TV room where it belonged.

The very next day that photo album was back on the kitchen counter, along with a book on travel.

But Beola wasn't quick enough to understand, because as she carried both books away to their respective places, every phone in the house began to ring. The one in the Red Earth office, the one in the kitchen, Kissi's mobile, her mobile. All ringing or playing their tunes, and no one on the other end when each was answered. It took one entire repeat of the whole pantomime the following morning before Beola got that message. She'd called Gary to ask for Jude's number and then, much later that same day, when she felt the time was right somehow, she'd called Edinburgh and found herself talking to Jos who was all grown up and home alone because Jude was out taking a poorly cat to see a vet.

And now the day had come!

Peter had been increasingly pervasive as this day drew nearer. There had been music, whole albums or just parts of songs played late at night. The Red Earth office files had been rifled on two separate occasions, information leaflets scattered, itinerary plans muddled... Nightingale was becoming more than a little wary, but mostly because her cigarettes had started going missing. She always kept them in the same desk drawer, but they had turned up in the downstairs bathroom which she never used because she always used the WC at the front door. They were discovered inside the photocopier, in the tub of instant coffee and, most recently, on the roof of her car. Ben was sweet on Nightingale and angry that she might flee as the previous admin assistant had after Peter used his books to communicate with her in a slightly different manner than Beola was used to and had even asked his mama to have a word.

But there was no reasoning with their enthusiastic ghost lately.

Kitchen cupboards had been emptied. The contents stacked on tables and chairs. Wall hangings had been rearranged and furniture moved. As if Peter had an excess of energy that he was expending on moving stuff around. The whole atmosphere in the house had become charged with a distinct sense of excitement. It was impossible to ignore and highly infectious. Beola had become much livelier, more difficult to be around according to her son. Cleaning, cooking, rushing here and there, and impelling everyone around her to do the same. And then there was the sex. Beola couldn't get enough of it! Kissi had ran off to Zambia with a baby rhino not to escape his wife's housekeeping demands, but to get a rest from her carnal desires. The poor man was exhausted!

But, last night, everything stopped.

Beola had checked the times and was almost certain that, as soon as Jos' plane had taken off, Peter had receded. Maybe he was simply waiting, gathering his strength so he would perhaps be able to communicate with his niece? Surely, he had something to communicate to Jos, otherwise why had he worked so hard to get her here?

Beola would wait and see.

CHAPTER FIVE

Jos climbed down from the Land Rover to stand on the paved area that ran parallel along the entire length of the porch, between it and the lawn. She was rooted to her spot, mouth open to catch flies, as she gazed up at brilliance from behind the safety of her sunnies. The white house was both beautiful and incredible. It looked like it had been teleported in from possibly another time or perhaps another dimension. Stark against the rich blue sky. Surrounded by an impossible array of lush greens and colourful blooms. No evidence of red earth here. No dust. Just tall trees, beautiful flowers, green lawns. Butterflies fluttered, insects buzzed, birds sang, and monkeys chattered all around. Everywhere Jos could see life and she could hear its voice. She felt a little overwhelmed looking at this paradise. Her heart was literally swelling inside her chest, beating fast, and she felt on the verge of tears. So emotional, she had to do some slow and deep yoga breathing to calm down.

Must be the jetlag.

Just then the front doors opened and Beola came rushing down the steps to greet their guest.

'Joslin!' she beamed. 'Welcome to Tanzania.' Beola took hold of both her hands, squeezing them before embracing her briefly. Standing back and taking hold of those hands once again, she said, 'You remind me so much of Jude.'

'She and my mum looked very alike…' Jos found herself rambling. 'They were often mistaken as twins when they were children though there's a couple of years between them. I suppose I must look like them both.' Laughing suddenly, she added, 'I definitely have the hair!'

'Beautiful hair.' Beola grinned and touched her own close-cropped afro which was salt and pepper grey these days. 'Mine not so much.'

'Oh, but it suits you.' Jos meant it. Beola was a slender woman, not quite as tall as her. She had a small head which lent itself very well to such maximum exposure.

'I trust Benjamin and Wendell have looked after you.' Beola eyed the boys for any signs this had not been the case.

'I was a perfect gentleman,' Wendell announced.

'So was I,' Ben was in a hurry to point out.

'They are afraid of me,' Beola told Jos. 'Men should always be afraid of their mothers. Wendell's mama is far away and so I have taken on this role on her behalf.' She winked, and then laughed when Wendell nudged her. 'Can you help Ben take our guest's luggage up to the garden room, darling?' she asked him.

'Am I staying for lunch?'

'Yes.'

'Then I can help.'

'Come, Joslin…' Hooking her arm, Beola guided her towards the stairs and up onto the porch. 'Are you hungry now?'

'Not really…' They were passing over the threshold. 'I had a big breakfast on the plane.'

Opening the inner door, Beola ushered Jos inside. 'Perhaps you are thirsty?'

'Mmmm…' Jos was distracted once again, absently removing her sunnies and looking around the entrance hall. It was cool. She could smell cooking, something spicy. She could also smell the scent of many flowers carried in on the light breeze pulled in from the outside perhaps when Beola opened the doors they'd just walked through. The general décor was predominantly white, but huge and vivid paintings graced the walls. Tribal women, dressed in colourful fabrics, danced among baobab trees. African wildlife gathered together around watering holes or marched across the horizon. Huge zebra heads in close up, one painted in golds and the other in silvers, gazed impassively down at Jos from high up on the entrance hall walls. In between the paintings were tribal masks and textile hangings. Oranges, reds, yellows, greens and blues. Carved wooden figures stood tall on the marble floor, in corners, at the bottom of the stairs. Animals marched across side tables, a bureau, and shelves. Huge leafy plants stood in enormous ceramic and terracotta planters.

Beola impelled Jos gently to their right to allow Ben and Wendell to pass by with the biggest suitcase she had ever seen. She then indicated along that hallway. 'Down there you will find the sitting room, the library… you know, games, books, music, it's all down that way. Red Earth Tours also have an office at the far end.' She then indicated the opposite hallway. 'Down there is my favourite room in the house,' she explained. 'The kitchen!' Jos was still looking around and not really paying any attention at all. 'Why don't we go outside?' suggested Beola. 'I have made us some juice.' She had to practically drag Jos across the hall and down the shallow steps towards the French doors and out onto the patio.

Jos didn't really want to leave.

She wanted to open every door, look into every room, every cupboard. She wanted to discover every single inch of this beautiful, amazing house. However, Beola was not to be diverted from her own goals and so she found herself outside once more, but at the back of the house.

The flagged patio area was enclosed between the arms of the house, currently well shaded, overlooked by numerous tall windows, and separated from the large kitchen garden by a strip of lawn around three meters wide. There was a large, round wooden table with six matching chairs on the kitchen side. Opposite was a matching set of traditional wooden sun lounger/deck chairs that might have come off the Titanic, along with a few low tables to hold those all-important cocktails. Huge canvas sails were folded against the walls either side of the French doors Jos had just walked out through. She could see they were attached to cantilever arms with winding mechanisms to open and position them as required. Presumably later in the afternoons when the Earth had turned around enough that the back of the house faced the sun.

From this vantage point Jos could see that one arm of the building had only one storey. She could also see clearly what she'd merely glimpsed on the outer facades as the Land Rover had made the final approach, there was a whole hanging garden thing going on up there. A mass of flowers cascaded down from the parapet running down the entire length of that flank. The elusive perfume she'd smelled inside was stronger out here due to the sheer volume of flowers. Thankfully, she didn't suffer from hay fever, but Jos pitied anyone who did if they ever came here! More windows ran the length of each side, interspersed with sets of French doors which all led out onto the pathways bordering the kitchen garden. Some of the kitchen windows were dissected by a flight of external steps leading upward from that side of the patio, past the overspill of flowers and onto the roof.

Jos really wanted to go up there for a look.

Beola was at the table, lifting a weighted net off the jug containing freshly prepared fruit juice and lots of melting ice. Stirring it first, she poured two small glasses and handed one to Jos.

Jos hadn't realised how thirsty she was and drank most of the tangy liquid gratefully. 'Delicious. Thank you.'

'Help yourself to more if you want it,' Beola instructed. 'You must try to make yourself at home here, Joslin. Peter made my family caretakers of this house, but it still belongs to him, to Jude… and so it also belongs to you.'

Jos tried to protest.

'Hush,' Beola told her. 'I merely want to get these things out into the open. After Peter died everything that had been because of him, carried on.' Seeing that Jos was opening her mouth to say or to ask, Beola raised a hand to stop her. 'There is much I believe you do not know about your uncle. I can help you with this. He was a good man, a rich man, a busy man. His many legacies are as flourishing today as when he created them. Peter planned for a future without him. Who knows, perhaps he knew he would die before his time. Perhaps he knew that, when he died, Jude would not want to remain in Africa without him. Whatever he knew, Peter ensured his white house would be protected by people who love it as much as he did. We did not expect to be the custodians here, but we are thankful as well as privileged for the life we have because of this. That life, and the family who live it, will now embrace you too.'

Jos wanted to but couldn't speak right then for fear of tears.

'Go anywhere and look at anything you please, Joslin. Open drawers, look at all the photographs, read the books. I will show you the room I share with my husband and ask that this space at least remain private, but you may explore freely. If you need anything… ask. If you wonder about anything… ask. But for now, I will show you to your room and leave you to settle in.'

'Thank you, Beola,' Jos nodded, blinking back tears. 'But please… will you just call me Jos.'

Beaming, Beola told her, 'Of course.'

Instead of heading back inside, Beola then headed for the steps that went up past the kitchen windows. She paused until she was sure Jos was following, and then carried on up to the top where she stood to one side to let Jos walk by, and into the garden.

*

Open mouth once again firmly in place, Jos gawped at the incredible spectacle laid out before her.

The explosion of colour which tumbled over the sides and down the walls was repeated up here, but with a different array of flowers wearing their own bright colours. The narrow pathways set between the central planters and raised beds were created from a mosaic pattern in hues of green. The planters held various different palm species all with huge fronds bending and wafting lazily in the sunshine. The beds were stuffed to overflowing with flowers and plants of such variety it was impossible to identify where one ended and the next began. Wooden benches were sited next to four of them, offering views in each direction. The air was heady with the mix of perfumes, alive with the hum and chatter of insects. Lizards darted here and there, crossing pathways, climbing the sides of the planters and disappearing into dense foliage. Birds swooped overhead.

'I don't think I've ever seen anything so beautiful,' Jos realised.

'Jude made this,' Beola told her. 'Peter wanted the garden spaces for growing food, but Jude wanted flowers and so this was the compromise.'

'Our Edinburgh garden is also beautiful,' Jos said, running her fingers through silky soft, bright pink blossom. 'Jude spends most of her time there. She grows a lot of vegetables too.' She wandered off along the little pathways, looking around and looking out across the views. From up there she could see across the treetops, see for miles across the shimmering landscape. There were no roads to be seen. No traffic. No other houses as far as she could see. Mostly she looked at the flowers, bending here and there to touch and smell. She thought about Jude, wondering how she could have left this place behind. Wondering too why Peter had denied this to his wife. Had Jude really left because she wanted to? Or had she been forced to because she was made homeless? Jos felt irritated suddenly, angry with her uncle.

How could Peter do that to Jude?

'And this is the garden room.' Beola had caught up and indicated the open doorway her son and his friend were just then emerging from. 'You're place, Jos, for as long as you need it.'

'D'you live in a bungalow, Jos?' Wendell wondered.

A little confused by the question, Jos told him, 'No.'

'How the hell did you manage to carry that case downstairs?'

'I didn't,' she laughed. 'I actually left the case at the bottom of our stairs and packed it right there on the floor. It just about killed me and Jude getting it in and out of the car! Thank you both for bringing it up here for me.'

'No worries,' they chorused.

Ben then added, 'You can buy us a beer sometime.'

'Definitely,' she nodded. 'And thanks again for picking me up from the airport.'

*

The garden room was furnished in French.

Jos knew this because Jude had a lot of French furniture at home in Edinburgh. Her big bed was ivory coloured rococo, with pale pink padding and intricately carved pale pink flowers and pale green leaves on both head and foot boards as well as down the sides. The bed was covered in pristine white linen and had a fringed crimson bedspread folded neatly across the bottom... presumably in case there was a cold snap. The entire bed was draped with mosquito netting. A beautifully upholstered green chaise longue stood at the foot, and a sumptuous brown leather, wing backed chair with a matching foot stool stood angled towards the window next to the door out into the garden. On the floor next to it she found a four socket UK plug board with an African connection. Handy. Her clothes and shoes were swallowed up now inside the lovely big, bed matching armoire which had a door either side of a full-length mirror, pale pink flowers and green leaves peaking above the mirror, and more pink flowers forming the feet. Her smalls were stored inside one dainty, bronze coloured three drawer table de chevet on one side of the bed. The matching one on the other side now held her jewellery, camera, iPod, chargers etc., as well as all her documents. A small docking station stood on top along with a bronze lady wearing nothing but a wispy looking piece of cloth as she held up a pale blue glass lamp shade. All her make-up, potions and lotions were in the en suite with its big claw footed slipper bath, separate shower as well as bidet. From the bath she could look out over the tree tops at the side of the house. There were large, leafed plants in the bathroom, but none in the bedroom. Instead, the bedroom was decorated with more tribal art and wall hangings similar to those seen down in the entrance hall. A door out onto the gallery meant Jos could go downstairs without going outside. There was a second window overlooking the side of the house like the one in the bathroom, as well as the much bigger window, overlooking the roof garden.

The garden room was going to be a lovely place to wake up to each morning.

Having retrieved her mobile from her bag, Jos sat down on the leather chair and called Jude. The connection hissed and whined a little, and the ring tone when it began was clear but very far away sounding. As the ring tone continued Jos pictured Jude moving through the house towards the ringing phone. There was only one, set on a table tucked in against the side of the staircase. Jude may have to come all the way downstairs from her bedroom, perhaps all the way from the kitchen. It would take at least six rings. Seven rings. Eight rings. Halfway through the ninth ring the answer machine kicked in and Jos heard her own voice suggesting that she try again later or leave a message after the beep.

She chose the latter option.

'Hi Jude, it's me. I made it! The flight was great, and Ben picked me up. Just unpacking in… is it the garden room? I think Beola called it that. Makes sense. Beola is very nice. But the white house is amazing! It looks so out of place it fits right in! I'm sitting at the window overlooking your roof garden. It is so beautiful, Jude. I really hope you had the chance to see it like this before… you know.' Pause. 'Anyway, I'm rambling. Hope you and the cats are all okay. I'll try again later. Love you.' Maybe Jude was in the shower, or out shopping?

Hopefully, she wasn't brooding.

*

Moody Judy could as easily be broody Judy.

Not so much in more recent years, because a younger Jos identified the twin triggers of Peter and Africa and learned to avoid them. At first, when she initially moved in with her aunt, she was consumed by the trauma of seeing her parents crushed to death, the survivor guilt that went hand in hand with that, and the general grief that filled so much of her mind it was a fulltime occupation. Her moods swung from sudden surges of hysterical anger to long periods of withdrawn brooding. Once she turned eighteen, Jos would demand the money that was hers by right… she wanted to set up on her own, buy a little flat, get a job, support herself. But Jude had fixed it so she couldn't get her hands on a penny until she was twenty-one, and even that was in the form of a monthly allowance. She wouldn't have access to it all until she was thirty! 'It's for your own good, toots,' Jude was fond of saying. 'You'll thank me later.'

At one time Jos broached the idea of going to university. She'd been clever at school. Top of her class. She'd always wanted to study ancient history at Edinburgh University. She'd surely be able to pass entrance exams with a little time and study. 'But how will you feel if you fail, toots? Maybe you could set your sights a little lower?' When Jos started looking for a job, any job, just something to relieve the boredom, Jude would look horrified. 'But you don't have to work, toots. You'd be taking a job away from someone who really needs it.' And then, when Jos gave up on those and any similar ideas, there would then be the stage-managed comforts, shopping, a movie that she got to choose, a nice dinner somewhere posh, the chance to dress up, maybe drink too much and have a laugh. 'It's for the best, toots,' Jude would tell her. 'We have everything we need right here.'

Jude did indeed have a beautiful home and garden. Every labour-saving device. Top of the range home entertainment. Days would pass, weeks, without seeing another living soul. They had cable TV as soon as it was available. It was the same with the internet. When shopping online became the norm, they had even less reason to leave the house that became Jos' bubble as surely as it had always been Jude's ivory tower.

But there was no history on show there.

Jos had boxes of photos from her childhood. Granted, it took years before she could look at them without wailing and crying, but she'd kept them because, one day, she knew she'd cherish them. Jude had nothing linking her to her past. Not a single photograph was on display anywhere. No curios, no souvenirs. When Jos asked if she'd saved anything from her African adventure, her aunt replied offhandedly that she'd returned to Edinburgh in the clothes she stood up in and began once more from scratch. Scotland and Africa were not compatible. But what about jewellery, accessories, keepsakes?

'Do you remember when I picked you up from that police station?' Jude barked at Jos, sneering. 'You wouldn't even go into your own home. I asked you… what should I pack, what do you need, want? You sat there shaking your head! It was nearly two years before you'd set foot inside that house, and even then, it was because you had to if it was to be sold. My husband died just as violently!' Her tone matched her anger by then, the mask slipping. 'Peter was the love of my life! When he was gone… I couldn't wait to get away from there… away from that house, from Africa, I couldn't stand it!'

Jude was typically a very cool calm and collected person, always smiling, always practical, and always optimistic as she glided through life. She dressed beautifully, always wore at least lipstick and mascara, and always Chanel number 19. This was the woman who introduced Jos to Yoga and Pilates, to spa days, aromatherapy massages and flotation tanks. During this outburst Jude bared her teeth and contorted her face in a scarcely controlled fury. Jos had apologised for causing upset and withdrew to the shelter of her bedroom. She stayed there for hours. It was winter back then, dark by four thirty. When Jos ventured out again a little after five, forced to by hunger, she discovered Jude standing in the dark sitting room at the window, back to the room, just looking through the glass into the blackness of the garden. The atmosphere in the room felt dense and corrupt.

Brooding.

*

Jos was standing looking through another window by then.

It was a bright and colourful view, nevertheless slightly tainted by the memory of Jude's hidden rage. Sighing, she plugged her mobile in to charge, and applied some factor fifty to her arms and shoulders. Swapping her heeled sandals for very comfy flip flops, Jos was ready to step outside again. A little bistro table with two chairs was positioned directly under the window. She hadn't noticed it before and decided to sit there for a few minutes before going back downstairs to find Beola.

Large and low planters were positioned around this little seating area, filled with lavender, mint and citronella to keep mosquitos at bay. Beyond that a low compartment jutted out from the wall a couple of feet. Behind its wooden doors lay a variety of gardening paraphernalia. Mounted on the wall above was a length of coiled hose, attached at one end to one of two taps fitted on the wall next to the storage. A second length of hose travelled straight down from the second tap, where it disappeared into a narrow, grid covered channel set in the mosaic. This was the start of the irrigation system that watered every planter in the roof garden with just a few turns of a single tap.

Jos chose the chair nearest the garden room door and turned it, so it had its back to the window. Sitting down she gazed across the garden, once more marvelling at how beautiful it was, as well as the work that had surely gone into creating it. She wondered if had looked this mature fourteen years ago, or had Jude left before her ideas reached their full potential. She thought about the work Beola must put into it to this day to keep it looking so beautiful. The deadheading alone was probably a full-time job. She yawned. Sleepy suddenly. Sliding her sunnies down from her head to her face, Jos relaxed against the chair back and closed her eyes. She could feel the heat of the sun against her skin. The warm breath of the breeze caressed her. She sighed. It was so very quiet by then. As if all the insects and birds had stopped for lunch. Maybe it was the midday heat?

Maybe it was something different altogether?

Unseen by Jos, as her eyes remained closed, the environment slowed down to a gradual stop all around her. The swallows that had been swooping overhead, flew off in search of insects elsewhere. Butterflies and bees alighted on the nearest flower or leaf, closed their wings and paused. Lizards stopped in their tracks. Insects either buzzed off or settled down. Even the breeze died, until not a sound, not a thing, not a breath of air stirred.

Waiting.

CHAPTER SIX

Back in Edinburgh, Jude was adjusting to having her home to herself again.

Life had been busy these past weeks; helping Jos apply for her visa, listening to tales of trips to the medical centre to be stuck with various needles, shopping for malaria pills, Deet and sunscreen, factor fifty and after-sun, tea tree, lavender and clary sage, Imodium, Diorolyte and Senacot… Jos had covered all those bases. Checking and rechecking travel documents as well as securing fifty thousand Tanzanian shillings through the bank, to go with the five hundred US dollars she was also taking.

Far too much even if Jos stayed a whole month in Jude's opinion.

'There's sod all to spend it on,' she'd warned. 'Clothes, jewellery, curios… it's all cheap as chips. Eating out is equally cheap… and highly dangerous without trusted recommendations. The cost of living is rock bottom because the standard of living is too. For Christ sake don't eat anything that isn't properly cooked and do not drink the water outside the house. There's a filtration system there, but everywhere else is roulette on tap. You better hope your every toilet is right next to a sink.'

Jude had presented a battery of such warnings regarding the dangers of Africa. Dysentery, sleeping sickness, cholera, insect and snake bites, wild animal attacks… there were only natural boundaries around the house so animal visitors were commonplace. Kidnapping, rape, murder, A.I.D.S. It was all commonplace. If Jude had been trying to put Jos off, it hadn't worked. Why would it? As Jos periodically pointed out, Jude had survived Tanzania for over a decade, and she was damned if she was going to pass up on this wonderful opportunity.

When the day finally arrived, Jude drove her to the airport.

There were tears in Jos' eyes as they said their goodbyes. 'I wish you were coming,' she moaned.

'Only because you're nervous about travelling on your own.'

No,' Jos protested. 'It's not just…'

‘Bollocks,’ Jude told her, fishing a fresh tissue from a pocket pack.

Dabbing gently, Jos asked, ‘Is my mascara buggered?’

‘Get used to it,’ Jude advised. ‘Once you get over there your make-up will just slide off your face.’

‘Nice,’ Jos sighed, looking very sorry for herself, and said a final goodbye.

Jude watched as her niece entered the airport and disappeared among the crowds, then she got back into her car and headed home.

The by-pass hadn’t been too horrendous on the way there, so Jude retraced that route back to the Biggar Road exit and turned north on the A702. Passing through Morningside she stopped off at Waitrose to pick up supplies. Newbattle Terrace and Whitehouse Terrace took her to Kilgraston Road, and she was nearly home. The closer she got, the bigger the houses, the taller the trees and the quieter the streets. Any parked cars wouldn’t belong to the residents. Residents had driveways leading to double or even triple garages.

Reaching the gates into her own drive, Jude pressed the remote and angled the car while the gates swung smoothly open. Driving in she paused to ensure the gates were closing behind her again, then parked at the side of the house. She went in through the boot room, past a bank of cat litter trays, and then into the main kitchen with her shopping.

Nicolae and Imelda were waiting and immediately started mewling, encircling Jude’s feet and rubbing against her legs. As soon as she’d put away her shopping, she fed the cats. When the sounds of those dishes being prepared reached feline ears, they came running from all over the house, as well as in from outside. Seven of the little buggers. There was always dry food available, but they all preferred the wet food sachets. Once the food dishes were on the floor of the utility room, the mewling stopped. After the meal there would be group grooming and purring.

Just like their much bigger relatives.

While the cats were busy, Jude went upstairs to shower and change. There hadn’t been time for that earlier with Jos in panic mode. Did she have all her tickets? Where was her cash? Where was the visa? What if she hated Africa? What if she hated the food? It would be weird food, wouldn't it? Jude had already said a hundred times that Beola was a great cook, so she ignored that question along with all the others. Instead, she took command of Jos' document pack and laid out the contents on the kitchen table. Two flight tickets, a visa, passport, sterling, dollars and shillings, vaccine record. Everything was there. She then made Jos put the pack into the purloined Fendi bag ready for the off. The enormous suitcase had been opened and reclosed three times before it made it into the boot of the car, because Jos checked, rechecked and checked the contents again. It was the same with the bag. Jude had simply breathed deeply and slowly and counted down the minutes.

Would she miss Jos?

Miss the occasional loud music, the abandoned and half read books, the near constant indecisiveness, and the constant reminder of the woman she herself had become? Somehow. In her day Jude had cut a swathe through everything and everyone in her path, but not anymore. Now she and Jos were like peas in a pod — two loners who ventured out from their cloister only when necessity demanded it. Back at the airport, as they made their goodbyes it had certainly felt like she was losing someone, or maybe even something important. As if something fixed was finally unravelling. Jude didn't want to dwell on what that might be, so she went back downstairs, made herbal tea and took it into the conservatory to make the most of the pleasant afternoon and a brand-new book.

It was September and too chilly to sit outside even with the intermittent sunshine. Sitting there she couldn't help thinking about Peter, about Africa, about loss. She'd thought of little else since Beola had crashed back into her life after all these years but now, without Jos to distract her, the book was abandoned unopened, and memories came flooding in.

*

It was 1970.

Judith Johnstone was still eighteen when she left Edinburgh with her ginger afro and travelled down to Bristol to see her best friend, April, who was at University there — much to her parents' chagrin. Old fashioned, working class parents who believed their daughter shouldn't be gallivanting around the country on her own, asking for trouble. Jude didn't give a toss. She'd saved up enough money from her job in a local chemist for a single train fare with a little left over to live on for a couple of weeks. She intended looking for work down south in the hope she wouldn't ever have to return.

April had offered to put her up until she got on her feet, so it was all good.

Within days of arriving in Bristol Jude found herself in the back of a Volkswagen camper van, with April and a bunch of her fellow students.

They were on their way to a house party in Bath. It was the end of their exams, and the start of the long summer break. They were celebrating.

The house party was also a garden party because the weather was glorious. There was booze, plenty of nibbles and plenty of weed to smoke. Everyone was drunk, stoned or both. At some point Jude realised she was being watched. As soon as they made eye contact, he extricated himself from the gaggle of girls surrounding him and sauntered over. He wore scuffed Chelsea boots, faded jeans and a T-Rex T-shirt. He wore his straight, glossy looking blonde hair down to his shoulders. The kind of painfully beautiful hair Jude usually coveted when seen on other women.

He was drop dead gorgeous and his name was Peter.

Charming and funny and a real flirt, he pretended to read her palm… she wasn't ever going to meet a tall dark stranger, just this blonde one. His accent was unusual. It seemed very English at first, but there was a hint of something else. Something blonde. Peter kept hold of Jude's hand and, after a time, led her out to the garden which was in darkness by then and a lot quieter. He brought along a bottle of red wine, and she carried the glasses. They sat on a low wall surrounding a large flower bed. Peter loved Jude's hair, her accent. He wanted to know all about her. The first thing she told him was that she didn't like wine. He laughed, delighted, and fetched her a few beers instead.

Armed with a cold beer, Jude discovered Peter had just completed a degree in Architecture at M.I.T., whatever and wherever that was. Previously, he'd completed a degree in Business and Commerce at Imperial College, London. He wasn't sure what he wanted to do with his life now he was done being a student, but maybe something to do with construction. He was following in his father's footsteps, so Jude just assumed his dad was a builder. His dad was originally from Aberdeen, and his mother from Norway. Peter spoke Norwegian fluently, and also a little French.

They spent the night together in that garden, talking until dawn. The party wound down and people either drifted off or found a corner to crash in. Peter and Jude wandered out into the bright morning instead and walked to a café nearby where they ate breakfast. He then took her to the train station and saw her onto a train back to Bristol, but not before she wrote down her address. There was a lot of kissing while waiting for that train, but Jude wasn't at all convinced she'd see her half Norwegian, half Scottish Viking again.

Late the following Monday morning, Peter arrived with flowers and the promise of a picnic.

Jude climbed into his sporty little car… literally because the passenger door was stuck fast, and they drove off with the top down. Leaving Bristol behind, they headed east taking the main roads before veering off into narrow lanes bordered by high hedgerows. Eventually they came to Dragon's Hill Road where Peter parked up close to the gate across a pathway. The landscape was high, green and rolling. Jude climbed back out of the car and then over a style before they walked along a vague path to a flat-topped hill. This was where St George had slain the dragon, according to Peter. But he turned the still standing Jude around to see something even better. The Uffington White Horse was high up on the hillside opposite, its pure white chalk looking brilliant against the green, green grass. The sight of it took Jude's breath away.

Peter took Jude's breath away. The way he treated her, the way he cherished her, the way he loved her. Mind body and soul. She hadn't had much experience of men before meeting her half Norwegian Viking, but he was undoubtedly different. With Peter, Jude discovered the true meaning of pleasure.

After a summer of picnics and parties, trips to the seaside, delicious meals in weird and wonderful locations, intense sex on a variety of drugs, Peter dropped a bombshell. 'I'm leaving, Fluff.' He'd been calling Jude that for weeks, mostly in reference to her unruly hair. She did not approve, so he mostly saved it for when they were alone, as they were then, in the middle of Bristol Zoo having just visited the penguins.

The bottom fell out of Jude's world as soon as those words were out of his mouth, and she realised she was in love. She was eighteen years old, she had no job, no family support, and now the love of her life was leaving. She felt like going straight to Clifton Suspension Bridge and chucking herself right off. Not that she let on. Her face was a perfect mask of indifference.

Thinking he would say Brighton or London or something equally local, Jude kept her face and tone impassive when she asked, 'Where are you off to?'

'France, initially. My dad has a project. I'd like to take you along.'

It was then very difficult to maintain that cool calm exterior, but Jude gave it her best effort. 'Really?'

'I'm in love with you,' Peter stated matter-of-factly, because these games were best played in twos. 'But first… I'd like us to get married.'

'WHAT!' Jude tossed away the mask and looked as incredulous as she felt. 'Why?'

'I'm an old fashioned kinda guy.'

'Rubbish!'

'That's what lovers do, Fluff.'

'But… I can't…'

'I know. You're a modern woman. You can't tie yourself down. I mean, if your parents ever found out you did anything so conventional…' Peter looked horrified on Jude's behalf.

Jude laughed loudly, and then said, 'My parents are not coming!' 'To France?' Peter wondered.

Two weeks later they were married in the registry office in Marlborough. April was maid of honour and Gary Preston, Peter's own best friend from childhood, was best man. There were no other guests. Jude had called her little sister with the news… at least, she'd called their neighbour who fetched Julia from home to take the call. Julia had been overjoyed and wanted to be a bridesmaid. But there wasn't to be a big wedding, with a fancy dress, lots of bridesmaids and a busy reception. Jude tried her best to explain, but Julia got upset and then angry. Jude was selfish and horrible, and Julia was never going to speak to her again. Jude would call again once Julia had the chance to cool down. In the meantime, Peter made miss her become missus him and, after a long lunch in a restaurant close to the registry office, Mr and Mrs Sinclair drove off, heading south.

*

When their brief honeymoon was over… deliciously sweet and spent in a pretty little hotel close to the Jurassic coast of Dorset, it was time to travel to France to meet the in-laws.

The newlyweds sat near the front of the aircraft where the seats were roomier than those farther back. Drinks were served in glasses and came with little dishes of nibbles. Upon landing, they were met by a young man holding a board bearing their name. Once Peter had identified himself, the man took charge of their luggage and escorted them to a fancy looking car parked nearby. Handing over the keys, he then stowed their luggage and bid them au revoir et bonne route.

Leaving Nice, they took the coast road travelling in the direction of another airport but turned off before reaching it. They then travelled up into the hills of Fabron. The roads narrowed as they climbed. The crowded houses began to thin out, get bigger. By then Jude was nervous. Working class roots jingle jangled a tune about inadequacy. She was out of her depth. Out of place. 'You're rich,' she declared suddenly. 'And your parents are gonna hate me!'

'They won't. Trust me.'

Jude spent the final few minutes of the journey feeling fit to vomit. When the car slowed to turn off the road and head down a steep drive towards a large pale orange house, perched on the edge of a cliff overlooking the sparkling Mediterranean, she pictured herself jumping for it and making off into the undergrowth. But two people had already appeared. A tall dark-haired man and an equally tall blonde woman. They were smiling, waving. Peter had barely stopped the car before he leapt out and enjoyed a group hug.

He hadn't seen them in months.

Jude was stuck in her seat, wide eyed and terrified. Then Peter's dad came to her door, opened it and reached a hand out. Johnny had a thick head of very dark brown, wavy hair which was just beginning to show grey at the temples. His eyes were brown, and, with his summer tan, he looked almost Spanish. His smile was the same cheeky grin he'd passed on to his son. 'You must be the wee Edinburgh lassie Peter married.'

Jude laughed, trying to conceal her shock. Taking the offered hand, she climbed out to stand before her very ordinary, working class sounding father-in-law.

Johnny kissed Jude on both cheeks, French style, then said, 'Welcome to the family, Jude.' Turning towards his smiling wife, he went on, 'Meet Astrid, Peter's mum.'

'Welcome to France, Jude.' Peter had inherited her blonde hair and beautiful blue eyes. Astrid also kissed both cheeks before embracing Jude briefly but tightly. 'Welcome,' she said again, before letting her go. 'You must be hungry. I'll show you to your room so you can freshen up and then we can eat dinner on the terrace. The views are so beautiful night or day. We love it here, and we're sure you will too.'

Astrid's accent was mostly heavy Norwegian vowels with the rolling and throat clearing consonants common in Scottish dialects thrown in, so Jude had to listen intently to try to piece together what she was being told. Luckily, Peter seemed to know what was expected so she just followed her husband's lead until her ears grew more attuned to her mother-in-law.

During a boozy dinner, Jude had Johnny and Astrid's story that very first evening.

He'd grown up in Aberdeenshire but had no interest in crofting like his parents. Instead, he went onto the trawlers at fifteen. When he wasn't at sea, he was laying girls and laying bets. A gambling man Johnny was also a lucky man and managed to buy his own trawler before he turned twentyfive. Soon after that war broke out and, like a lot of trawler captains, his boat was taken over by the MOD. Johnny became a gun runner for

Churchill, taking arms as well as medical supplies across to Norway and sometimes France.

Astrid fled Norway during the winter of 1942, but not on Johnny's boat.

From 1941 until the end of the war, many Norwegians were able to escape using The Shetland Bus: Fleets of small fishing vessels, with a few light machine guns concealed inside oil drums as their only defence, and courageous crews disguised as humble fishermen. They sailed at night, often in dreadful conditions, with no lights and the constant threat of discovery by German patrols. But the risks for the passengers were often less than those faced in Norway. Astrid's parents were active in the Norwegian resistance. Her father had been betrayed and subsequently executed, so she was escaping with her mother. But their boat was blown off course in an almighty storm. Several passengers and crew were swept overboard, her mother among them. Lost to the sea. The survivors were lucky to make land at all, pitching up on Black Dog Beach, north of Aberdeen. The locals lent a hand during the rescue and some also took in refugees. Astrid was bereaved and alone, seventeen years old, and taken in by the parents Johnny had left behind.

'I slept in his bed, read all his books, gazed out across the view he'd grown up with.' Astrid's smile was wistful, remembering. Then she made a face. 'I also ate his mother's dreadful porridge.'

'She knew me well before we even met,' Johnny smiled lovingly at his beautiful wife.

Jude watched her in-laws, the way they touched and smiled and looked at each other. Obviously still in love after all these years. They got to know one another during the course of the war and, once it was over, quickly became lovers and were married as soon as Astrid suspected she was pregnant. Peter arrived eight months later, and Johnny got on with inventing ways to support his family.

Taking advantage of the political and economic chaos in the immediate aftermath, Johnny carried on doing what he'd come to know as business; buying and selling armaments. 'I was a smuggler,' he admitted. 'An arms dealer.' But that didn't readily settle with his conscious, especially after the birth of his son, so, after a few years, he got out of destruction and into construction.

Having no experience of such things, he simply invested in those who could build, housing, factories, schools. Demand was high, opportunities plentiful. Johnny put up the cash for as many projects as he was able to, and the returns snowballed. By the dawn of the sixties, he was a very wealthy man. They did the predictable things; spent big, travelled, sent their young son to the best school, and they bought a big house in the Wiltshire countryside.

'But we'll only ever be common,' Johnny shrugged. 'Unless you're born into your money the British rich just look down their long, snooty noses at you. At us.' He and Astrid were ostracised by the affluent and by the ordinary. They weren't invited to any of the dinners or the posh parties, and they weren't welcome down the local pub. They didn't fit in anywhere. 'It's better over here and in the US,' he went on. 'The French and Americans aren't snobs like the bloody English.'

'What about Scotland?' Jude wondered. 'Do you ever think about going back there?'

'My folks died before I made any real money, and I don't have any other close family to speak of. But I do go back now and then. We set up an emergency fund for the trawler fleets. Anything from boat repairs to funeral costs. You see, Jude, once you reach a certain point in financial terms, you can't spend it. It just sits there being as useless as money is, without something to drive it forward. So, we use some to make the lives of less fortunate folks a bit better. We've set up scholarships so clever kids from poorer families can go to university, and we're building a library in Astrid's home town. The German's burnt it down, books and all, in 1941. We just try to do a bit of good. But I won't be getting any younger, and now it's Peter's turn to step up and show the world what he's good for.'

Before rising to the challenges of his father, Peter and Jude had some

fun.

They enjoyed trips to the theatre and ballet, as well as the odd concert. They went for long walks along the beaches of Cannes and Nice, stopping off for delicious meals and cocktails along the way. People watching. They wandered the medieval streets of Antibes old town, ducking in and out of the endless artisan shops.

In upmarket Juan Les Pins, they trawled the boutiques, trying on clothes, hats and the latest designer shoes. Jude's first big purchase with her very own Master Card was a dark green Coco Chanel pants suit. She felt fit to burst every time she caught sight of herself in a mirror!

Jude Sinclair underwent a huge transformation in a relatively short period of time. When October came around with her nineteenth birthday, she carried herself with an elegance and calm that belied her youth. She wore expensive clothes, shoes, make-up. A very expensive hair salon in Cannes had turned her bright orange afro into deeper orange spirals and curls that drew admiring glances instead of the looks of horror or ridicule she'd grown up with. She was, head to toes, a new woman. And, though she didn't get over her dislike of wine, Jude did become a big fan of Bollinger.

*

The present displaced the past when big ginger Benito jumped up onto Jude's lap.

It was late afternoon by then, time to feed the cats. Time to potter and tidy round for a while. Time to prepare and eat dinner. A glass of wine or three later helped Jude sit still long enough to watch a crappy movie on TV. Another glass helped her to sleep the slumber of the insensible but woke her at four am with a thumping headache and a full bladder. Taking care of both she then managed to get back to sleep and didn't wake until nearly eight! By the time she'd fed and watered the cats and eaten her own breakfast, she realised that Jos must be in Tanzania by now. Maybe she had even made it to the white house.

When the phone rang moments later, Jude jumped a little.

But she didn't leave the kitchen and cross the hall. Didn't pick it up. When Jos began to speak, her familiar voice only slightly muted by the distance, she simply got up from the table, and closed the kitchen door.

CHAPTER SEVEN

Still waiting.

The soft sigh that escaped from between Jos' lips was the only sound. Floating and yet deeply rooted, lighter than air and heavy like lead, drifting in place. She felt everything and nothing. The air drawn slowly inside her felt soporific, its effects felt throughout the entire roof garden and for some little distance beyond. Every living thing caught up inside a mysterious bubble, and Jos was at its focus. Heart beat ebbed and blood flowed. Mind calmed, thoughts faded, until she was barely mindful of her own existence.

She sat, perfectly still and silent for long drawn-out moments.

Wake up.

A little voice inside suddenly piped up. A frown flitted across her brow. Hitching in a little breath, this time Jos made a small moaning sound. It reached her ears and awakened her thoughts. The quiet was surely not natural, considering the air had been filled with the voices of teeming life as she stood in front of the white house. She remembered too the sounds of buzzing insect life which should be surrounding her here and now. Something was different. The air felt heavy and almost cloying now. It seemed to be pressing against her, holding her in place. Jos knew she needed to open her eyes… but she was afraid to.

Of course, she had to.

Peter Sinclair was seated on the bench opposite her. Dressed in habitual jeans and the sky-blue cotton shirt he'd died in. He'd removed his battered old Tilly hat and placed it on the slats next to him. He cast no shadow because the sun did not acknowledge him any longer. As soon as she opened her eyes, he said, 'Hello, Jos.'

Jos recognised him immediately from a framed photograph her parents had kept in their living room. She hadn't seen it since the morning before their deaths, but Jude's dead husband was a striking looking man and there was absolutely no doubt that it was he seated directly opposite. She cried out in fright, jumping up from the chair like it was burning hot and knocking it over with a loud clatter. She then almost fell over it as she tried to get away. 'You're dead. You can't be here,' Jos told him, her voice high in her panic. 'Go away.' She wagged a hand at him, diving in through the garden room door, and slamming it shut behind her. 'Go away,' she wailed, her back pressed to the door.

'Wait until she sees my burnt-out husk side,' Peter told the sky, and then immediately disappeared.

Just like that.

A sudden breeze puffed into life, and immediately the garden bounced back into action. Stalled lizards dashed for cover, butterflies and bees spread their wings and resumed their floral business. Insects chittered and chattered. Swallows reappeared as if by magic, swooping and soaring in the air above the garden.

As if nothing at all had just happened.

Beola had heard the disturbance from the kitchen and raced up the outside stairs as fast as she could. She paused at the top, seeing nothing except the overturned chair under the window. Crossing the space on quick and silent feet, she knocked on the door, and asked, 'Jos… Can I come in?'

Jumping in fright from her new position at the side of the armoire; hiding like a child, and then immediately relieved that someone else was there. Someone who was actually alive! She crossed the room and opened the door.

'Are you all right?' Beola asked, her face a mask of concern. She could see Jos' hands were shaking, and that she looked like a person who'd just had a bad shock. Perhaps she'd seen a ghost? 'I heard you cry out.'

'I don't know.' Rational mind had intervened by then. There was no such thing as ghosts. The heat, the bright sun, the journey. All these things had conspired to fool her into seeing something which could not be there. 'I must have fallen asleep,' Jos reasoned. 'I nearly fell off the chair. I gave myself a fright.'

'Are you hurt?'

'No,' Jos shook her head. 'I'm fine, honestly… just a bit…' Scared?

'You are tired after your journey.' There was no point in trying to force an issue that wasn't ready to be dealt with, so Beola suggested, 'Why don't we all have something to eat and then you can relax, perhaps have a little nap.'

‘Sounds good,’ Jos nodded, relieved to have an excuse to leave the scene.

*

Lunch was served on the patio.

Vegetable curry, spiced pilau rice, chapattis and little sweet potato and courgette patties served with a rich red dipping sauce which was hotter than Jos expected. She could feel the sweat prickling out of her facial pores and had to gulp down a couple of glasses of water.

Beola laughed almost as hard as Ben and Wendell. ‘Perhaps a little less chilli the next time.’

‘That is lethal!’ Jos declared.

Having been asked about her journey, she spoke about her plane neighbour and all the money he’d raised for charity climbing Kilimanjaro eight times already. ‘Such a lovely old man,’ she said. ‘I really do hope to catch up with him for a drink after his latest climb. Richard Isherwood, he’s a…’

‘Retired teacher!’ Wendell remembered. ‘He’s been on at least two of our tours. Maybe three.’

‘Has he really?’ Ben asked.

‘He’s the old fella who jumped into Lake Chala to rescue that little American kid who’d hit his head on a rock.’

Ben remembered. ‘Mum and Dad were too busy taking pictures and we were setting up the barbeque.’

‘Small world,’ Wendell declared. ‘He always stays at the Kilimanjaro

Wonders. Pretty good bar and restaurant there.’

‘Mimosa is better.’ Ben thought. ‘They apparently serve the best cocktails.’ Wendell was looking at him as if horns had sprouted on his head. ‘What? I hear things, I read the reviews. And the food is supposed to be divine.’

‘Better than my cooking?’ Beola was wondering.

‘There is no better cook than you, Beola,’ Wendell told her, winking at Jos.

‘Lunch is delicious,’ Jos agreed. ‘I cook,’ she revealed. ‘Though I’m better at baking. Great biscuits and cakes.’

'Biscuits and cakes!' Wendell was delighted. 'We should have a cook
off.'

'As long as I can judge all the dishes.' Nightingale breezed through the French doors. She was tall and slim, her long, narrow plaits collected up into a knot at the back of her head. With a musical 'jambo' for all, she went to Beola first, then Ben and Wendell and shook hands with each of them. When it was the red head's turn, Nightingale, also said, 'Nafurahi kukuona, Jos.'

Jos was at a loss, and just beginning to feel awkward.

But Nightingale burst out laughing, clapping her hands in delight. 'I'm just messing with you. My English is a lot better than your Swahili.' Throwing herself onto a chair, she pursed her lips, batted her lashes and leaned in towards Beola.

'Help yourself,' Beola laughed. Then, when Nightingale reached out towards the patties, added, 'Get a plate.'

Nightingale made a dash for the kitchen and was back in seconds. Gone long enough for Jos to notice how Ben's eyes had followed her.

'Nightingale is our assistant.' Ben had noticed Jos watching, and was trying to hide his tracks.

Snorting, Nightingale said, 'If it wasn't for me these two would not know where they were, never mind where they were supposed to be going. I organise everything. I even built them a proper website. They had a book... HTML For Dummies.' Sweeping a hand high over her head to indicate even that child's play book was way over Ben and Wendell's combined head, she added. 'My mama didn't raise no dummy.' 'Hey!' Beola protested.

*

Ben, Wendell and Nightingale went off to their office as soon as everyone was finished lunch... but not before checking with Beola about required help clearing up. Jos took her opportunity and insisted she would take care of that. Luckily, there was a dishwasher. The kitchen wasn't ultra-modern by Jude's ice blue, high gloss finish and frosted glass counter tops standard, but rather it was bleached wood farmhouse style with pots and pans hanging from a ceiling grid, a red tiled floor and a big oak table. After loading the dishes, sticking in a tab and pressing the indicated button, Jos wondered,

'What's next?'

'Are you tired? Maybe you would like to go upstairs for a little nap?'

That was the last thing Jos wanted to do. 'Can't I have a tour instead?'

'I shall show you the important landmarks now,' Beola agreed. 'The rest of the house you should discover for yourself.'
'Okay,' Jos supposed.

Important landmarks in the east were where the food stuffs were stored, where the washing machine was, the dining and kitchen linen and towels. Upstairs Beola showed Jos where to find fresh bedding and bath towels as well as which bedroom was her and Kissi's. Back downstairs western landmarks included the TV room which was also where the internet could be accessed. Books were, naturally, stored in the library. From there they exited through the French doors onto the far end of the patio from where they'd eaten lunch and wandered around the kitchen garden.

Courgettes, lettuce, radish, tomatoes, potatoes, carrots, cauliflower, sweet potatoes, green beans were the vegetables Jos recognised. Melons, strawberries and blueberries the easily identified fruits. An irrigation system snaked up and down the rows, connected to a nearby tap. 'We turn the tap on every morning and leave it for around half an hour.' Beola explained. 'If it gets very hot, we do it again as the sun is going down. There's a similar system upstairs in the roof garden. The taps are just outside the garden room.'

Jos made a mental note to try to remember to turn the water on at least once a day. 'Do you grow all your food?'

'As much as we can. Supply is better now, but when Peter and Jude started this garden it was out of necessity. They kept chickens too, but I don't like them…' Beola shivered. 'I cannot bear the sight of their feet,' she said.

'So, you got rid of them?'

'We ate them.' Laughing along with Jos, Beola then led her out from within the arms of the house, across the sun-drenched rear lawn, and on until they came to a gated fence. Pointing to where they could just be seen, she said, 'These solar panels provide all our power.' 'Why the turbine?' Jos wondered.

'Even here we sometimes miss the sun. Storms are not unknown. The wind blows and the lights stay on. Mostly.' They then walked a little further along the fence line, heading west until they could see the hives. 'I hope you like honey.' Seven hives holding around four hundred thousand busy little bees. 'Jude planted the garden so that there would be flowers for every single month of the year.'

'Did she look after the hives?'

'She was a better beekeeper than Peter. At least the bees thought so. Sometimes Jude never wore any of the gear at all… except she would wrap her hair up into a scarf, otherwise bees would get all caught up in it.'

'Jude the beekeeper…' mused Jos. 'Who knew.'

Next, they came to a side door in what would soon be revealed as the garage block.

Inside there was a wide grid across part of the floor. Pipes came up through, or possibly went down into it. Those pipes came from… or went into, a large metal unit with lots of buttons and a few circles of light in greens and ambers. More pipes crossed the ceiling, went down the wall close to the door, and disappeared into the floor. 'This is the pump and filtration system,' Beola explained. 'All our water comes from the well.'

She pointed to the grid. 'It's safe to drink straight from the tap.' Through a second door, they entered the garage.

There was a very old dark blue, two-seater jeep parked side by side with a newer, larger green one. A big red ride on mower sat beyond that, and a push bike was leaning against the back wall next to a petrol strimmer. There were wall mounted shelves holding jerry cans, ear defenders, visors and goggles, and several big plastic bottles of various motor oils. There were reels of strimmer cable, a big green funnel, a bicycle pump. Various grades of rope were hung in neat coils from hooks. There was a huge, wheeled toolbox standing beside a pile of what looked like new and unused tyres in a corner. There were also boxes of batteries, mostly double and triple A, and a row of hurricane lamps for when the lights went out.

'Feel free to borrow a jeep whenever you please,' Beola told Jos.

'I can't drive.'

'Well, if you want to go into town, I will take you.'

'Sorry,' Jos made a face. 'I'm so useless.'

'I am sure that is not true!' Beola told her firmly. 'And anyway… I go marketing every two or three days. Ben is often going into town in the evenings, so you can hitch with him. He and Wendell visit all the hotels and bars looking for new customers. We will work it out.'

As they were walking from the garages around to the front of the house, Jos saw the little log cabin. 'Who lives there?'

'Jude and Peter did while the house was being built. Then I moved in with Kissi and Ben… and now Ben lives there alone. His bachelor pad.' Rolling her eyes, Beola added, 'Sometimes I wonder if he will ever settle down.'

Rounding the corner of the house, Jos saw the lion for the second time, and realised she'd forgotten about it in all the excitement. Heading straight for it, she reached out to touch the raised paw. The metal was warmed by the sun and gave the illusion of a living thing. Her hand held the massive paw for a few seconds, and then travelled down the leg, across the partially exposed chest, up the throat and onto the muzzle. The mouth was slightly open, relaxed looking. Just the merest suggestion of teeth. Indentations and whiskers, wide flat nose, half closed eyes, rounded ears. The detail was incredible. Continuing to explore Jos smoothed her hand down the back of the huge head, along the powerful neck, across one shoulder and on along the one and a half meters of muscular flank. She then trailed her hand along the gently winding coil of tail which hung lazily off the stone plinth. Aware that Beola had joined her, Jos said, 'This is really beautiful.'

'Lulu,' Beola told her and, when Jos obviously didn't have a clue, she added, 'Lulu is the reason Jude and Peter stayed in Tanzania.'

CHAPTER EIGHT

When the autumn of 1970 arrived in the south of France, and just after Jude's 19th birthday which was celebrated on a yacht on the Med, Johnny and Astrid headed off to California, and it was time for Peter to take on those projects.

Having always been interested in architecture, he had recently also expressed a desire to resurrect old buildings, so Johnny had purchased three near derelict properties in the south of France. Three ancient chateaux left to fall into rack and ruin. Peter had a reasonable budget and instructions to bring these beautiful buildings back to life. Once the renovations were complete, he could sell them for as much as possible, pay Johnny back the total budget and invest the rest as he saw fit.

It took until September 1972 to renovate, market and sell all three properties. So, while Jude was learning useful French phrases… pouvezvous me melanger une margarita s'il vous plait, or… pouvez-vous apporter une autre bouteille de Bollinger a la table, learning to cook cassoulet and boeuf bourguignon, and refusing to enjoy even the best Bordeaux reds, Peter was getting down and dirty with his three French mistresses.

Rather than try to restore the chateaux as family homes, he transformed each one into a boutique hotel. Beautifully finished bedrooms all had en suite facilities, there were cosy bars and smart dining areas overlooking sweeping lawns and unspoiled acres of parkland and forests. Fish filled lakes, rivers and moats. Entrance halls became modern reception areas with fully restored, ornamental staircases. He retained as many original features as possible and married those with the most up to date furnishings and materials. Old met new and fell in love.

When each chateau neared completion Jude and Peter moved into the management suite to get a feel for the building and what it needed to turn it from a project into a needful thing. This is where Jude came into her own. Dying of boredom by then, she relished the chance to finally play a part. Drapes to complement upholstery, whole rooms decorated around an antique chandelier salvaged from an out of the way Brocante. Antique French beds, gilded mirrors, huge armoires, delicate dining furniture. Jude had an eye and began to do some restorations herself after watching and learning from the old men who came to sand and plane, and polish battered old pieces back into life. She also discovered a talent for gardening.

It was all very well having rich and beautiful interiors and massive windows to gaze out across the lawns, but there was only so much green the eye wanted to see. Colours were missing and so Jude went off the Jardinières to investigate flowers. From bedding plants to shrubs to trees, she was able to picture how they could look when brought together and plan flowerbeds, window boxes, secret gardens and sweet-smelling orchards. By the time the hotels went on the market they looked stunning outside as well as in. After repaying Johnny's original investment, property taxes and other fees, Peter and Jude walked away with over fifty thousand pounds.

Next stop America.

*

Taking a break from renovations and restorations Peter turned his attention to technology.

Gary Preston, was a very talented computer programmer, and flew with them to Washington DC in October 1972. Jude celebrated her twenty-first birthday at Old Ebbitt Grill, washing down oysters with ice cold beers and spotting the actors and politicians also dining there. Change was coming according to Gary and Peter.

'Whatever happened to miniskirts and the contraceptive pill?' Jude wondered.

'This is the biggest advancement in communications since the printing press, Fluff.' Peter was animated in his excitement. 'Bigger than the telephone.'

'Bigger than Jesus!' Gary declared a little too loudly for the allAmerican palate.

It was the eve of the International Computer Communications Conference where there would be the first ever public demonstration of something called ARPAnet; a revolutionary packet switching system which was destined to become the internet. Computers would talk to each other using gateways, irrespective of borders, regardless of operating systems. Peter didn't know what exactly, but he could almost smell the possibilities and had money to invest in the people on the verge of changing the world. Gary was there to advise his friend on the most viable options from the hundreds available.

Three days of networking and demonstrations later, Peter and Gary were on first name terms with William Gates and Paul Allen. Three years later, Peter would invest a chunk of capital into setting up a company called Micro-soft. One year after that he would make a similar investment in the Apple Computer Company. The dividends generated from stocks held in these and similar companies, formed the continuing foundation of the Sinclair family wealth.

The shares that just kept on giving also came from capital Johnny had invested previously. IBM, Coca-Cola, McDonalds, Walmart, Proctor & Gamble to name his big five. However, Johnny didn't expand his portfolio the way Peter intended. He saw investments as a kind of career. He had a good nose for a great idea and, if he heard about something interesting, he hopped on a plane and went to see for himself, talk to the people behind it and, if they were open to it, help them to make it happen in exchange for shares.

Stocks and shares became his craft, and Peter scoured the markets constantly. He read never-ending newspapers and journals, books, magazines. He bought and sold based on research into various trends that he believed were predictable. The Monday effect was a consistent anomaly in any market; bad news released the previous Friday night, negatively affected share price the following Monday. Peter made modest profits simply collecting stocks on Mondays, sitting on them for a few weeks, and then offloading them on chosen Friday mornings. There was the January effect, the holiday effect, momentum effect, value effect. The predictabilities were often self-fulfilling, and Peter was right enough of the time to justify the time he put into it. Sinclair wealth grew in relation to their rapidly expanding stock portfolio.

*

After three years back and forth between the US, Europe and the UK, Jude was fed up.

'I'm so bored,' she moaned. She didn't mind the first-class travel, or the luxury hotels and apartments, or the amazing food she was taking for granted by then. But there was only so much shopping a girl could do while her husband ogled new bits of technology or poured over indexes of stocks and shares. 'Can't we spend some time together? Just me and you. No more dinners out talking computers with all those weedy guys you seem to be collecting.'

'How about a holiday?' Peter was surprised his wife had put up with it all for so long. 'You choose, Fluff.'

Jude slept on it, and the following morning decided, 'I'd like to go to Africa — on a safari.'

Peter booked them a two week stay at Amani Lodge on the slopes of Mount Kilimanjaro, inside the national park, in northern Tanzania. They could go on safari every day if Jude wanted and, if they got bored with that, the town of Moshi was less than thirty miles to the south with its selection of bars and restaurants for the tourists. He bought Jude a professional grade camera for her twenty-third birthday, so she could document their adventures.

*

Having arrived after dark, Jude got her first view of Mount Kilimanjaro when she stepped out onto their wide terrace a little after dawn. Wrapped in a red and black shuka against the chill, she gazed out across the tops of the dense tree cover between her elevated position and that beautiful view. A great, flat topped pyramid of hardened lava and ash, dark against the brightening of the African sky. A snow-capped wonder, dominating the landscape. At 19,341 feet it was the highest peak in Africa. Three peaks actually, Shira, Mawenzi and Kibo. A stratovolcano. The tallest freestanding mountain in the world. Jude had been reading all about it on the journey. Peter slept like a baby on every plane he travelled in. She rarely even napped, so always carried a selection of reading material, usually related to their destination.

She'd barely slept last night either, lying in the dark listening to the roars and bellows and shrieking and who knew what animals! She was so excited. Africa had been an unobtainable dream for a little girl borrowing picture books of lions and elephants and hippos from her local library back in Edinburgh. Marrying Peter had made her every dream come true and, as the sun rose high enough to waken the day shift, Jude watched the near view burst into life. Insects, birds, lizards and monkeys were all wide awake and foraging, and her heart swelled watching them. 'I love Africa,' she decided. Then she ran inside to jump up and down on the bed until her husband got up and took her on safari.

*

Second week.

Even Jude wouldn't sit in a hot, dusty vehicle trying to spot lions every day. There were lakes to swim in, and waterfalls to stand under. There were markets to browse and weird and wonderful foods to sample. There was also a lot of relaxing to be done around the pool or on their own terrace, armed with cocktails and paperbacks. And lots of loving to do too. It was a fabulous holiday, in a wonderful place. Jude had taken endless photographs, and Peter was thinking he should probably buy shares in Kodak.

Fourth safari.

A small group of six tourists all seated in their respective couples in the back of an open Land Rover. They had their driver and an armed ranger. They spent the morning visiting two different waterholes, parking at a distance they were able to watch water buffalo, antelope, zebra and a troupe of monkeys visit the first. The second appeared devoid of life, until the telltale nostrils of a crocodile appeared on the water's surface. Another broke cover on the shore where it had been invisible among some rocks until beginning a slow waddle down to the water where it slipped inside with barely a ripple. The day was hot, the distance shimmered, the air thrummed with the constant noise of chirruping insects.

The lunch venue was inside the safety of a boma made from the thorny acacia. The Maasai staff were friendly and welcoming, their food basic but very good given that they were using a few camping stoves to cook. There were chilled drinks and even basic toilets. It was just heavenly. They were used to the best… accommodation, food, service… Peter and Jude routinely experienced the finest of everything the world had to offer. But sitting there, under flapping canvas shade, troubled by flies and watching the biggest creepy crawlies on the planet make off with any dropped crumbs, they were united in feeling relaxed and content.

'Feels like we've always been here,' Peter said, squinting up at the deep blue sky.

Nodding, Jude said, 'Like we came home.'

While they were preparing to leave for that afternoon's safari, word reached the boma that a large herd of elephants was on the move nearby.

Everyone quickly piled back into the Land Rover and the chase was on.

It didn't take long to find such large creatures and, once the vehicle had caught most of the way up, they followed at a slow and very respectful distance… Jude was practically sitting in their driver's lap by then to get her very best photographs. Matriarchs, young males, and several youngsters of varying ages being guided along by the adults. Trunks dipped to the ground or lifted to the trees. Always investigating. They noticed their escort but seemed relaxed and unconcerned, some even showing off a little for the cameras. Such huge and gentle beasts. Everything was perfect and beautiful and awe inspiring.

Right up until a gunshot shattered the peace.

Birds screeched, taking off from hidden perches in the highest trees. Monkeys shrieked, and scattered into the tree tops, zebra and antelope bolted. The elephants also moved off, some at speed, having taken fright, the rest following at a more sedate pace. Just as well, because, with barely any warning, a jeep burst forth from the undergrowth close to where the elephants had been. A second jeep was in hot pursuit, and both passed close to the safari party vehicle. Their ranger recognised colleagues among the pursuers, and immediately got on his radio. The driver ordered the passengers to sit down and keep their seats, before roaring off after the two speeding jeeps.

Jude was as excited as she was scared, clinging more tightly to her wonderful new camera, than she held onto her husband. Following the plume of dust, they soon caught up with the other rangers a few miles east, because they'd beached their vehicle on some rough, rutted terrain. Getting them out was easy and quick, but they had lost their quarry. Poachers, they said.

Heading back the way they'd come, they followed the rangers at a more sedate pace, back to the scene of crime.

Jude groaned and covered her mouth at the bloody scene a few yards from where she sat. A lioness lay dying, shot in her flank, she was bleeding out into the grass. Panting, eyes rolling, tongue lolling. Beside her a tiny little cub, mewling for mama. Jude dumped her camera into Peter's lap and jumped over the side of the Land Rover before anyone could stop her.

'No missus…' One of the rangers tried to get in her way. 'You stay back now. Don't look.'

Jude just shoved past him and, as a different ranger prepared to shoot the mother, she scooped up the cub and shielded it from the sight. The poor little mite was trembling, covered in blood, but seemed unharmed. Jude just cradled it in her arms and, when Peter joined her, they cooed and stroked the tiny little orphan together.

Peter got to the bottom of it.

Poachers had killed the mother to get her cubs. They made off with two siblings, poor animals that would be sold as pets or worse; used as entertainment. The cub would not survive on its own, so the rangers were going to take it to a man they knew of. The Dutchman lived on the south side of the park and looked after many sick and injured animals. Peter wanted to meet this man for himself, and he managed to convince the rangers that if they wanted to get the cub to the Dutchman, then they would have to take Jude too. As Jude was his wife, he would also have to go.

The rangers didn't bother arguing, just made room in their jeep for the stubborn white people.

By the time they reached the small collection of fenced in buildings accessed via a gated arch bearing the legend Rhonda Rehabilitation Centre, Jude had determined the cub was female and had named her Lulu. Henk De Vries had been contacted by radio already and was there waiting. Peter shook hands, introducing himself before helping Jude and little Lulu out the jeep. 'My wife, Jude…' he told the oddly bemused looking Dutchman.

'And the poor little lion she's carrying is Lulu.' 'Close enough,' Henk nodded thoughtfully.

'Sorry…?' Peter didn't understand.

'Just thinking back to something an old friend told me recently,' Henk smiled all round, and then gestured to the small clinic off to one side, 'Let's get the little lion inside and get a good look at her.'

*

Not long after Henk de Vries set up his rehab centre, named for his recently deceased wife, a number of Maasai turned up. Four elders and eight warriors made up the initial delegation. One of the warriors, Joseph, spoke good English and always came along during these regular visits so they could all communicate. The elders had learned of Henk's work through the bush telegraph and wanted to check him out. They wanted not simply to ensure that this white man was good for the animals, but also for Africa. Too many white people had little or no respect. Henk was different, a qualified vet and passionate conservationist, he always put the animals as well as the environment first. Little by little they grew to trust the Dutchman, and they began to relax more, their visits becoming about friendship and an exchange of information.

They would all arrive unannounced, sit down in front of his house, smoking and drinking the chai tea they brewed on little cooking fires. There would be long greetings and introductions and then Henk would prepare food for all. Meagre meals based mainly around rice and beans, but this was always received with great ceremony as well as gratitude.

On one such afternoon, after the main delegation arrived, an antelope arrived on the back of a young warrior. A fresh kill that was swiftly prepared and then cooked for hours over a fire. Once more Henk provided the rice and beans. They feasted that night and drank too much of the honey beer also brought along, as well as a bottle of single malt whisky that Henk had been saving for a special occasion. It didn't get any more special than that night. The sound of the warriors singing and whooping under the stars was hypnotic, their voices as percussive as their spears. The beating heart of Africa.

The following morning, before they took their leave, Joseph introduced Henk to a previously unknown elder. He was their medicine man, their bearded laibon. His name was Laputo Edward Ngoyo and he wanted Henk to know that there was now trust between them and that they two would become great friends.

Henk felt suitably honoured.

Less than one week later, Henk awoke in the night to find the laibon standing in his bedroom.

The old man spoke loudly and clearly and in perfect Dutch. 'Wake up!

Get out! Your house is on fire.'

That was when Henk awakened for real and jumped from his bed. He began opening doors, sniffing the air for the tell-tale smells of burning, his ears straining for any crackle sounds a fire might make. But there was nothing. Just a dream. At a loss he stood still and silent in the dark of his kitchen. Then he heard the distinct sounds of someone moving about on his porch. He ducked low into the shadows just in time to avoid the gaze of the man who just then peered in through his window. As soon as the man moved on, Henk retrieved his gun, checked it was loaded, and took off the safety. He was ready and, when two armed men came into his home, he shot them both dead.

Three other men made their escape into the night.

When the police arrived with the dawn, they spoke of poachers. Henk had three rhinos, several young elephants and a number of big cats. He was a lucky man because he also had his life. After a cursory investigation, the bodies of the two would-be poachers were unceremoniously bagged and loaded into the back of a van, and Henk was left with the suggestion that he employ some rangers to help protect his business.

As soon as the authorities were gone, Joseph appeared from his place in the bush close by where he had been watching. The laibon had sent him to check on Henk. The warrior had left their boma around the time Henk had wakened up having been told in his dream that his house was on fire.

'The laibon saved my life,' Henk realised. 'Is he psychic?'

'He is laibon,' Joseph shrugged laconically. 'He sees many things.'

Life returned to the normality of capturing, healing, rehabilitating and releasing animals. A trio of dedicated rangers joined Henk's team of one, led by a young man called Kissiri Nyerere. Sometimes Henk could barely afford to pay these men, but he managed simply because he could afford even less to be without their support. In return, the rangers helped manage the day to day running of the clinic, cleaning out pens and assisting with operations both surgical as well as practical. His Maasai delegation also continued to call. But the laibon didn't come again until one day in October 1975.

It was the usual evening of dinner and drinks and musical interludes long into the night, but the laibon sat with Henk for much of it. They smoked, they drank, and they talked with Joseph's help as translator. They spoke about dreams and houses that hadn't caught fire.

'Got you out of bed quick though,' the old man chuckled, and then grew serious. 'Henk, a white man is coming. His name is Peter. He will be travelling with…' he frowned, unsure. 'I think her name is Lou… something of this sound. You must help him. Help him to stay. We need this man. Tanzania needs this man.'

'Another dream?' Henk wondered.

'I was looking through the fire that night. I see this man coming through the flames as clearly as I saw men coming into your home to kill you. Look out for him for me.' 'I will,' Henk meant it.

So, when the English couple arrived less than a month later with their little Lulu, Henk was not at all surprised. He also wasn't surprised when Jude refused to leave Lulu, on the grounds she needed mothering. He then took it all in his stride when Peter began negotiating a package deal of accommodation and food in return for help around the centre.

*

Henk determined that Lulu the lion was three to four months old, so would need milk for another three or four months, as well as a little meat. Jude and Peter were happy to take on roll of surrogate mothers. Initially they shared the little twin bedded room Henk had created from an old store room, with the cub, taking turns feeding her every two hours. They shoved the beds together so all three could sleep curled around one another in the time between. They had to share a toilet and shower block, and kitchen slash laundry room with the three rangers. Within the first week Jude had a cleaning rota on the wall and woe betide anyone who didn't adhere to it.

'Especially the toilet,' she told them, hands on hips, trying her best to appear bigger than she actually was, during a hastily arranged house meeting. 'I am not here to clean up after any man's shit.' Animal shit was a different matter entirely.

For the next six months the Sinclair's got up before dawn and collapsed into bed, exhausted, as soon as their chores were done and their bellies full. The rangers as well as Henk pitched in, but they were often called upon to release and rescue, and Henk had his patients to care for. Subsequently, the day-to-day slog of managing the thirty to forty animals the clinic had capacity for, fell onto Jude and Peter's shoulders. The single ranger who always stayed behind, couldn't help out much or often, because he was obliged to watch over them as well as the animals while his colleagues were off site. All these animals, from the smallest rodent to the largest Rhino, pooped freely all day and night long. So, they spent a lot of time dealing with poop.

Jude came to believe that, of all the disgusting smells in the world, cheetah poop was by far the worst! It was like black, sticky tar and had to be scraped and scrubbed away with a lot of elbow grease. Quite the challenge in the African heat.

They scoured bird shit off aviary floors and walls. They took buckets and shovels into countless pens as well as into larger enclosures and shovelled up dung to be added to the massive heap set away from the clinic and living quarters, because Henk earned a few quid selling it to various hotels who used it to fertilise their beautiful gardens. They also scrubbed out and replenished countless water troughs every single day. Feeding time was worse in so many ways.

Before the shit detail began, every single animal had to be fed, and no human ate until that was done. Henk and the rangers took care of the huge chunks of carcass they tossed in to the big cats from the back of their Land Rover on their morning rounds… the Sinclair's collected up those remains later and drove it all out to the 'vulture buffet' to be stripped clean by the vultures already gathered there, watching. Every morning, Jude and Peter handled hundreds of frozen chicks, and again every evening. These were fed to the raptors and the younger or smaller animals that Henk happened to be caring for at any one time. Sometimes the chicks had to be skinned and chopped up for ease of digestion. It was a gruesome task which, due to them just getting on with it, earned the two rich white people the respect of the rangers who could then be relied upon to follow Jude's rota.

Henk had never seen his place so clean and tidy.

Jude and Peter also took turns bottle feeding a baby giraffe while standing on the back of a flatbed truck holding up two litre bottles of formula. Two of those per feed, three times every day. Initially the other would sit on the flatbed to give Lulu her own bottle, so Lulu and the young giraffe, who Peter nicknamed Georgie, became great friends, face to face as they checked one another out. Georgie would lick Lulu and Lulu would purr.

Henk tolerated this friendship because wild lions don't often hunt giraffes, an adult giraffe can easily kill or seriously injure any lion with a single kick. But when he found out Lulu was also playing games with a new born zebra he immediately put a stop to it. 'Forming an emotional attachment to the pretty stripy horses will not help Lulu adjust to life in the wild,' he admonished.

By then it was obvious that Lulu was a little diverse in the physical sense too, because she lacked any tail end tuft; a characteristic of the lion species that should have been become apparent by the time she was five to seven months old. Nothing to worry about according to Henk. 'Lulu will just be easier to spot in a pride, so easier for her foster parents to keep an eye on.'

Then there was the live food.

Peter and Jude also had to feed the orphaned mongoose and bush babies, and this involved collecting hundreds of horrifically monstrous bugs every day and night. At first, they ran and leapt about like loons trying to capture large moths and any other flying insects attracted to the night-lights around the compound. Then they grew wiser, and, with the aid of a torch and a collection of empty jars, they sat back and let the night creatures come to them. One little mongoose in particular seemed much taken with Jude and would snuggle between her boobs to be fed… and consequently dropped countless creepy crawlies into her shirts. Cue Jude shrieking and freaking out as Peter tried desperately to fish half eaten critters out of her bra.

A gang of thugs, also known as six serval kittens, were by far the most challenging.

The young servals couldn't digest the little yellow chick feathers, so Jude and Peter had to chop and peel one hundred and twenty little Easter chicks, every single day. Six dishes, ten chopped chicks each, twice daily. Having initially viewed these beautiful creatures through the enclosure fencing, Jude decided they were adorable, with their huge ears and beautiful stripe and spot markings. They would all run up to the fence, full of curiosity, purring and even meowing as they rubbed up and down the chainlink. A serval can jump up to six and a half feet from a standing start, Henk warned. They hide in long grass, and pounce on their prey. They eat insects, small birds, frogs and rodents. Jude was a full-sized human. There wouldn't be a problem. That first morning, she carried three dishes in each hand like a pro and waited as Peter opened first one gate and then the other, closing each behind her. The grass in the enclosure was so long it was up to her waist in places.

'Here, kitty kitties,' Jude cooed, moving boldly forward. 'Mama brought some chickies.'

Before Jude knew what was happening four of the servals all pounced at once. They came leaping at her face, her back, and one even landed on her shoulders before bouncing right off again. They were after the chicks, not Jude, but she didn't care. Shrieking, she hurled all the dishes away as far as possible. Lumps of chick went flying. An airborne buffet distraction as she ducked, turned and fled, still shrieking for the gate. Her arms, neck and one shoulder bore the scars of this encounter for weeks afterward. From that day on, Peter carried the dishes, and Jude backed him up with a large broom.

Eventually, when Lulu was old enough to stick up for herself, she was introduced to two other young lionesses whose mother had suffered a similar fate. These two were sisters and slightly older than Lulu, but they all bonded well and were housed together in a huge enclosure. They had trees to climb and rocks to ambush one another from behind. They had wild birds and a variety of rodents to practice their hunting instincts on. Jude and Peter missed their little girl a lot, but Lulu was getting big and bold by then, and really needed to learn how to be a lion if she was ever going to make it out in the wild.

They still broke her out at least once every day to go for a walk.

*

Throughout their stay, Henk taught the Sinclair's a great many skills when it came to catching, caring for and rehabilitating wild animals. He rewarded their hard work with half decent meals and a well-stocked bar, so… on the odd occasion they had some left-over energy, they would sit on his veranda swapping life stories and looking out for shooting stars. There were daytime trips into town on animal feed and medical supply buying excursions. Sometimes Peter would go along, sometimes Jude. When it was Peter, he would take the opportunity to call his parents, his best friend, his stockbroker. Jude would sometimes call her little sister; telling Julia warts and all tales about their adventures, but she always popped into the local store to buy treats for everyone at the clinic.

Having extra help allowed Henk to take on more animals than he could manage previously. As a result, they'd all been so busy he hadn't paid much attention to the passing of days. Life was like that in his business. Every day cycled into the next, driven by the necessities of routine. He hadn't even realised five months had passed since he'd last seen his Maasai friends, until he returned from early morning rounds one day in March 1976 to find the delegation already smoking pipes and brewing chai tea on the patch of grass outside the clinic.

The laibon was with them, but it was not Henk he had come to see.

Although he greeted the Dutch man with all the warmth befitting their friendship, it was the other white man the laibon had come to see. Laputo Edward Ngoyo was a patient man and so, eager as he had been to meet the man he saw coming through his fire, he had stayed away to allow that man time to realise that Africa wanted him to stay. That wasn't to say that he hadn't regularly despatched the occasional warrior to keep an eye on things, but by that day he was sure the man called Peter had come to a decision.

They met on the dirt track that passed by the enclosure housing Georgie the giraffe.

Peter was walking along with Lulu, squatting low every so often so she could leap up onto his back and then springboard off. She was so heavy by then; they would have to stop this favourite game pretty soon. Jude was trailing behind, taking photographs of the cloud formations crowding around the peaks of Kilimanjaro. Lulu saw the old man first and hid behind Peter as she usually did when encountering a strange human. He wasn't the first Maasai Peter had seen, but he was the first elder. Instantly recognisable in simple garb and close shaven head, his earlobes stretched into large loops, his beard bushy and unkempt looking.

'Supai, Peter.' The laibon greeted him in traditional Maa language which gave his people their name. Then, as they shook hands, he asked, 'Errabioto?'

Smiling apologetically, Peter said, 'I'm so very sorry but I don't understand.'

Nodding, the laibon kept hold of Peter's hand in both of his own, searching in his blue eyes. He could tell he was making the white man uncomfortable, but that wasn't important. When the lioness tried to come between them, he looked down at her and waited until she settled quietly to the earth and then he resumed his search of those blue eyes. Satisfied at last that this was indeed the man he had seen in the fire, Laputo turned back the way he'd come and whistled loudly. In a few moments, a warrior appeared and came trotting towards them.

Joseph arrived at the same time as Jude.

Joseph handled the introductions all round and, seeing Jude twitching over her camera, he added, 'Please ask permission before you take any photographs.'

Jude immediately asked, 'May I take some photographs?'

Joseph asked the laibon, then told her, 'The laibon said that it is fitting that you document this moment because foolishness must come before wisdom.'

Jude was only really sure she had permission, when the warrior started posing for her, grinning and posturing with his spear. She got busy.

'What's happening, Fluff?' Peter wondered. The old man was still holding his hand. Lulu was still lying quietly on the ground by their feet… the quietest he'd ever seen her unless she was sleeping. He was unsure what to do, or what was going on.

'Who cares?' Jude was snap happy. 'Pose with the laibon. What's a laibon, Joseph?'

'Medicine man. Sage. Judge. Shaman. Healer. Laputo Edward Ngoyo is our most gifted laibon.'

'He seems very taken with my husband,' Jude noticed, smiling encouragingly at the old man who rewarded her with a big smile. 'Smile, Peter.' And when they were both grinning and still locked in their handshake, she took half a dozen pictures. Then she took photos of all three, and then had Joseph take some of her with Peter and the witchdoctor.

When Laputo let go Peter's hand, he lifted his own in a brief gesture.

Joseph said, 'No more photos now.' He then translated for the laibon, telling the white man, 'Now that you have decided to stay, Africa welcomes you. I welcome you. We are destined to be great friends. The next time we meet we will talk longer. I will provide honey beer and tobacco and you will provide the whisky.'

Looking around, Peter wondered where he might come by a bottle of malt in the African bush.

'Try one of the hotel bars,' Joseph winked, smiling.

'Okay. Thanks.' And then Joseph and the laibon just turned and headed off in the direction of the clinic compound. 'Wow.'

'Wow, indeed.' Jude caught Lulu's front paws when she jumped up to nuzzle her, face to face with their cub now. She was big and heavy and could easily knock Jude off her feet. 'Is it true?'

Moving close so he could help his wife support their errant lion child, Peter asked, 'Is what true?'

'You've decided to stay.'

There they stood in the hot African morning, Lulu pawing at them, chewing on their fingers, their clothes. They held onto her, held onto each other. They laughed and smiled and exchanged kisses. Or, in Lulu's case, big licks.

Grinning into Jude's beautiful eyes, Peter wondered, 'Haven't you?'

CHAPTER NINE

'Hey Jos…' Ben had seen her, and his mama admiring the lazy lion and had just stepped out from the office onto the porch. When she looked his way, he asked, 'D'you fancy a game drive this Thursday? One of our bookings just cancelled so the seat's yours if you want it.' 'What day is it today?' Jos asked Beola.

'Tuesday.'

'Yes, please!' Jos called to him. Then, once he'd gone back inside, she asked Beola, 'I don't suppose Lulu is still out there?'

Shaking her head, Beola said, 'But Lulu lived for sixteen years, Jos, and had many sons and daughters. Her descendants are still out there and some of them even bear her mark.' Jos looked confused.

'Lulu had no tuft at the end of her tail,' Beola explained. 'Some of her descendants share this same trait.' When they had returned to the kitchen, she set about making them camomile tea. She'd caught Jos yawning several times by then. 'You should try to have a nap,' she suggested.

Letting her shoulders drop, Jos pouted. 'Do I have to?'

'You are tired and yet you do not wish to sleep. Or maybe you do not wish to return to the garden room… where perhaps something has unsettled you?'

Sighing loudly, Jos gave in, 'I didn't drop off earlier. I closed my eyes for a few moments and… well, when I opened them again, I saw Peter Sinclair as clearly as I can see you now. I know it was him, because my parents had a lovely, framed photo of him and Jude on our mantle. I tried to convince myself it was a dream, but it wasn't. Dreams fade and this one is as clear as can be, and right at the front of my head. Is he really still here, Beola? Is he a ghost?"

'I have seen him too,' Beola admitted, joining Jos at the table. 'He comes to me when I need him. We talk. At first, I was afraid, but then I was grateful to still have my very good friend here with me.'

'He gave me the fright of my life. If I hadn't peed just minutes before

I'd have probably wet my pants right there and then.'

Beola burst out laughing. 'I ran from the house screaming the first time,' she told Jos, with wide eyes. 'I think they heard me in town, I screamed so loud.'

'Did the world stop?'

'Yes.' Eyes wide, and Beola knew exactly what Jos meant. 'As if every living thing took a break. Even the air stopped.'

'Where did you see him?'

Pointing up to where the roof garden topped the kitchen, Beola said, 'I have seen him in here too…' Jos started looking all around her as if Peter would suddenly jump out from one of the cupboards. 'Mostly he makes his appearances up there.'

'And you gave me that room!' Jos was incredulous.

'Jos…' Beola sighed and thought a few moments before continuing,

'As long as you are in this house, I think Peter will seek you out.'

'But why?' Jos nearly laughed then because her voice had sounded so whiny.

'Only Peter can tell you that.'

'Oh, come on! You know more than that.' And when Beola continued to not speak, Jos said, 'Please tell me, or I'm catching the next plane home.'

There was nothing else for it. 'I believe it was Peter's idea to have you visit.' Beola then told Jos it all. The matches, the footsteps, the books, the music. She told her about the photograph album, the travel books and the phones ringing. 'As soon as I contacted Gary the nonsense stopped.'

'Gary?'

'He and Peter grew up together. Gary looks after the estate. If we need anything we call, and he sorts it out. I imagine the same is true for Jude.'

'I thought Jude looked after her own affairs… and mine.' Jos told Beola about Jude's handling of all the financial affairs after the deaths of her parents. 'Though, when I think back on it now, I don't think she actually ever left the house. Just made a lot of phone calls.

'Jude is a very capable woman in the practical sense.' Beola knew. 'But she had no interest in the financial side of Peter's dealings. Not ever. When Peter died it was Gary who took over the business…'

'I thought you said estate.'

'Isn't it the same thing? Peter's estate was run like a business while he lived, and it still is. There are legacy projects which he set up that are still running today.'

'What kind of projects?'

It was easier to show Jos and so Beola led her west and along the hallway between the sitting room and the library which was lined with dozens of photographs in colour as well as black and white. Pictures of Lulu the lion, were prominent, but Jos could look at those later. Beola guided her to a picture of Henk de Vries, smiling broadly as he cut a thick ribbon that had been strung across the arched entry into his clinic compound. He was flanked by three men in camo gear, two wearing green overalls and wellie boots, and two young women in white scrubs. 'Peter and Jude helped Henk set up as a trust. Some funding came from private donations, but most came from the students who came from all over the world to work there. They pay to work so the clinic can support itself.'

Moving on, they passed several photos of Jude with the Maasai people. One showed a dubious looking Jude having her hair pleated and beaded by a pair of amused looking women. Another showed an unrecognisable Peter in full Maasai dress, including face and body paint, as part of a small gathering of colourfully attired warriors seated around a fire, all smoking pipes. There were several more pictures of Peter painted like a warrior, bare chested, armed with a spear and joining in a tribal dance. When Jos paused to look more closely, Beola said, 'They had a lot of Maasai friends who used to stop by the white house from time to time…' Nodding towards the front of the house, she went on, 'There would be gatherings out on the lawn which lasted for days sometimes.' She recalled the sounds of their singing long into the nights, how the Sinclair's would sit and eat and drink with them, how there would be groups of warriors, dressed in all their finery lazing around on the porch or sitting on the grass. 'The day Peter died…' she went on, '… the Maasai arrived at sunset. They were a solemn gathering. Their voices sang and their fire burned as the elders cleansed the white house of sorrow.'

'Where was Jude?' Jos wondered.

'The police came for her. To tell her, you know. I think she stayed in town. We went to stay with Kissi's father for a few weeks. When we returned, Gary was here to tell us that Jude had returned to England with Peter's remains and would not now be coming back. He told us that the white house was still our home…'

Jos dialled it back a bit, 'So no one was here for weeks, except a tribe

of Maasai carrying out some weird ritual.'

'Spirituality is part of our everyday culture, Jos,' Beola told her. 'The physical world is joined with the spiritual in the same universe. And so, in Africa, the supernatural is not otherworldly, but rather part of everything that we see, feel and hear. These things became very important to Peter, and he forged tight bonds with his Maasai brothers. When Peter died those brothers came to pay their respects in traditional ways.'

'Sorry,' Jos felt ashamed. 'I didn't mean to be so white.'

'Don't worry…' Beola advised with an elbow to the ribs and a big grin. 'A few weeks in the African sun and you'll stop being so white.'

Jos couldn't help laughing. Knowing right then that she and Beola were going to get along fine.

Next on the tour were the photographs taken of the deep well installed between clusters of rural communities who had previously relied on the watering hole their animals also used. 'That man with his hands in the air…' in triumph as well as joy, '… was trained to install, maintain and repair these wells. He went on to create many more, and now thousands of people have access to clean fresh water.' There was a little school house that shared a compound with a bush clinic. 'The students at the school promise that, at least once in their adult life, they will sponsor one other child to attend this same school. Many of them have sponsored many more children by now because they are now doctors or lawyers or teachers and they want the next generation to follow them. The clinic supports itself in much the same way Henk's does. If Peter was here, he would tell you that there is no value in throwing money at something only to turn your back and walk away.' Opening a door, she ushered Jos into the library. 'He read like most people breathe.' The room was lined with floor to ceiling shelves, all packed with books. 'In here Peter found ways to make his plans work.' 'He was a generous man,' Jos realised.

'He was a gift to us all, Jos, and mourned greatly, far and wide, when he died.'

'How did he die?' A car accident, was all Jude had ever said.

Sighing, Beola sat down in the overstuffed armchair Peter used to spend hours in, reading, planning. No one really knew how Peter died. 'It was an accident.' She repeated the mantra. 'His jeep left the road and collided with a tree.' A tree that was nowhere near that road. So far from the road some had even suggested that Peter had killed himself. 'His jeep caught fire…' Exploded. 'We hope that he was dead before…' Beola shook her head, clearing the image.

Jos could tell she was upset and felt responsible. 'Jude hasn't gotten over it either.'

'Come.' Beola got up, beckoning for Jos. 'Our tea is getting cold.' They returned to the kitchen via the patio.

Over a cup of very nice tea sweetened with a little honey, Jos discovered more about Peter. How his mother, Astrid, was still alive and living in her native Norway. She had returned there soon after his father, Johnny, died. Astrid, like Jude, lived on an annual income paid through the estate that was being managed by Gary Preston.

Jos was sure there must be more to it. Houses in Edinburgh and Norway, significant others on yearly incomes, a brilliant white mansion built atop a hill, a man working fulltime somewhere managing property, money and numerous projects. Of course, Jos could try calling Jude again, and ask her the one hundred and one questions racing around in her mind by then. Or… she could ask the ghost.

Moody, broody Judy or petrifying Peter.

Having finished the tea by then, Jos said, 'I think I will try and have that nap.'

*

The breeze was warm, stirring delicately among the flowers of the roof garden, filled with the insignificant sounds of a thousand tiny creatures going about their business. Birds sang from the trees, and swallows swooped and wheeled overhead. Somewhere a monkey chattered with its neighbours. The sun was high, and Jos was closer to it than she had ever been, sitting on the very bench she'd seen Peter sitting on just a few hours previously. Exactly two hundred and forty miles south of the equator, and she had no idea how she knew this.

Sunnies were firmly in place against the white house glare, while waiting and listening. Here and there a scuttle and a rustle as something, or perhaps more than one thing, stirred amongst the flowers inside the big planter behind her. Sliding along to the end of the bench, farthest away from where her uncle had appeared previously, Jos took a deep breath to prepare herself, thinking, for the umpteenth time, that she must be stark raving mad.

But if that was the case, then surely Beola was just as mad, and Beola seemed like a very nice and very level headed person. She was matter of fact about their ghost, and so Jos would endeavour to be so too. 'Okay,' she told the afternoon softly. 'Let's do this.' Little by little, nothing happened.

That same sense of absence crept in and encircled her slowly, wrapping Jos up inside a cocoon of silence. Skittering, scuttling sounds ceased. The breeze ebbed away; the air grew heavy. It felt thick and liquid as she breathed it in. Out. Her heart beat the only animated thing in a world of stillness. She had to gather herself to find her voice and, when she spoke, it was in the merest whisper, 'Beola says I shouldn't be afraid.' Sighing. 'But I am afraid…' Shifting. '… because you are dead…' The strangest feeling. '…and being dead…' A sensation of drifting. '…usually precludes…' Feeling fixed. '…any ability…' In space. '…to walk…' In time. '…or talk…'.

'I don't mean to scare you, Jos.'

Her reaction was as immediate, and involuntary, as the first time.

Jumping up in fright, onto feet that wanted to flee the scene because every fibre of sense was screaming at them to escape, Jos clutched herself, holding herself in place just a few feet away from her end of the bench, while loudly blurting out, ‘What the very fuck!’ Large as life and in full technicolour.

Peter Sinclair, deceased, was sitting exactly where she’d seen him earlier. Like he was the most natural thing in the world. He was tanned and handsome. Bright blue eyes sparkled with a life he no longer had, with crow’s feet in their corners from years of squinting in the sunlight. As well as his casual outfit, he was wearing a wide and amused smile. Raising his palms towards her, he assured, ‘I understand, truly I do. The first time Beola saw me she ran away yelling her head off.’ He laughed a little. ‘She didn’t come back into the house for nearly a week. But I’m not actually scary, am

I? It’s simply that I’m not really supposed to be here.’

Jos had her palms against her cheeks by then, shaking her head a little.

‘I don’t bite.’ He smiled a little, then asked, ‘Won’t you sit down?’ Jos shook her head more firmly.

Peter shrugged, his smile a little sad looking.

Jos felt bad to think she’d upset him, so, clearing her throat a little, she clasped her hands under her chin and asked, ‘Why has everything stopped?’ Looking quickly around she saw that the world had indeed remained still and silent despite her own cacophony. ‘It’s like time is standing still.’

Looking up at the sky, Peter watched a distant cloud move slowly on its personal journey, and knew his effects were local. ‘Gaia disapproves of me,’ he spoke softly.

‘Who is Gaia?’

‘Life, the heavens, the sea and the mountains. She is Nature, and she declines to have anything to do with me.’ Stretching a hand out in front of himself, Peter added, ‘Even the sun refuses to acknowledge me.’

‘No shadow,’ Jos realised. Then she realised something else and laughed, delighted. ‘Because you’re peter-natural.’

‘You seem to be getting over your fear.’

Peter smiled right at Jos then, and it was like the sun coming out. His whole face lit up and he looked beautiful and happy and very, very real. And she just loved his accent, very posh, but with a hint of what she supposed must be his maternal Norwegian. At that moment she was able to release a lot of the tension she’d been holding. Letting her hands unclasp and drop down, she said, 'I've faced worse.'

Peter knew all about those losses. He had known even before his own death, because an old friend saw it coming in the flames. He and Jos were connected somehow. A shared path into the future, the laibon had described, but his niece would have need of a safe haven before that time came. 'I'm glad Jude was there when you needed her.'

'Me too.' But Jos didn't want to talk about that. 'Can you just show yourself to anyone?' She wondered.

'I've only ever intentionally shown myself to Beola, and now to you. But one time I was up here alone, practising my visibility technique I suppose, and Ben's friend saw me.'

'Wendell?' Peter nodded, and Jos then asked, 'Is it easy? Showing yourself.'

'No,' Peter told her seriously, shaking his head. 'At first I was almost nothing. A collection of molecules held together by will and driven by vague memories. I clung to the white house like mist. It was this house that sustained and protected me until I was able to gather myself into something more coherent. I had a lot of obstacles to overcome before learning how to achieve something as complex as this visible organisation. For a long time, I thought I'd never be seen again, never be able to communicate directly, so I worked on manipulating objects. You've no idea how difficult it was to move just a single little match.'

'Beola told me all about the matches, and the books. I'm finding out a lot from Beola. About you mostly.' 'Jude doesn't talk about me much.' It was a statement.

'Do you… see her? Maybe watch over her?'

'I can't see much beyond the confines of this place I consider home.'

When he didn't say anything else, Jos said, 'Jude won't talk about you, Peter. She tells me that she can't, that she's never gotten over you. She gets… angry. I suppose she's angry because you died and left her all alone.' Peter sat there quietly, refusing to look at her. His shine was gone, just like his smile. 'What happened to you?'

‘I lived fast and died young,’ Peter declared tersely. Sagging a little, before adding, ‘Unfortunately, I did not also leave a beautiful corpse.’

Jos sensed she’d hit a nerve, although it was odd to think of a dead man having any to hit, but her very first day in Africa had taken a strange turn and she would just have to go with the flow. ‘You look pretty good for a ghost.’

‘I’m not a ghost.’ Peter was sure about that. ‘The term conjures up images of a suggestion of humanity, don’t you think? Something fleeting, something lost and sad, or perhaps angry and destructive. I don’t feel any of those things.’

‘So, you can feel?’

Peter looked up and around, pursing his lips, considering how best to respond. ‘Well, obviously I have no sense of touch…’ His hand swept across the slats of wood next to where he was seated. ‘I don’t feel heat, cold, rough, smooth… but I do feel sensations of reality. Like static electricity. Some objects are better conductors than others, so they feel more apparent to me. As for my emotions, those are limited within my current actuality which is somewhere between life and death. I call it my In-between. All one word, capitalised.’

‘I’ll try to remember that.’

Peter laughed at her dry response. ‘Why don’t you sit down, Jos. You’re not really afraid at all now.’

‘Can you feel that?’

‘I feel your emotions rather powerfully. Right now, your curiosity is far greater than your fear.’ He was right.

Sitting down gingerly at the far end of the bench, Jos asked, ‘So why haven’t you just gone on?’ Then she slid her sunnies up onto her head, pushing her hair back, so she could see him better. ‘Over the rainbow bridge… or into the light… or wherever it is dead people usually go?’

Peter had watched the big reveal, and saw that Jos had her mother’s bright green eyes. Julia had looked a lot like her big sister, but Jude’s eyes were more hazel than green. When he’d met Jude, he’d thought she was surely unique, built like a fairy, with incredible eyes and a great cloud of bright orange frizz. But there was two of them. Scottish sisters with crazy hair and cat’s eyes. Now there was two of them again, only Jos was taller, and her hair was darker, sleeker, a cascading and curling dark amber mass that fell around her shoulders like some storybook princess. Seeing her stirred emotions inside that Peter had thought as dead as his body; remorse and loss felt paramount. If he had breath, he'd have to hold onto it. Change was coming, but she was waiting, and it took an effort to speak. 'I wanted to stay here,' he said, finally.

'Why?'

Peter shifted around to face Jos, pleased that she didn't shrink away from him. 'A very long time ago a Maasai shaman, or laibon, to give him his correct title, predicted my future,' he began. 'He foresaw not simply my death, but the complications that would arise from it. There would be a void, he said. All the work going into the projects I created would be wasted, because there wouldn't be anyone here to protect them. I was determined that, if the old man was right about my future… or lack of future, then I wanted to stop that from happening. The laibon agreed to help. I had the legal documents drafted and appointed my executor. The laibon gave me the power to remain fixed when the world wanted me to fragment. He used his magic to tie me to the house.'

'Black magic, white house,' Jos snorted more than laughed, and covered her mouth, blushing. 'Excuse my pig,' she giggled. 'She's a friend.'

Peter was a little mystified, because Jos had gone from outright apoplexy, to laughing and joking in just a few short hours. Then he recalled Julia again, and how she was the funny one. Jude was the relentless force of nature. Her little sister, the comedian. He'd only spent a few short weeks with Julia, but remembered always laughing, listening to her jokes and her cheek, and watching her and her husband, Mike, bounce off one another. He and Jude had invited them to Africa many times, but the time hadn't ever been right for Julia, Mike and little Jos.

And then time ran out.

'Is your old friend still around?' Jos wondered.

'I hope so.' The laibon would surely be ancient by now. However, he was an essential component of what needed to happen next. Peter was depending on that.

‘So…’ Jos settled herself against the back of the bench. ‘Apart from playing with matches, and using books to communicate… do you miss it? Being alive.’

‘Oh yeah,’ Peter nodded. ‘I miss so many things. Eating, drinking, smoking weed. It would be so great to be able to taste food again. Oh…’ He sighed. ‘A really good glass of wine. Or a cold beer! Oh man… I would give anything to drink one more margarita.’

‘Really?’ Jos managed to laugh without bringing her pig. ‘I’m quite partial to a margarita or three myself.’

‘Three?’ He laughed. ‘Two is perfect, but three is dangerous.’

The silence that followed was palpable, not only because they were two strangers thrown together in this weird situation and neither one really knew what to say or how to communicate, but also because there were mysteries between them. Secrets that only Peter could reveal.

After a time, he said, ‘Tell me about yourself, Jos.’

For the second time in the same day Jos felt acutely aware of her shortcomings as a human being. Selfish, weak, ungrateful. These were ways Jude had often described her. Times when Jos had inadvertently upset her aunt because she forgot to walk on the egg shells. She sighed loudly, her breath puffing out her cheeks as she sagged visibly, eyes cast downward.

‘Has your life stopped?’ Peter wondered in a whisper. ‘My life ceased to be, but your life has stopped on route as it were. At least, that’s what I was led to believe would happen.’

Looking up sharply, Jos wondered, ‘By your laibon?’

Peter nodded. ‘He told me that loss would make you retreat.’

‘My parents were crushed to death right in front of me. My mum saved my life. She tried to save my dad too, but he had a broken leg, and he couldn’t move. She just held onto him instead. She could have followed me onto the floor, but she chose to die with my dad. For the longest time I thought that was because my mum just didn’t love me enough.’ Jos felt the tears slide down her cheeks, overcome with emotion wrapped up in the memories. She hadn’t cried over it in years. ‘Jude used to say just put one foot in front of the other, toots. You’ll get through this, toots.’ Pausing, Jos wiped at her face, her eyes, her nose. ‘And I did.’ She fought to keep her voice steady. ‘I got through it, and then I didn't get any farther. I've been stuck in Jude's ivory tower, so… in answer to your question, I don't do anything.' That feeling of hopelessness was so acute it forced a sob from Jos, and she was crying all over again.

Peter would have given up all the margaritas on the planet to be able to hold her right then. His memory of heart was breaking for her. 'I'm so sorry I've upset you.'

'It's not your fault…' She wiped her eyes, face and nose all over again. 'I'm feeling so emotional today. No idea why.'

'You're tired. You've travelled a long way to get here.'

Nodding, Jos said. 'I think I should go and lie down. Sleep maybe.'

'That's a good idea.'

'Will I see you again?'

Smiling, pleased that she wanted to, Peter said, 'Of course.'

And then he was gone, as quickly as he'd appeared. The garden immediately burst into life. Bird song, insect buzz and hum, and the warm breeze conspired immediately to banish the stillness.

Jos noticed none of it, she felt weary and troubled, an emotional wreck. It had been years since she'd got this upset over the loss of her mum and dad. Years since she'd taken herself off to bed, to lie down and curl up in a ball like a child, holding onto herself.

Inside the garden room, that is exactly what she did.

*

At first Jos liked her dream.

She was at home with her parents. They were all in the kitchen. Her dad was cooking a Sunday roast dressed like Prince Charming aka Adam Ant. Not an unusual choice of attire for a big fan of Adam and the Ants, because Mike Ferguson wore that get up every chance he got, Halloween, fancy dress parties, Hogmanay. The radio was on. Jos and her mum were singing, laughing, dancing, and jumping around like idiots. That was how life had been when she was growing up. Julia was loud and funny and full of energy. Jos was the same. It was all Mike could do to keep his wife and daughter from spinning off into outer space when they were both at full volume. Every day was an adventure, surprises at every turn.

But the dream shifted as they do, and Jos found herself sitting in the diner across from her dad, her mum at her side. You Don't Own Me by Lesley Gore was playing and she and her mum were singing along, singing to her dad as they held up chips as if they were little wands, waving them in the air above the table. As the song ended, Jos stuffed the chip into her mouth and then lifted up her chocolate milk shake. Her mum shoved her hard and suddenly right then, and Jos landed on the floor on her backside. In real life she had sat there, covered in chocolate shake, wondering what was going on, not even aware of the danger when the glass started to fly. But in that dream, as in so many others, she opened her mouth and screamed

NOOO!

Then something else happened, something new.

Jos felt hands slipping in to her armpits, strong hands which lifted and pulled her up and away into a peaceful darkness that enfolded her. She felt strong arms around her. All her anguish faded away, as she filled up instead with surging feelings of love and wellbeing. Soaring higher and higher, like a bird. And then, suddenly, it wasn't dark any more.

Jos burst forth into a bright blue sky, stretching out all around her. She held out her hands, but there was nothing of herself to see. Looking around she saw nothing, no one, but she could still feel the safety of those strong arms embracing her. Looking down, she saw the white house, the colours of its gardens, the greens of its lawns and the cordon of trees far below. She would have gasped, had she the breath to do so. Instead, Jos simply trusted in her dream to carry her. The sensation that she was safe and cherished, was intense. Her movement across the sky slowed and became more like the feeling of floating, undulating, circling. Perhaps birds of prey feel like this when they ride the thermals. Around and around, she circled, even higher now above the white house. It was the colourful pupil in the green eye of the hill it was built upon. She saw movement down there, someone leaving by the front door, getting into the Land Rover that had collected her from the airport, driving it around the lawn, and then disappearing into the trees. Wendell Cooper she realised.

Sure, right then, that she was no longer simply dreaming.

*

Having forgotten to set an alarm, Jos slept through her first African sunset.

She was wakened sometime soon after dark by the sound of Beola screaming. Jos sat bolt upright at the sounds, heart pounding in her chest, but quickly realised Beola's shrieks were cries of excitement. Ben's voice could also soon be heard, and Jos wondered what was going on. Feeling groggy, but rested and strangely content, she undressed… pausing when she remembered that her dead uncle might be watching but pushing such thoughts aside in favour of a quick shower.

It was as she was showering, that Jos tracked memories of her most recent dream, inspired probably by the emotional state she'd worked herself into while talking to Peter. A dream like a thousand other dreams since that terrible day, only this one ended differently. For her at least. Standing naked under the cool water, she recalled feelings of soaring, rushing, flying and, closing her eyes, she let the experience wash over her once again. Just like the cool water raining down.

It took her breath away.

As she dried off and then dressed in a long, cool cotton dress, Jos found herself grinning. She felt good. Fantastic! She felt excited to be in Africa and glad to be alive. She felt inspired. For the first time since her parents died, she was able to look back on their memory with the fondness and joy they deserved, instead of wallowing in misery. They were dead, but they'd been two wonderful people and she was lucky to have been born to them, lucky to have had them for fifteen years. She wanted to run around, she wanted to laugh and shout. She felt fit to burst!

Ready to run downstairs and face whatever was waiting, Jos stalled a moment to try Jude again.

This time Jude answered. 'Hi Jos. I got your message. Glad you made it safely. How are things?'

The whole tale of Peter was ready to spill from between Jos' lips, but instead she checked herself, and said, 'Really good. It's so beautiful here. It's dark now. I just woke up actually.'

'Did you sleep on the plane?'

'For a few hours. Not sure I'll ever be able to fly in the cheap seats again though.'

'That good, huh?'

'Ben is taking me on safari on Thursday.'

'You're in for a real treat.'

'Are you all right, Jude?'

'Yes… the cats are keeping me busy.'

'Were you out earlier?'

'I forgot to pick up some shopping on the way home from the airport, so I popped out this morning instead.'

'I miss you.'

'Miss you too, toots.'

They said their goodbyes, and then Jos put up her hair and went downstairs to see what all the noise was about.

*

Jude stood next to the phone for several minutes, lost in thought.

When she returned to the dining room she sat back down at the table and resumed going through the small pile of photographs that were all she had packed when she'd left the white house. They'd been wrapped up inside an old T-Rex T-shirt, stored inside a box, hidden away from view, up in the highest shelf in the darkest corner of a forgotten cupboard up in the gods. A box buried inside a bigger box. Safe from harm.

She saw her younger self, saw her laughter, her smiles, saw the way she looked at her husband in complete and utter adoration. Jude may have wronged Peter, but she had always loved him. He looked out at her from other photos, sparkling blue eyes and mischievous smiles. His tan, his dimples that only ever appeared right before a smile became a laugh. She could almost hear the sound of his laughter. She could almost smell him on that old T-shirt.

She buried her face in it, and she cried.

CHAPTER TEN

'Jos!' Kissiri Nyerere got up from the table smiling, arms outstretched in welcome, and went to meet her as soon as she strolled into the kitchen from the patio. Shaking her hands in both his own, he said, 'Welcome my darling, welcome.'

'Thank you.' Jos matched his smile and tried not to want her hand back. Tanzanians, she was learning, were very big on handshakes. The longer the shake, the better they like you. Just another random piece of information that popped into her head from who knew where, like being two hundred and forty miles south of the equator, and ninety-four million miles from the sun. Kissi was wearing army type fatigues with his bare feet. Presumably Beola had made him remove his boots outside. His hair was close cropped and salt and pepper grey — just like his wife. 'I'm very happy to be here, Jos told him firmly and sincerely.

'Sit,' Beola commanded, watching Jos as if seeing her for the very first time. She had lit up the room when she walked in. Her smile as bright as her eyes. She looked beautiful. A confident and happy young woman. Something had changed. Smiling knowingly to herself, she then told Jos, 'My husband has come home a whole day early without bothering to let me know. Now I must cook extra food to feed him.'

'I can help.' Jos was eager to do something, anything to burn up some of the energy surging through her veins, but the look on Beola's face put paid to that idea.

'Sit with me.' Kissi guided her to the table. 'Would you like a beer?'

Making a gargoyle face, she told him, 'I don't like beer.'

Laughing at her expression, Kissi suggested, 'Wine then.'

'Oh yes,' Jos grinned from ear to ear. 'I like wine.'

Once she was seated Kissi fetched a couple of glasses and a bottle of white, South African wine from the fridge. Pouring two glasses, he handed one to his wife and placed the other on the table in front of Jos. He wondered what had happened to the shy girl with the uncertain smile his wife had described. The girl before him looked as effervescent as all the hair she had piled up on top of her head. Joining her at the table he said, 'It is a very long time since we've had a red head in the white house, Jos. If you don't mind me saying, you look a lot like Jude.'

'I already told her that,' Beola said, stirring a big pot of rice.

'And I already told Beola I look as much like my mum, because Julia and Jude looked very similar.'

Kissi asked, 'How is Jude?'

'I actually just spoke to her before coming down. She's fine. Keeping busy and missing me apparently.'

Jos could hear herself and realised that, although this was really little more than polite conversation, it was different somehow. She was different. Changed by coming to this place. Recalling the overwhelming feelings that filled her up when she first stood outside looking up at this very house, she wondered if the white house was just as powerful as the man who built it. Maybe Peter and the white house were interchangeable? Maybe it was Peter who had saved her from yet another replay of her parents' death. She had so many questions! Her mind felt fit to explode. If it had just been her and Beola she would be venting, every word that passed between her and Peter, analysing what it all meant, marvelling that it had happened at all. Her dream of floating high above the white house, seeing Wendell leaving. Was it real? She remembered it as if it was real. It hadn't faded and fragmented like every other dream she'd ever had.

Without waiting for any more questions, and the associated risks those posed, because bland no longer seemed an acceptable life choice, Jos looked Kissi in the eye and suggested, 'Tell me about your work as a ranger.

It sounds fascinating.'

Kissi enjoyed talking about his job because he loved it.

And so, while Beola cooked and served a meal of roast chicken and vegetables on a bed of rice and beans, he told Jos all about his career. How he had joined the ranger service at seventeen years old, trained for two years, and found himself leading a small group of three men at a small rehab centre close to Mount Kilimanjaro National Park by the time he was twentysix. That was back in 1975 and where he first encountered

Peter and Jude. It was those five, along with Henk de Vries, who released Lulu, her two adopted sisters and a sassy young male into the safety of the park fourteen months later. There was joy in his eyes as well as his smiles as Kissi spoke. 'I have dedicated my life to freeing and protecting animals,' he told Jos. 'There is nothing better for a man to do with his life.'

'Except for the time spent with his family,' Beola admonished.

Over a rich, cardamom scented almond paste and butter pastry dessert, and some wonderful coffee, Kissi talked about his most recent deeds. Relocating a young male black rhino to Zambia where he was to be the star of a breeding program in Kafue National Park, in the north of the country. They took the one thousand five-hundred-mile journey over six days, with five overnight stops at various animal shelters where their young stud was able to stretch his legs and recuperate. But the rhino had been a patient traveller and there had been few issues to overcome on route.

Ben had arrived by then, helping himself to dessert as well as beer. 'Jos is coming with us on Thursday,' he told his father. 'Kilimanjaro.' With a wink, he added, 'We'll take her to meet some of the clans.'

'In Africa, the clans have female chiefs,' Kissi revealed.

'Really,' Jos said flatly. 'And I suppose they wear kilts and hunt haggis on holidays and high days.'

They were talking about spotted hyena.

Hyenas, Jos soon learned, live in clans. Cleverer than apes they use complex, non-verbal forms of communication, and their spotted coats are as individual as the human fingerprint. The larger females are more muscular and aggressive, with three times the testosterone of their male counterparts. Females lead, with even the lowliest female ranking above the highest-ranking male. In fact, the female hyena is so far in the lead, she wears her sex organs on the outside as a pseudo penis until she's ready to mate. Her milk has the highest protein and fat content of all carnivores, so she can leave her babies for up to a week between feeds. This enables hyena to range far and wide to hunt. They are fast as well as durable and, despite popular belief, they rarely steal kills from other predators. In fact, it is lions who steal around fifty percent of their own food from hyena.

'When they eat…" Kissi told Jos with wide eyes, '… hyena eat it all. A group can devour an adult zebra in less than half an hour, leaving nothing but the blood smeared on the grass as evidence that zebra ever existed.' 'Gruesome,' Jos said.

'Efficient,' Ben thought. 'I adore them,' he admitted. 'They are so misunderstood. It has become my mission to make sure people appreciate them a little more.'

'Well…' stifling a yawn, Jos told them all. 'I'll look forward to seeing some on safari.'

*

Everyone assumed Jos was tired after her long journey, so it was easy to excuse herself for an early night. She was tired, but she was also more determined than ever to get some answers from Peter. The night air was warm and still, the moon high, and the walls of the house shining with a pearlescent white that lit up the kitchen garden below as she moved down that side of the garden towards the garden room.

Inside, she found her mobile and checked the time. It wasn't even eleven o'clock, which meant it wasn't even nine in Edinburgh. Plenty of time. The passing of time was a thing for Jos at that moment; something she was eager to keep track of. Sitting herself down on the same bench… though not jammed quite so much at one end as previously, she asked the night, 'Can we talk again, Peter?'

Instead of closing her eyes and giving in to the soporific effects which became apparent almost immediately, Jos forced herself to focus, accessing her phone's stop watch function and activating it. She could feel the world slowing down all around her, hear the sounds of the night fading until there was only silence. She refused to be distracted, refused to become affected by it. She concentrated all of her attention on the counter and, though she'd suspected as much, was still utterly gobsmacked to see the number count slow significantly, until the seconds were creeping by at around one quarter standard speed. 'Fuck me,' she breathed.

'Your language is appalling,' Peter remarked from his end of the bench.

'Whatever.' Jos made an impatient face, then held up her stop watch display briefly. 'This is science fiction.' Once more watching those seconds drifting by, she lifted her arm and turned her free hand this way and that.

Waggling and waving it about as if trying to shake off something sticky.

'What are you doing?'

'Trying to see if I'm slowed down.'

'Clearly you can move at normal speed.'

'But why? How?' she demanded to know. 'It doesn't make sense.'

'Does it have to make sense?' Peter wondered, tilting his head to one side, watching his niece resisting the deceleration of his special effect.

He hadn't been positive until Jos introduced a clock into his bubble but suspected. Once he'd had a long conversation with Beola about her many concerns looking after the white house, the well, the solar panels, the hives. It was a big undertaking for a woman and mother who often found herself alone for long periods, because her husband ranged for his living. That had been on the patio and, just before Peter joined her, Beola had gone into the kitchen to put on the kettle. The water was still hot enough for her tea after Peter withdrew once more into his In-between.

Now there was Jos, with her dark orange hair and her bright purple dress, clutching the evidence in one hand. 'Can't it just be?' he asked.

'How very zen,' but Jos gave in with a sigh anyway. Relaxing at last because that was simply what was required. Letting it just be. 'Beola tells me you and Jude decided to stay here because of Lulu the lion.'

'We wanted to see her free. It was a long process… fourteen or fifteen months, I think. The day we watched her, and her new family walk away into the bush…' Peter paused, smiling, recalling how Lulu had turned and held his eyes for a long moment, lifting her massive head finally in a kind of salute, before turning and moving off after her sisters. 'I knew that I could drop dead that very moment because my life was complete.'

'Kissi said something similar over dinner,' Jos remembered. 'There is nothing better for a man to do with his life.'

'Now you've met the whole family.' Peter smiled. 'Some of my favourite people in the whole world.'

Nodding, Jos agreed, 'They are easy to be around. I was nervous about coming. You know… strange country, people… strange everything. I mean, I've existed in a bubble for the past nine years so this is a big deal for me.'

'You are a courageous soul.'

'You think?' Jos laughed a little, slumping a little more. Closing her phone and setting it aside, forgotten. 'I don't feel brave.' She sighed. 'Most of the time I feel… anxious.' Which reminded her, 'I had a very strange dream earlier. A variation on an old, familiar one actually. My very worst day replays in glorious technicolour but, instead of staying until the gruesome end, something… or perhaps someone, gathered me up and took me away.'

'I could feel your distress.'

'I have no idea how, but you took all of that distress away. I felt… safe… cherished.' Loved. Jos knew that what she felt most of all was uncomplicated love. The kind of love felt when wrapped up inside the arms of an adoring and affectionate parent. A love she hadn't felt since her own parents were wiped out by a horrible twist of fate. She was beginning to feel emotional again but was hopeful she could keep it in check this time, because she had a lot to say and questions to ask. 'I haven't felt that content since I was a child.' She went on. 'Since I had parents who loved and wanted me. That feeling is still in me. Like you took all the bad stuff out and replaced it with joy. I felt happy for the first time since my mum and dad died. I still feel happy. I'm able to remember them now without feeling the loss. I used to try never to think of them, because I hated that I couldn't have them anymore. I resented being alone because they went off together and left me behind. But now… my head is just bursting with lovely memories of my younger life. I remember Hogmanay parties with the neighbours, barbeques, and picnics. Stuff I'd forgotten… or repressed probably. It feels like you set those memories free.' Jos paused, watching Peter watching her, beginning to realise that she was beginning to feel as if being with him was perfectly normal. As if she'd known him all her life and they were just having a chat. If someone were to ask who she'd prefer to stay with now, Jude or her dead Uncle Peter, he would win hands down simply because, in a few short hours, he'd made Jos feel better about herself than Jude ever had. 'But it wasn't simply a dream, was it?' 'Not after I intervened,' Peter admitted.

'So, you really were inside my head.'

'Long enough to steal you away.' Looking up at the stars, Peter added, 'By the time we were up there, you were in my world.'

Jos sat quietly for a few minutes letting that sink in. Eventually she whispered, 'Inside your In-between, looking down on the white house. I felt like a bird. Maybe being you isn't so bad.'

'It isn't.' Peter sounded a little surprised. 'I never really thought about it in those terms before. But then, being me was never as apparent as it is now.'

'What do you mean?'

'Just as I am having a positive effect on you, you are having a similar effect on me. Being here is easy.'

'Really?' Jos couldn't help smiling because the thought pleased her.

'I was always so focused on reaching this point.' Focussed on waiting long enough because remaining was a near constant battle. Like swimming against the tide, walking into a hurricane. It took everything Peter had just to stay within the boundaries of his home. But things were changing now. The battle was over, because having Jos near had given Peter more strength than he'd had since living ended and waiting began. An unexpected benefit. 'Now we're together…' he told her with a smile. '… I can relax and enjoy an existence again.'

'Which brings us back to what you said earlier about us sharing a destiny.'

'It's about succession.' Peter shrugged as he continued, 'Jude and me planned to have children, but I was always busy looking after existing projects, setting up new ones, and planning more.

It always felt like we had our whole future to have kids. And then we didn't. When I found out my number was coming up sooner than expected, I put my affairs in order so that the void would be filled until you were old enough to take it all over.'

Jos was shocked. 'Are you saying I'm in your will?'

'You are my will.'

'I don't understand. What about Jude… your mother?'

'This is about the future, Jos. All of this can't be allowed to just fade away. You saw it for yourself. You heard it from Beola. It's all still going on, but it needs managing. I've stolen fourteen years of Gary's life. He allowed me to do that because I promised him that it wouldn't be forever.'

'But I can't manage a business. I wouldn't know where to start.'

'I can help you.'

'A crash course in being humanitarian?' Jos wondered. 'Why didn't you just leave it to Jude?'

'Jude was never interested in business. In the beginning, I tried to teach her how to make things work in the longer term. Projections, planning. Every project is set up to run itself in the long run, but they still need managing. Not everything can be foreseen and so someone has to act as guardian. It's time now to pass on the responsibility to someone young, with new ideas, and a better understanding of how much the world has changed in my absence.'

'Why did you leave the white house to Beola?'

Jos' change of tack was sudden, but not exactly out of the blue.

Peter sensed she was irritated by that fact, probably because he should have left the home he'd built, to the woman he'd built it for. 'Thanks to my magical old friend I had reasonable warning of my impending doom,' he explained. 'I didn't really believe him… I didn't want to believe him, but there were other things that Laputo predicted that did come to pass, so I gave his predictions for me the respect they deserved, and I prepared. He told me that Jude would leave Africa soon after I died and that she would not return for many, many years.'

'So, Jude will come back then?'

‘As predicted by the man who told me I was destined to die at the side of a road.’ Peter knew it would be soon, and he knew why his wife would come, but kept those things to himself for the moment. ‘He was right about me, so I believe he’ll be right about Jude too. But this was all years ago. I didn’t want to be alone through my years of waiting for you to grow up and come looking for me.’

‘But I didn’t come looking for you, Peter… according to Beola, you sent for me.’

‘I did,’ he admitted. ‘I became… impatient.’

‘So, you summoned me all the way here for a job interview.’

‘I suppose you could look at it like that.’

‘Peter… I haven’t worked a single day in my life. I know nothing about running a business. I have trouble reading my bloody bank statement. I’m pretty useless at everything financial. I wouldn’t know where to start.’ ‘I will help you,’ he repeated.

‘How… exactly, can you help me?’

‘I have a very clear instinct about what I have become, Jos. I am pure energy with none of my corporeal self to impede progress. You have the same energy animating you too, body and mind, trapped inside you for the most part. Our energies are compatible as proved by our shared experience earlier today. It was as easy as rain falling into a river, and just as easy for my fluid self to flow back out again. I wasn’t looking for you then, but I felt your distress and it was my instinct to comfort you. That instinct carried me into your mind, and I saw not simply your dream, but also the memories powering that dream. I could escape all of that easily, and so I chose to take you with me. And you came… just as easily. Your energy freed itself and bonded with mine and, when you were ready, that energy just returned to where the rest of you was still curled up and sleeping on the bed. I had no idea any of this would be possible until those moments. But now that I see it, now I have felt it working, I know I can give you all of the memories, and the knowledge I retain still. That will allow you to pick everything up where I left it as easily as you can reach out and pick a flower. I have a lot of information for you, Jos. I prefer to give it to you quickly and directly. Telling it could take weeks, and then it may take you years to process and remember it all. We don't have years. I'm not even sure we have weeks.'

'Why?'

'Your arrival has been a catalyst.' He smiled regretfully. 'Events are now in motion which are destined to overtake and extinguish me.'

A frown creased her brow, as Jos considered the possibility of losing peculiar Uncle Peter so soon after finding him. His love had cleared away the years of pain clogging up her mind and left her happy and contented and able to forgive the world for taking her parents away too soon. Was the world going to take him away too?

Of course, it was Jude who had rescued her in the real world. Jude had given her a home, fed and clothed her and held onto her in the night when her own screaming wakened Jos from the nightmares. But living with Jude was mercurial, dependent upon how her aunt was feeling and those feelings could change day to day. It was all right as long as Jos didn't ask questions. But, now she'd escaped, Jos knew she couldn't go back to living like that.

She didn't want to.

Something had to change.

'I'm twenty-four years old!' Jos exclaimed suddenly, and as if this had just occurred to her that very same moment. She was on the verge of tears again. 'I really need to get a grip.' Looking at Peter directly, she asked, 'Do you really believe that I can do it?'

'You can do anything, Jos,' Peter told her sincerely. 'Believe in me and then let me help you to believe in yourself.'

Before thinking herself out of the confidence she suddenly felt, Jos said, 'All right, I will.'

Smiling his biggest, brightest smile, Peter told her, 'You won't regret

it.'

'Would I have to live here?' she wondered.

'Maybe some of the time? I suppose that's up to you.'

'Can you tell me anything about it now?'

'Beola has already shown you the types of projects you'll be involved in. Each one has an individual or small group of managers on site. You will need to meet these people let them teach and guide you. Your job will be problem resolutions that, for whatever reason, cannot be achieved by those individuals. It's about relationships, Jos, and getting the best results for the greatest number of people involved.'

'That terrifies me,' she admitted.

'Then practice pretending to be confident,' Peter advised. 'You need to relax more.'

'I am relaxed.' If she relaxed any more right then, Jos worried she'd slide right off the bench.

'That's sort of a side effect of being here with me.' Peter looked up and all around, looking at the view he knew like the back of his hands. His entire world as seen from various points in and around the white house. It wasn't a bad place to be stuck. 'I didn't know how to stop until I came here, Jos. I was always on the move, always busy. Some would say that never changed even after I settled right here, and they would be right. The difference lies in how this place can make you feel on the inside when you let it in. Mind, body and soul. It changes you for the better.' Sensing that she was weary, and knowing he hadn't said it all yet, Peter asked, 'Can I try something else while you're sleeping?'

'Like what?'

'You can come into my world. I'd like to see if I can come into yours.'

After a few moments' consideration, Jos said, 'That sounds suspiciously like you want to borrow my body.'

'I do.' Peter nodded, serious faced. 'Just for a short time.'

'To do what exactly?'

'An experiment. I'd like to sneak downstairs and eat some of that food Beola prepared. Drink a beer maybe.' Jos wasn't looking at all convinced, so he went on, 'I really just want to know if this will be possible. I didn't know I was able to visit your dream until I tried and, if you think about it, it'll be a lot easier to teach you about handling things if I can go along with you when you visit the projects. We can be a team.'

'A team,' Jos repeated quietly. After a moment, she added, 'This is insane.'

'Maybe, but you and I are not insane, we're simply in a crazy situation that surely deserves to be properly explored. This is science, Jos… without the fiction. Let's test the boundaries and find out what we're capable of when we pool our resources.'

Jos wanted to know how it would work, how long it would last, would she remember it, would she know it was happening, would it change her in any way?

Peter couldn't answer a single question.

'At least you're honest,' Jos said, yawning her head off. 'As long as I wake up tomorrow perfectly feeling me… and as long as I get a blow-byblow report of everything you do while driving my chassis, then okay.'

Eyes shining, Peter said, 'Fantastic!'

'This is permission for this one time only,' Jos told him seriously. 'Any future teamwork will have to be freshly negotiated and will very much depend upon your behaviour this time around.'

'Got it,' Peter told her softly. 'Sweet dreams.'

He winked out before her eyes, and the night breathed into life to replace him.

Picking up her phone Jos saw that less than five minutes had passed and, as she sat there marvelling at her very own science fiction, she heard Ben wishing his parents a good night. Then she heard him cross the porch and descend the steps, heard the gravel crunch as he moved off parallel to the front of the house on his short walk towards the lodge.

And then there was just the night.

A trillion tiny voices joined in chorus under the stars. An unceasing, and vibrating trill and whistle which filled the dark as far as she could not see. An owl hooted from the trees surrounding the white house and Jos found herself standing, looking through the darkness to where it would inevitably meet the morning. She had no recollection of moving from the bench to walk across the garden to where the flowers spilled over to tumble down the walls. Maybe she was already asleep? Already dreaming. Maybe it was all just a dream? When she heard Beola giggling like a randy schoolgirl somewhere inside the house, Jos went into the garden room and closed the door.

CHAPTER ELEVEN

Beola was not sleepy at all.

She found it hard to get to sleep after sex. Unlike her husband who was already snoring beside her. She lay in the dark thinking about love and life and eventually her thoughts turned to the more immediate things. She wondered about Jos? Wondered about Peter's intentions. Clearly, he was up to something, because he had made such a fuss about getting her here. But why now? Why? But it was beyond her imagination to guess what was going on. She only hoped that it wouldn't affect her own peace with the world. She liked her life, liked things the way they were. But she was beginning to experience a vague sense of foreboding. She'd been too busy preparing for Jos' arrival to notice before, but now their guest was here Beola had the distinct feeling that things were about to change.

Before trying to get to sleep, Beola got up to use the toilet and, on her way back to bed, she smelled the unmistakable aroma of cigarette smoke. Knowing her son was prone to the odd cigarette she wondered if perhaps Ben had been the one moving Nightingale's cigarettes, smoking the odd one and then leaving the packs in odd places so their resident ghost would get the blame. Back in her bedroom she pulled her dress back on and went downstairs to investigate.

Finding the French doors open onto the patio from the entrance hall, she followed her nose and was shocked to find Jos lying on one of the loungers, wearing nothing but a T-shirt and a pair of skimpy knickers, puffing away on a cigarette. 'I had no idea you smoked, Jos.'

'Beola. I didn't mean to disturb you.'

'I thought it was Ben.' Beola frowned because something was off. She hadn't known her long but was familiar enough with her face to know that Jos looked odd; her expression seemed more fluid than fixed as they regarded one another, as if Jos couldn't decide what she was feeling or how to show it. Maybe she was simply feeling guilty, caught out like a naughty child? 'I came down here to tell him off…' Beola went on. '… but I don't suppose I can tell you off.' Then she noticed that the doors into the kitchen were also standing open and all the lights were on. The place would be filling up with insects. Tutting to herself, Beola crossed the patio to close the doors and switch off the lights.

Entering the kitchen, she saw that Jos had taken the dinner leftovers from the fridge. Dishes of roast chicken, vegetables, spiced rice and beans, all left standing on the table. She didn't seem to have bothered with a plate either, just dug in with the large spoon that was still lying next to the dish of chicken. Beola tried not to feel put out, but manners were important in Tanzania and guests especially should display good manners. With just a hint of the irritation felt, she said, 'I suppose I should be glad you used a different spoon for the tart.'

'Fyrstekake!'

Beola spun around at the sound of that singular and clearly spoken word, and saw that Jos was heading quickly across the patio towards her, cigarette in hand, and wearing the strangest smile.

'I taught you how to make that, Bee. My own mother's recipe.'

Beola had no time to be stunned, because she was suddenly swept up into a bear hug and lifted up off her feet. Then she was spinning around and around, held tight in that strong embrace. Peter used to do that to her a lot. Now Beola was feeling afraid. 'Put me down,' she demanded, struggling to free her arms. 'Put me down!' Back on her own two feet she was dizzy, but she brushed away the hand that sought to steady her. 'Don't touch me.' She backed away from the person who was not Jos.

'Sorry about the mess…'

Beola watched not Jos jam the cigarette in her mouth and then begin collecting the dishes from the table.

'…it's been so long since I last tasted anything.' Spoken around the cigarette, with one eye closed against the smoke. 'I don't suppose there are a few beers lying around? I could murder a cold beer.'

'Peter?' Beola spoke tentatively, quietly, watching not Jos stashing the leftovers back in the fridge where there were no beers to be seen, because Kissi and Ben had finished them earlier.

'Wine will just have to do.'

Watching then as wine was drank straight from the bottle, Beola spoke again, louder and much more sharply, 'PETER!' She then watched not Jos' face light up in a big grin.

'Surprise!'

'What have you done?'

'Relax, Bee. It isn't permanent.'

'Do you have permission to use Jos in this way?'

'I do.' And the excited smile on his borrowed face was entirely Peter

Sinclair. 'She's asleep now… but before she went to bed, we had a chat…'

By then Peter, wearing Jos' skin, was on his way back out to the patio taking the wine along. Beola followed, still open mouthed, watching. The gait, the tiny gestures, the tilt of the head. The next cigarette… from a pack she recognised as Nightingale's, was being lit from the last.

'We've been meeting up in the garden.' Peter puffed rapidly, before inhaling deeply. 'She likes me.' Pausing again to allow smoke to billow out. 'Well…' smiling coyly at Beola. 'I am adorable. So anyway… first I slipped into her dream. I did that earlier too… she was very upset you see…'

'Upset?'

'Very bad dream. I slipped inside and carried her away. My heart was breaking for her… so young, too young for all that pain. Anyway, I realised a few things about the connection we share, and we talked about that this evening. Jos is my heir, Beola. I need her to be more like me. We're working on achieving that with this little experiment.'

'I thought that you left everything to Gary.'

'Gary is my executor. In charge only until such time as she can find my other, more recent will which states categorically that everything, lock stock and barrel, belongs to Jos. Except the white house, Bee. That will only return to Jos after you and Kissi are dead. After that, it's up to Jos what she does with it. Obviously, I'll be telling her where I hid that will so she can just go and fetch it, but I can't do that yet… not until…' That little grimace again. 'Oops… I can't go revealing all my secrets just yet. Suffice to say that I need to borrow Jos from time to time so I can get all my little ducks into a row.'

'Does Jos know one of your ducks is a smoker?' Beola wondered.

That comical grimace again. 'I nearly coughed these lungs inside out taking the first few puffs. But I persevered.'

'How dare you!' Beola was very angry suddenly. 'How dare you contaminate a body that you have no right to be inside.'

Sagging visibly, not Jos stubbed out the fresh cigarette.

Pouting, Peter sat back down on the lounger hugging the bottle. 'Can I at least finish the wine?'

'How can you be so… so…' Beola was so angry she could barely speak. 'Oh, I don't know what you are, or what you are doing. But it is wrong! This is wrong.'

'Not for me, Bee.' Suddenly, Peter's borrowed face was a mask of seriousness. 'This is what I've been waiting for.'

'To possess Jos?'

'To give her what she needs to pick it up where I left off.' After a second of silent staring, Peter relaxed and said, 'Can't you be just a little bit pleased to see me?'

'I don't see you, Peter. I only see Jos.'

*

Jos woke just before dawn.

She turned over, discovered her head hurt, groaned, and then realised she also had a foul-tasting mouth. Disentangling herself from the sheets, she saw dirty marks where her feet had been, because the soles of her feet were filthy! 'What the very fuck?'

Getting up, she went to the bathroom and brushed her teeth before bothering to pee. Pulling on a pair of shorts, Jos then went down to the kitchen to have a large glass of that homemade fruit juice she knew was in the fridge. As she was fetching the juice, she scratched an itch by her nose and, sniffing the scent of those fingers a small noise escaped her throat. 'Oh my god, oh my god, oh my god.'

Beola arrived right then after a very restless night, surprised to find her guest already up and taking a jug of juice from the fridge. Memories of last night's carry on swept in and maybe it was still going on? Maybe Peter was still using Jos? When the young woman's eyes met her own, she saw only confusion in them, and that wasn't an emotion she'd ever associated with Peter. 'Jos?'

'Sorry…' Jos was far too distracted to notice Beola's uncertainty about her identity. 'I don't feel well. I feel like I had lots to drink last night… and… and… I think I was smoking. But I only had two little glasses of wine and I don't smoke. I've never smoked. Except for the time I had a puff on a fag one Friday night after the ice rink, but it was horrible, and I felt sick… and… and… oh my god I'm going to be sick.' Covering her mouth with a hand, Jos looked around wondering if she might make it back up to the garden room to puke in private.

Not a hope.

Beola watched with a mixture of horror and concern as Jos vomited copiously into the kitchen sink.

Jos stayed slumped over the sink for several minutes, her forehead resting on the outside rim so neither her eyes nor her nostrils would be offended by the regurgitated contents of her stomach. Beola was at her side with a glass of juice by then, encouraging her to drink and sit down. Jos would rather the floor opened up and dropped her into the centre of the Earth, where she could never again embarrass herself. 'I am so sorry, Beola.'

'Don't worry, Jos. Are you unwell? Do you still feel sick?'

'No…' Rolling her head to one side Jos saw that Beola had set a chair close by, and she sat down gratefully, taking the juice and sipping just enough to disguise the acrid taste of vomit. 'I'll be fine,' she assured herself more than Beola. 'I have no idea why that happened. I'm so sorry. I really can't remember the last time I was sick.'

'Please don't worry, Jos.' Beola suspected she knew more about what was going on than poor Jos did, and felt guilty. 'Why don't you go and take a shower, brush your teeth…'

'I'll clean my mess up first.'

'No…'

'Yes,' Jos told Beola firmly. 'You are not cleaning up after me.' When Beola opened her mouth to protest, she added, 'Please, just let me do it.

Show me where the cleaning things are.'

Beola fetched a little caddy from a nearby cupboard, containing a selection of cleaning products and some cloths, which she set down next to the sink. She also fetched a roll of kitchen paper and a plastic bag, and once it was all ready, said, ‘I’m going to take a shower and then I will make us coffee, would you also like something to eat?’

‘Maybe some toast.’ Jos was feeling better by then and, taking regular sips of juice, managed to clean up her mess without adding to it. The act of cleaning helped to focus her mind and helped her recover some memories from last night. Memories she felt unusually disconnected from; as if she was telling what had happened as opposed to remembering it. A jumbledup mish mash of excitement, food, drink and cigarettes. After tying up her sick bag and dumping it into the bin, she replaced the caddy and then went back up to the garden room to brush her teeth again and take a quick shower. Dressed and feeling much better, Jos stood in the bedroom and said, ‘What the fuck did you do to me, Peter?’ She then had to sit down due to the soporific effects, which were tedious right then, because she was angry, and she didn’t want to lessen the effect of that. Nevertheless, her legs refused to fully support her weight, so she sat down heavily in the chair by the window.

‘I’m sorry.’ Peter appeared with hands already raised, palms outward in supplication. ‘Please believe me…’

‘How many bloody fags did you smoke with my lungs?’ Jos wanted to know. ‘I don’t remember agreeing to fags. You swanned off wearing my body, and then you polluted me! I remember sitting downstairs, half dressed. For fuck’s sake, I just got here, I don’t know these people and they don’t know me. My god, Beola must think…’ Pausing to allow a small collection of images to flit across her mind, she realised, ‘Beola was there too. Christ, no wonder she wasn’t sure who was about to puke into her kitchen sink.’

‘I apologise, sincerely.’ Turning, Peter walked through the open door, out into the garden and sat down on his usual bench facing the garden room window.

Jos trailed after him but sat at the bistro table instead.

Face to face with her nemesis, but irritated that she’d followed him like a puppy. She waited quietly, watching him intently. He looked so real, like she could reach out and touch him. Maybe she could? Would her hand pass through him like he was a TV ghost? Perhaps touching him would shatter his illusion? His blonde hair was loosely tied back this morning. Unable to resist, she asked, 'Did you have to tie your hair back before puking up into your In-between?'

Peter looked away, trying not to laugh.

'Seriously…' she went on. 'Don't ever do that to me again. And don't ever eat seafood. I hate seafood. The thought of it makes me want to puke.' 'How can you not like seafood?'

'How can people ever eat it, is what you should be asking. The sea is the world's dustbin, Peter. Fish are fucked.'

'I'll promise not to eat seafood if you promise not to swear.'

Jos shot him a look. 'My body, my rules.'

'Fair point.'

'What I really want to know is… if we do that again, can we do it awake? Me awake; I mean. So, I can stop you if you reach for any fags… or fish.'

Grinning from ear to ear, because Jos was proving to be a lot more fun than initially anticipated, Peter asked, 'Wanna find out?'

CHAPTER TWELVE

There was a raft of rules and regulations governing what Jos insisted on referring to as body snatching.

No seafood, no fish of any kind, as discussed previously. No body snatching until Jos was showered, dressed, and made up, if and when appropriate! No sex. No drugs. No illegal activities at all. No dangerous activities such as mountain climbing or caving or jumping out of planes. Definitely no bungee jumping. Peter needed to have that one explained and knew he'd definitely have been first in the queue inside his own body, but agreed that, should they encounter a bungee jumping operation on their travels, he would avoid it. Fortunately, Jos had no allergies and wasn't taking any medications, otherwise they'd have been there all day.

When she was finally showered, factor fiftied and dressed, Jos applied a little mascara and a smudge of lippy in honour of the exciting day ahead. She then twisted and coiled her hair up onto her head, fixing it in place with a few Kirby grips and a big black claw. Then she remembered Beola and the toast. 'I have to go down to breakfast,' she told the garden room. Almost immediately she felt profoundly impatient. 'Are you in me already?' Standing, listening intently, feeling just as intently, awaiting the expected inertia. Instead, she just felt a defined sense of urgency. 'Okay, okay.' Jos exited her bedroom via the internal door and went down to the patio that way.

'I thought you'd fallen asleep.' Beola had already finished her breakfast and was on her second cup of coffee. Pouring a cup for Jos, she asked, 'Are you feeling better?'

'Much.' Jos sat down and helped herself to two slices of toast, which she slathered in honey before getting stuck in. Pausing only to gulp coffee and juice in turns.

Bemused, Beola wondered, 'Are you in a hurry?'

Looking sheepish, Jos said, 'Not particularly.'

'Well, it certainly seems like you are in a rush.'

'It's such a lovely day.' Jos tried to sound relaxed and casual. 'I thought

I'd go for a walk.'

'A walk.' Beola repeated flatly. 'You do recall that we are surrounded by African bush, and there are leopards and cheetah also going for a walk.' Jos failed when trying not to laugh.

'Tell me,' Beola demanded. 'Something is going on and, after last night, I want to know what.'

'Oh yeah, last night. You were there. It was an…'

'An experiment.' Beola knew the tag line. 'To what end?'

'Peter wants to do some sort of mind meld thing…' Jos waggled a hand next to her temple. 'I suppose it'll be like uploading information from the internet onto your PC. My brain is the PC, and his memories are going to be uploaded into mine. That's how I understand it anyway.'

'And you are okay with this?'

'So far, so good,' Jos shrugged.

'It isn't natural.'

'Moving matches and books and appearing before your very eyes isn't natural either, Beola, but you were okay with that once you got used to it. I can't truly articulate what is happening between me and Peter, but it has changed a lot of the negative stuff for me.' Jos explained what had happened to her yesterday afternoon, and how it made her feel. 'I still feel happy. I feel loved! It's like I got my life back… or at least all the positive emotions I seem to have missed out on since losing my parents. I've spent a decade of my life just… floundering! Since coming here I've begun to feel like me again. The real me, not the me I became because living with Jude didn't really heal me. Peter has been waiting for me, and perhaps I've been waiting to come.' Pausing, for a moment's realisation, Jos then said, 'I've felt more at home here in the past twenty-four hours, than I ever felt living with Jude.' 'At least Jude was there for you when you needed her.'

'It's strange that you mention her now, because whenever I mentioned her to you yesterday you changed or avoided the subject. I've spent years walking on egg shells and avoiding some of my own subjects. Peter, the white house, and even you. Whenever I mentioned you in the weeks before coming here, Judy got all moody. The atmosphere became chilling. I'd find her in dark rooms, just staring into space or staring out of a window into the night. It would be my fault. I was the one who'd upset her, because I'd reminded her of painful memories. I needed to stop being so selfish. I lost count of the times I retreated to my room to weep. At least once a week I came close to cancelling the whole thing. I wanted to hide, to lock myself away, to never speak again. But I didn't... because something else inside me was braver, and that is what got me here!'

'I'm sorry.' Beola was a little surprised by Jos' vehement reaction. 'I didn't mean to make you feel bad. I didn't know how things were between you and Jude. I just think you need to...'

'Please...' Jos interrupted her. 'Just let me handle this as I see fit.'

*

Back upstairs, Jos practically ran through the garden, so excited was she to explore those boundaries. 'Peter...' she whispered loudly. 'Where are you?' *Tucked neatly inside.*

She stopped dead, looking all around, mouth open to catch those flies.

I thought you'd realised. I know you felt my impatience. It was me scoffing your breakfast so enthusiastically.

'Fuck,' Jos whispered, then laughed softly, delighted. *Stop swearing or there will be calamari for lunch.*

Giggling like an idiot, Jos went inside the garden room and closed the door. In the bathroom, she stood in front of the mirror, momentarily disappointed that Peter wasn't staring back at her as he probably would've been had this been a movie. 'What now?' She wondered.

First, we need to find out if I can leave the white house with you.

'Okay... and?'

The keys for the jeep are kept in the drawer of the sideboard down in the hall.

'I can't drive.' *I can.*

'But...'

Let me worry about that, Jos.

Finding the keys was easy, even if it did take two trips.

In all the excitement Jos forgot to grab her bag and they had to retreat to the garden room to fetch it. Whatever powers Peter might possess, she doubted they'd get very far without money. Back in the hall, they simply walked up to the sideboard and stretched a hand out. Peter guided that hand to open the correct drawer. The keys were in their hand before she realised, and they were heading towards the garage seconds later. In through the side door, they climbed into the little dark blue jeep and Jos felt very strange sitting in the driving seat.

You're going to have to relax now, Jos. Recede a little. When Peter sensed she was about to speak, he told her, *Close your eyes as well as your mouth and think about letting go. Remember how it felt when I carried you away. You felt safe, loved. I do love you, Jos. I would never allow anything bad to happen to you.*

His sound inside was soothing, calming. Once more Jos felt herself filling up with love and joy and allowed her mind to simply drift away. When her eyes opened, she watched one hand activate a button on the key fob which sent the garage doors rolling upward. When that same hand keyed the ignition as the other put the jeep into gear, Jos saw it all as if she was watching it on a screen. She wasn't looking at her feet and so was only very vaguely aware that one had depressed the clutch, and the other was the pressing the accelerator. When the jeep began moving forward, she closed her eyes. *Shit*

The jeep stalled.

Jos… you need to keep your eyes open.

'Sorry.' Without waiting to be told, Jos felt around inside her head for all that love and joy, finding it flowing through her like a river, she let it carry her away once more.

Peter started the jeep up again and this time they managed to drive out of the garage and around the lawn. When they noticed Beola coming through the front doors, they raised a hand and waved to her before driving into the trees. In the rear-view mirror, Beola ran out onto lawn, waving her arms about and calling something after them. They ignored her. Following the gravel drive as it wound around the hill to meet the red earth track, they felt increasingly exhilarated as well as apprehensive. Would they escape? Or would the white house anchor Peter as it had done since the laibon united them? Nearing the foot of the hill, they pressed harder on the accelerator, bursting out at speed from among the trees, passing through the invisible boundary and taking their hands off the wheel to punch the air with both hands, whooping in delight.

We did it!

It was just after ten when they reached Moshi, slowing the jeep down so Peter could look around at how much had changed over the years. A golf course and a supermarket. Garish billboards lined the roadside between the trees. Bars and restaurants set back from the road advertised aircon and chilled drinks, hot food, best food, food served all day. On they drove until reaching a round-a-bout where they turned south onto Arusha Road. When they saw yet another sign advertising best breakfast, they pulled in to the little car park.

'Surely not,' Jos commented as they got out the jeep and began the short walk into a leafy garden area where more than a dozen tables were set at random, under big, thatched umbrellas, in front of an open-air bar with a small building housing the kitchens behind it.

I haven't had a decent breakfast in fourteen years, Jos. Indulge me.

'I am gonna get so fat.' Jos tried to sound irritated, but really, she was having the best time. The drive was amazing, though Peter had to keep telling her off for trying to look around, while he was trying to watch the road. But for Jos it was all so exciting, so free. To all intents and purposes, she was an independent woman pleasing herself. In reality she had her constant, inner buddy, looking after her every step of their way, but the world didn't know that.

They were greeted by a pretty French waitress. Flawless skin the colour of gold, pouty looking pillow lips, huge brown eyes, perfect bobbed hair, wearing nothing more exciting than a pair of faded jeans and a tight black T-shirt, but carrying the ensemble off with an easy aplomb. Drop dead gorgeous.

Sickening, Jos thought.

Peter fixated on her arse like a dog on heat as they followed her to a table near the bar.

'Merci bien, mademoiselle.' Peter had to assert himself to produce the coy smile he deemed fitting for the occasion. 'J'ai vraiment faim, ce matin. Que pouvez vous recommender?'

Jos didn't waste time marvelling at the new language skills because she was too busy trying, unsuccessfully, not to pout and flirt.

Responding just as coyly, the waitress wondered, 'Vegetarienne ou carnivore?'

'Carnivore.' And that single word sounded so lewd to Jos it was embarrassing.

The waitress didn't mind. She smiled just as lasciviously back at the red head and began reeling off her menu de jour like it was a bill of fare for sex. 'Mais…' she said, finally. '…si vous avez tres, tres faim, je recommande le steak, les champignons, la tomate, les pomme de terre sautees et les oeufs.'

'Ca a l'air formidable!' Peter had both of Jos' hands gripping the side of the table, trying not to pounce.

Wetting her lips with her tongue, the waitress said, 'Je sais.' Then, wafting herself with a launguid hand, she wondered, 'Qu'est-ce que vous voulez boire?'

There was a short period of 'Mmmmmming.' With matching eyes and batting lashes, and then, 'Café… s'il vous plait, et une bierre blonde.'

Watching as the waitress made her way over to the bar, looking back over her shoulder and smiling as she went, Jos grabbed the menu lying on the table and held it up high enough to hide her face. 'Stop it!' she whispered vehemently. 'She thinks I'm a bloody lesbian.' *Have you e…*

'Shut up.'

Breakfast arrived soon after the beer, and it was so big it was spilling over the sides of an already large dinner plate. Jos looked at it with dismay in her heart, but Peter was ogling it like a cat watching a big fat mouse and filled her head with a ravenous lust that allowed her to consume the entire meal. They washed it down with the rest of the beer and were done in time for the coffee to arrive with the bill… and the waitress' phone number!

'Josette.' Peter sighed, tucking her phone number safely inside Jos' shorts.

Jos couldn't get out of the place fast enough. *Where next?*

Back in the driver's seat of the car at least, Jos spoke quietly but firmly, 'I'm going back to the white house. I need a lie down after eating half a cow.' She could sense Peter's frustration, but she wouldn't be swayed. 'Enough for today. We can go out again tomorrow.' She found herself placating as if he was a child. 'I'm booked on a safari with Ben and

Wendell.' *Where?*

'Mount Kilimanjaro National Park I think.' Her head filled then with a defined sense of satisfaction, and she remembered this was where Lulu had been released all those years ago.

Before heading back, they made a quick stop at the Total station. Jos thought this was a nice gesture; it seemed only right that, after their grand theft auto, they at least replace the fuel. Peter just thought Jos was far too naïve for her own good.

*

Back at the white house Beola had filled Kissi in about everything that had happened since Jos' arrival so, when she returned in the little jeep, they were a united front on the white house steps.

Kissi had been angry until that moment; his wife was upset, afraid, unsure what was going on and what would happen next, and he didn't know what to think or believe. All he knew for sure was that whatever was going on then, had begun the night after Peter died. A strange night indeed, filled with tribal ritual and a black and angry sky that had concentrated its rage upon the very house they now called home. And then came Jos, just as she was coming right then, walking slowly towards them, looking so shamefaced he suddenly wanted to laugh.

Whatever was going on, it surely wasn't her fault.

'Well…' Kissi tried hard to maintain a stern façade when Jos reached the foot of the steps. 'For a woman who cannot drive, you certainly managed to drive that jeep.'

'I would explain.' Jos shrugged a little. 'But I'm not sure you'd believe me.'

Beola also felt deflated by then. 'I have told my husband everything. So, whatever is going on, we can deal with it together.'

‘I’d like that.’ Stepping up onto the porch, Jos sat down on one of the cushioned basket chairs arranged around a low table. She felt very tired suddenly. Empty. Searching her mind, she found no trace of the love and joy flowing through and knew that Peter had returned to his In-between.

After a moment Kissi and Beola joined Jos, aware she seemed drained. Her head hung off her neck and her shoulders sagged as she sat there, slumped and quiet. ‘Are you all right, darling?’ Beola wondered. ‘Can I get you something? A drink? Some food?’

‘Oh god no…’ Jos waved it away. ‘I am stuffed. He made me eat steak for breakfast.’

‘Who made you?’ Kissi wondered.

‘Peter,’ Beola and Jos chorused.

‘So, he really is… inside you?’ Kissi tried not to sound as troubled as he felt.

‘Not any more,’ Jos said softly. ‘He doesn’t hurt me,’ she assured. ‘It’s kinda fun. There are boundaries, rules. He didn’t want to come back so soon. I did. It won’t be forever, just until… until…’ ‘Until what?’ Beola asked.

Sitting quietly for a few moments, Jos then repeated the gist of what Peter had told her, ‘Until events overtake and extinguish him.’ She then got to her feet. ‘Can we talk about this later? I really need to sleep.’ She yawned to prove the point. ‘I’m so tired.’ Must be the jet lag.

As she got up from the chair, she fished a small square of paper out of her shorts pocket and gave it to Beola. ‘Can you hide that for me, or burn it… yes, please just burn it.’

Reading, Beola wondered, ‘Who is Josette?’

‘Peter has a hankering for more than just food, and I am drawing a big fat line under that one.’

Looking at one another, Beola and Kissi laughed heartily.

*

Jos would’ve been quite happy to lie down and sleep right there on the porch, but she climbed the stairs to the garden room, dropped her bag on the floor as soon as she closed the door, kicked off her sandals and flopped, face down on top of the bed.

She was asleep inside a minute.

*

Peter was directly responsible for Jos' fatigue, because he was draining her energy by making her mind work twice as hard. But she was young and healthy and, when all of this was over, would be able to return to her normal sleep patterns with no lingering effects. He was one hundred percent sure of this, and so didn't waste time worrying that Jos was having to sleep a lot of extra hours to counter his effects.

As soon as she started to dream, he slipped inside her mind like rain into a river, joining her for a pleasant dream of driving. He was in the passenger seat, and she was laughing in delight in complete control of a sporty little car. She turned to smile at him, pleased to see him. Top down, shades on, hair wild in the wind. She was happy. He adored the sound of her laughter. Pure joy. When the dream morphed into an indoor scene populated by people he didn't know, Peter receded without causing a ripple, and then stimulated only her conscious mind to wake. Just as he had the night before.

Little by little Peter merged his free energy into Jos' mental energy, becoming just another series of action potentials, flowing through the great plethora of electrochemical activity that was her intellect. Positively charged ions flowing into cells, and negatively charged ions flowing out, in the same perpetual motion as all the oceans of the planet.

It was like breathing.

When their rhythm was mutual, he opened Jos' eyes and saw only the landscape of bedding, because Jos was still face down with her head turned to one side. Her head was fuzzy, her limbs heavy with the chemicals all human brains use to stop sleepers acting out all those dreams. It took time to strike a balance, time to dial this brain into a groove between theta and delta waves, and into a suspended state between dreaming and not dreaming. By achieving this particular level of cognizance, Jos' mind was able to accept Peter's activities inside her physical self as a dream. At the same time, her body was able to function, because it wasn't being immobilised by a brain cycling too slowly in delta waves but had just enough of the extra speed afforded from theta.

When her body was sufficiently restored, Peter impelled Jos to roll over and sit up. Then he lifted her hands and flexed her fingers. In doing so his energy was compelled into her physical self. Muscles and tendons and organs. His flow was carried then inside the rivers of her blood and the firing of her neurons. If she was going to awaken fully, going to reject him, it would be then. She did not, and so Peter was then able to stand up from the bed, retrieve her bag from the floor and find that little mobile phone he had no idea existed until Jos brought it into his sphere of awareness to prove that his time differed from real world time.

Knowing something exists and knowing how to work it are two very different things, so it took Peter a few minutes of pressing buttons and listening to beeps, before he discovered both the number he wanted and how to make the phone dial it.

Four and a half thousand miles away a phone began to ring.

When the ringing stopped, a voice said, 'Hi, toots.'

'Hey… Jude.'

'Jos?' Jude wasn't entirely sure despite the fact Jos' name and familiar number was showing on caller display. The cadence was off. She wondered if maybe her niece was drunk because it didn't sound like her at all. Jude didn't allow space to the thought regarding who it did sound like.

'And guess who else.'

'Is this some kind of joke, Jos? Are you drunk?'

'Do you recall… way back when… you and I were in love?'

'Stop it, Jos!' Jude still refused to acknowledge that distinctive accent. 'I don't need this crap. I…'

'Oh, do shut up, Fluff!' Peter then had to hold the phone away from Jos' ear, in case Jude's wailing and shouting disturbed her dreaming.

Needless to say, Jude then hung up.

So, he called again.

This time the answer machine kicked in and Peter could almost see Jude standing next to it, listening. 'It's a shock, I know.' He said after the beep. 'I'm shocked myself after all these years. But Jos is making this very easy for me, Jude. Jos has turned into a lovely young woman, hasn't she? A bit fucked up in the head, but we're working on that. We're becoming very close. Next, we'll be swapping secrets.'

*

In Edinburgh, Jude's legs had given way, and she was slumped on the stairs listening to her dead husband's words coming from the mouth of her niece. That unmistakable and singular, very English with a hint of Norwegian accent filled the hallway. There was no doubt in Jude's mind that she was listening to Peter. Somehow. He spoke about time running out, about secrets being uncovered, about Jos finding out the truth. And Jude's perfect little world came tumbling down inside ninety short seconds that the answer phone allotted Peter to communicate his threat from beyond his grave.

Even after the call ended, Jude sat there for over an hour, transfixed and very afraid. So afraid, she was unable to think or act. Frozen in place as her mind struggled to grasp the implications. Some of her little cats stopped by to rub and to purr and perhaps even to see if Jude was all right.

But she continued to be unmindful until the crunch of gravel path outside signalled the arrival of the postman. There was a glass door and a small vestibule between her and the front door, so she watched as a sheaf of brown and white envelopes fell from the letterbox, down onto the tiles. When she was sure the postman had moved on, Jude got up from the stairs, opened the inner door and collected her mail. Bank statements for her, as well as Jos, a mobile statement, gas, electricity, something from Edinburgh District Council, probably letting her know the council tax would be going up again next year.

Back in the kitchen, where she'd been when the phone rang the first time, Jude found her abandoned breakfast of cold coffee and soggy cereal. Her laptop was asleep but woke as soon as she touched it. The screen displayed an array of flowering shrubs on a garden centre web site she'd been browsing.

Opening a second page, Jude began browsing airline websites instead.

CHAPTER THIRTEEN

Jos didn't wake up until after four.

After another quick shower, she dressed, and was about to head downstairs to find her hosts, when she noticed her mobile lying on the bottom of the bed next to her bag. She remembered quite clearly dropping that same bag on the floor before passing out and hadn't even looked at her phone since using it to prove time with Peter was slower than time in general. Frowning, Jos picked up the phone and opened her calls list. Two calls to Jude she had absolutely no recollection of making. 'You did that,' she told the garden room. No response whatsoever. 'I'll find out.' One way or another.

Heading down to the patio moments later, Jos saw Kissi was lying back on one of the patio loungers with a newspaper and a bottle of beer. The site stimulated a memory of her lying back on that same lounger late last night, smoking fags and quaffing wine. Another memory flitted across her mind then like a tiny little butterfly, but Jos couldn't stop to follow it, because Kissi had noticed her coming down the stairs.

'Jambo, Jos…' He greeted her warmly, meeting her on the patio where his eyes searched hers'. 'Are you all right, darling?'

'I think so.' She nodded, knowing what he was referring to. 'How about you?' she wondered. 'Are you all right with all this… weirdness?'

Sitting at the table and indicating that Jos should join him, Kissi said, 'I have lived with Peter for close to thirty years, darling, despite the fact the man has been dead these past fourteen years. I like him. We became friends quickly, and I was very sad when he died.' Pausing to laugh a little ruefully, he then added, 'Of course we were all unaware at that time that Peter would be staying with us all the same. It took him a while… you know, to let us know he was still here. But I am sure my wife has told you all of this already, Jos.'

'Yes.' She nodded.

'Tanzania is a superstitious place…' Kissi went on. 'It wasn't easy for us to come to terms with our resident spirit, and we have had some trouble because of it.' Kiss then told Jos how he and Beola and Ben managed to keep everything within the family, right up until Ben and Wendell set up their business. 'It made sense that they use one of the rooms in the white house as their office.'

'Even then it wasn't a problem until they were making enough money to employ someone else.' Beola joined them, sitting down and taking hold of Jos' hand in friendship as well as reassurance. 'The first one lasted a week.'

'Her name was Rachael, and she was going into all the downstairs rooms,' Kissi explained.

'She was free to use the kitchen as well as the little toilet at the front door, but everywhere else was private,' Beola explained. 'Ben told her, and

I also told her.'

'Brave girl to have ignored you.' Jos winked at Kissi.

He laughed heartily, then picked up the story, 'I don't know about bravery, but she was certainly a nosy girl and Peter threw some books at her when she was snooping in the library.' Jos gasped, wide eyed.

'She ran out of here like all the lions in Africa were chasing her down.' Beola grimaced. 'And then she went into town and told everyone who would listen that evil spirits lived in the white house and that I was a witch. We put up with a lot of finger pointing and rumours for many months afterwards.'

'You must be very concerned that my own strange activities don't bring more trouble,' Jos realised.

'That is not why we are telling you this,' Kissi told her quickly. 'We simply want you to know that Peter's ghost is old news around here. Please do not feel that you have to keep things to yourself. We are here for you if you need our support.'

'I'm grateful,' Jos told them both. 'I really am, but I'm fine with it all. It makes me very tired… he makes me tired. I'm not sure why, but a wee nap, sorts that out. Of course, I don't want to sleep through my holiday…'

'Jos?' Beola was still holding her hand, but she squeezed it to get her attention. 'Are you sure you know why Peter is doing these things with you… to you?'

'You mean, is he up to something apart from ascertaining whether or not he can impart all his wisdom directly into my memory?' Jos shrugged. 'Probably. I think he also might be trying to get Jude here.' Beola and Kissi exchanged a look.

'What was that?' Jos wondered. 'That look.'

'You've barely been here twenty-four hours, Jos…' Beola told her. 'And so much is going on. We're just having to adjust, darling.'

*

Jos insisted on making dinner that evening. Her way of trying to make up for all the upheavals she was causing. She didn't believe for a moment that Beola and Kissi were cool with the idea that Jude could breeze in any day. But they wouldn't be drawn on the subject earlier and then Ben arrived with tales of a feisty and frisky American woman who'd been trying to get into his shorts all day! Besides, Jos wanted to find out why Peter had called her aunt, before asking the Nyerere's any more questions on that subject.

When Ben then went on to tell tales of woe related to how hungry he was after his busy day fighting off an American invasion, Jos took the opportunity to tell Beola to sit down, have a glass of wine, and let her do the cooking.

There was an abundance of chicken as well as honey available so, after also finding some garlic, soy sauce and vinegar, Jos set about preparing one of only three dishes she'd perfected. Her honey garlic chicken was crispy on the outside and succulent inside. Served with steamed veg from the garden and egg fried rice. She was glad she'd made extra, because Ben ate enough for three, and it wasn't beyond the realms of possibility that Peter would later use her to consume another late-night feast. For that reason, Jos ate sparingly… much to Beola's chagrin.

'I'm still trying to digest my enormous breakfast,' Jos reminded.

'I'm lucky if I get toast,' Ben moaned.

'If you want something more substantial then you could try making that in your own kitchen,' Beola pointed out. 'There is nothing but beer in my son's fridge,' she told Jos.

Conversation then turned to the impending safari drive the following morning.

'You'll need to be up early,' Ben told Jos. 'Wendell will be here around seven to pick us up, because we then have to collect the rest of our tourists from their hotels in town.'

'I'll set an alarm,' Jos promised.

It was a relaxed evening of good food, good company and good conversation. Jos managed to forget all the weird goings on, and even forgot about Peter for a while. The Nyerere's were a really nice family, they laughed and carried on together, and reminded Jos of her own family life. Her mum who had always been laughing and singing, and her dad who watched his wife with nothing but adoration in his eyes. She was happy letting those memories back in again, contented now because, finally, she understood that her parents were still right there, inside her body and soul, and she was free now to enjoy that. Still smiling as she climbed the stairs back up to the garden room planning another early night, still clutching a last glass of wine.

But when Jos went into the garden room, she saw her phone and remembered she had a bone to pick.

Back outside on the usual bench, she said, 'If you don't come and explain those phone calls I won't go on that safari.'

After the usual lethargy, Peter arrived, saw the glass of wine between them, and wondered, 'Another experiment?'

'You're driving me to drink.' Jos had actually forgotten all about the glass set precariously on the bench in case she dropped it during the general lassitude. Picking it up again, she sipped and asked, 'Why did you call Jude?'

'I thought it would be nice to catch up.'

'Did Jude see it like that?'

'She hung up on me.'

'On me more like.'

'Oh no…' Peter shook his head slowly. 'She knew it was me.'

'And you called her back. What did you say… and please, don't lie? You're using my head and, though I seem to have some initial trouble recalling when you hijack my sleep, it does all become apparent eventually.' Naïve maybe, but definitely not stupid.

When he was still waiting for Jos, Peter had been so wrapped up in his reasons, he'd not given space to the idea that he would care for her quite as much as he did. Jos turned out to be as fragile as he was obsessed, because she'd only ever succeeded in repressing her past woes. A lost and innocent little girl, who hadn't been properly nurtured since the day fate stole away her parents. He'd inadvertently forced those memories to the fore, and her later dream replayed the entire, horrific scene right in front of the fifteenyear-old who still resided inside the adult Jos. Forever destined to be on the floor of that diner, watching as her parents were crushed to death, because no one had ever freed her from that terrible burden.

Peter had felt her anguish, recognised it, and rescued Jos because he couldn't bear what it embodied inside his own past! It had been his instinct, his will, and she had melted into him so completely they became spiritually and emotionally entangled. The experience, as far as he was concerned, had inspired a deep and affectionate love for Jos. She was the daughter he never had, his child, and now his responsibility. The time had come to tell her the truth, and he was acutely aware that she had no one in the real world to turn to when she inevitably felt the force of it. But it had to be done.

'I called Jude…' Peter plunged ahead because he had no choice. '… to tell her I'll no longer be letting her get away with my murder.'

Before Jos could protest, he was inside her mind, and they were travelling up into his In-between to take a journey back in time.

CHAPTER FOURTEEN

Nicolae Ceausescu died peacefully in his sleep.

Of course, the real Ceausescu's died the death of one hundred and twenty bullets thanks to a firing squad, but Jude's saggy old boy hadn't shown up for breakfast that morning and was found curled up on one of the dining room chairs early that afternoon. He looked so peaceful, and it was this small death that clarified what now had to be done. He was still warm when Jude sat down on the next chair so she could scoop him up and cradle him on her lap. Just for a little while, before she had to go outside and dig another grave by the back wall where past decedents already rested in peace beneath the flowers and shrubs.

Jude cried a lot of tears sitting there. Not just for her saggy old boy, but for herself, for her life, for all the crap she was now going to have to deal with, because her dead husband was incapable of staying bloody dead. She wept too for all her other beloved cats, because Jude knew by then that she would have to leave them. Africa had called once more, and she had no choice but to face the terrifying consequences of Peter's resurgence.

When she felt ready, she carried Nicolae's furry little body through to the utility room where she wrapped him up in a clean towel. Leaving him there for the moment, she went out into her garden, fetched a fork as well as a spade, and began to dig.

Jude chose a spot close to the back wall where it was peaceful, secluded, and overhung by mature trees. She dug it deep, otherwise the foxes would only disinter the remains and she couldn't have that. She piled the dug earth onto a sheet of plastic laid out next to the grave and, when she was done, she went back inside to fetch the dead cat. His grave was four feet deep, around two feet wide, and four feet long. Far too big for the little cat gently laid in the bottom, all wrapped up in his bath towel shroud. Covering little Nicolae then with just a few inches of earth, she finished off with a single flower, and then covered the entire grave with a folded pasting table that usually lived inside the shed. Finally, she added some large stones to weigh it all down.

The remaining six cats had all attended the funeral, saying silent farewells to their fallen comrade. Some crouched on the wall watching. Others observed from the nearby shed roof. Only Imelda bore witness from the ground next to the grave. When it was done, they dispersed, going about their feline business.

Imelda was the last to leave.

CHAPTER FIFTEEN

Jos was up before six.

She was exhausted, emotionally drained and still in shock. Back to putting one foot in front of the other and once she'd showered, dressed, plaited her hair and gathered up a few belongings into her bag she then let Peter inside. His presence immediately took away all the pain and confusion, filled her with energy, and Jos knew she would be able to navigate the day ahead.

Together they went downstairs and, inside another drawer in a side table close to the foot of the internal staircase, they found the key to the cellar door. Opening it, they flicked on the lights and went down the thirteen steps into a wide, brightly lit space packed full of boxes, crates, suitcases and rails of clothes. Long wooden poles were affixed to the ceiling to hold even more clothes, gathered into clusters and covered up in dust sheets. It took nearly fifteen minutes to find the battered old Tilly hat, but it fitted Jos' head well and wearing it filled Peter with a defined sense of comfort; like finding some small solace in an old friend.

Back upstairs, they locked the door and replaced the key before heading to the kitchen. They then set about making a stack of pancakes and a variety of delicious toppings.

Ben arrived around six thirty, saw the Tilly hat on top of Jos' bag where she'd left it on a chair by the kitchen door, and was about to ask how she'd come by that particular hat, when he spotted the breakfast. 'Pancakes!' he declared. 'Are these for me?'

'Ben!' Jos' face lit up in a wide smile.

They dropped everything and went to hug him immediately, but Jos intervened on route, because she and Ben had only just met. She restricted Peter's joy and simply pecked Ben on the cheek as she gave him a brief little hug. She and Peter had spent hours together last night. Past and present. As for the future, Jos had insisted on an active role at all times. If they were going to proceed with agreed plans then it had to be an equal partnership. Today was going to be their watershed, and so far, so good. 'Sit down,' they said. 'Would you like coffee? Juice?' 'Everything,' Ben laughed.

Kissi arrived, and then Beola, both steadfastly refusing to acknowledge the fact that Peter was the world champion pancake maker who'd habitually left his kitchen looking like the bomb site discovered that morning. Bowls, pans, spoons and spatulas littered every work surface. There was bacon cooking in the oven, eggs frying on the hob, and pancakes piling up. The table was covered in dishes of fruit compote, honey, jam, syrup, and yogurt. There were lemons, mangoes, berries. Coffee was brewing and juice was chilling. They simply sat down and enjoyed the feast.

When Wendell arrived, he was a little surprised by the warm welcome received from Jos, who seemed to have gotten over her initial shyness. She was quite the ball of fire, jumping up from the table when he walked in. Fetching him pancakes and coffee and telling him to help himself to toppings.

'Reckon you need to up your breakfast game, Beola.'

'Reckon you need to mind your cheek, Wendell Cooper.'

As they were readying to leave, Jos asserted herself so she would remember her bag as well as Peter's hat. That was when she noticed the state of the kitchen. She really wanted to clean up the horrendous mess before leaving, but Ben and Wendell had already put their plates into the dishwasher and were heading for the door. Catching Beola's eyes, Jos grimaced.

'Go,' Beola told her. 'Kissi will take care of it.' 'I will?' he wondered.

But Jos was already turning towards the door because Peter was driving again.

*

They were finally on their way to the park by eight thirty.

Viv and George; middle aged, Canadian, quiet in a friendly way, their first time in Africa. Sally and Amanda; twenty somethings, English, bubbly back packers having the time of their lives before going back home to find proper jobs. Christina and Erica, nineteen and eighteen, American, spoiled rich kids passing through on their way to Europe from Japan, on their slow way back home to start studying law, both daddies were senior partners in corporate law, jobs in the bag no matter their grades, lives all mapped out, kept everyone waiting for twenty minutes so Christina could straighten her hair. Gregor and Rudi, thirty somethings, Russian, polite and reserved, it was also their first time in Africa. Jos, twenty-four, Scottish, radiating an infectious enthusiasm for the day ahead, taking life one day at a time, sat at the back in the three-seater along with Viv and George.

It took just over an hour to reach the gate at the south west of the park, passing through the rich, fertile and mountain watered lands all the way. This was a zone of agriculture, settlement and huge coffee and banana plantations. The peaked wooden entry way mimicked the mountain and, once Ben had taken care of the formalities, they were waved on through by the park entrance staff. There was a quick stop to allow anyone who needed to, to use the toilets.

Then they set off through the jungle and rainforest zone. At first, they were in a small convoy of similar vehicles filled with similar groups of wazungu; the local word for white people and tourists, all photographing everything from the signposts to the lush vegetation. Birds and animals could be heard in abundance, but the forest was just too good a hiding place. Little by little the vehicles lost sight of one another and soon it was just Red Earth Tours and the ever-climbing route through the fabulous flora growing around the knees of the highest free-standing mountain in the world.

Ben handled all the questions with cool expertise, while simultaneously keeping an eye out for any wildlife. He spotted turaco birds with their vivid blue and green plumage, which showed red under their wings when they took flight. Red billed hornbills roosted in the trees, and a striking black and red ground hornbill was spotted hopping around close to the road. He pointed out at least three species of cuckoo and entertained his audience by mimicking the female red chested cuckoo call which had a male perched on the Land Rover's bonnet in no time at all. Colobus monkeys could be seen flashing black and white through the trees, and a troupe of blue monkeys stopped them completely when they decided to sit down on the road for an impromptu grooming session.

Jos was having a wonderful time. Peter was completely dormant inside, and she busied herself taking some great photos with her brand-new digital camera which had an impressive range. She was also enjoying the company of Viv and George, who had left their sons looking after their farm in Ontario to take a holiday for the first time in over twenty years! It would no doubt be another twenty before they took the next holiday, so they were making this trip count and spending three months touring Africa to fulfil a lifelong dream. Jos took photos of them for their album, and they took some of her sporting that battered old Tilly hat which, for them at least, marked Jos down as a seasoned traveller.

Little by little the forest began to thin out, the views opening up. The wildlife also changed, and antelope as well as zebra could be seen grazing on the moorland, while giraffes browsed among the tree tops.

'Where are the lions?' Christina wanted to know.

Rolling his eyes at Wendell, Ben presented his best smile to their annoying guest of the day. 'Big game, are a lot rarer in this park.' 'But we want to see lions!' Erica chimed in.

Ben tried not to sound like he was addressing small children but allowed himself some measure of condescension when pointing out that, when Erica and Christina booked directly with him, and Wendell the previous weekend, they had explained that the trip to Arusha National Park would suit them better for big five opportunities. 'But you didn't want to get up at six am and drive nearly two hours. Do you remember? The morning at Arusha is also a game walk, and you two definitely didn't want to walk either.'

Christina and Erica conceded these points without a shred of grace or diplomacy. Tutting and sighing, and generally behaving like the spoiled brats they were. 'When are we stopping again?' They wanted to know. 'We're bored. And hungry.'

Thankfully, it was time to break for lunch by then, and moments later Wendell drove into a picnic area set among the fringes of the forest. The mountain dominated up ahead, while the views south, east and west were wide and stunning from their three-thousand-meter elevation. Everyone got out. Their guests all had packed lunches provided by their various hotels and, after pointing out the location of the toilets, Ben suggested that they take around forty-five minutes break. He also asked them not to leave any rubbish unless it was in the bins provided, to recycle what they could in other bins and not to leave any processed foods like bread and potato chips behind as animal food. If they wanted to leave things like fresh fruit and nuts that would be fine with both the birds as well as the monkeys that were a permanent fixture around the place.

Ben and Wendell then took Jos with them into the squat wooden building bordering the picnic area. Inside there was a well-stocked snack bar with a large dining area reserved for all those who worked in the park, rangers, scientists, ecologists, and guides like them who needed a break from the tourists for a while. 'Today you are our trainee,' Ben told her.

Jos was already on her way to the hot food counter.

As soon as the smells of food reached her nostrils, Peter jumped right into the driving seat. 'Jambo,' she said to the smiling lady in charge of all the fayre. 'Habari gani?'

'Nzuri,' the lady replied, smiling even wider.

Ben and Wendell watched in bemusement as Jos then discovered what was on offer that day and opted for kudu meat pie with sweet potato mash and sweet corn. She ordered mango juice and coffee for drinks and then later insisted on paying for all three of them.

'Thought she didn't speak any languages?' Wendell wondered. 'Her Swahili is better than mine.'

'And there's the hat,' Ben spoke softly to himself more than his friend. The hat was Peter's, and back when the man was alive and wearing it practically every hour of every day, there would be a joint concealed inside the inner secret pocket and maybe a cigarette tucked into the band. It had been found close to where Peter died and returned weeks later by one of the officers who'd attended the scene. Ben's mama had laid that hat on the big easy chair up in Peter and Jude's bedroom, which was one of his favourite places to sit, looking out at the mountain. There it had stayed until his parents found the courage to pack up all Peter and Jude's things for storing in the cellar.

On the verge of asking Jos how she'd come by that hat, Ben thought better of it, realising that he didn't really want to know. It was the same as Nightingale's cigarettes. The same as Rachael;

the Red Earth Tours very first employee who was pelted with flying books when she had no business being in the library. It was the same as not being able to sleep in the white house because, night after night, Peter's ghost had disturbed the peace there.

The afternoon game drive took them off across the landscape following well-worn tracks across some rough terrain. They saw hyena feasting on a recent kill, their muzzles bloody, and their voices yapping excitedly to one another. There were several fights, and some of the guests, perhaps unsurprisingly, had nothing positive to say regarding this behaviour. Ben naturally defended his beloved dogs, dispelling the myths and educating these visitors regarding the many saving graces of the humble hyena.

It was Sally who accused them of thieving kills from lions and, right on cue, five lionesses turned up.

They came from higher up the slope, bounding down from rock to rock until they were right on top of the dogs. Backed by their king and a pair of younger males, who watched from a rocky outcrop as the females effortlessly routed the hyena before making off with great chunks of what remained of the carcass. The hyenas howled barked and snarled in frustration, giving chase until three of the lionesses dropped their booty to join forces with the pair of juvenile males. These five big cats turned to face the pack of angry dogs, and a quick and bloody battle ensued. Voices roared, teeth bared, jaws clashed, claws slashed, and fur flew. Combatants collided, and then fell to the ground in a tangle of ferocity.

But it was the poor hyena who suffered the worst casualties, rapidly forced to back off in the face of mobhanded leonine strength and fury. One poor dog was caught in the jaws of two of the lionesses for what seemed like a very long time to the group of human observers. The noises she made were terrible to hear. But her fellow clan members did not desert her. They banded together to launch a counterattack, nipping relentlessly at the rumps of the lionesses with their stronger jaws, until the cats let go of their comrade. As she then ran off limping and bloodied, the clan closed around her retreat and faced off against the lions who were all about bravado by then. The king was already feasting on the plunder, and they were eager to join in the meal.

‘Wow.’ Jos had managed to video some of the event as well as get a lot of what she hoped would prove to be great stills. It had all happened so fast she’d not had time to worry about focussing, relying instead on the camera to sort out its own focus when she just kept pressing the buttons. She felt horrified and elated. She also felt privileged to have witnessed the cold hard facts of living wild.

‘Okay,’ Sally said. ‘Now I’m a believer.’

Ben smiled, knowing his day’s work was done.

*

On the way back to Moshi and just outside the park Jos spotted three Maasai warriors walking along by the road up ahead. As the Land Rover approached, Peter slipped back into the driving seat and asked Wendell to stop.

Wendell assumed Jos wanted to take photos. Pulling over at the side of the road, he was just about to tell her to ask permission first, when she leapt over the back of the Landy and down onto the road in one fluid movement. ‘What is going on with that young lady today, Ben?’

‘I’d rather not speculate, my friend.’ Though he would certainly be asking questions once he had Jos back at the white house.

All eyes were on Jos as she approached the warriors, shook hands all round, exchanged the usual battery of polite greetings and then chattered away with them for five full minutes in rusty Maa peppered with much fresher Swahili. ‘I’m looking for a laibon,’ she told the one called Macari.

‘Laputo Edward Ngoyo is his name. Is he still alive?’

‘Yes,’ said the one called Ezra. ‘He is my father’s little wife’s uncle.

Very old now, but still breathing.’

‘Why do you look for him, little sister?’ Macari wondered.

‘He and my uncle were great friends. I have important news to bring him, news of my uncle.’

‘And who is your uncle?’

‘He was Peter Sinclair.’

The three warriors looked to one another, nodding slowly. None had met the man, but they had heard his name and tales of his endeavours. After some quick, muted discussion between them, while the white woman waited patiently, the warriors gave her the name and location of the laibon's village where, in their opinion, he was now living at the mercy of his wives.

Getting back into the Land Rover in the conventional manner, Jos sat back down between Viv and George, knowing for sure that the encounter was exactly what Peter had been waiting for. He may have receded inside her once more as soon as they took their leave of the Maasai trio, but she was brimming with a residual satisfaction that forced a Cheshire cat smile upon her face.

Thankfully, Viv and George assumed that smile was for them, and they got back to telling Jos all about their planned trip to some hot springs the following day. Just the thing after spending all day bumping along in a Land Rover.

Wendell resumed the drive back to Moshi after offering the three Maasai a ride, but they were turning off soon to go to Marangu to visit a friend who was in hospital there. So, Wendell simply retraced his route of that morning, returning his passengers to their hotels and lodges.

Ben turned on the charm at every drop off point as usual, hoping for great reviews as well as greatly appreciated tips. They received over eighty US dollars in gratuities that day, split fifty-fifty back at the white house, where he and Wendell went into their office to check the itinerary for the following day, and read any messages Nightingale may have left. Ben didn't invite his friend to stay for dinner as he often did, because some air needed clearing.

'I'll see you tomorrow at seven,' he said, walking his business partner back to the front door.

'What?' Wendell grinned. 'Not stopping by Mountain View bar this evening?'

This was where Nightingale also worked part time and Ben had taken to swinging by towards the end of the night so he could spend some time with her. 'Not tonight.'

CHAPTER SIXTEEN

Jos found Beola and Kissi collecting vegetables and fruit in the garden. They all exchanged pleasantries, mostly concerning how Jos had enjoyed her trip and, while waiting for Ben to join them, she showed off some of her photos, a few of which were pretty spectacular.

In truth Jos felt sick to her stomach, and so very tired. She felt weighed down with her burden of knowledge, and knew she had to have a difficult conversation with the Nyerere's, because she needed to know what they knew, regarding Peter's death. She had to collect as much information as possible, before challenging Jude.

The night before, Peter must have anticipated Jos' reaction to the news that Jude was a cold-blooded killer. Telling her was not enough. She wouldn't have believed it! So, he'd resolved to show her. There had to be no doubt, because, when the opportunity for retribution arrived, he needed Jos on his side. All of this and more was communicated directly into her mind as she was being swept up into Peter's In-between and propelled upwards once again. But this time it was different.

This time there was no sense of riding the thermals around and around like a bird on high. There was no comfort, no sense of deep love. This time, as soon as Jos became aware, she was looking down upon the white house far below… the vision so clear she could see herself still seated on the bench, her head bent as if she'd fallen asleep… than she felt them travelling downwards again. Fast. The white house was rushing upwards to meet them and, just as Jos feared they would surely crash into it, they passed harmlessly down through and into it. As if it wasn't a solid thing.

For long, drawn out moments, Jos felt that she was everywhere in the white house all at once. Every wall, every room was apparent to her. The view from every window could be seen all at once. Every stick of furniture, every book, every single object inside that house was strewn out around them, expanding in a small universe of existence. Then her awareness became focussed on the entrance hall, which became like a hub around which the white house fell into ordered place. People moved through the hallway in fast-forward mode. She saw numerous versions of Jude, Beola, Kissi and Ben all younger than the people they were now. She saw Peter too. They all moved to and fro, upstairs and downstairs, in and out of the house.

She also saw numerous Maasai in all their finery.

At first Jos wasn't sure what she was looking at when the Maasai appeared, because they flowed so quickly by, they appeared as flowing ribbons in reds and oranges, pinks and purples. Then she noticed the odd spear, a shield, beads, painted faces and incredible ochre-coloured hairdos. They flowed in the front doors, around Jos and then out through the back doors. They repeated the process in reverse. Over and over, they passed through. One Maasai in particular came to stand out, he was tall and very thin with a bald head and bushy beard. His ear lobes were stretched, and his robes more blue, than pink. He looked very old. He was standing as still as Jos was, fixed in place upon his bare feet and looking right at her. Unlike everyone else passing through Peter's white house, moving in a constant flux between them, this man could see her. As Jos watched he smiled, nodding and then he raised a hand to beckon to her.

Soon.

She heard his voice inside her mind, speaking perfect English.

Bring Peter to see me very soon, little sister. My journey is coming to an end.

The microcosm of the white house contracted back in upon itself, suddenly, like elastic snapping back into shape.

Jos then felt only Peter, growing inside her mind. His memories flooding in at the speed of thought. Images, sound bites, smells and sensations all rushing in, in a sensory excess. Driving, walking, eating, drinking, sleeping under the stars, sitting staring into fires with the old, bearded black man Jos recognised as her beckoning man. His laibon. Peter had forged strong bonds with the Maasai. They called him brother. He cooked and ate with them. He wandered with them. He helped repair the bomas which kept their precious cattle safe from predators each night. He spent weeks residing in the manyatta; the warrior village where Peter learned Maasai songs and their infamous jumping dance. He had the respect and friendship of their elders too. Especially the laibon whom he continued to supply with the odd bottle of single malt whenever there was a fire that needed looking into.

The laibon had often looked into a fire on Peter's behalf, foretelling the destiny of his many plans. Whole projects were either progressed or abandoned under the laibon's guidance. On a more personal level, the old man predicted the death of Peter's father, four months before the event, as well as the subsequent retreat of his mother to a house by a lake in a land of ice and snow.

Peter trusted the old man implicitly and had never felt more at home than when he was immersed inside the wilderness of Africa; the people, the land, the culture. Combined it all became more important than his own life. And that is why, when the laibon saw death approaching in the hands of his wife, Peter decided to face it. He looked for ways to overcome the financial finality of death so his work could continue on into the future, despite the fact he did not have an obvious heir. Little Jos Ferguson was the sole familial option, but she was only nine years old at that time, and anything could happen to her before she was old enough to assume any kind of role in Peter's long-term plans. As for his wife, if Jude did end him as the laibon predicted, she would surely be found out and punished.

But the laibon told Peter she must be allowed to go free.

Jude's destiny was entwined around that of the child chosen as his heir. Without Jude, Jos would be in danger of disappearing from Peter's sphere of influence and may become lost to him forever. That was when Peter began to think in terms of waiting, and of a dish best served cold. For the first time in his existence, he began to value the depravity of wealth and how he might use it to advance his own negative ends.

So, while the laibon prepared the spiritual rituals of binding Peter to his white house so he might be anchored to it beyond the limits of his physical existence, Peter prepared the legal rituals governing succession and death.

A complex will was drafted, leaving the bulk of the working estate to his oldest and most trusted friend. Gary Preston would be employed by the business as well as run it, and he would use his IT skills to continue to develop resources to help maintain the legacy projects Peter left behind. His mother would retain the generous income she'd inherited from Johnny. Jude would be afforded the same income, on proviso that she relinquish, any and all claims on the white house as well as every other property belonging to the estate at the time of her husband's death. Should the laibon be successful, Peter did not want to share his sanctuary with the woman who murdered him, and so he bequeathed the white house to Beola and Kissi Nyerere for their lifetimes. The house would then revert back to the estate, just like everything else, in the hope Jos was already there, able to pick it all up where he had left it.

A second will was then drafted by the same lawyer, offering the same terms to Jos Ferguson. This will was witnessed by Gary and Henk de Vries. Gary also made a sworn statement to the effect that he understood the implications and that he promised to hand everything over to Jos on production of that second will. Peter then concealed that document inside the white house, knowing that no one would ever find it unless he was in a position to disclose its whereabouts. If the laibon failed, the second will would remain lost, Jos would never inherit, and Gary would be free to pass on the estate as he saw fit.

That took care of succession.

Manipulating events after a death that was yet to happen, was a lot more complicated than managing a multi-million-pound estate. Fortunately, Peter was destined to die in Tanzania where his money would facilitate just about any desire he aspired to. Fortunate too that he had good friends. Most of the burden was offered to Henk who, because the laibon was their mutual friend, agreed to help without asking too many questions. Peter made a sizable donation to The Rhonda Rehabilitation Centre in the months preceding his murder, on the understanding that Henk would be using a percentage of this money to complete his allotted tasks, including bribery. His Maasai brothers would handle everything else until Gary Preston reached Tanzania to finalise the terms as they affected Jude.

Jos received all of this information, all at once because Peter had lived it, remembered it. She wouldn't be able to recall it all at once though. Her analogy of uploading information into a computer was a sound one. It would take time for her to read it, and she had no time right then, because they were on the move again, flying high, travelling across the tree tops and out over the open ground towards another, lower hill which could be seen from the roof garden.

Then, quite suddenly, Jos found herself sitting next to Peter as he drove what she assumed was the same little blue jeep they'd taken to Moshi earlier that same day. He was on the far side of that hill, on his way home from Arusha Chini. The town lay to the south of the white house, and he'd been meeting with a small group of women interested in starting up a business co-op of their own. Peter would provide start-up funds as well as small, interest free loans which the women would pay back beginning from their third year in business. After five years, the women would start a savings plan, and in the tenth year they would begin loaning to other women to set up businesses of their own. It was a sound idea, enthusiastically met, and he was a very happy man on his way home.

As they rounded the hill, Jos saw Jude standing on the track about fifty yards ahead. She said as much, but her words went unheeded. She understood suddenly that she was there to observe only, and that could mean only one thing.

In the driving seat, Peter Sinclair had reached a similar conclusion, and braked hard at the same time as his wife was raising her arm to display the gun she held, in one outstretched and steady hand. The sound of the first shot was heard clearly above the noise of the jeep's tyres skidding across the loose earth at the side of the track as Peter fought to turn it around using the handbrake, while ducking as low as he could. The bullet missed, but not by much. He was vaguely aware of it whizzing past his hat. A second and third shot followed almost immediately, both going wide. Abandoning the planned one-hundred-and-eighty-degree turn, Peter settled for ninety and simply drove off the track and down the hillside, fighting to keep some control of the jeep as it lurched from side to side over the steep and rough terrain. He didn't dare look back, because he was driving towards a line of trees, and he didn't want to slow down either, because his wife was still shooting. He heard the next shot… sixth, seventh, maybe even an eighth, a fraction of a second before a bullet punched through his right shoulder and erupted from his chest in a concentrated gush of blood, bone and incredible pain.

That was when Peter lost control of the jeep and hit a tree head on. The collision was powerful enough to whip him forward and slam his forehead down onto the dashboard. His beloved Tilly hat was knocked to the ground where it rolled away to one side. He was knocked unconscious, but only for a short time, because the pain in his shoulder was too excruciating to avoid for long.

But the time was enough for Jude to reach Peter on foot, and she was at his side, pressing the trigger again and again, her face a mask of fury because she was out of ammo. Pocketing the useless Glock, she tore a bandana off from around her neck, unscrewed the petrol cap and poked the scarf down into the tank. Pulling the sodden end out again, she switched it around and pushed the dry end in. Then she took a lighter from her shirt pocket.

Peter was much more aware by then; he could see what was happening and he was trying to get out of the jeep. But the door was jammed, just like the door in his old sports car that he had taken Jude out on their very first date. He would have to climb out. But he was dazed and in a lot of pain and his time was running out. He couldn't get the seatbelt undone, and she was getting ready to torch the jeep with him in it. 'No…' he told her. 'Please, Jude… not like this.'

'Damn you, Peter,' Jude told him as she touched the little flame to the bandana and held it there. When she was sure it had caught, she turned and made a dash for a boulder that had probably perched a short distance away for thousands of years just waiting for her to need its shelter.

As for Peter, he was fuelled with pain numbing adrenalin and fighting for his life. But he couldn't escape the clutches of the seatbelt in time to avoid the explosion, or the flames that engulfed him moments later. The pain was exquisite and utterly complete. His screams drew fire down his throat and into his lungs, silencing his voice but not his suffering.

It felt like aeons before death finally freed him.

*

Peter's end of life also brought an end to the entire experience for Jos.

He retreated to the sanctuary of his In-between, and she was left behind on that roof garden bench, holding onto herself and trying not to sob too loudly in case she attracted the attention of the Nyerere's. Jos had no idea how long she stayed there, feeling the same anguish as experienced in the wake of her parent's own violent ends, because she'd been forced to watch yet another horror.

Her place next to Peter on the short drive had shifted just before the jeep hit the tree, and she found herself standing next to the same boulder Jude would hide behind. She had shouted warnings. She'd pleaded, begged, but it was all pointless; like shouting at actors in a movie who are destined to follow the script no matter what the audience did or said. She screamed as Peter screamed, because she couldn't bear it. She screamed at Jude, as

Jude watched him burn, with an expression of cold detachment on her face.

Back on her bench, as the sobbing subsided, Jos exchanged horror for hatred. Hatred for Jude who had burned her husband alive, walked away and never looked back. But Jos also hated Peter right then, for not sparing her the terror or the details.

Yesterday it all seemed like a game, a fantastic adventure with an extraordinary companion. But by then Jos was beginning to realise that whatever Peter was playing at, she was now along for the ride whether she liked it or not. She felt sad and let down. She felt used and she felt stupid.

Making her way inside the garden room, Jos crawled onto the bed and cried mostly for herself. And, when she had no more tears, she lay in the dark thinking things through and trying not to focus too sharply on the horrific images that were still crowding the fringes of her imagination, eager to assault her senses again, if she let her guard down for even a moment.

At some point the familiar sensations of Peter's presence inside her mind made itself felt. Their connection was stronger than ever now; a twoway bond. Jos felt his sorrow and his regret as clearly as she felt her own anger and disappointment. He didn't try to erase any of those negative feelings, and she was grateful for that. They were united in misery, and that actually made her feel a little better. After all, she wasn't the one who'd been shot and burned to death. She was just the one finding out about it.

Obviously, there was more to Peter's intentions than disclosure; right before the devastating revelations he'd stated categorically that he was no longer going to let Jude away with it, and Jos realised that this must be the price, the counter balance to all the fun and games. Was she to be Peter's means of exacting his vengeance? 'Is that what you want?' she whispered to the darkness.

But Peter didn't answer, Jos soon slipped into a natural sleep with ordinary dreams and, when she'd wakened that morning, she resolved to find out every side of the story.

Now it was the Nyerere's turn to tell. Ben had come out onto the patio, and immediately began telling his parents about the hat, the Swahili, the encounter with the Maasai. Jos just let him get it out his system and, when he invited her to comment, she said, 'Why don't we all sit down?' Mistaking her invitation as a prelude to revelations, Ben sat.

Beola and Kissi exchanged another one of their looks, and then joined their son at the patio table.

'Ben obviously has some questions, but there's one question that I'd

like answered before I say anything else.' Once all eyes were on her, Jos asked, 'Did any of you know that Jude murdered Peter?'

'What?' Ben laughed, incredulous, looking from his mama to his papa and back again. But his parents were looking only at one another. 'Mama… Papa?' he asked. 'What is going on?'

Resting a hand on her son's arm, Beola hushed him. Then she asked Jos, 'Do you know for sure that Jude killed him?'

'He showed me,' she told them all. 'A no holds barred, completely uncensored front row seat, as my Auntie Jude shot and wounded her husband. Then she watched him burn. He was still alive when she started that fire. I can still hear his screams inside my head. Jude can be a right moody cow, but I'd never have believed she was capable of such ruthless cruelty if I hadn't seen it with my own eyes.'

Kissi put his head into his hands, shaking it slowly.

'But you must have been dreaming.' Ben shook his head because he didn't believe a word of it. 'Jude would not have done such a thing.'

'I am the one who taught her how to handle a gun,' Kissi admitted, still shaking his head because he was desperate for it not to be true. Reaching out for his wife's hand, he went on, 'We suspected it might have been, you know… we have had a long time to wonder and, yes, we have wondered many times if it was Jude.'

Ben felt as horrified as he looked, staring at his parents as if they'd gone mad.

'We didn't even consider that to be a possibility at all until weeks after,' Beola said quickly. 'We weren't even here… I mean, I was here that day. But the Maasai came. They told me we had to leave…'

'I don't blame you, Beola,' Jos told her. 'I don't blame any of you and I know Peter doesn't.'

'How?' Ben asked. 'How do you know that?'

'Because you were right, Ben. I am finding my niche… right here in this house. And Peter has found a little latitude through me too. We have met, and we have had a very frank exchange of information. So much information lately I'm still trying to unravel it all, but I know enough to understand why Jude will come back now.' 'Why will she come?' Kissi asked.

At that point Jos allowed Peter to guide her.

Getting up, they went into the kitchen and out the other side. The Nyerere's followed. Reaching up to the top of the second door frame they came to, Jos retrieved the key to the walk-in cupboard that was always kept locked. Inside she reached behind a shelf and retrieved the key to the cabinet which was fixed to the wall opposite. Opening the door, she stood aside so the Nyerere's could see the single rifle inside, and the empty space next to it. 'Where's the Glock?'

'We don't know.' Beola shook her head. 'We didn't even realise it was missing for many months after.'

'But you were here when Jude came back,' Jos remembered.

'I was cleaning in the sitting room. I saw her return through the window. She'd been marketing and had a few bags, but not so many that I went out to help her,' Beola shrugged. 'She looked perfectly normal. I didn't see her again for a time… an hour, maybe. I heard noise coming from the kitchen. Crashing, banging about. When I got there, she was emptying cupboards so she could clean. I offered to help but she asked me to change the beds instead. I was still upstairs when the police came.' After a moment, she added, 'We have looked after and cleaned this house for years, Jos. If anything was hidden, we would have found it by now.'

'Maybe she got rid of it before she came back?' Kissi suggested.

'Maybe I should just ask Jude?' Jos wondered, locking the gun cabinet again, replacing the key and following the Nyerere's back into the kitchen where she sat down at the table with them. All united in silence, as they considered the implications of knowing the truth.

Ben was most upset of all; he'd spent a lot of time with Jude while he was growing up. It had hurt him that she hadn't said goodbye when she left. He'd missed her, and now he was finding out she was a killer! 'Why didn't you tell me?' he asked his parents.

'We didn't know for sure,' Kissi told him.

'What good would it have done you to know we thought a thing, but had no proof, no…' Beola couldn't find the right words.

And yet, even when those words were pointless and circling round and round without clarity or direction, they just kept coming as the Nyerere family exorcised that demon amongst themselves.

After a while, Jos had had enough. She told them, 'I am so tired.' 'Then you should sleep,' Beola spoke more sharply than intended.

Jos didn't care. She returned to the garden room to do exactly that. There would be another outing that night and she needed to rest ahead of it.

They were going in search of his laibon. Her beckoning man.

His journey was ending, and it was time to bring Peter to see him.

CHAPTER SEVENTEEN

It was nearly ten p.m. when Jos wakened.

She showered and then dressed in jeans, a T-shirt and tied a sweat shirt around her waist. She then dug a pair of socks out the bedside drawer and laced her feet into a pair of comfortable walking boots. She didn't even consider what she was doing, until catching sight of herself in a mirror. 'Are we going on a hike?' she wondered.

Just a long drive.

Downstairs the white house was quiet, the remains of half-eaten meals abandoned on their plates by the sink. Jos didn't really want food, but Peter insisted they had a long night ahead. She had to eat something. As some bread was toasting, she scraped the plates and stacked the dishwasher and generally tidied up. She felt guilty.

Why?

'Why me?' she wondered. 'If I walked away, if I just got the next flight home, would you hate me?'

Go to the library.

Leaving the kitchen and heading west, Jos found the library by finding the same photos she and Beola had been looking at before going in there the day she arrived. 'My god…' Jos whispered to herself. 'I haven't even been here three full days and, already, I've turned this family upside down, mind-melded with a ghost and discovered my aunt is a psycho-killer.' Inside by then, she closed the door before feeling for the light switch. 'What now?' *Go to the bookcase between the French doors.*

Once standing before that bookcase Peter directed Jos' hands.

Reaching up to slide the fingers of her right hand behind the ornamental moulding in its top right corner, finding a small nub there, and pressing it firmly until a shallow drawer popped out from the centre of the crown moulding above her head.

Inside, Jos found the first of the three white house secrets.

A fat white envelope, addressed to her in neat handwriting. Unable to take her eyes off it, Jos felt around behind her until she found Peter's other favourite chair and sat down in it. Turning the envelope over she looked at the seal for several breaths before daring to open it. She then removed a hefty document as well as a second, slightly smaller envelope which was addressed to a firm of solicitors in Bath. Glancing at the script on the front page of the document, she said, 'Your will.'

If you want to leave, you have my blessing. You'll find contact details for Gary Preston on the back page. Call him. He'll advise you what to do next.

Well, it was certainly an option.

But, after a few moments' consideration, Jos decided against taking the coward's way out. Replacing everything inside the envelope, she returned it to the hidden drawer, pushing it closed with her finger tips. And it was once again as if that drawer didn't exist. She then retraced her steps to the kitchen where cold toast awaited. Spreading a little honey on it she began to eat. It felt like cushion foam in her mouth; dry and chewy and impossible to swallow. She poured some juice from the fridge and forced the wad of sweet wet bread down her throat that way.

Soon after they were back by the little blue jeep that Jos now knew belonged to Jude.

She and her husband had had one each, but Peter's was destroyed by fire all those years ago. Before allowing Peter to take over so they could drive it, Jos looked inside every nook and cranny of that Jeep until, inside the seat pocket behind the passenger seat, she found a single hairclip. She didn't know for sure that it had once held Jude's ginger cloud in place, but she doubted Beola had ever had a use for it. Casting it aside with an expression of distaste, Jos readied herself for whatever was coming next.

Ready, now all possible trace of Jude had been eliminated.

*

They headed north to the A23. They then turned west there, heading in the direction of the airport for a time. Just before Boma Ng'ombe they took a right, driving due north around the western fringes of Mount Kilimanjaro National Park. The drive was long, and Jos slumbered as Peter drove.

He was following an old and familiar route through the night. Passing through the settlement of Engare Nairobi, and on through Matadi. Farther north, the road skirted along the border between Arusha Region and Kilimanjaro Region. He turned off the main road there, heading east on a dirt track, going directly towards the mountain which loomed large and darker than the night.

He reached the manyatta close to one a.m.

A small collection of mud, clay and animal dung huts, topped with ragged thatch. This was the village where the youngest warriors lived without need of a boma… or their mothers, to protect them. Two of them were waiting and, when he slowed down the jeep, they jumped into it. One sat in the passenger seat, while the other squatted down in the little cargo space at the back.

'We must hurry.' The one in the front told the white woman. 'He is waiting.'

As they approached the family village, surrounded by its thick enclosure of thorns, the one in the back stood up and whistled. Almost immediately two sections of the boma were pulled aside, the jeep drove on through, and the gap was sealed behind them again. The two warriors then jumped down from the jeep and went to join the pair who had opened the way for them. They stood in silence, watching as the jeep moved off slowly between the collection of circular huts containing their mothers and their sisters, their elders.

All hidden, all waiting, all knowing change would come before the dawn.

Peter drove slowly, heading into the middle of the village. When he got there, he saw an elder come out of the shadows. He stopped and turned off the engine. It was as he was getting out of the jeep that he realised, 'Joseph?' The last time he'd seen this friend, Joseph was a proud warrior with a mane of ochre plaits, decorated with numerous beads and baubles. This man wore a simple shuka with few adornments. His head was completely shaved, and he had the beginnings of an impressive beard.

That told Peter three things. 'You are an elder now.' Joseph nodded. 'And about to change. Are you becoming laibon?'

'Soon…' Reaching out, Joseph took Peter by the hands. '… and you come at last, brother.'

Peter drew his friend into an embrace. 'I came as soon as I could.'

If Joseph thought it was odd to welcome a strange white woman as warmly as he would an old and trusted male friend, he showed no sign of it. 'Come,' he said at last. 'The laibon is waiting. The sacrifice will be soon, and we must begin the summoning.'

Ducking in through the low doorway, Peter followed Joseph around the short, curved passageway into the main room beyond. It was brighter in here thanks to the low fire burning in the central pit. The air was thick and heavy with the smoke that helped keep insects and parasites away. It was sparsely furnished, with only a few modest belongings on display.

Laputo Edward Ngoyo was seated on a low slung, woven stool, close to the fire. His beard was bushier than ever, but his head was as bald as the head of his apprentice. He was so thin and frail, the sight of him was a shock to Peter. He went to his old friend, kneeling down by his side and embracing him carefully. Afraid the old man might crumble to dust in his arms.

'Welcome, Peter.' The laibon let go of the white man, and instead held the woman's pale face in his hands, smiling into her green eyes. 'And you too, Joslin. We meet again.'

'Again?' Peter wondered.

'Shhh,' the laibon hushed his friend. 'Little sister is sleeping. You are a demanding spirit, Peter. I should know…' The old man laughed, but his mirth soon turned into a wracking cough.

Joseph quickly fetched chai tea from where he'd set it aside just before Peter arrived and helped the old man to drink.

When the laibon trusted himself to speak once more he bade his companions to join him by the fire. 'Peter on my left. Joseph on my right.'

'I'm not sure I can put Jos through this,' Peter told them. 'She doesn't…'

'Our little sister knows all she needs to know for the time being,' the laibon assured. 'It has to be now, Peter. I have only a few steps left.'

'Thank you,' Peter told him sincerely. 'Thank you for everything you did and thank you for all you are about to do.'

‘You have assured my place in history, my friend.’ The laibon grinned, delighted. ‘Joseph has a long, long road ahead if he wants to catch me up.

Now be still.’

Barely breathing.

The laibon’s companions were just as still, just as silent, united in their contemplation of the flames. United in their recollection of the past. Far off nights and far away flames. A pact made then, that was about to be realised. This night. This fire. The only sounds came from the crackling of its voice, and their breathing, which deepened and slowed until they were completely in sync. They remained like this for long minutes until, finally, a knife appeared in the laibon’s left hand. The blade glittered in the orange light as he held it up. Raising his right hand to meet it, he used the knife to cut deep into the palm. Blood welled and flowed. Reaching out, he held his cut hand above the fire and allowed drips of his blood to fall to sizzle and spit among the flames. ‘Sit behind her, Joseph,’ the old man commanded. ‘Keep her still.’

Taking a firm hold of the little sister’s right hand, the laibon made his cut.

The pain catapulted Jos into full consciousness. She lunged forward, her eyes and her mouth opened wide and her voice roaring,

‘Aaaaaaagghhhhh…’

It took all of Joseph’s strength to hold her back.

The laibon cast his knife away and gripped her wounded hand with his own, their blood mingling, palm to palm. He then used nearly all of his remaining strength to force their clutched hands out and over the fire.

Jos heaved in enough of the smoky air to fill her lungs and roared again. Much louder this time. A sound of fear and desperation and pain. She had no idea where she was, who she was with or why they were hurting her. She roared right into the old man’s face, trying desperately to get her hand away from the fire.

The laibon used the heel of his uncut hand to smack her hard in the middle of the forehead.

A shockwave passed through Jos rendering her entire body limp and her voice silent. She folded at the waist, and Joseph was then struggling to hold her upright so the laibon could keep their bonded blood above the flames.

The laibon began to sing. His song invoked the spirits of his ancestors. He called to them, pleaded for their guidance. Singing incantations and murmuring spells, the cadence of his voice rose and fell like the fire. But, as his voice grew stronger, the fire began to climb higher, licking at their hands. When his voice reached a crescendo, the laibon forced their joined hands down into the belly of the fire and held them there for a few seconds. When he retracted their hands, he relinquished his grip on the little sister's hand, and Joseph laid her down.

Minutes later, the still unconscious Jos was curled up in foetal position close to the fire, her injured hand wrapped up in a clean piece of cloth. Joseph would tend to it as soon as he could, but before that he had to help with the summoning. He was on the cusp of becoming a laibon and had spent many years studying for the transformation, but he'd spent the previous three months rehearsing for this ceremony and he knew the song off by heart.

The summoning was a relatively unremarkable ritual.

The laibon began to sing again. A different song to invoke different magic. His voice was weak because his life was fading. Joseph also sang, his voice stronger, louder. The flames rose and fell once again, dancing in time to the cadence of this new spell, writhing and swaying, climbing higher and higher with the progression of the melody. Together the two men rose up onto their bare feet, the younger helping and supporting his elder. Their two voices continuing to sing, enticing the fire to grow, inviting the flames to dance higher. Their three elements united in invoking an ancient rite which would take hold of a free spirit, carry it across a distance to an intended destination, and then bind it with another.

Many years previously the laibon had performed a similar spell to gather his friend's spirit from the border of death, so he could then bring it to, and bind it with the white house. Of course, the white house had no spirit of its own with which Peter's could be bonded. But Peter had already put enough of himself into the house he'd made so, when what remained of him was brought back, the laibon was able to fix it all in place long enough to complete the ritual. The rest… the years of remaining fixed in that place, were testament to Peter's strength. Since that night, they had been waiting for Peter's niece to set them both free.

It was now the laibon's destiny to go forth so he may then return and repay the debt. As he and his successor sang the final incantation, he gave silent thanks to the earth the sky and all that dwells below, for his life, his loves, his children and his power. Then he crumpled down to the floor. His human journey was over.

*

On the other side of the mountain a single lioness woke suddenly. Her belly was full of a meal taken just a few hours previously but, instead of rolling over and going back to sleep, she stood up and sniffed the night air. Turning her head, she looked to her sleeping sisters for perhaps the final time. Then, turning south, she padded silently away without looking back.

Her journey was just beginning.

CHAPTER EIGHTEEN

Before dawn, a bull was slaughtered during a ceremony attended by Maasai elders.

A great number of elders attended, all gathered in a clearing close to the family village. They had come from all the many villages situated on the west side of the mountain. They came to pay their respects to the laibon who had healed their children, quashed their fears, charmed their women, judged their follies and looked into their futures. The bull was butchered expertly and swiftly, the meat then cooked over an open fire. When the feast was ready, they sat down together and ate in his honour, swapping tales of their dealings and celebrating the journey just ended.

Once the feasting was over, a small group of elders from Laputo Edward Ngoyo's own village, led by Joseph, separated from the group. They collected the laibon's body and also various vessels containing the blood and fat of the slaughtered bull. Carrying everything in their hands and arms, they walked for a time into the forests at the feet of their great mountain. In another clearing, they laid the remains down and smeared it all over with the blood and fat before returning to the gathering.

Predator Burials were rare by then, but it was the laibon's wish and no one would disobey for fear of evoking engooki; a curse on the entire tribe. Joseph would simply revisit the site in two days to ensure the remains had been taken by the animals. If the remains were left untouched the old man would then have to be buried, and bad fortune would surely follow.

*

Back in the laibon's hut, Joseph checked Jos' hand before waking her.

The cut was already healing, and there was no trace of damage from the fire. This was good because it proved that the flame was pure and the magic good. 'Shhh,' he hushed as she stirred. 'You are safe. You are well.'

‘Where…’ Jos looked at the strange man in obvious apprehension, snatching her hand away. ‘Where am I and what did you do to me?’ She saw the cut on her hand, but there was no sign of burns. ‘But…’ Looking at Joseph, she shook her head. ‘It can’t be. I saw it. He put my hand into the fire. I felt it burning.’

‘You felt it in your mind because your eyes wanted it like that. But our fire was pure. Good magic. Even your cut will fade quickly. No scar.’

‘Really?’ she wondered distractedly. Jos felt confused by then, and profoundly sad. Her mind reached out for Peter, but he didn’t respond.

‘You have my word on it as laibon.’

‘Where is the old laibon?’

‘That journey is ended.’

‘He’s dead…’ Jos realised. ‘Peter is grieving.’

‘He and the old laibon were great friends.’

‘What do I do now?’ she wondered, frowning. ‘I should really go back to the white house.’

‘Your jeep is still outside, little sister. You can leave when you wish.’

‘I can’t drive.’ And with that Jos began to cry quiet tears, feeling suddenly alone and overwhelmed. Sitting in that dark little place, stinking of smoke, she had no idea where she was, or even what lay beyond the little room she felt trapped inside.

Joseph comforted her as best he could, before fetching her inheritance from the old man. Handing it over, he said, ‘Laputo Edward Ngoyo wanted you to have this.’

Jos took the folded cloth from him, recognising it as the pink and blue checked shuka the old man was wearing when they met in Peter’s Inbetween form of the white house. ‘For me?’ Joseph nodded, smiling.

Wrapping it around herself, Jos began to cry again. Tears of loss this time. But this was the last time she would shed tears within this shuka. Jos would treasure it for the rest of her life and, whenever she was unsure, or sad, or confused, or angry, she would wrap it around herself, and it would always make her feel better.

‘Are you hungry?’ Joseph asked. ‘Thirsty?’ ‘A little.’ Jos nodded.

'Please wait here.'

'I also…' Jos grimaced a little, then told him, 'I really need to pee.'

Laughing softly, Joseph said, 'I will send one of the women. She will show you.'

Perhaps that woman was already waiting outside the hut because Joseph returned with her almost immediately. 'This is my wife, Naserian, she will look after you.'

Naserian was tall, slim and beautiful. Her hair was cropped, and she wore a beaded circlet around her forehead. Her ears were elaborately beaded, and she wore layers of beads, some coiled tightly around her slender neck and others hanging lower. She wore an orange shuka as a dress and a sky blue one as a type of shawl. She had bracelets around her biceps as well as her wrists, and leather sandals on her feet. Smiling broadly, she stretched her hand out, beckoning to Jos to follow her.

Outside the day was hot and very bright, and the village was bustling with activity. Children ran around, shrieking and laughing as they streaked on by chasing one another. Elders stood or sat around in small groups, smoking their pipes, talking their talk, and generally relaxing. There was a small group of young teenage boys watching curiously from nearby. Too old for games and too young for manhood. Mostly there were the women.

Dressed in their colourful shukas, which were arranged into an incredible variety of garments, the Maasai women were gathered into several groups. Some were cooking, while others washed pots as well as children. Some were weaving, as others were busy making the colourful, intricately beaded jewellery they all wore but also sold to earn their own money. Everywhere Jos looked she was rewarded with smiles and waves, and she began to feel a lot more relaxed being there.

No sign of the toilets though.

When they reached a gap in the thorny enclosure surrounding the entire village, Naserian collected two backpack water carriers from a collection of similar carriers all hanging upside down from the branches of a low tree. They were empty and light then but destined to hold five gallons of water each. She gave one to Jos, because they would be making a small detour on the way back from their toileting.

A few hundred yards out into the bush, the two women walked into a small thicket of trees and shrubs. Setting her backpack down, Naserian indicated that Jos should do the same. She then pointed Jos in one direction and indicated that she would be going the opposite way. Jos got the idea easily enough and took herself off for a short distance to relieve herself among the bushes… after having a quick scout around for snakes and rodents and anything else that might bite her on the bum. She then made her way back to the backpacks and followed Naserian on through the thicket and out the other side.

A little way into the next clearing stood the well.

A dozen women were already there, pumping clean water into the same backpacks, with the help of some younger girls who were helping their mothers and their aunts and their older sisters. Collecting water was a lot easier from this communal well. Previously they had to walk miles to the nearest river… farther in times of drought. They had shared the river with the wildlife so it was always a risky endeavour, avoiding both larger animals that might hurt them as well as diseases brought about by parasites living in the water. They had to collect that water in jerry cans and buckets which then had to be carried back to their villages on their heads. The well water was clean and plentiful, part of a small network of similar wells serving all the villages in the region. No one had to walk more than half a mile now, and the backpacks made it much easier to carry water home. A few simple changes that had massively improved the lives of both the women and girls who carried out this task every single day.

This was one of the projects Jos would soon be getting involved in, started when Peter was alive, and still being improved upon as and when new ideas were being put into practice. The backpack water carriers were a relatively new invention based on five-gallon backpack pump bags used in the USA by men and women fighting forest fires. The idea was brought to Gary Preston's attention two years previously. He'd then commissioned a small business in Arusha that already manufactured heavy duty nylon tote bags, to make the backpacks and fit them with food grade polythene liners which could be easily replaced as required.

They were an instant hit with all the tribe's women who now had access to them.

Jos was welcomed into the group with more smiles and even a few kisses, and she marvelled at their joy as the women sang together and clapped their hands, even doing little dances in small groups to entertain one another as they all patiently awaited their turn on the pump. The women helped one another constantly, pumping, filling and then securing the backpack lining bags, before holding them up between two so the carrier could then get her arms into the straps and position the load comfortably onto her back before setting off back to her village. Soon enough it was Jos' turn, and she discovered that five gallons of water weighed around forty pounds. 'Jeezo,' she gasped. The women laughed, delighted, sending the white woman on her way with Naserian, with yet another song.

Jos had no idea how she managed to get back to the village without falling flat on her face. The water got heavier with every single step, and she was practically bent double and sweating profusely with the effort. Her back was soaked beneath the outer nylon of the backpack. She was stumbling more than walking and falling more and more behind.

Naserian, on the other hand, walked tall and as elegantly as a supermodel carrying nothing more challenging than a handbag containing a lipstick.

Jos received a small round of applause from the two women waiting to relieve her of the burden, when she finally made it back into the village. While she took a few moments to reach for the sky and stretch her back, the women stood on a wooden bench and emptied the backpacks into a large, elevated water butt cube which had a tap close to its bottom and a secure lid. Jos was then led to a fire where she sat down on a woven stool. Naserian gave her a little tin mug of chai tea sweetened with honey and a bowl of ugali ladled straight from a large pot; a maize-based porridge which Jos didn't particularly enjoy but ate because she was absolutely starving by then.

The rest of Jos' morning was spent in the company of the village women and children. Her hair and clothing were examined closely, and her attempts at beading were cheerfully critiqued by all.

It was while she was attempting yet another bracelet, that Jos suddenly realised she could understand some of what the women around her were saying. Someone was pregnant, someone else was getting married and a little brother was in trouble with the elders, because he hadn't asked their permission for something or other. 'Peter,' she said softly. 'About bloody time,' She smiled, and nodded to the old woman sitting opposite who perhaps thought Jos was speaking to her. The two of them grinning and nodding like a pair of loons. 'Yes,' Jos told her. 'I'll have to poo soon and, if I'm still here, I'll also probably have to carry another forty pounds of water on my back to compound my mortification. That won't be happening, sister, oh no, no, no. Not if I can help it.'

Getting to her feet, Jos made driving motions with her hands.

Someone called out, and Naserian came out of a nearby hut, cradling a baby in her arms. The two women embraced carefully, the tiny baby between them. They then walked back to where the jeep waited, the leather seats burning hot in the sun. Joseph emerged from the little hut Jos had spent the night in, carrying her pink and blue check shuka, which she took gratefully. It then took a few minutes to say goodbyes and thank you's to everyone who came to see her off, but Jos was soon sitting in the jeep, turning the keys to start the engine and waving wildly as the jeep moved off… and immediately stalled.

Why not let me drive?

Jos laughed as heartily as her Maasai farewell party, thinking she really must learn to drive while telling Peter, 'Get on with it then, and can we find a proper toilet please? As soon as possible, because I need to… you know.'

CHAPTER NINETEEN

As Jos was beading bracelets, Jude was coming to terms with the fact she would be returning to Africa after all. She wasn't sure what was going on at the white house beyond knowing that her dead husband was able to use Jos to contact her and, if he could do that, then it was only a matter of time before Peter told Jos the truth about his death.

Perhaps he already had?

The only thing Jude had going for her, was knowing where the gun was hidden.

She'd concealed it that day, as soon as she returned home, knowing the police would come looking for her as soon as Peter was found. She also knew that wouldn't be long because the smoke would attract attention from a long way off. So, she hurried. She hid the gun in the first place she thought of which, as it turned out, wasn't such a bad place, because it hadn't been found since. Just as well, because in her rush to conceal it, Jude didn't wipe it clean. It was her intention to do that later but, when she was finally able to return home later that night, the Maasai closed ranks around the white house and wouldn't let her near it!

Jude hated the Maasai by then because they stole her husband.

Peter spent so much time in the company of the warriors he became like them. All he wanted to do was wander around the African bush tending cattle, singing songs and jumping up and down as part of his adopted lifestyle. It was a boys' own adventure living with Maasai warriors who had a very easy life compared to their women. Maasai women did all the hard work; they built the huts, fetched and carried water, cooked, cleaned and looked after the children. They also submitted to having their clitorises removed! Without anaesthetic. It was barbaric. There was even some talk of Peter taking a second, little wife, from among the Maasai women. All a big joke to Peter, but Jude was outraged. The thought of him being with another woman sickened her. And the thought of all the money he gave away frightened her.

Jude may have grown up in a poor family, but she'd fallen in love with

and married a very rich man. Peter had given her years of extravagance and indulgence by the time they reached Tanzania, all of which Jude was happy to give up temporarily when they got all caught up with Lulu and Henk and the Maasai people, who soon became like an extended family. Then Peter built their beautiful white house, made from his love for Jude. That's what he said! He would call Jude his goddess, his queen, his Fluff, the only woman he would ever love. Peter even said he would die for her, and it really did come down to that.

In the end.

Peter had never cared much for material things but, by the time he died, he was spending huge amounts of money on his endless projects to improve the lives of tribesmen and women. Meanwhile his wife… his one and only wife, waited alone at home with nothing but bees and flowers to occupy her time. Jude knew that vaccine programs, education and clean water was much more important than one woman's happiness, but she didn't understand why they couldn't do both. They had left Tanzania one single time since arriving, and that was to attend Johnny's funeral. They were gone less than a week, and the only shopping she got to do was at the airport.

There wasn't any internet shopping back then, so Jude had to buy everything either locally, or drive to Arusha which was a six-hour round trip. A trip she had to make countless times just to buy decent toiletries! Moshi was a lovely little town, but it was mediaeval when it came to sourcing modern sanitary protection. And if it was lingerie you were after? Forget it! Jude tried to arrange a number of trips to Europe, planning to take along extra luggage so she could stock up on feminine toiletries, pretty underwear and decent hair products, but Peter always bailed on her at the last minute. She pleaded with him, promising that, once she was able to stock up on a few luxury items she wouldn't hassle him so much. She just wanted a break.

Peter didn't understand why Jude didn't just go alone. Why didn't she go to Scotland, visit her sister? But why didn't he, she would ask? He was always taken with little Jos, always saying they must have children of their own one day. Maybe if they actually spent some quality time together, they could make a baby!

But for that they'd need to have sex.

Despite having a fun and varied sex life for years, by the time Jude was reaching the end of her tether, they were hardly having sex at all. Peter was either out playing in the bush with his warrior pals, or he was shut up in his library surrounded by his books, nurturing ideas and formulating plans for his next enterprise. Jude tried to seduce him up to bed, or down onto the floor, or even just to fuck him on that damn chair he spent most of his home time sitting in, but Peter rejected her. He was too tired, too busy. 'Later, Fluff.' But later never came.

She wondered if he was having an affair with Beola, knowing this was a distinct possibility because they two definitely had the hots for one another. But in reality, it was improbable simply because Beola was always in and around the white house, and Peter was often away for days at a time. Eventually, Jude resorted to kicking her husband out of their bed altogether in an effort to shock him to his senses. She even told him she wanted a divorce and, if that threat bothered Peter, Jude wasn't ever aware of it.

His response was to spend more time away from home, more time with his warriors, and more money on his projects. Jude's frustration turned into sorrow for a while. She became depressed. She stopped engaging with Peter at all, even when he was in the same room. She spent her days tending her garden and her bees, and her nights curled up with dark thoughts. She avoided Beola and Kissi and even Ben, who she had watched grow up and adored completely. She drank too much, and she brooded constantly until, eventually, she hated Peter just enough to want him dead.

Jude spied on him then.

Listened in to his telephone conversations so she could ascertain where he was going to be and when. Weeks passed. Months, before his plans revolved around somewhere she knew, somewhere close enough to home to predict which road he would travel and at what time. During that time Jude gave Peter every opportunity to come back to her. She stopped banging on about trips to Europe, stopped ignoring him. Instead, she made an effort to heal the rift between them. She cooked favourite foods for him, meals that often went uneaten because he didn't come home. She tried to take an interest in his latest ideas, but he was, understandably by then, not keen to share. Then, for their twenty first wedding anniversary, Jude booked a table at a favourite restaurant. She'd really have liked to have gone away for a weekend of debauchery but knew that would be pushing it. Surely, they could manage an evening out together? But, while they were getting ready to leave, Peter got a call about a broken well and went off to take care of that instead.

That was two days before she killed him.

If Peter had just put her first that single time, Jude wouldn't have gone through with it. But he didn't. Instead, he disregarded his wife, their marriage, yet again, and so Jude followed him south towards Arusha Chini a couple of hours after Peter set off. She'd made the drive enough times to know the lay of the land and had a sound enough plan based on that knowledge and her ability to handle a gun.

Living in Tanzania, surrounded by African bush had seen both Jude and Peter learn to handle a hand gun as well as a rifle. Kissi Nyerere had been their teacher, and Jude was a pretty good shot when it came to wounding trees. Of course, she'd never shot anything living before, or anything moving, but she had a full clip of eight rounds in the Glock 1911 inside her glovebox, and the determination of a woman filled with hatred, as well as the will to take whatever was left of Peter's money and get the fuck back to civilisation.

Parking her matching little jeep among some nearby shrubs, she made her way to the dirt track encircling the hill to the south of the one the white house sat upon. Jude then climbed to the top to watch for her husband. She didn't have long to wait when the tell-tale plume of red dust showed a vehicle moving towards her. Before she was spotted… her orange hair really was a dead giveaway, Jude hurried back down to take up position on the track, so she was ready and waiting when Peter drove around the bend.

Naturally, it didn't go exactly as planned.

The plan was to kill Peter up on the track. A couple of decent shots when he came around the bend, and he'd either crash the jeep into the side of the hill, or he'd go over the side. If the jeep just stopped, then Jude would have to push or drive it off the track and down into the trees crowding along the slope beneath where she ambushed him. Then, if the jeep didn't burst into flames by itself, she would set the fire to destroy any evidence. Best laid plans.

But Jude's first, carefully aimed shot went wide, and Peter reacted so fast she just keep firing, trying to hit the fuel tank as much as her husband. At least he drove off down the slope and crashed into a tree under his own steam, but the jeep did not explode as hoped. Jude had lost count of how many rounds she'd used by then, but could see Peter was slumped over the wheel, and with blood all over his back, so perhaps she'd got him after all.

She ran down the slope as fast as she could to check.

But Peter was just wounded, unconscious and already coming around as Jude stood there trying to shoot him over and over with an empty gun. He was watching her, trying to speak, and she saw a terrifying hatred in his bright blue eyes. Then he was trying to get out, to open the door. Jude started to panic then, knowing that she couldn't let him get away, because she'd be done for attempted murder and spend years in prison. Even if by some miracle she managed to survive years in an African jail, she'd come out to nothing. No one. She'd have to go back to Scotland and back to poverty. She watched in horror as he stopped trying to open the stuck door and started trying to undo his seat belt so he might climb out. Her life started flashing before her eyes. What had she done, what was she doing? But it was too late; she was committed.

From that moment, everything Jude did was in a mechanical haze.

Her bandana came off from around her neck. It then went into the petrol tank, before being removed, turned around, and threaded back inside with the soaked end hanging out. The lighter seemed to appear in Jude's hand, its little flame jumping greedily onto the petrol-soaked cotton. Peter was speaking to her by then, but she had no idea what he was saying. She was turning, running for cover and just making it behind the boulder before the loud WHOOMP exploded into a ball of flame which receded back into itself almost immediately. An unremarkable fire with a flailing man shape at its centre. Peter's screams were horrible to hear, but it was that or it was prison. From burning the jeep with Peter in it, to getting back to the white house with a few bags so Beola would assume she'd been shopping, to getting rid of the evidence. It all happened in something of a daze.

Once she'd concealed the gun, Jude just had to keep going to avoid dwelling too much on what had just happened and what might be about to happen. She went into the kitchen, and she started cleaning, scrubbing, just a busy housewife at her chores. It was easy enough to get rid of Beola and then, when the police finally arrived, it was easy to breakdown, because it was a relief to give in to the horror of what she'd done. Real tears, but only for herself, for the trauma yet to come as Jude navigated her way through the impending investigation.

The police were kind, gentle, they delivered their dreadful news and then invited her to come back to Moshi. They needed her to formally identify a few of her husband's possessions. No, they said, she wouldn't be required to identify his remains, because his injuries were too severe, too upsetting. But there were other formalities to be dealt with. Would she come now? Beola wanted to come too, but Jude told her to stay at the white house and call Gary Preston, because he was Peter's best friend, and he should be told what had happened. She also knew that Gary was Peter's executor and, the quicker Gary got to Tanzania, the quicker Jude could pick up the pieces of her new life.

Leaving Beola to handle that, Jude followed the police back to Moshi in her little jeep that was no longer one of a pair. She identified Peter's old Tilly hat, his wedding ring and the remains of his wallet. She drank the sweet tea provided to help her deal with her shock and she answered their questions to the best of her ability. She knew what time he'd left home, and she knew where he was going. She hadn't expected him back at any particular time because Peter was always such a busy man. He spent a lot of his time helping others. The police knew all about that, because everyone knew all about Peter's efforts on behalf of so many living in the region. His death was a great loss, and possibly every officer on duty that afternoon came by the chief's office to give Jude their sincere condolences.

It took longer receiving all the well-wishers, than it took to deal with the few formalities necessary after such a tragic accident, so Jude wasn't on her way back to the white house until it was dark. By the time she was driving down off the ridge she could see the storm clouds piled up over the hill, see the lightening, and the tell-tale orange glow of a big fire. Wondering too if the house was on fire, she put her foot down, eager to get there before she got soaked in her open topped jeep. Eager to retrieve the gun and bury it somewhere safer before the rain forced her to wait for daylight.

But Jude never made it to within fifty yards of the white house, because a whole battalion of Maasai warriors… some armed with spears, and others with wicked looking pangas which they beat rhythmically against their shields, were waiting for her at the top of the drive. They knew everything, of that Jude had no doubt. How they knew she didn't stop to wonder about. She made one attempt to drive through their ranks, satisfied with how quickly they dispersed to avoid being mown down, and then she turned her jeep around and got the fuck out of dodge.

Jude was allowed back into the white house the following evening, when the newly arrived Gary escorted her there from her hotel in town. He took her set of keys. He even took the keys for the jeep. He was in full executor mode, he had the paperwork to back up his instructions, and he didn't leave Jude alone for a second. She was allowed to remove only her personal belongings and even then, those had to fit inside two suitcases. Excess personal belongings would be packed up on her behalf at a later date and delivered to her in due course. The white house was now part of Peter's estate and Jude would have to return to England with his remains as well as Gary. Gary would make all those arrangements, and the will would be read after Peter's funeral.

Jude often worried that Gary knew of her crime, just as she wondered if the Maasai knew. But how could they? No one could possibly have known because she hadn't confided in anyone. She didn't believe in Maasai magic, or their witchdoctor. The old man may have turned up at the rehab centre all those years ago, telling Peter he'd decided to stay, but it was probably Henk who'd told him that. Peter and Henk used to spend a lot of time smoking, drinking, talking. Henk told the laibon, and the laibon simply used that to his advantage.

Later, finding out Gary was Peter's main beneficiary had sent Jude into an exquisite rage. She'd threatened to contest and, when she discovered she would lose her allowance the moment she took such action, Jude had resorted to vitriolic letters and phone calls. Gary simply ignored her, and that drove Jude to plot his death too. But what would happen to her allowance then? Gary would have his own beneficiaries and she would lose the only income she had. All she had to do, to keep receiving that allowance, was to remain single. No second marriage, no cohabiting.

In the end Jude counted herself lucky to walk away with the same income her mother-in-law enjoyed. Even so, for years afterwards, she lived in near constant fear that the gun would be uncovered. Every time the phone rang, every letter that dropped onto the mat, she was sure was destined to become her undoing. When her sister died, Jude was forced back into the light and still she survived. The years went on by and she was free and well off and, as long as she didn't think about Peter or about Africa, she could almost consider her life to be normal and good.

Right up until Beola called.

And then Jos called, only it wasn't Jos, it was Peter.

Somehow her dead husband was still a possibility, and Jude had no idea if her fingerprints or DNA, or whatever else would still also be a possibility in terms of evidence. She had no choice but to go back for the Glock 1911 after all those years, no option but to move it and get rid of it far away from the white house. The UK had an extradition treaty with Tanzania and, if she was charged with murder now, she might yet have to spend the rest of her life in a filthy Tanzanian jail.

So, Jude had booked her flights, as well as a modest suite in a five-star hotel. The hotel had also agreed to have a hire car waiting for her at the airport. She had even started packing, despite the fact her first flight wasn't until Sunday afternoon. She'd exchange currency once she was on route.

All that was left to do now, was take care of all the little dictators.

*

Benito Mussolini was another victim of the firing squad.

His feline counterpart was destined to be despatched with similar speed and efficiency, because Jude had learned how to put a small animal out of its misery from her old friend, Henk de Vries. A distasteful task that, once begun, must be completed.

A bit like killing Peter; once that first shot was fired, Jude had no choice but to see the whole thing through.

It was impossibly expensive for Henk to use drugs to put every single dying animal to sleep and so, if the animal was small enough, he would simply tug and twist in one fluid motion to break the animal's neck. He'd demonstrated many times and, one time, had supervised as Jude used the technique to despatch an adult mongoose that had been hit by a car and was obviously in a lot of pain.

Jude had wanted Henk to take the animal from her and do the deed, but he pointed out that she was delaying the inevitable. 'It is an act of kindness,' Henk said, both of them crouched at the side of the road where they'd discovered the animal. Jude, as usual, had jumped from the jeep first and had the animal in her arms before Henk could tell her not to move it. Taking it from her would only increase the suffering, and so he'd spoken with force. 'Do it,' he commanded. 'Do it now or leave the animal to die in pain at the side of this road.'

Jude found the right spot with her fingers and, once her hands were in position, closed her eyes, held her breath, tugged and twisted. It was over in less than a second.

Jude took a lot more time to prepare herself that morning.

Before settling herself in the conservatory she laid her tough leather gauntlet gardening gloves on the side table beneath the lamp next to the easy chair. She placed a cardboard box containing an old towel on the floor under the table. She prepared Benito with a dose of antihistamine in his favourite food. When he curled up to sleep on the sofa in the sitting room a little later, she scooped him up and carried him into the conservatory. Once she was sure it was just her and Benito in there, she closed the door, and settled down in the easy chair with the gently purring cat on a cushion on her lap.

After a brief battle with her conscience Jude refused to hesitate any longer. She had no choice. She couldn't have anyone coming in to look after her cats and she couldn't just leave them to fend for themselves. She certainly didn't have time to rehome them. It was for the best, for her as well as for them. They'd all had five-star lives living with her, and now Jude would give them as peaceful an ending as was in her power.

Pulling on the gloves, she stroked Benito, his head, his neck. Once she was sure he was oblivious to her movements, she gripped him at the base of his neck with her left hand, while her right tugged hard and forward, while twisting downward. It was over a split second after little Benito stirred. Quick and clean.

It was just past noon.

*

It was just after two p.m. local time, in Mount Kilimanjaro National Park.

Gabe Sanders had just come down off the mountain after a week-long trek up to the summit. The stepped path had just brought him down through the lush green rainforest and, though he was walking on air because of his amazing achievement, he was dog tired and looking forward to getting back to the lodge, to a hot shower and a cold beer. There would be a slap-up dinner later on with the whole group, where they could share experiences and look at one another's photos. But, right then, he just wanted to get back on the transport bus and have a nap.

Having just signed out at the ranger station under Mweka Gate's steeply pitched roof, he was now approaching the car park. It was full of people as well as vehicles; freshly arrived trekkers on their merry way up the mountain, and done in trekkers such as himself, on their weary way off the mountain. He saw the lioness as clearly as he saw the people milling around, but he couldn't quite trust his eyes that she was as real. A full-grown lioness standing right next to a colourful looking minibus wasn't something he expected to see. He stopped dead, and peered at her, watching to see if she moved… maybe she was a mascot toy, or an optical illusion brought on by his fatigue?

'What's up, Gabe?'

Gabe resisted the urge to look at his friend, Nick. Instead, he pointed.

'Look, over there by the green and yellow minibus… what do you see?'

Looking, Nick said, 'I can see a lion, Gabe… what do we do?'

'I think we run.'

'Couldn't run to catch a bus even if my life depended on it, mate.'

'Think that's the point.' Gabe then did the only thing he could think off. Putting the index finger and pinkie of one hand into his mouth, he whistled loudly. When he was sure he had the attention of at least some of the people, he yelled, 'Watch out people. There's a lion on the loose.'

The people looked to where the shouting man was now pointing and, sure enough, there was a great big lioness and, as if their attention was her trigger, she opened her mouth and began to roar.

All hell broke loose.

Those who thought of it, jumped into vehicles and closed doors. Others just scattered, with most running for the gate and the safety of the rangers who would surely have guns. The rangers did indeed have guns and, as soon as they realised what the disturbance was about, they were unlocking gun cabinets, and loading ammunition. Radios were crackling, and orders were given. Four armed and ready rangers exited the station and made their way into the car parking area, fanning out as they approached the lioness who was still roaring her head off but making no moves on the running people.

'How the hell did she get out?' the chief ranger wondered, wishing she hadn't because now he would have to shoot her, and he really didn't want to do that.

His men rounded up the closest people, encouraging them around and behind them. Those farther away they told to take cover. The lion was pacing by then, making no real moves away from her position by the minibus and, most importantly, not making any moves towards the people who were frozen in their fear and closest to her. The rangers began to close in but, just as the chief raised his rifle to take aim, the lioness turned tail and bounded off into the undergrowth at the east side of the car park.

Taking his radio from its holster, he called all rangers in the vicinity. They had an escaped lion on the loose. They needed a tracker, they needed more men, and they needed more guns.

Within minutes the area was being cleared. Every bus and car was loaded back up and the people made to disappear. There would be no trekking today. Calls were made to the various camps on the lower slopes. Those people were told to stay where they were, to stay alert. Calls went out to the settlements to the east of the gate, the local people told to get inside and stay inside, to close and lock gates if they had them.

Inside thirty minutes a team of twenty armed rangers had assembled in the car park in five vehicles. After a brief meeting, they set out, some on foot and others in the vehicles, to track and find their errant lioness.

Two rangers stayed at the Mweka Gate to meet any trekkers still on route. One of the rangers went to the toilet as the other was on the phone to his wife to let her know he would likely be late home that evening.

While both these men were distracted, a lioness came out of her hiding place among the ferns at the bottom of the path just inside the gate. Sniffing the air momentarily, she then trotted silently through the gate and vanished into the undergrowth on the west side of the car park, directly opposite where another lioness had so recently disappeared.

*

Jude had allowed herself the luxury of some silence and contemplation before getting on with what came next. Benito was wrapped and boxed and carried out to the shed. She left him there, while she went back inside and counted cats. All but Imelda were lazing around downstairs. Jude assumed Imelda was upstairs on Jos' bed as she'd started sleeping there a lot since Jos left. Imelda had slept with Jos every night since she'd come to live with Jude, so she was probably pining.

Closing the cat flap so none could use it, she went back outside, and uncovered the large hole in the ground already containing one small occupant. Having then retrieved Benito from the shed, she carried him to the grave, removed his little body from the box and squatted down to lay him next to Nicolae. Finally, she covered him over with a few inches of earth and topped him off with a flower. Replacing the folded table and the stones, Jude then went back inside taking the box with her.

Imelda was not upstairs.

Imelda was in the garden the whole time. She had watched through the windows of the conservatory, as her human murdered her comrade, and she had then watched him buried. Once her human was back inside, Imelda went to the grave and crouched down on the cover. She stayed there for many hours, thinking her thoughts and feeling her emotions. Finally, when hunger commanded it, she made her silent way back inside the house that was no longer her refuge. She ate her fill of the dry kibbles and then, avoiding the human completely, made her way up to where her favourite human had slept before leaving.

Avoiding the comfort of that bed, Imelda slipped underneath and settled down to wait.

CHAPTER TWENTY

Jos got back a little before five.

Peter had taken them on a detour to a restaurant that no longer existed, and so Jos had to wait a while longer to find that proper toilet that she craved so badly by the time they arrived in the car park of a different establishment. Thankfully, the waiter didn't take it personally when Jos cut him off mid welcome to request the location of said toilets. Thankful too that Peter left her alone from the moment the jeep was safely parked. Peace to use the facilities, and freedom to choose to eat food that she liked, in more frugal quantities, and to forego the beer completely.

In her entire life, Jos had never eaten alone anywhere other than in her own home but had done so twice since arriving in Africa. Obviously, she wasn't alone on the inside at those times, but to everyone else she was Betty no mates, and attracted a few curious stares from many of the tourists dining in couples or in small groups. But Jos didn't give a damn by then. She was discovering an entirely different world to the insular existence she was used to. She had the companionship of a dead man, had taken part in a fire ritual, and had spent the morning with Maasai women, getting along just fine despite the obvious language difficulties. She was no longer the frightened little girl who'd left Edinburgh, and Jos was ready to tackle Peter's projects head on.

Once they'd resumed their journey back to the white house, he made her understand that was why he'd left her in the village all morning, to meet some of the people the projects were aimed at and walk in their shoes for a time. He was glad she'd enjoyed it because that was half the battle. Being there because she wanted to be there. He also knew that Jos had toilets on her mind but told her to forget that. That would be imposing her Western preference on people who were perfectly happy dealing with those hygiene issues in their own way. It isn't just the bears that shit in the woods, and she would just have to get over that.

Jos resolved never to stay more than a single night in any Maasai village as long as she lived.

*

At the white house she found Beola alone. 'Where is everyone?' Jos wondered, clutching the folded shuka to her chest.

'Where have you been?' Beola believed to be the much more pertinent question. She felt rather put out that Jos had taken off last night without bothering to let anyone know where she was going, or when she would be back. 'You stink of smoke.'

'Fire not fags,' Jos assured, picking up on that irritation, she explained her night and morning as best she could as they sat on the patio sipping some of Beola's tea which, in Jos' newly formed opinion, was not as good as Maasai chai tea. 'The old laibon gave me this…' She indicated the shuka which was on her lap. 'Joseph passed it on to me this morning.'

'Joseph? Speaks very good English?' After Jos nodded, Beola went on, 'I know him. He used to come here a lot. He was always with the old man.' She hadn't seen the laibon since the night after Peter died but felt some regret hearing of his death. Beola also felt a more distinct irritation because Jos seemed to know so much while she was no longer involved as far as events surrounding Peter were concerned. For years she'd been sharing some form of communication with her friend and benefactor, and now Jos was getting all that attention. But Beola couldn't give in to how much this bothered her. She had to listen and smile and be a friend to the young woman. So, she carried on talking, 'I cannot believe he has been alive all this time,' she went on. 'Was he waiting, just like Peter was waiting? And, all this time, Jude has been free. Perhaps we should have done more… reported the gun missing perhaps? Maybe there would have been an investigation?'

'No,' Jos shook her head. Picking up on Beola's idea had sparked a connection inside her mind and she'd found another batch of Peter's information inside her own head. 'Jude was right where she was supposed to be. I needed her, and Peter made sure she was there. For me.'

'And now that the laibon is dead?' Beola wondered. 'What happens if Jude does come back?'

'I'm not sure…' Jos spoke slowly, distractedly, looking out across the lawn and the kitchen garden and into space, as she considered the possibilities based upon what she was still remembering from her Maasai magic experience. 'There were two rituals…' She looked down at her hand, and the wound that had hurt so badly at the time, and now looked days old. Her hand felt hot suddenly, not burning, but in memory of the fire perhaps. Pure fire that had hurt like hell at the time but, somehow, hadn't damaged her skin. Good magic. 'A sacrifice… and a summoning.'

'Perhaps he was summoning Jude?' Beola wondered.

Jos shook her head slowly, spoke softly, still thinking. 'Peter did that.'

'So, who, what?'

'I don't know.' She focused on Beola again, shrugging a little. 'But I think he gave his life to make it happen. I think that's what he was waiting for.' Looking inward again, Jos allowed her mind to wander on, following ideas and suggestions and whispered little memories that did not belong to her until Peter left them, like breadcrumbs, for her to find. 'This is about revenge,' she declared at last. 'Jude only ever got away with it because I needed her farther down the line. I'm here now, and Peter can avenge his murder.'

'If she does come here for the gun, do we take her to the police?' Beola doubted that this was the sort of revenge Peter had in mind. 'She would spend the rest of her life in prison. How do you feel about that?'

'Not brilliant,' Jos shrugged a little. 'But I saw how it happened, Beola. She burnt him alive! I don't think I will ever be able to forget the sound of Peter's screams for as long as I live.' She shuddered involuntarily. 'He chose to allow her to get away with it this long, not me. If I have any say in what happens now, then I suppose seeing her tried for murder is as good a revenge as any. It's not like Jude can't afford a good lawyer.'

The two women sat in silence thinking about murder and revenge and everything in between for a while, and then Jos remembered, 'Where is everyone?' she asked again, stifling a yawn.

'Ben and Wendell are working but they will be back soon I am sure, and Kissi has been called to the Kilimanjaro park because a lioness has escaped.'

'Really?'

'A trekker spotted her a few hours ago but she took off before the rangers could stop her.'

'Will they capture her?'

'They may have to shoot her.' It was a sad fact that, sometimes, predators escaped from the parks and the reserves. When they did, their journeys often brought them into contact with local populations. Attacks were not unknown, and so the escaped animals often had to be killed.

The tea finished; Jos excused herself for a time.

She went up to the garden room, turning on the tap to water the garden as she went. She took a long shower, washing the smell of smoke from her skin and from her hair. Once dressed again, she stripped the sheets from her bed, dirty after Peter's first body snatching incident, and added them to her washing pile. She fetched clean sheets from the cupboard Beola had shown her on arrival day, remade the bed, and then had a general tidy round, brushing her hair periodically until it was dry.

Jos was trying to be a good guest, sensing Beola was pissed off and supposing it was because she was the source of so much upheaval. This was a pattern of behaviour she'd learned around Jude. Unintentionally piss Jude off, make up for it by being a good girl. Of course, Beola hadn't verbally shut Jos down in between the way Jude did, but the resulting feelings inside Jos were the same, she felt guilty and miserable and confused about what she'd done in the first place.

Once she'd hurriedly put her hair up with a big silver clip, Jos went outside and turned the tap off again. Back inside the garden room, she collected up her washing into a bundle, and sat down on the bed with it in her arms. Then she said, 'Peter.'

After a few short moments of lethargy… much shorter than previous encounters, he appeared sitting right next to her on the bed. 'You rang?'

'Fuck off,' Jos laughed, and then laughed again at his obvious irritation. She felt instantly better with Peter around. 'I like swearing,' she told him. 'I'm Scottish… it's a national pastime.'

'Just promise me that, when you're doing business, you'll converse with a little more dignity.'

'You are such a snob.'

'Old fashioned maybe… but I am no snob.'

Rolling her eyes, Jos told Peter, 'I really need a break. I'm beginning to pick up on some of the information you uploaded into my head now, and I need time to digest it.'

'What things?'

Jos frowned, thinking, then she said, 'It's imagery mostly. And seen through your eyes, so ever so slightly disconcerting for me. The outfits…' She made a face, rolling her eyes. 'I can timeline some of it based on the outfits alone. I know what your parents look like. You really look your mum, but your dad was gorgeous… all dark and mysterious looking. He looked more Spanish that Scottish. And I would recognise Gary too if I met him… he suits a beard! I think you went to University in America… but maybe it was London?'

'Imperial College, London was first, then architecture at MIT in Cambridge, Massachusetts.'

'Well, that explains how I now know what an oriel window is,' Jos laughed, delighted. 'And the difference between Corinthian and Doric columns.'

'I love buildings,' Peter told her seriously. 'And bridges!'

'You certainly built a beautiful white house. And you seemed to spend a lot of time meeting a lot of people, in a lot of different buildings. Then again, you spent as much time driving around, shaking hands… there can be so many voices in my head sometimes, and they're not all talking English! The weirdest thing is, when I concentrate, I can understand what's being said no matter what language it's in. I've begun to think of it in terms of the Peter Sinclair Memorial Mind. That's four separate words, capitalised. I'm thinking of having some signage created.'

Jos was learning to recognise and then compartmentalise all those memories.

It was becoming just another mental process, a trigger would initiate a walk through a building, through a door, a person waiting, and then a conversation. Or maybe it was a journey, an arrival, another person, another discussion. As soon as Jos realised what she was remembering had happened to Peter, she packaged it up, and stored it inside a specially created structure inside her mind, to be accessed later. At first, she pictured this structure as a drawer, and she would toss little packets of information into it. The drawer was soon stuffed and so the structure changed. The drawer became a bureau, became a room, a house, a small storage facility. Lately she had begun to despatch all Peter's memories into a high-rise building full of lofty rooms. These rooms were full of images, snatches of conversations, music. Whenever Jos sent a mental messenger into these places, there was an immediate, complex and often perplexing response as everything crowded her consciousness at once.

It was like opening the door into a soundproofed room, where a band was playing live in one corner, a heated discussion was going on in another, a party was in full swing in the third, a quiet conversation was taking place in the final corner and, in the middle of all that, some kind of stock exchange was trading at full tilt. Added to this were all the random extra manifestations darting around in the resulting chaos. As soon as she opened the door it was all there and all at once.

Jos was just trying to learn to focus on one corner at a time, categorising in terms of period as well as importance. Jousting with punts on the River Cam might have been important to Peter at the time, but she could get along fine without it. On the other hand, the man in the short sleeved white shirt who appeared again and again with bright smiles and firm handshakes was someone Jos was learning about. This man, his predecessor and his successors, all belong to The Municipal Council of Moshi. Land is not for sale in Tanzania. Land belongs to the state. The white house stands upon borrowed land, and that land… as well as the surrounding acreage, attracts what Peter calls a ransom which must be paid annually through both official as well as unofficial channels, to ensure the preservation of the status quo for the white house, it's residents and all the wildlife living in the estate surrounding it.

Clearly, Jos needed a second, high rise; one for the dross and the other for the deals.

'It can get overwhelming,' she admitted to Peter, touching her temple. 'It's chaos in here right now. Sometimes I wonder if I'm not just going mad. And I suspect there's a lot more to it than a few projects that you need looking after.'

'By the time I died it was all second nature to me, Jos. And by the time this is over, it'll be the same for you. Don't waste time worrying about what it means… just let it happen.'

'How can you say that?' she wondered, irritated a little. 'One second I'm wondering if I need to charge up my phone, and the next I'm wondering how the commodities markets are trading, and should I be changing my investment strategies. Goals, risk, tolerance.' She stopped to glare at Peter because he was laughing quietly. 'It really isn't funny. I'm supposed to be on holiday.'

Laughing louder, Peter wondered, 'How can you be on holiday when you haven't worked a day in your life?'

Looking affronted, Jos said, 'Well… it still makes me really tired.'

'I understand,' Peter said seriously. 'You're doing wonderfully well.

We make a good team.'

'What about Jude?'

'We'll have to wait for her to begin making moves before plans can take on any focus.'

'Are we sure she's coming?'

'She'll come.' Peter knew it. 'I told her that we will rip the place apart until we find the gun and, when we find it, we… you, will take it to the authorities.'

'That simple, huh?' Jos wondered.

'I have no idea, Jos.' Peter watched her looking down at the bundle of washing in her lap, feeling her apprehension, her confusion. 'I'm simply trying to get Jude to take the bait.'

'And you're sure the gun is here?'

'It's here. Somewhere.'

'And yet you can't find it.' Jos recalled what the white house was like in Peter's In-between. 'This whole place is like a sum of all its little parts, for you.' She explained how it had been like that for her too, in the moments before they'd zoomed off across the tree tops to watch Peter's murder. 'Wouldn't it just show itself like everything else seems to?'

'You saw it like that too…' Peter was impressed. 'I was just pulling you along with me. But first, I had to gather it all up and go back towards that day. I'd no idea…' he mused.

'What about the other stuff?' Jos wondered. 'Ninety-four million miles from the sun, two hundred and forty miles south of the equator. I've been finding random stuff like that inside my head since I got here.'

'I think you've been gaining access to whatever passes for my mind these days.'

'Isn't that the point? Isn't that how you can give me all your mad info?'

'Undoubtedly, but I didn't anticipate these reverse effects.'

'Maybe I'm psychic?'

'Or maybe your inner formidable woman is simply getting more scope these days.'

Jos laughed, then made a face.

'Don't be so quick to put yourself down,' Peter admonished. 'You need to be strong. We need to be strong.'

'Because Jude is coming to get her gun.' Jos sighed. 'And yet you can't

find it.'

'It must be concealed in the earth.' Peter knew that because he had a secret of his own concealed in the earth. Something else that never showed itself inside his In-between.

'We need a metal detector,' Jos thought. 'Maybe I can pick one up in Moshi?'

'Let's just allow Jude to lead us to it.'

'She might shoot me too.'

'There aren't any bullets in it. She fired them all at me. Remember?' Jos nodded.

She was quiet, looking down again. All formidable locked up inside and the little girl was sad and afraid. A long lock of hair hung down like a coil of deepest amber and, instinctively, Peter reached out to brush it back from her cheek.

With a loud intake of breath, Jos slid off the bed and onto the floor, where she sat open mouthed, surrounded by her dirty laundry, looking up at Peter. With a hand on her cheek, she then asked, 'What did you do?'

But Peter was rubbing his hand, which wasn't even real, but felt a little real right then in the sense it was tingling. Then he looked down at Jos who was looking back up at him with a dazed expression, and he burst out laughing.

‘What?’ Jos wondered, scrambling to her feet so she could look in a mirror. Her whole head felt funny, but her right cheek in particular was smarting a little, as if she’d been slapped. ‘Oh, for fuck’s sake!’ She was looking at herself in the bathroom mirror by then, and all her loose hair was standing on end at the roots. She looked like Sideshow Bob. ‘Look at the state of me!’ She then started laughing, going back into the garden room and taking her brush with her. ‘What did you do?’ she asked again.

‘Your hair was hanging down. I didn’t think. I… I touched you.’

Jos undid her hair and started brushing it, dispersing all the static tingle as she did. ‘Feels like you slapped me.’ When he grimaced, she added, ‘Not the slap exactly… just the slight sting that comes later. Jude slapped me a long time ago. I was hysterical. It was soon after my mum and dad… you know. I was having a bad day and screaming at Jude for some reason I can’t even remember. She slapped me. My cheek felt like it does now for quite a while afterwards.’

‘Sorry… I’ve only ever tried to touch inanimate objects before now, never people.’

‘Give me some warning next time.’ Jos rearranged her hair on top of her head and clipped it more carefully back into place. ‘I’ll bring a hat.’

Peter was laughing again, watching his niece. Her freckled nose and cheeky smile. She was tall, but she was slight. Undoubtedly strong, but she looked like she might blow away in a stiff breeze. He was filled with the urge to protect her, which was in direct conflict with his desire to unleash what he knew to be inside Jos; that formidable part of her that belonged to her absolutely but was just as surely being nurtured by the elements of his own psyche which were flourishing inside her mind now. Their team, destined to become an ensemble of one, because the bond was growing stronger every day.

‘Thank you, Jos,’ he told her sincerely. ‘Thank you for staying. Thank you for believing. Thank you for allowing me to experience living again before I must finally succumb to death.’

‘I honestly wouldn’t have it any other way,’ Jos sounded slightly surprised, because that was actually how she felt. ‘I never realised how dull my life was until I came here. Even if I do seem to spend an inordinate time sleeping just now.' She yawned on cue. 'I really need a break. I just want to sleep the clock around. Though I hate to abandon Beola all over again now Kissi is away chasing lions.'

'Is he?'

Jos told Peter the latest news, then wondered, 'Maybe she's a relative of Lulu?'

'That is a distinct possibility. She was a prolific mama.'

'Let's not dwell on that too deeply,' she suggested. 'It's likely this lioness will be shot on sight.'

Thoughtful, Peter said, 'Then we must hope Gaia will protect her.'

'Hippy,' Jos grinned. 'But seriously, I really need to sleep. Please don't disturb me unless Jude shows up with a spade and a box of bullets.' 'I promise.' Peter smiled, and then winked out of existence.

*

Having collected up all her washing again, Jos went downstairs and loaded up the washing machine, before looking for Beola.

But it was Ben and Wendell she found first, meeting them in the hallway as they came through the front doors on their way to their office for their usual end of day checks.

'G'day, Jos.' Wendell greeted her with a big smile and a small peck on the cheek. 'Been out fraternising with the natives again?'

'As a matter of fact, I have just got back after spending the night in a

Maasai village.' Jos then smiled sheepishly at Ben. 'Are we good?' 'We are,' he assured, nodding.

Wendell wondered, but he didn't ask. If it was his business he'd get to know when one or both of them was ready. Instead, he said, 'You're getting quite a tan there, Jos.'

'Am I?' She looked at her bare arms. 'Sure, it isn't just my freckles, all joining up?'

'Where are my parents?' Ben asked.

'Your papa has been recalled early…' Beola had been sitting in Peter's favourite chair in the library when the voices reached her. Mulling over everything that had been revealed over the past few days, and wondering how much of the past could have been prevented? A waste of her time no doubt, and so she was walking along the hall towards her son, their friend and their guest trying to think only of the future. '… because a lion has escaped from the park.'

CHAPTER TWENTY-ONE

Jude was in the kitchen using the pestle and mortar to crush antihistamine tablets again, because she would have to despatch at least one more of her cats today. She had five more dictators and just two days within which to carry out her gruesome tasks. She then mixed the powder into the meat waiting in one dish. Placing them all on the floor for the four already mewling around her legs, and letting fate decide.

Eva Peron died of cancer, but it was little Eva cat who stepped up to the drugged dish and began to eat her downfall. Joseph, Augusto and Elena tucked into the unlaced dishes and Imelda continued to play hard to get.

Soon after, back in the conservatory with her handy box and her sturdy gloves, Jude laid sleepy little Eva on a cushion and placed the cushion on her lap. Once again, and with the same ruthless speed and efficiency, Jude held, tugged and twisted the dozy cat into a premature death at twenty minutes past five.

Once again, Jude counted cats, ensuring they were all safely inside before adding Eva to the grave by the back wall. Still no sign of Imelda but she had always preferred her own company and would no doubt turn up eventually.

Jude was unconcerned.

Jude was becoming increasingly focused on the task in hand. Her method had worked well for two cats now, and so she planned to repeat the same process until she was done, or until it failed to produce the desired results. As soon as she returned to the house, she crushed another tablet into powder and checked to see how long she needed to wait before giving the remaining cats their supper.

*

At seven twenty p.m. a lioness was sighted just outside Mountain View Secondary School.

One of the teachers, Gloria Juma, was on her way home for the evening. She should have been home hours ago, but the temperamental old photocopier in the staff room decided to play up when she was trying to get the following week's workbooks printed out. She spent at least an hour struggling with that, and then her colleague Charles Kayombo came along. He was having trouble with one of his students, so they'd had a coffee and a chat about that. Before Gloria knew it, it was after seven p.m.

Had Gloria known she'd be working so late, she'd have brought her car, because not only was it dark already, but the land all around the school was forested. Even the bright moon couldn't ease the blackness of her road ahead, and the little light on the handle bars of her bike was only slightly better than useless. But she knew the road well, it was less than a ten-minute ride to her home in nearby Machame Magharibi and, if any cars happened to be passing she would easily hear them coming or see their headlights from a good distance. So, Gloria decided to just get on with it.

She'd been cycling less than a minute when she encountered the lioness.

There was no mistaking that the animal was a lion, even in the restricted light. Her golden pelt and spotted belly, her paler muzzle, her mouth hanging open slightly as she panted softly. Her huge head and paws. Her eyes alternately narrowing to slits, and glowing dully in the feeble bike light, as she sat in the middle of the road less than ten meters from where Gloria had stopped dead.

There was a reason lions were locked up inside the parks. Lions did not play well with others and poor Gloria was frozen in fear for what felt like an eternity. She stood stock-still staring at the lioness as the lioness stared back. The animal just sat there, looking completely carefree, but Gloria wasn't fooled. She didn't dare scream, or run, or move in any way. To do that would be to declare herself prey, and the lioness would spring into deadly life. She would run Gloria down and she would eat her. What to do?

What to do? Gloria didn't know what to do.

Praying for divine intervention, Gloria prayed for a car to come along or, better still, a truck loaded up with big strong men carrying big powerful guns. She whispered to God to intervene on her behalf; she was a good woman, a good Christian and a good teacher. But nothing happened. No car, no saviour, no hand reached down from heaven to pluck her to safety.

She was on her own, and God helped those who helped themselves.

In an effort to break the spell that had fixed her on the spot, Gloria twitched her mouth, licking her lips slowly… difficult when every bit of saliva has dried up in fear. She moved a hand just as slowly, sliding it along to the middle of the handle bar and back. The lioness was every inch the disinterested cat. Playing with a mouse called Gloria. But Gloria began to tell herself she wasn't going to be that mouse; she was going to get through this. Somehow.

Once again, moving painfully slowly, Gloria got off her bike, never taking her eyes off the lioness for a second, thinking that, if the lion did leap at her, she could maybe throw the bike and possibly get away. It had been a while since Gloria had run any races, but she was fit enough due to cycling regularly, and maybe she was also fast enough to make it back to the school and into the safety of the grounds? It couldn't be far, a few hundred meters to the gates perhaps. How long would it take her to also close the gates, she wondered. Maybe she would be faster climbing the big tree just inside the gates. Who was she kidding! Gloria hadn't climbed a tree in forty years, and lions slept in trees. Her heart was pounding by then and the panic beginning to rise. Gloria knew that if she didn't do something right there and then, her life would end very soon and very badly.

The lioness rose to her feet and shook her massive head.

Gloria Juma screamed, pushed her bike uselessly to the ground, turned tail and ran up the road still screaming her head off and waving her arms in the air. She didn't dare look back. She didn't want to see the massive and powerful animal that was bounding after her, gaining quickly, so quickly she could hear its breath, feel the heat of it at the back of her neck. Any second now Gloria would feel those massive jaws close around her throat. She would have the life choked out of her. She would go limp. She would be carried off into the forest where the lion would tear her body limb from limb. Her bones would be picked clean by vultures. The horrifying images and thoughts just kept on coming, and Gloria just kept right on screaming!

Charles Kayombo heard her a long time before he saw her, though he didn't know it was his colleague that he was hearing. He'd just driven out the school gates when the terrible sound of screaming shattered the peace and quiet. The sound of it chilled the blood in his veins and filled his soul with fear. Stopping his car just beyond the gates, he opened the door, and stood up… keeping one foot inside the car in case he needed to get away quickly. The screaming was getting louder and so nearer. A woman, no doubt.

A second later he was almost relieved to see it was Gloria running into his headlight beams. He was afraid to see her so frightened and wondered what had happened. But she didn't look injured in any way, and he was unable to see anyone or anything chasing her. Feeling braver, he moved forward and away from his car to intercept her.

'Gloria,' Charles shouted to make himself heard over her racket, putting both his hands out to stop her.

Gloria ran right into her colleague and then hid behind him. 'Lion!' she wailed, clutching the back of his jacket. 'There is a big lioness chasing me. Please… please we must get inside your car.'

'But…' Charles peered back the way Gloria had come. His headlights were on full beam, and he could see all the way down to the first bend in the road. He couldn't see or hear anything in the least lion like. 'Are you sure…?' He turned to speak to Gloria, but she was already inside his car, and in the driving seat. 'Gloria?' As he watched, she made a three-point turn and drove back through the school gates. She then kept on going. 'Gloria!' he called out, waved. 'Stop! Wait…' Clearly something had scared her very badly, and lions were expert hunters who liked to sneak up on their prey. Gloria's lioness could be watching him right then and he wouldn't even know it. Looking nervously back down the road again and all around at the myriad dark spots in the undergrowth surrounding him, Charles decided to err on the side of caution. He hotfooted it back into the school grounds, closed the gates for good measure, and chased his own car all the way back to the main building.

Gloria would not get out of that car even when Charles was at its side and the door into the building was just a few steps away.

‘I am telling you…’ she spoke through the tiniest gap at the top of the window. ‘There is a lion out there. Why is there a lion out there? I can’t be expected to deal with lions. Call the rangers. Call them now!’

Resigned to a very late dinner that evening, Charles nodded. ‘I will go and call the ranger service now.’ And he went back inside the school to do so, if only to get his car back. He was also beginning to think his colleague had perhaps scared herself with a shadow or something. She shouldn’t have been cycling home alone in the dark. She had probably just seen a stray dog. Going through the motions he found the relevant number and dialled.

However, the ranger service took the report very seriously indeed.

‘Stay where you are,’ the ranger manning the switchboard told the teacher. ‘We will send a team as quickly as possible, but it may take them some time to reach you, as most of our men are deployed to the east of your position this evening. She must have doubled back.’ ‘Who has doubled back?’ Charles wondered.

‘A lioness escaped from the park earlier today…’

‘Why were we not informed?’ Charles demanded.

‘Because we have been tracking her to the east,’ the ranger explained. ‘Now… please… just stay where you are. The men will come into the school to find you.’

It was almost an hour before Gloria was finally surrounded by the big armed men, who took her to the place she had encountered the escaped lioness. Two got out of the truck and began trying to track her movements away from the road, but it was too dark to see anything. Instead, they collected Gloria’s bike and loaded it into the truck between the knees of the men still sitting inside. As the truck progressed downhill toward the settlements and villages scattered down there, they jumped down from the truck in pairs and began going door to door, warning the residents to remain inside, and to be vigilant.

The hunt for the escaped lioness would resume at first light.

CHAPTER TWENTY-TWO

Beola called Kissi as she was making dinner for one. 'Where are you now?' she wondered.

'East of the Mweka Gate trying to track our runaway.' Kissi had just spent a stressful half hour explaining to the tourist coffee pickers that they would have to spend the night in a nearby church, because a lioness was on the move beyond the park boundaries. She had been seen heading in the direction of their camp and remaining in the tents was not an option. Some of them thought it was exciting, others thought it was a ridiculous overreaction. 'And not five minutes ago another call came through telling us she was spotted more than an hours' drive west of here,' he told his wife. 'It doesn't make sense!'

'Will you get home tonight?'

'I doubt it. Tomorrow we must begin tracking all over again, and some of us will be needed inside the park to count heads. We need to find out how many lions are missing and how they are getting out.'

'Take care of yourself, my darling.'

'I will. Did Jos show up yet?' Kissi wondered.

Beola offered a much-abbreviated version of recent rituals and the death of the laibon. 'She's in bed already. She wouldn't even wait to eat dinner. I'm getting a little worried about her.'

'I'm sure she'll be fine.'

'It's Peter,' Beola told her husband. 'I am sure of that.'

'Well, that is up to Jos,' Kissi reminded his wife. 'And maybe it's for the best. If Jude killed him then it's about time that was known. I'm not sure what will become of this truth, but at least we know now.'

'Jos would like to see Jude tried for his murder, but we will need to find the gun for that to happen.'

'Beola…' Kissi voiced a gentle warning. 'Leave this to Jos to deal with.'

'But Jude will come here!' Beola reminded. 'To our home!'

‘And we will deal with that when it happens,’ Kissi told her firmly. ‘Right now, I have other things to worry about.’

‘I know,’ Beola said softly. ‘Sorry. I will let you get back to your job.’ Before ending the call, she reminded her husband that she loved him, and that they all needed him home safe.

She then finished preparing and eating a meagre meal that she didn’t really want.

After clearing away her dishes, Beola chose to return to the library, thinking that, if Peter wouldn’t appear for her, then he would have loads of books to communicate with instead. ‘Peter?’ she asked, sitting down at the little table instead of in his chair. ‘Please come to me. I need you, my darling.’

Beola soon sensed the daydream qualities that always heralded Peter’s arrival and felt glad he hadn’t forsaken her. She sat quietly, letting the silence take shape all around her as her mind grew relaxed and calm and peaceful, in a deep and satisfying way that had been denied to her, since before she made the call to Edinburgh to invite Jos to come and stay.

That all seemed like such a long time ago.

‘I can’t stay long, Bee.’ Peter was standing at the French doors, smiling when she opened her eyes to see him.

‘Why?’ she asked, pouting.

‘I promised. We’ve gotten all tangled up, and Jos needs to rest.’ ‘Why isn’t she out chasing boys?’ Beola wondered.

‘Because I stimulate her intellect,’ Peter smiled, beguilingly. ‘Our attraction came from a different place entirely and so your response was different entirely.’

Sighing, Beola said, ‘I’m losing you, all over again and there isn’t a damn thing I can do about it.’

‘Don’t take it personally. Jos has to take up the reigns of the estate when this is over, and that means she needs to hit the ground running. She needs to know everything I know, how to think, how to act. I’m giving her a huge amount of power as well as information, and she needs to know what to do with that. If I just pass on the inheritance without the tools, it will all fall apart. Decades of hard work, years of labour in absentia. I owe it to Gary to prepare Jos for what is coming to the absolute best of my abilities, because she needs to take the responsibility away from him. Before she came, I wondered how I might be able to cast her into a version of myself as far as the business is concerned. I worried it might take years, knowing we wouldn't have years. But then she came, and she could be mine, Beola… Jos is like the child I never had, because my wife murdered me before we had any children of our own. She thought it would all go to her…'

'Is that why she did it? For the money?'

'Jude only ever saw the smaller picture. Only money spent, never money generated. Jos will be different, and she'll do a better job than I did, because she's learning from all my mistakes. She knows more and more every day. Right now, Jos even knows what I'm up to. She'll recall this conversation later as if she witnessed it. It's a kind of telepathy. I like it. I feel increasingly real…'

'But you're not real!' Beola almost shouted, she was so frustrated with what was going on. 'Not any more. Life lost you all those years ago, Peter. You were still here, and I got used to having you around, but you're not real. You are using Jos… you're manipulating her into becoming another you.'

'Don't let jealousy cloud your judgement, Bee,' Peter winked out.

Leaving Beola more frustrated than ever. Clenching her teeth as well as her hands, she gave voice to her frustration, thumping her fists down onto the table as she did so. She wanted to go straight up to the garden room and shake Jos into her senses.

Instead, she went outside.

Walking the short distance to the gate, Beola went to the little outhouse closest to the bee hives. Dressing in a bee suit, she prepped a smoker with dried lavender and eucalyptus leaves and, once the aromatic smoke was puffing nicely, she began inspecting the hives. Lavender and eucalyptus smoke didn't make the bees afraid their environment was burning. It calmed them, which calmed her. She had put the super boxes on the day before Jos came, and the busy little bees would only take a few weeks to stuff them full of honey laden comb. Beola spent the next two hours telling the bees all her troubles, inspecting the super frames, while they inspected her. The late afternoon sun, the gentle buzz, the aromatic scents of lavender and eucalyptus.

The joy of focusing upon something good and sweet and productive.

*

Ben and Wendell were in Mountain View Bar a little later.

It was filled with a Friday evening crowd. Busy with groups of younger tourists who were visiting the region. There were the backpackers and the climbers, the rich kids and the students, and there were also the older ones who still preferred the noise and excitement of a busy bar-cum-disco, to the library quiet of the hotel lounges and cocktail bars.

Nightingale and her two colleagues were constantly busy mixing drinks behind the bar, and bar snacks were being served all over the seating area by the two waitresses. The little dance floor in the back was empty despite the music blaring through there, but that would change once people had consumed enough alcohol to want to let their collective hair down.

Red Earth Tours had a pop-up booth in the bar every Friday night, thanks to Nightingale's influence as well as cut price tour seats for the owner and his family. They set up around seven p.m. before the bar got too busy, and usually closed up around nine p.m. because after that people were just too drunk to be bothered with. It was always better to catch people sober so they'd have a chance of remembering the spiel when they dug the flyers out their bags and pockets the following day.

They had a permanent spot at a window side seat close to the bar because Nightingale simply slapped a reserved sign on the table when she came on shift at six. Ben and Wendell then got their pop-up signage and their boxes of flyers out from a store cupboard when they arrived soon after and they were good to go.

That Friday had been very productive, because they managed to confirm new bookings with four separate groups for the following week. One was a group of eight! Lots of other people seemed very interested if not actually willing to book there and then. After packing up for the night, Ben and Wendell held onto their table, and got in a few rounds to celebrate.

'Jos seems different,' Wendell said eventually, not really fishing for what had gone on between her and Ben, just an observation of fact. 'She seemed like quite the shy Sheila when we picked her up from the airport. Next thing she's talking like a native and spending the night in one of the Maasai villages.'

'Not to mention stealing cars.' A single pint and Ben's tongue became so loose it was a wonder it hadn't just fallen right off.

'What?' Wendell wondered. 'When was this?'

After mentally kicking himself a few times, Ben sighed and said, 'Look… I can tell you some stuff, but you have to keep it to yourself, okay.' 'Cross my heart, mate.'

'Jos isn't just Jos… She's Peter Sinclair's niece.'

Wendell had heard the name mentioned in the exchange between Jos and the roadside warriors. 'Who is this bloke… Peter Sinclair?'

'He built the white house,' Ben explained. 'He built it for his wife. You see, we didn't always live there… we started off living in the lodge. Peter and his wife, Jude, lived in the big house. My mama was their housekeeper for years. But Jude murdered Peter and now my…'

'Hang on…' Wendell stopped Ben with a raised hand. 'So, this Auntie Jude killed Uncle Pete.' When Ben nodded, he asked, 'Is she in prison?'

'Edinburgh.' Ben said, as if that explained everything. 'Everyone thinks Peter's death was an accident.'

'Except you?'

'Jos told us the truth last night.'

'So, Auntie Jude confessed?'

'Wendell… shut up.'

'Okay.'

'Peter told Jos…' Stalling the next interruption with his own raised hand, Ben said, 'Just listen… Peter might have died fourteen years ago, but he's kinda still around.'

'Big bloke? Longish blonde hair? Repairs irrigation systems when he's not busy haunting white houses.'

'I had to tell you something.' Ben couldn't help laughing. 'And now you know what I'm telling you is true. But… and trust me on this, things have gotten a whole lot more complicated now Jos is here. We found out about the murder for one thing. Jos went straight for the gun… or rather where the gun should be, but it isn't. Peter is telling her everything. I think he's taking her over.'

'Like… possessing her?'

‘Not in a demonic, spewing pea green soup while demanding coitus sort of way.’

‘That’s good.’ Wendell nodded, sipped his beer and then added, ‘I thought for a second back there we were going to have to call in a priest.’

‘Actually, the most dangerous thing Peter does is let Jos drive.’

‘Did you really just say coitus?’

‘My mama brought me up not to swear,’ Ben explained. ‘Anyway, back to my point. Jos can’t drive, but she drove into town on Wednesday morning, and she’s been up west visiting the Maasai… a tribe Peter was an honorary member of before he died. As well as speaking in tongues and cooking all those pancakes we ate for breakfast yesterday.’

‘Yeah?’

‘Yeah.’ Ben and his folks had a long chat about what was going on with Jos the night before. ‘I remember Peter’s pancake breakfast extravaganzas. I was even involved in some. Pancakes on the ceiling, the floor, wrapped around hanging pots. That was definitely Peter bouncing around in Jos’s body at six a.m. I’m telling you; it’s all going on in the white house. Has been since the day he died. That night a Maasai laibon conjured a whole storm right above us.’

‘A witchdoctor?’

‘Don’t say that,’ Ben told his friend. ‘That’s a white people word. Laibon’s are spiritual men, they are healers, teachers…’

‘Okay, okay, I get the picture. But you said conjured so I was thinking magician.’

‘This laibon was a true legend, Wendell. His name is known all over Kenya as well as Tanzania. Most laibon’s are just old men who know a bit about healing herbs and are maybe good at listening and helping people solve their problems. But this laibon…’ Ben puffed out a breath. ‘This laibon had real power! Supernatural power. He and Peter were great friends, and my folks think he is the one to help Peter stay after his death. That was a very strange night. I was there. We were there. A whole tribe of Maasai turned up. They lit a great big fire, and the laibon was up in the roof garden shouting up at the sky. The wind was howling, the rain was lashing down. It seemed like the whole world was a storm, and we were right in the middle of it. And then we weren't. The wind, the rain…' Ben was looking at his friend earnestly. 'I swear. It all stopped as soon as we were off the hill. We were on our way to my grandfather's, and we stopped up on the ridge and got out the jeep. We were still all soaked from the lashing rain around the house, but the night beyond was clear and still and dry. We just stood there watching a storm raging right above the white house.' Ben sat quietly for a time, thinking about that night, then he said, 'It was magic. The most supernatural and mystical event I have ever witnessed. And I have seen things since. Heard stuff too…' He gave Wendell a quick run-down of Peter's general tricks that he'd been trying his best to ignore for years. Right up until Peter started messing with the woman he loved. 'He's the one moving Nightingale's fags, I'm sure of it. He was a smoker, so he's probably trying to sniff them or something.'

'It's not like they can give him cancer.'

'But what if she gets scared?' Ben asked, looking across to the bar where Nightingale was smiling and beautiful. 'What if she leaves like Rachael did?'

'What really did happen to Rachael?'

'She was snooping in the library, so Peter threw books at her.'

Wendell burst out laughing. 'Is that all? Christ, she told anyone who would listen that the devil himself told her to get out of his home.'

'You fancy her, don't you?'

'Rachael?' Wendell looked as incredulous as he felt. 'Gimme a break.' 'Jos,' Ben said patiently.

'Oh.' Wendell nodded. 'Sadly, yes.'

'Why sadly?'

'She'll go back to Scotland. No future in it, mate.'

'I don't think Jos will stay there. You heard what she said… she doesn't seem to have much of a life there. She really has been waiting to come here. Peter's been waiting for her, and now they're together… well… watch this space,' Ben advised. 'Something is about to go down.'

*

In Edinburgh, Jude's best laid plans were going down the toilet.

Augusto Pinochet may have died of a heart attack, but fat cat Augusto refused to be despatched in such a pedestrian manner.

Fat cat Gus put up a fight.

The latest batch of antihistamine was mixed in with some tasty tuna. Once again Jude let fate decide and it was Gus who got stuck in to the laced batch. But he didn't eat so much and neither Elena nor Joseph would go near it afterwards. Imelda was still refusing to show herself, and Jude was beginning to think the old girl knew what she was up to.

Finally, Gus curled up on her bed to go to sleep.

Jude had been following him around the house for over an hour by then. She was eager to get on with her packing, and there were a few little jobs that needed doing before leaving. The cold tap in the utility room was dripping again, and she had to bleed all the radiators, because the nights were getting chilly, and she wanted to come back to a warm home after her trip. She could have left Gus alone, but she only had one more full day before setting off, and there were still four cats awaiting despatch. It was gone eight p.m. by the time she arrived in her bedroom armed with those gardening gloves, that box and another old towel.

As Jude prepared herself, she caught sight of her reflection in the armoire mirror. A simple black dress, expensive opaque black tights, pretty high heeled shoes and a long string of genuine, chunky amber beads which complimented her orange hair perfectly. A chignon today, held in place with crystal tipped hairpins. Jude always liked to look her best, and she was very proud of how youthful and trim she looked at fifty-three. Close up she had the tell-tale signs of age, but it was nothing a good plastic surgeon wouldn't be able to erase.

Jude had plans in that direction now. At first, she'd felt terrified by Peter's implications, but by then she'd come to realise that all she had to do was get rid of the evidence and no one could prove a thing. There wasn't a jury on Earth who would convict on the testimony of a ghost. Peter could manipulate Jos all he liked, but without the gun they had nothing. She would retrieve the Glock, toss it into Lake Victoria, get back to Edinburgh and restart her life after a fourteen-year hiatus. She was rather looking forward to the challenge. She had the money, and she had the looks.

The world would once again be her oyster, and Jude intended to devour it.

But, by the time fat cat Gus was dead, Jude's hair looked like raptors had been nesting in it, her beads were scattered, her tights were shredded, she was missing the heel off one shoe, one sleeve of her dress as well as its neck line was torn, she had a cut lip, and her legs, arms and neck were covered in scratches some of which were deep enough to bleed freely.

It was a doomed attempt from the get-go.

Gus woke up when she lifted him, and he was definitely suspicious of the gloves. He hissed a little, but Jude persevered, soothing and stroking, trying to get him used to the gloves. It seemed to work, and she was able to sit with him on the bed. She even managed to lift him onto her lap. But maybe she was tense by then? He must have sensed something, because as soon as she tightened her hand around his neck, he became a ferocious beast. Every single hair on his body stood out on end as he yowled and screeched, hissing and struggling, and digging in with vicious claws as he fought to get free.

The sounds he made scared Jude, and she had no choice but to relinquish her hold. She jumped up off the bed, pushing him off as she went. But his claws got caught up in her clothing and, instead of fleeing, he turned on her. Gus used her dress as a ladder. She felt his claws digging through the fabric and into her skin, and soon she was making as much noise as the cat, howling and swearing as he hissed and scratched. Somehow, she managed to get him off, but he took one of her gloves with him. He then stood on the rug between Jude and the bedroom door, shaking and batting his paw until the glove flew off.

Then Gus stood watching Jude with malevolent eyes. So unsettling was his expression, she found herself backing away, putting the bed between them.

But Gus was having none of that. Ears back, mouth open, baring his teeth, he sprang through the air, bounced once on the bed and flew at Jude's face like the wild animal he was only ever a few steps away from being.

Jude yelled and fell backwards, knocking into her dressing table and sending perfume bottles and cosmetics flying. Grabbing blindly, she felt something in her hand and lobbed it at the cat with a loud grunt. It was the heavy hand mirror she used for checking the back of her lovely hairdos, and it bounced off him and sent Augusto racing for the door. But the cat couldn't get out, and looked set to launch another attack, so Jude picked up anything she could reach and started tossing bottles and tubs and jars at Gus, until he forced himself behind her bedside table, nearly tipping it over in his panic.

Jude was the one making for the door then, hauling it open and striding out onto the landing. She needed to get away, to regroup. But Imelda was right there in the doorway, as if she'd been listening at the door like a little spy. Jude tripped over her and went down, breaking the heel off one of her shoes and twisting her ankle. She narrowly missed crashing through the balustrade as she fell. It was as she was on the floor, out of breath and tasting blood, watching Imelda run for cover into Jos' room that Gus came back for another round.

Fat cat Augusto came tearing out the bedroom and used Jude's head as a springboard to the top of the stairs. She roared, feeling the needle point claws digging painfully into her scalp. 'You little bastard,' she yelled after his tail as it followed him at speed down to the bottom of the stairs. Standing up, Jude caught sight of herself in the landing mirror. She saw a dishevelled mess looking back at her. Her face was contorted with all the rage she felt. Her lip was cut, swelling and bleeding. Her ankle hurt like hell. One sleeve of her dress was torn from shoulder to elbow. The arm underneath was scratched and bleeding. Jude was really angry by then and, kicking off her broken shoe, she took the other off and held it like a weapon as she limped downstairs to look for that cat.

Bigger and smarter she soon caught up with Gus in the boot room.

He was trying desperately to get through the cat flap, but she'd locked it. Just like she locked the boot room door. Locking them two inside. Augusto on the floor, yowling and hissing up at her again, ears flat and tail swishing. Jude on her feet, stiletto in hand. 'Come on then,' she told him, reaching out to one side to unhook an old jacket from the coat pegs on the wall. There wasn't a lot of room in there, and she knew it was going to be rough, but she was fuelled with hatred by then. Hatred for Peter. 'Damn him,' she shouted at Gus. 'Fuck him for making me do this!' With that, she threw the jacket at the cat and launched herself after it, pinning Gus to the tiled floor. It almost worked, but he wriggled and scratched himself free. Jude had to use her shoe to force him off. She struck at him wildly, whacking at him with the heel.

But Gus was fuelled by fear, fighting for his life. The cat was feeling no pain, despite sustaining some serious injuries. By the time Jude managed to pull a heavier jacket down off the pegs to use in a second, more successful attempt to pin him down, he had three broken ribs and a broken jaw. But he was still fighting. Even when he was covered by the jacket and the weight of her as she knelt on top of him… even when he was unable to dig his claws into anything but the tiles… his claws breaking and his toes tearing as he did, Gus continued fighting.

Once Jude was sure he couldn't get out from under the jacket she tossed aside her useless shoe and grabbed for a boot on the shoe rack next to the backdoor. Inside the boot was a wooden tree. She managed to shake it free with one hand. The other hand and one knee were holding the cat in place under the coat. Once she had a firm grip on the boot tree, she began swinging it up and bringing it down, up and down, up and down. Over and over again. Until she was spent, trembling, crying, snot and spittle all over her mouth and nose, hunched over the jacket which was too dark to show much of the staining.

All that was left of Gus was barely discernible beneath that jacket.

Jude sat on the floor next to her mess, leaning back against the backdoor, catching her breath. Looking up at the clock above the door leading into the kitchen, she saw that it was only twenty-five minutes past eight. In the space of twenty minutes, she'd turned from a calm and elegant woman into a savage monster. 'Four down, three to go.'

*

In Moshi, Ben and Wendell were sitting at the bar by ten thirty p.m.

It was still busy at Mountain View, but many of the people sitting and standing in the bar area were now on the little dance floor getting down to some Kylie Minogue. Nightingale had been chatting to them in the longer breaks she was getting by then, between customers, but right then she was out collecting glasses.

As Kylie was still spinning around, Muhammed Asraf burst into the bar with such force he stumbled into and then knocked over the table closest to the door, spilling drinks and cheesy nachos all over the couple sitting there.

The girl of the couple sat looking down at herself, dripping with beer and strewn with shards of tortilla chip covered in melted cheese as well as a few splodges of salsa. Her guy jumped up onto his feet, also dripping beer but none of the food. He bore down on Muhammed, calling him stupid and threatening actual bodily harm.

Muhammed ignored him. 'Lion…' he shouted, reaching for

Nightingale's denim clad leg as she approached to begin the job of cleaning up. 'Lion…' Muhammed pointed in the direction of the door. Gaining Nightingale's full attention by clinging onto her leg with both hands, he looked up at her, eyes wide, and told her, 'There is a lion outside.'

'Are you sure?' Nightingale knew Muhammed fairly well. He was a local man, and a taxi driver. He was neither stupid nor clumsy, so she turned to the bar. 'Ben,' she called. 'Muhammed says there is a lion outside. Will you check?' And when no less than four customers all got up from their seats to make for the door, Nightingale used her empty tray to bang it on the side of the fallen table. 'STOP!' she yelled at the top of her voice. 'No one is going anywhere! Sit down and shut up.' When a man decided he knew better, she called after him. 'If you open that door and step outside, I will lock you out. Lions have escaped from the park today. They hunt at night. They eat idiots like you for supper.'

The man turned to see the feisty barmaid, his hand on the door. He looked through the glass panel at the view beyond, but it was dark, and he could see more of the bar behind him than the car park. Other voices were shouting at him by then, others backing up what the barmaid said about lions on the loose. Then he could see that a large man had come up behind him. He turned to see this man, his hand already dropping away from the door handle as he thought better of taking on the brick shithouse.

'Step away from the door,' Ben told him firmly. 'I am a licensed ranger, and I am in charge here. Sit down.'

By then Kylie had been silenced and Wendell was helping Muhammed to his feet. Nightingale fetched a few bar towels and gave them to the beer and nachos couple to clean themselves up a bit, and then she and her colleagues started getting the rubber necked customers away from the door area.

'Did you seriously see a lion outside?' Wendell asked Muhammed quietly.

'Oh yes,' he said, hands visibly shaking. 'I pulled in after dropping off a fare at the hotel opposite. I was hoping to pick up another from here, but I got out of my cab to smoke a cigarette while waiting. I was just standing there minding my own business when she walked out from the side of the building. She was only a few meters away from me, and she just walked by, looking at me… looking right at me…'

'Where did she go?'

Muhammed pointed in the general direction of the street.

Ben was on the outside of the door by then, keeping his back against it, as he peered into the poorly lit parking area. He couldn't see much, but enough to see the place was mostly empty. Most of the customers were tourists so, especially at night, the car park wasn't used much. He could see Muhammed's cab parked next to Red Earth Tours Land Rover and, at the other end, a couple of small cars, one of which he knew belonged to Nightingale. He went to the cab first, careful to keep his back against the wall. Before approaching the cab, he got low to the ground so he could peer underneath. No sign of any lions. Getting up onto his feet again, he began to approach the Land Rover, feeling in his pocket for the keys. Just as he was realising that he didn't have those keys, he heard the bar door open.

'Mate…' Wendell whispered loudly. 'Keys.'

Ben caught the tossed keys. 'Thank you.' Wendell then ducked back inside, and Ben continued moving towards the Land Rover. After a quick perimeter check, he got inside, unlocked the metal box on the floor between the front seats and removed his side arm. He checked it was loaded but kept the safety on. He removed the holster, put it on and put the gun into it. He then pocketed a box of spare bullets and his ranger ID. As he got back out of the Land Rover, he took the radio from its holder and retreated back to the wall next to the door into the bar. Back firmly against the wall, eyes sharp, he then switched to the frequency he knew his father could be contacted on, and he called in the possible sighting.

While his sighting was accepted as possible indeed, it was nevertheless met with incredulous indignation from the other end. Not again! Not another one! What the hell was going on?

It was while Ben was sympathising with the difficult situation they had all found themselves in, that a cry was heard farther up the street. That cry was followed by a scream, and then more screams and the sounds of general panic.

'I think our escapee just tried to check in at the hotel,' Ben told his contact. 'I'll investigate and report back.'

*

By then Jude had pulled herself together. She got herself up and, without looking down at her mess, quickly went back upstairs to retrieve both gloves and box. She wouldn't be needing the towel after all, so left it on her bed. Back inside the boot room she pulled on wellies and a hooded coat, making sure the hood was up, before she scooped up whatever was left of Gus, trying her best to keep it all contained inside the jacket. It was wet and hot and mushy. Bits of congealed fur left behind on the floor, blood dripping. The smell was hellish. Jude gagged several times, but persevered and got the whole stinking jacket contained mess into the box.

Back at the feline graveside, she moved the rocks and slid the folded table aside before dumping the contents of the box unceremoniously into the grave. She used her hands then to dump enough dirt from the pile to cover it. Before returning to the boot room, she replaced the table as well as the rocks. Back inside she set the box on the floor by the gore and dumped the gloves into it. She then removed both wellies as well as coat, and fetched rubber gloves, a mop, disinfectant, a roll of kitchen towel and a mop bucket filled with boiling water.

Back in the boot room she cleaned up as much of the gore as possible, using the paper towels which she dumped into the box. That done, she took the box back outside to leave it in the shed. She would burn it all tomorrow. She then went back to the boot room and cleaned the floor thoroughly. With a fresh wad of kitchen towel, she then checked every inch of skirting, walls and fittings in there, cleaning up every last trace of fat cat Augusto.

Only when she was satisfied there was no tell-tale reminders of her latest homicidal act, did Jude take herself upstairs to bathe and clean her wounds.

CHAPTER TWENTY-THREE

Jos woke bright and early on Saturday morning.

She felt fantastic. The best she'd felt since arriving in the sense she felt both rested as well as comfortable in her skin, stretching like a cat before getting up. She didn't go for a shower after using the toilet, instead she dressed in loose cotton shorts and a vest and took her yoga mat out into the garden. It was cool and shaded close to the garden room and perfect for a twenty-minute yoga routine.

Before going back inside, she turned on the tap to refresh the garden, and then went for a long cool shower. Wearing a short summer dress and her flip flops she then went down the outside steps to the patio, her long hair wet and loose to dry in the warm breeze. In the kitchen she had just got the kettle and the toast going when Beola arrived. 'Good morning,' Jos grinned.

'You look rested.'

'I am. How is Kissi? Have they found the lioness?'

Shaking her head, Beola said, 'There must be more than one lioness out there.' She then nodded to Jos' silent offer of coffee and filled her in regarding the second sighting reported in the opposite direction the previous evening. 'And then, last night, a third sighting outside the bar Nightingale works in.' She then told Jos that story as relayed to her late last night by her son. 'She ended up in the grounds of the hotel opposite! There was panic.

People running around, screaming. I almost feel sorry for the poor lioness.' So did Jos. Hopefully, she asked, 'Did they catch that one?'

'She vanished. There are a lot of plants and bushes all around the hotel grounds, but there is also a wall. Maybe she jumped over and got away like that, but Ben said she disappeared in front of his eyes.' 'Like a ghost,' Jos mused, distractedly.

*

In Kilimanjaro National Park, at the ranger's station, an emergency meeting was taking place.

Six men were in attendance, five heads of teams, and a sixth, who was chief ranger of the region. His name was Julius Chokala, and he was as tired and confused as his men. 'Three sightings in the past seventeen hours and not a single trace found,' he spoke, looking up at the map of the region which was on the wall and marked with the location of each sighting. 'Either we have three lions on the loose or one very fast animal.'

'I'd like to take my team into the park and count heads,' Kissi Nyerere spoke from the back. 'We need to know how many animals are out there. My son told me not ten minutes ago that Kilimanjaro News have set up an outside broadcasting team in the Sunandah Hotel car park.'

'That is all we need.' Julius Chokala clamped a hand to his forehead, then rubbed it back and forth across his bald head. After a few minutes watching his distinguished career drop off the edge of a cliff, he sighed and started giving orders.

Nyerere's team were sent to find the three prides living in the park and ascertain how many were missing. The next team were sent to check the perimeter fencing to find out where they were getting out. The three remaining teams were sent back to square one, back to the place each lion was spotted and, now they had daylight, two of the best men from each team were to track and trace as fast and as discreetly as possible. The remaining men were to continue door to door enquiries and issue the usual public safety warnings. He would meet and greet the news team personally.

'Placate pacify and reassure,' Julius told himself. 'Hopefully, the mountain will wake up and erupt before I get there.' Anything to direct the spotlight away from him.

*

Ben and Wendell were on their way back to the white house after spending the night at Nightingale's.

After calling in the sighting at the bar, Ben had crossed the street to the Sunandah Hotel, which was set back from the road and surrounded by lavish gardens. He'd gone in there, gun drawn and cursing the fact he'd forgotten to also take a torch from the Land Rover. He tried not to think about the fact he was also wearing his flip flops. He hadn't fared well trying to chase Jos down in his flip flops at the airport, so how he was going to cope with a marauding lion was anyone's guess.

A handful of guests were running towards the street from the south side where the hotel pool was sited. He identified himself, directed those people to the Mountain View across the street, and tried to find a member of staff. Thankfully, the staff uniforms were brightly coloured, so he soon located the hospitality manager; a young woman who took the time to tell him that there was a lion in the poolside bar, before following the guests heading for Nightingale's bar.

As he passed the wide reception area, Ben saw more staff inside, blocking the closed doors to keep the gathered guests inside. Flashing his ID to the one wearing the badge that identified him as the duty manager, Ben spoke to him through the glass doors. 'Keep everyone inside. Are all entrances secured?'

'I don't know.'

'Then find out. Make sure every door and window on the ground floor is locked tight.' He paused long enough to know the duty manager was delegating this simple task, and then he continued on around to the side of the building.

The poolside bar was at the far end of the pool from where Ben rounded the corner. That end was fairly well lit, as was the pool itself, but the gardens bordering it on three sides were full of shadows as well as places to hide. Most of the sun loungers lined up around the pool were undisturbed, bar one that was floating in the water at the far end. And then he noticed a second being used as a shield by a young couple who were crouched low in the bushes close to where he stood. Moving closer, keeping his back to them, and his eyes sharp, Ben asked, 'Where is she now?'

'At the bar,' a woman's voice told him.

'Cocktails are on promo,' a man added, laughing nervously. 'Maybe she wants a mai tai?'

'Shut up, Stewart,' the woman admonished in a vicious sounding whisper.

Stewart tutted.

Ben considered asking them to move around front and go across the street, but they started a whispered argument, so he decided they were probably safer where they were for the time being. He spotted the lioness in front of the bar, partially hidden by all the furniture between it and the pool. She was wandering slowly among the tables and chairs, her nose sniffing at the abandoned drinks and bags and other things left behind by the fleeing guests. She looked calm and curious, not at all like she was stalking anything or anyone.

A bit like Gloria Juma earlier that same evening, Ben didn't really know what to do.

He was well trained and well versed with procedures surrounding the containment of escaped animals, but not when that animal is at a poolside bar. Not to mention the fact he was alone. He was still standing considering his options when he heard a new sound.

'PSSSSSSSSST.'

It was coming from another bush a bit farther down the pool and closer to the bar. Ben went to investigate, moving slow and quiet. But the lioness saw him, tilting her head as she watched him. He stopped, and waited until she lost interest, before looking again for whoever was trying to get his attention.

'Why don't you just fucking shoot her?' asked Mr. Psssssssst from inside his bush.

'Why don't you just stay quiet and calm and let me deal with this,' Ben suggested to the bald, bespectacled man peering out at him from a clump of oleander.

White people were really easy to spot in even the darkest corners.

'Hey, cobber… what's the John Dory?'

Ben turned round to see Wendell had managed to sneak up on him in his own flip flops, and the sight made him burst out laughing. The noise of which he tried his best to stifle with his free hand.

Wendell had watched his friend disappear into the grounds of the hotel, and then helped Nightingale and the other bar staff to get the fleeing guests inside and quieted down. Then he began to realise he couldn't just leave his friend with his arse in the breeze, and so he told Nightingale to call the incident in to the rangers, the police, anyone who might come and lend a hand, and then headed for the door. But Nightingale asked him to wait, then disappeared into the office behind the bar. She was gone for several minutes and returned with a couple of useful items. So, Wendell had arrived poolside with a rusty old spear in one hand, and a flat metal, circular dustbin lid in the other.

Ben was still laughing.

Wendell started grinning, posing with his new battle gear.

'I'm glad you two are finding this funny,' said baldy in the bushes. 'My wife and I…'

'Strewth…' Wendell peered into the bush. 'Are there more of you holed up in there?'

'No. My wife had gone to the ladies when…'

'We're here too.'

Ben moved a few feet farther down and saw three faces peering out from behind a piled-up devil's tongue cactus plant. One was a child. 'It's okay,' he spoke to the child who looked terrified. 'The rangers are on their way, and we will stay right here with you until they get here.' The child nodded his head up and down, rapidly.

Meanwhile the lioness was still browsing among the tables. As Wendell watched, she stuck her snout into an abandoned handbag that lay open in the ground, sniffing the contents for a time before moving on a little. She then sat down and began to lick her forepaw so she could clean her face. She appeared to be absolutely harmless. Of course, lions were like that… until they were hungry, or threatened. 'What's the plan?' he asked Ben.

'Containment.' Ben nodded towards the end of the pool at their side. 'That side is fenced off.' A high fence, not just to stop the guests wandering around behind the hotel, but to stop their eyes being offended by garbage bins, or smoking staff, or laundry, or deliveries. 'The rest of the area is walled off…' A six feet high, stone wall enclosed the gardens surrounding the pool. 'Her only way out is down this end, so we keep her up that end.'

'What if she doesn't want to stay up that end?'

'Then, my friend… we shall dissuade her.'

Wendell nodded, looking impressed. Then he said, 'Buckley's, mate.' 'Let's just watch and wait,' Ben said.

Just then, a few floors up above, a window opened, and a head came out, calling out, 'Why is it so quiet? Is the bar still open? Where is everyone?'

'Bloody drongo,' Wendell muttered, looking up.

Most of the guests hiding in the bushes also looked up.

Ben didn't.

Neither did the little boy.

Both of them hadn't taken their eyes from the lioness, and they saw her glance upward towards the voice for a second, before turning tail, trotting towards the wall and then springing up, arching through the air towards it as if she would clear it completely. But she didn't. She just disappeared.

Now you see her, now you don't.

The little boy stood up, smiling. 'Cool,' he declared, immediately before being dragged down again by his mother.

Ben was standing staring at the place she winked out of sight, mouth hanging open, unable to speak or even move. 'She…' he said softly.

'What's up?' Wendell wondered, looking around for the lion. 'Where'd she go?'

'She disappeared,' Ben told his friend, still staring at the place he'd last seen her.

'Like magic,' the little boy said.

His parents were busy telling him off, telling him to stop talking nonsense.

'But…' The little boy, looked imploringly up at the nice man with the gun. 'We saw her.'

'She can't just have disappeared,' Dad told his son. 'She must have got over the wall. Is it safe now?' he asked, looking between the Australian and the African. 'Can we go? My son needs the toilet… so do I as it happens, and I'd really rather just go to bed. We've had enough excitement for one day.'

The police arrived then, closely followed by a small team of rangers, all of whom Ben knew well. After briefing them… leaving out the part where the lioness disappeared mid-air, he and Wendell handed the responsibility over and headed back across to the bar.

They'd followed Nightingale home a little later, to ensure she got there safely, and she'd invited them in for a night cap. Nightingale lived with her parents, who were both still up after hearing about all the commotion in town. They welcomed Ben and Wendell with beer and then tea. Then insisted they spend the night in the little one room cabin in their garden which they rented out to tourists now and then to supplement their income.

Single beds and not much sleep, especially for Ben who was still trying to come to terms with his disappearing lioness.

The following morning, on the way back through town, Wendell and Ben passed by the hotel and saw the TV station van parked close to the entrance. There was camera, sound and a glamourous looking reporter, all surrounded by various groups of guests eager to be interviewed about last night's excitement. They were on their way back to the white house to shower and change before driving back into town again, to collect a gaggle of six young women who were due to visit Materuni Falls & Coffee Plantation. They had less than three hours to get there, but luckily Materuni Village was only fifteen kilometres north of Moshi.

'She didn't disappear into the undergrowth,' Ben told his friend for the tenth time. 'She just disappeared in front of my eyes.'

'Maybe she ducked down to repair the irrigation system?'

'You are never going to let me forget that, are you?' 'Nope.' Wendell shook his head slowly.

*

At the white house Ben went to the lodge to shower and change.

Wendell dug out the change of clothes he always kept inside the storage box under the rear seats, then went into the main house. 'Beola?' he called. 'Is anyone home?'

'In the kitchen.' Beola called back and when Wendell walked in, she asked, 'Is Ben with you?'

'He went to the lodge to shower and change. Is it okay if I have a shower?'

'Wendell!' Jos walked in from the patio and offered her cheek for pecking. Laughing, she then asked, 'Where are you off to today?'

'Materuni Falls… village tour, short hike through the rain forest, eighty-foot waterfall and swimming in the pool below.

Lunch and then a spot of coffee picking, grinding, roasting and drinking.' 'Sounds amazing!' Jos said.

'We have spare seats.'

Jos was grinning from ear to ear, and then she turned that grin on Beola.

'Maybe we could both…'

Beola didn't look sure.

'I'm not swanning off again and leaving you here alone all day worrying about Kissi. If you're not going, I'm not going.'

'Well…' Beola was thinking it would do Jos a lot of good to get away from the white house as well as Peter's sphere of influence. '… if you are putting it like that.'

'Pack your cozzies,' Wendell advised, and then laughed as Jos ran off shrieking with excitement, presumably to pack her cozzie. Then he turned to Beola, 'How are you holding up?'

'Kissi has been out hunting down wild animals since before we met. I am sure he will be fine.'

'I mean about the other stuff. The Jos stuff.' Beola looked a bit put out.

'No worries, Beola,' Wendell assured her. 'Ben confided. He of course swore me to secrecy, but I reckon you're slap bang in the middle anyway. Besides… I can't keep secrets from you.'

'You are a good boy.'

'And I am also here if you need anything.' Wendell kissed her cheek, then took himself off to shower and change.

*

Jude got up just before six a.m.

She'd had a dreadful night, because some of the worst scratches sustained during her battle with fat cat Gus were painful, the welts swollen and ugly looking. She had to get up repeatedly during the night to apply aloe gel to cool and soothe. By the time she limped downstairs on her swollen ankle, Jude knew she wouldn't be crushing up any more antihistamine tablets.

She had a new plan.

Having an extensive vegetable garden necessitated extensive storage and preservation facilities too. There was the American style fridge freezer in the main kitchen, the chest freezer in the small servant's kitchen and a second chest freezer inside the utility room. The latter freezer was mostly empty at the time because it was only ever used properly when there was a bumper harvest and this year conditions weather-wise had been pretty poor and so the yield of tomatoes, courgettes etcetera was poor. Inside Jude found a few boxes of various soups and a few part baked potatoes. She relocated all of that into the other chest freezer and turned the dial on the now empty freezer all the way to minus thirty degrees.

She then went into the main kitchen and put the kettle on.

*

Materuni Village was a centre for cultural tourism, run by the Chagga people who lived there.

At 1800 meters above sea level every wooden house was balanced precariously on the south eastern flanks of the mountain and surrounded by the lush greens of the forest. David, their guide, told the all-female group about the home gardens and the cropping system, which was both ecological as well as successful in the socio-economic sense of farming. He described their methods as creating a diverse and multi-storeyed agro-forest of plenty.

The canopy of palms above were newtonia buchananii; planted to provide shade for the coffee. Its leaves fed livestock, and trunks were perfect for making charcoal. The smaller macaranga kilimandscharica with its heart shaped leaves, was used primarily for wood; construction, making furniture, crates and even beehives. They also grew passion fruit, sweet potato, sugar cane, taro and beans. The village women earned money selling any excess bananas, milk and vegetables at the local markets, while the men sold the coffee, eggs and poultry. There would be a homecooked and organic lunch served after the waterfall visit so they could all taste a traditional Chagga recipe; goat and banana stew.

The waterfall was a forty-minute hike from the village.

The views were stunning when the forest allowed, the landscape rolling out beneath them and on into the distance, where the emerald, green horizon met the deep blue sky. Jos took loads of photos, even getting Beola to pose for a few, and take some of her. They heard the waterfall a while before they saw it. Thousands of gallons of water per second, jumping from the river bed eighty feet above to tumble down the cliff and into the pool below. It was narrow at the top, fanning out as it fell. A grey, white plummet similar to the Grey Mare's Tail near Moffat in Scotland… except for the lush foliage. And the sun. And the heat.

Beola was happy just to sit on one of the big flat slabs of rock surrounding the pool with her lower legs in the cool water. Jos, on the other hand, was first in. The water was only really deep enough to swim in closest to the falls, but the cold was invigorating and wonderful. After spending a few minutes splashing around with the six Spanish girls who made up the rest of their party, Jos got out and joined Beola on her rock. 'That was fab!' she said. 'Cold, but great.' Lying back so the sun could warm her cold skin. 'This is my first ever visit here,' Beola told her. 'So beautiful.'

'I live in Edinburgh,' Jos said. 'A real tourist magnet and I can count

on one hand the touristy places that I've visited there.'

'Are you all right, Jos?'

'Better than I've ever been.'

'You seem to be spending a lot of time with Peter.'

'A means to an end.' Rolling onto her side, Jos propped her head up and leaned on an elbow. 'I know you're worried about what he's doing to me. But I'm not. I like it.'

'You're even beginning to sound like him.'

'Is me sounding like Peter such a bad thing?'

'Peter was a powerful man; Jos. Oh he was sweet and funny and charming too… but he was also used to getting what he wanted. Right now, he wants you to…'

When she stopped, Jos asked, 'What, Beola? What does he want?'

'I don't know,' Beola frowned. 'I don't know anything for sure. I just think he wants you to… to…'

'You think he wants me to avenge him.'

'Don't you?' Beola wondered, looking at Jos intently, her voice quiet but passionate. 'Would you?'

'For the first time in my adult life I'm free, Beola.' Jos stretched out her bent arm and turned onto her back. 'I won't be risking that.'

The sun was hot, but it felt good. Jos hadn't factor fiftied in days, but Wendell was right, she was beginning to turn a golden brown. Usually, she had to be very careful in the sun, the tiniest bit of over-exposure would see her turn from a lobster into the singing detective overnight; her reddened skin sloughing off in great big flakes. Not anymore.

Even her skin was changing.

*

Elena Ceausescu died in the same hail of bullets as her husband, but little Elena cat had a far more chilling fate in store.

Fetching one of several cat carriers kept in the under-stair's cupboard, Jude then fetched Elena off the sofa and put her inside it. Elena didn't mind. She was always an easy-going little cat, always good during trips to the vet, always affectionate. She simply curled up on the little fleece blanket lining the base of the plastic box and purred away as Jude carried her through to the utility room, opened the chest freezer and placed the carrier containing the unsuspecting Elena in the bottom.

Jude then closed the freezer and left the room, closing the door behind her.

It was nine forty-five a.m.

*

Back at the village by then, and Beola had been a little distant since their chat.

Jos made a concentrated effort to just be herself. It wasn't difficult. A matter of closing the doors on the high rise, ignoring any stragglers, and suppressing her own curiosity where Peter's life was concerned. It wasn't forever, just until Beola got over her envy.

Confused again as to why Beola was so obviously pissed off with her, Jos had done some inner investigations. Once she stumbled upon the abrupt ending to the little tete a tete between

Beola and Peter the night before, it was a hop step and jump to the answers. There had been an ongoing flirtation between those two for years before Peter died. That was what came between Beola and Jude in the end. Jude knew that Beola had the hots for her husband. No wonder she was eaten up with rage to that day; her husband left the house he built for her to another woman. As for Beola, Jos also knew she'd been shagging Kissi to within an inch of his life recently, because her connection to Peter made her horny as hell. Now that connection belonged to Jos, and Beola hated that.

Tough.

Homemade fruit juice and little fried patties were first on the menu, followed by the promised goat and banana stew, served with rice. It was indeed a lot nicer than it sounded, spicy fruity and delicious. Clean bowls all round. Then it was time to make coffee.

Red berries were put through a hand turned grinder to remove the skins. These lighter beans dropped into a bath of clean water and would be left to soak for three days before being air dried… for up to eight weeks!

'Not to worry…' David grinned. 'We have some dried beans for you.'

Two women arrived with a gigantic, wooden pestle and a mortar as tall as Jos. They all then took turns grinding the husks away from the precious beans while the women, David, a second much older man, and two young boys, sang songs and clapped hands to motivate the grinding process. Beola seemed much more relaxed by then, smiling and laughing, joining in.

The ground coffee was then tipped into a bowl of woven banana leaf. One of the women showed how to spin and flip the beans to get rid of the powdered husks. Two of the Spanish girls had a go, and one was declared to be a natural. The beans were then tipped into a small cauldron-like-pot and placed on top of a trio of stones with a smouldering little fire in the centre. Mum wafted her banana leaf sieve at the fire, and it soon flamed into life.

While the beans were roasting, the four generations of David's family sang songs back and forth as the air began to fill with the familiar coffee aroma. The roasted beans were then returned to the banana leaf bowl to be tossed and sifted again, with another song to help this process along. After that, the shiny dark brown, split beans went back into the mortar for the final grinding, until they became that amazing dark brown powder so familiar to coffee lovers all over the planet. Water was boiled, the powdered coffee went in, and another song helped stir it. The coffee was then decanted into a big yellow jug and shared out among the group. It was the best coffee Jos had ever tasted.

An opinion shared all.

Before they took their leave, Ben and Wendell collected tips for the village, and those were given generously, in keeping with the spirit of the people who had welcomed and entertained as well as educated and fed them all. 'Thank you so much, muchas gracias,' said the Spanish girls, shaking hands all round.

As soon as they got down off the mountain one of the Spanish girls got a phone call. Earlier she'd revealed that her brother worked nearby. She was in Tanzania to visit him, her friends along for the ride. She soon started getting all animated about something.

Wendell, who'd spent over a year living and working in Madrid understood that she was talking with her brother then, and relaying news of yet another sighting. 'Another lioness sighting,' he told Ben.

'Where?' Ben asked.

'Donde estaba el leon?' Wendell asked.

'En un lugar llamado… Marangu… mi hermano es medico en el

hospital alli. Creo que dijo que el leon estaba en una calle del mercado.' Beola was already calling her husband.

'I've been trying to get you,' Kissi told her as soon as he answered. 'Farther east in Marangu this time.'

'I know…' Beola explained where she was and how she'd found out.

'It is also all over the TV and the radio,' Kissi said. 'It was at midday. She just wandered along Market Road in broad daylight, without a care in the world. Dozens of people saw her. It doesn't make any sense. Once again, miles from the last sighting. It's as if we have lots of lions wandering around out there, but there is only one missing. We checked in with all three prides this morning and just one female is missing… from the Mandara pride.'

'Does she…'

'No.'

The implications unsettled Beola. 'What is going on, Kissiri?'

'I will be home tonight. We can talk then.'

Saying her goodbyes, Beola then updated the front of the Land Rover, without mentioning the name of the pride the missing lioness belonged to, or her distinguishing feature. The Maasai say that there is no point gathering fruit when a dance is taking place and, in Beola's mind, she believed firmly that past as well as present were gathering around the white house for just such a dance.

CHAPTER TWENTY-FOUR

Jude returned to the utility room.

Over two hours had passed since she'd left Elena in the freezer, so Jude was confident the cat would be dead when she lifted the lid, but she wasn't about to take anything for granted, so she did that slowly and carefully. Half expecting the little cat to come flying up at her, all claws and teeth.

But the freezer was as quiet as it was cold and, when she lifted the carrier back out… using a dish towel to protect her hand from the severely chilled handle, she saw that little Elena looked almost peaceful. She had obviously tried to escape from the carrier, because the little rug was bunched up at the back, but the cat had perhaps slipped into a hypothermic sleep eventually, and looking at her, her fur sparkling with frost crystals, Jude wondered why she hadn't thought of this in the first place.

'Five down and just two to go,' she said to herself, transporting the cat to the graveside, still inside the carrier.

Flies were buzzing around inside the grave, no doubt attracted by the mess fat cat Gus became inside the jacket. But, apart from that, things looked undisturbed. Getting Elena out the carrier was a lot harder than getting her into it, because a solidly frozen cat is not at all a flexible thing. In the end, Jude was forced to break the carrier apart using a spade in order to get the cat out. That done, she put Elena in with the rest, covered her over with soil, added two flowers, and then covered everything over again with the folded table and the rocks.

Jude then stashed the broken carrier inside the shed, collected the box containing the bloody mess of kitchen towels as well as her blood-stained gardening gloves, and took it all across to the other side of the garden where she had a compact brazier for burning the garden rubbish.

It was drizzling a little but, before Jude lit the fire, she went back inside and upstairs to check through the back bedroom windows that none of the neighbours had hung any washing out. It wouldn't do at this stage to have an irate neighbour on the doorstep. Satisfied there was nothing and no one, she returned to the garden with a bottle of lighter fluid, doused the box and contents and tossed in a lit match.

There was a satisfying WHOOMP, rather like the WHOOMP when the petrol in the jeep went up and engulfed Peter. However, this little fire burned down quickly. Without all that human fat to sustain it, it was gone in a matter of minutes.

*

Back inside Joseph was wandering from room to room mewling. Looking for his little friends no doubt. Jude eyed him, wondering if she should just plonk him into the freezer there and then. But Joe wasn't a fan of the cat carrier, and she had enough scratches to tend to thanks to fat cat Gus.

She went back up to her bedroom first. Dressed again in jeans and long sleeves, two layers. Back in the kitchen, she forked the remaining tuna into one of the cat dishes before going into the boot room to pull on first leather gloves and then put on a pair of woollen ones on top. Finally, she wrapped a scarf around her neck. If she'd had a motorbike helmet or a hockey mask Jude would have put that on too, but she didn't. Instead, she returned to the kitchen and called for Joseph, shaking the plastic tub of dry kibbles for good measure.

There hadn't been any food that morning, so Joseph was hungry and came out from under the missing human's bed where he'd been snuggling with Imelda since finding her there hours before. He didn't know where their other friends were and, although he waited a few moments expecting Imelda to also follow the sound of food, he was alone when he went downstairs. He smelled the fish before he found it in the usual place, bypassed the other human without a thought, and tucked in, purring contentedly.

Jude had been waiting in the kitchen, using her body to conceal the white metal cage style carrier. This one could be collapsed flat for storage, so its entire top was also the lid. Much easier to get a protesting cat down into it… and a frozen one up and out of it. Without delay, she simply entered the utility room as soon as Joe was eating, closed the door, set the open carrier on the floor next to him and, with just a hint of a struggle, managed to scoop him up and get him inside it with only a little fuss.

From there it was just three steps to the empty chest freezer.

Jude had intended preparing dinner after that, but even with the door closed, she could hear Joe yowling inside the freezer, and so she replaced gloves and scarf in the boot room and then went back upstairs. She undressed again and had a nice lavender bath instead.

When Jude came back down to the kitchen half an hour later everything was peaceful.

*

Kissi arrived home around four p.m.

He felt as tired as he looked, having managed to catch just a few minutes nap at a time, as his team were moving around the park tracking the three different prides living there. There were no radio collars or other fancy tracking devices in use because there were no funds available to supply these things. Instead, rangers like him had to do a lot of the tracking on foot, looking for imprints in the earth, disturbed grasses, patches of urine and faeces. He also sniffed the air just like the beasts themselves. Kissi knew lion scent as well as he knew the smell of his wife. The metallic scent of a fresh kill was unmistakable. After forty years in the job, he was an expert tracker.

The last three decades of his career he'd spent in and around Mount Kilimanjaro National Park. He knew every member of the extensive ranger service operating twenty-four seven, he knew every hiking guide, every porter, every cook working the numerous routes up and down the mountain. He knew the trees, the plants and the animals. He knew every path. Kissi even knew the rocks; the ones that were comfortable to sit on, the ones that offered the best views. Armed with binoculars, their senses and one another, he and his men had tracked down every lion in the park… except for a single six-year-old female, conspicuous in her absence as well as her complete lack of any tail end tuft.

Kissi had been home less than an hour when Ben and Wendell came rushing into the kitchen with the latest news bulletin.

'A lioness was seen on the golf course!' Ben said.

'Eighteenth hole,' Wendell added. 'Three players were so busy yacking they almost tripped over her lying on the green.'

'It's on the news,' Ben said. He and Wendell were curious after seeing the TV station van outside the hotel, and so they'd tuned in to the news channel to find out what was being said. 'Reporters are there now but it was just after four apparently.'

'Your boss is there,' Wendell added, thumbing back over his shoulder in the general direction of the small sitting room which was home to the one and only TV in the white house. 'Looking extremely uncomfortable.'

Within the next few minutes everyone in the white house was either seated on the sofa set before the TV, or standing behind it, all watching the report being broadcast live from not only the golf course and club house, but from every place the lions had been spotted in the previous twenty-six hours.

Gabe Sanders was back at Mweka Gate being interviewed in the same car park where he'd spotted the lioness that had sparked the excitement. No, he hadn't felt afraid for his life. He'd called out the warning on instinct. The lioness hadn't acted aggressively at all… sure, she'd roared a bit, but then she'd simply turned tail and bounded off into the undergrowth.

Gloria Juma was standing on the road close to the school gates where she'd seen her lioness last evening. She was posing with her bike although the TV van had transported it up there for her, and she'd driven up in her little car to meet them there. Of course, she'd been terrified! A dark road on a dark night… a woman alone… she'd ran for her life! God be praised that she was still alive to tell about it.

A small group of hotel guests were gathered together around Muhamed Asraf outside the Sunandah Hotel. He'd been smoking a cigarette in the car park outside the bar opposite and had been lucky to get into the bar before being attacked! Lucky too that an ex-ranger was inside that bar and able to cross the street and rescue the hotel guests when the lioness went there too. 'She was at the pool bar,' one guest added.

'We were having cocktails…' said another. '… and next thing we knew a lion was coming at us from the bushes. We were terrified. We ran for our lives.'

‘We hid in the bushes…’ a little boy revealed, his eyes shining. ‘Then the nice men came, and we all saw the lion disappear.’ ‘Disappear?’ wondered the reporter.

‘Oh, don’t pay him any heed…’ advised the boy’s mother. ‘… it was way past his bedtime.’

‘But Mum…’ the little boy protested vehemently. ‘… I saw her jump into the air, and she disappeared. It was like magic.’

Magic for some maybe, according to the reporter, but a very real threat

to life for others.

Another gathering was being interviewed outside Marangu Post Office after spotting a lioness strolling down the road there earlier that same day. One had not been able to believe her eyes! Another had to run out onto the street to scoop up his child and then get his little daughter inside the safety of the butcher’s shop on the corner. A nurse on her way to begin her shift at the local hospital had hurt herself when she jumped over a wall to escape certain death.

Cut back to the Golf Course and the reporter there wanted the very uncomfortable Julius Chokala to explain to the viewers what the Ranger Service were doing, and why so many dangerous predators had been allowed to escape the park.

‘My men have been into the park this morning…’ the chief explained for the second time since arriving at the golf club. He looked as under as much pressure as he felt bearing down upon him. ‘…and I can assure the public that only one animal is missing.’

‘Surely you don’t expect our viewers to believe that just one animal is roving around the countryside… popping up here there and everywhere, and disappearing completely between sightings?’ The reporter looked affronted that this man believed her viewers could possibly be so stupid. ‘Even a humble reporter such as I, knows that lions cannot run that fast!’

‘Perhaps the lions have come from elsewhere? A private individual perhaps…?’

‘What?’ she asked. ‘Who?’ she demanded. ‘Who is this person?’

‘I just mean that if… if there are more lions at large, then they have not come from the park. My men…’

‘What exactly are your men doing to protect the public?’

‘Everything in their power!’ Julius had had enough by then, and he grabbed the mic from the reporter’s hand and spoke directly into the camera. ‘Myself and my men are doing everything we can to protect the good people of this region.’ She was naturally trying to get the mic back, but the camera was still pointed at his face, and he was holding onto that mic with all his might. ‘Please do not panic. Stay…’ He had to jostle a little to keep holding onto that mic when she tried another tack. ‘Stay at home!’ He spoke quickly. ‘Stay indoors! If you see an animal…’ He stopped to tell her. ‘Please madam, let me speak.’ To the camera he added, ‘Call us… call the ranger…’

‘Give me that!’ The reporter hit the chief ranger with her clip board and, once she had her mic back, she hit him with that too. ‘That’s quite enough from you, you incompetent…’

Kissi could not believe what he was seeing, and stood gawping at the little screen, his mouth hanging open to catch some of the flies Jos was also after with her wide-open mouth which was then laughing heartily. Beola didn’t know whether to laugh with Jos or cringe with her husband. Ben pressed his lips tightly together.

‘Will you apply for the chief’s job when it comes up?’ Wendell wondered, watching the reporter and the chief slapping at each other with three flapping hands and one microphone. ‘Reckon that could be any minute now.’

‘What is happening?’ Kissi asked the ceiling and then, standing up, added, ‘Our small part of the world has gone crazy, and I need to sleep.’

Jos watched Beola follow her husband, and then she asked Ben, ‘Is your dad all right?’

‘He’ll be fine,’ Ben assured. ‘He’s been awake more than thirty hours so a sleep will do him the world of good. He’s not the only one…’ He yawned as if to prove a point and then he and Wendell made arrangements for the following day, when they were taking a group to Lake Chala. ‘See you at seven then.’

‘Hoo roo.’ Wendell shot Jos a wink and a smile, and then left the building via the French doors and the porch.

*

Having not explored the white house at all since arriving, Jos decided to do that now.

Leaving the TV room, she crossed the hall and entered the room directly opposite. Board games on shelves, playing cards, chess sets, backgammon. There was an antique marquetry card table by the French doors out onto the patio, open to reveal the green baize playing surface. There was a full-size roulette table complete with wheel, chips and dice.

Next to that a semi-circular black jack table.

'This has to be the games room.' Jos spun the roulette wheel.

However, one end wall was fitted floor to ceiling with pigeon hole shelving, each section stuffed full of black vinyl albums in their colourful sleeves. Fleetwood Mac, The Kinks, The Stones, Pink Floyd, The Mamas and Papas, America, Slade, 10cc, Nina Simone, Janis Joplin, The Small Faces, T-Rex, David Bowie, Roxy Music, Barry White, The Jacksons, The Doors.

The old fashioned, top of the range once upon a time, Bang and Olufsen stereo cabinet stood quietly by. It had a cassette player as well as radio. Headphones. Gigantic speakers. Jos saw the plug lying on the floor below the socket, so she plugged it in. As she did so she knew that Beola had unplugged it not so long ago to stop Peter playing music in the middle of the night. And no wonder because the volume was almost all the way up. Adjusting that first, she opened the lid and saw LA Woman on the turn table. She then had to fanny around for a bit trying to get it to work. But she got there in the end and, once The Changeling was playing, she sat down at the card table and asked, 'What's happening, Peter?'

There was no pause, no lethargy, no hiatus within the surrounding nature to make space for the man who had no right to be there. Had Gaia given in? Or had she simply passed the responsibility on to Jos by then? Peter appeared seated on the chair opposite her, as if they were about to play a card game.

Jos wondered how high the stakes were becoming.

'Did you have a nice day out?' Peter wondered, with attentive politeness.

‘I did. I helped to make some really delicious coffee. I also swam in a freezing cold pool at the foot of a massive waterfall. What did you do?’

‘Oh, you know…’ Passing his hand across a stacked set of cards, Peter watched them fan out before adding, ‘… hung around the white house.’

Jos barely noticed. ‘Beola reckons you’re trying to manipulate me into offing Jude.’

Raising his eye brows, Peter asked, ‘Perhaps as a last resort?’

‘Nope,’ Jos told him. ‘Besides… if I’m in jail how can I manage all those projects you love?’

‘A man can dream, can’t he?’

‘No doubt,’ Jos agreed. ‘But you’re looking at manhood in the rearview mirror.’

Peter threw his head back and laughed, delighted.

‘So, what is the plan?’

‘I am awaiting a sign from our old friend.’

‘Doesn’t anyone stay dead around here?’

‘Are you tired?’

‘Not particularly,’ Jos realised. ‘I feel quite lively and, typically, everyone else is too tired to play.’

‘Fancy a drive?’

CHAPTER TWENTY-FIVE

A little over an hour later, they drove through the gates of The Rhonda Rehabilitation Centre.

It was dark by then, but easy to see that nothing much had changed to the layout of the main compound since the photograph Beola had shown Jos just five days ago, had been taken. The arched legend was still over the gates. The flower beds either side were simply more mature, the buildings hadn't moved. It was just another journey back in time to a place from Peter's past.

As soon as the jeep came to a stop outside the clinic, Peter receded, and Jos got out and approached the group of young men and women seated on the clinic steps. They were all similarly dressed in khaki shorts or jeans, sturdy footwear and rehab centre T-shirts of various shades of green. One of them had a little furry brown creature perched on her shoulder. It joined the humans in looking up at Jos curiously.

'Can I help you?' A young woman in blue scrubs popped her head out from the clinic.

'I'm looking for Henk,' Jos told her.

'I am here,' said an accented voice from somewhere inside. A moment later Henk arrived at the door, drying his hands on a small white towel. He had collar length white hair and a neatly trimmed white beard. Slim and fit for his seventy odd years, and with a great smile. Bright eyes sparkled behind his glasses. 'Hello.' He smiled at the red head, and it was as if he was being kicked all the way back when Jude's hair was lighter, brighter. Diminutive Jude who would think nothing of popping into the rhino enclosure armed with nothing more formidable than a pointy stick. The resemblance was truly striking, but the young woman standing watching him intently right then was taller, darker. 'What can I do for you?'

'Can we talk somewhere private?' Jos wondered, fighting the surge of emotion inside her that was Peter's reaction to seeing his friend.

‘Of course.’ Henk set his towel aside, and descended the steps between the seated students, all waiting on the pickup truck to arrive to take them to the other side of the reserve where the new accommodation blocks and cafeteria were sited in a separate compound. It wasn’t too dangerous to walk there, even after dark, but there was always the possibility someone would stand on a snake, or trip over a rock, so the students were always transported between compounds. ‘This way.’ He bade the red head follow him next door to his office. Once she was inside, he asked, ‘How may I help you?’ He indicated that she should sit, but she didn’t, she stood there, with her back to the door and her face went through so many different expressions, Henk began to wonder if perhaps she was a little crazy.

‘Oh, for fuck’s sake!’ Jos exclaimed suddenly, her face a mask of irritation for a moment before she relented. Peter burst into her mind, and she was then propelled towards the old Dutchman, embracing him tightly, cheek to bearded cheek and telling him, ‘It’s so good to see you, Henk! Man… I have missed you!’

Henk was rooted to his spot, arms at his sides, contemplating calling for help. ‘I don’t…’

‘It’s me…’ Jos’ mouth told him, gripping both of Henk’s upper arms, shaking him. ‘It’s Peter! Peter Sinclair.’

Henk was pulled back in time once again… remembering his friend, the mystery, the laibon… before pinging back into the present. ‘It worked,’ he realised, sitting down in the chair the red head had refused. ‘Are you…’ he stopped, then started again, ‘Who are you?’

‘Me.’ Peter laughed, then realised what his friend meant. Indicating the woman’s body, he was wearing, he said, ‘But this is Jos… she’s my niece and she’s giving me a ride. Otherwise, I’m stuck in the white house. She made it, man. I made it. We finally came together and now she’s finding out the truth. I thought it would be fun to come visit you, so you know all your hard work back then was worth it. I won’t be around like this for long, you see. Now Jos is here I’ll have to move on finally… whatever that means. A great big expanse of nothing I imagine, but I made it this far with your help. Thank you, by the way. Maybe you can tell Jos what you did back then, Henk.’ It had all come out in a big rush.

'I…' Henk blinked. 'I…'

'Hang on…' Peter held up a stalling hand, receded and then Jos retracted that hand, smiling uncertainly at the Dutchman. 'Me again,' she said, half smiling, half grimacing. 'I'm Jos, Jos Ferguson, and I'm really sorry to descend on you unannounced, but Peter made me. He gets very excited and, right now, he wants to play.'

The difference was significant, demeanour, tone of voice, expression. It had all shifted to become someone else wearing the exact same face. 'Hello, Jos,' Henk told her. Reaching out, he took her hand in both his own. 'You look a lot like…'

'Please don't say that,' Jos told him. 'I just found out she murdered him and, if I get out of here alive, I might just have to dye my hair or something.'

'Don't do that.' Henk smiled broadly, shaking his head. 'Your hair is beautiful.'

'Thank you for saying…' Jos spoke quickly. 'But he is like Tigger inside my head at the moment. I'm guessing you too got along famously because Peter is really excited to see you. It's taking a lot of effort to stop myself grabbing you again so I can hug and kiss you. I really want to jump up and down and then lift you up into the air. It's happening inside my head, so I know Peter has done that to you before…'

Henk started laughing. 'Peter did that a lot. He would grab, lift, spin and kiss. I don't think I ever met another human being who was so happy to be alive.' Then his face fell into sadness. 'She really did do it then?' Henk's eyes filled with tears, and he let them fall, unashamed. 'I didn't want to believe it. Jude was such a… such a…'

'Tell me about that night.' Peter had deflated completely to see his friend so unhappy, and Jos was able to focus properly. 'Tell me everything. Please.'

'Are you hungry?' Henk wondered, drying his eyes with a paper towel from the dispenser above the little sink on the wall behind his desk. 'Why don't we go over to my little house, and I will cook. Nothing fancy, but I make pretty good spaghetti and meatballs.'

'Sounds brilliant.'

Henk's kitchen was small and compact, with a little flip down, wall mounted table and one chair which Jos sat on as he prepared their dinner. He poured them each a glass of white wine and talked as he worked. 'It began months before.' He wiped his eyes again, but these tears were from chopping onion. 'Peter came to me with the laibon… I heard just yesterday that he died. Did you meet him yet?'

Jos nodded. 'I was there when the laibon died… we were there. Four people, three bodies, two rituals and one fire. It was a strange night.'

'I am sure.' Henk began making his own meatballs as he talked. 'The laibon foretold Peter's death a long time before. They told me that I was needed to get his body back to the white house and also to pay the police chief not to proceed with an investigation… and any other expenses…'

'So, the police knew it was murder?'

'Even after being so badly burned the gunshot wound was apparent, Jos. Money secured a revised death certificate to go with the revised report, and finally an open verdict at the later inquest. The judge insisted upon that. It would have been funny if it wasn't also so serious that this judge was morally corrupt enough to take the bribe, but principled enough to refuse to record perhaps a death by misadventure. This was important because the police chief was very reluctant to allow Jude to leave the country. He only agreed to accept his bribe on the understanding that, if Jude sets foot in Tanzania again, he can arrest her.'

'Jeezo,' Jos said. 'So, there's an outstanding warrant on my aunt, and not just any old warrant… a warrant for murder. Does she know that?'

Henk nodded. 'I believe so. There was another man, from England… erm…'

'Gary?'

'Yes. He came for her. He escorted Jude back to England. He promised to ensure she would never return.'

'How many people were involved in letting her away with it?' Jos wondered, incredulous. Also hungry, as Henk had begun frying off his meatballs and they smelled amazing. A touch of Peter leaking into her consciousness perhaps.

'Peter wanted it that way. He said he had his reasons.'

'Me,' Jos told Henk. 'He was protecting me. It's a long story for another time because Peter reckons Jude is coming back.' 'Then she will be arrested,' Henk said flatly.

'Well, this could be a lot less stressful than I imagined.'

'Being arrested is not the same as being charged. To charge Jude with murder, the police will have to have evidence.'

'The gun.'

'Where is it?'

'We don't know. Peter reckons she buried it close to the white house, but it could be anywhere within his sphere of awareness. There's eight thousand acres out… oh.' Jos stopped talking.

'Is something wrong?' Henk wondered.

Shaking her head, she said, 'I'm becoming all Peter-natural these days. I'm his heir you see, and Peter is filling my head up with just about everything and anything he had inside his. It's his closing down sale, and I get to mind my own business one minute and stumble into his memories the next.' Indicating her head, she went on, 'There are literally two people living in here at the moment.'

'That sounds exhausting.'

'Oh, it is.' She nodded, wide eyed. 'My poor brain has never had to work so hard. But it's also fun. I wish I'd met him… I did once, but I was only a few weeks old, so I don't remember, but he does. It's kinda the same thing for me now. I know I sneezed and farted at the same time while he was holding me, and Peter thought that was both amazing and hilarious.' Henk thought it was pretty funny too.

'He's getting me into all sorts of trouble!' Jos carried on. 'He's fond of reminding me of all the things he hasn't done in fourteen years… these little outings for example. He made me flirt outrageously with a French waitress who then gave me her phone number! He abandoned me in a Maasai village, so I had to pee in the woods and carry water back from the well. And he made me smoke… I puked my guts up after that one, and he thinks it's all a big game…' Jos stopped talking, because Henk was pressing his lips together so tightly, and his face was becoming very red. 'Go on then,' she told him. 'Laugh.'

Henk laughed his head off.

‘Peter was such a lot of fun, Jos.’ They were eating dinner out on the veranda by then, and Henk was reminiscing. ‘He was also a clever, honest and interesting man. I count myself privileged to have known him, and it was my honour to help him when he needed me. I would do it all again if I had to. When the laibon told me, Peter was on his way… I mean before he’d even set foot in Africa, it was my job to keep him here… right here in this centre, until he realised, he wanted to stay in Africa. Those were some of the best times of my life. My wife had died some years before. This was her dream. We were both vets. We met at vet school, and we fell in love. We had a successful practice near Rotterdam, but my wife was killed by a police car involved in chasing a suspect. There was a great deal of compensation paid to me because of that, and so I came here, and I opened this centre for her.’

‘Rhonda,’ Jos realised.

‘It was a struggle for me alone, at first, but I made friends with the Maasai, and they helped me. They also protected me. The laibon saved my life once, by shouting loud enough in my dream to awaken me. Some poachers broke into my home moments later. They came to kill me, but I was ready for them thanks to the laibon. After that the warriors watched over me, and they still do. Poachers will not come here. Not ever. When the laibon later asked me to look after a white man called Peter who was coming soon, I never doubted it for a second. He even knew the name of the lion… well, nearly. He called her Lou. But, one day, Peter and Jude arrived with little Lulu. Jude was another force of nature. She knew how to get things done! They stayed here for over a year; you know! They transformed this place, and me with it. Together they moved mountains, Jos.’

‘So, what happened to them?’ she wondered. ‘How did Jude get to a place where killing Peter was her answer?’ ‘I am afraid you must ask Peter that.’

*

Jos stayed at the rehab centre until around midnight.

She passed a very pleasant evening listening to tales of Jude and Peter and their time working there, sitting on the same veranda they had all shared back then. The animals they'd cared for. The operations they'd assisted with. Apparently, Jude had been a competent veterinary nurse, as opposed to her husband who'd been so squeamish Jude often had to deal with the gorier incidents alone... sometimes while Peter lay on the floor in a faint.

Henk also revealed details about the night after Peter died. How a Maasai warrior arrived with the news that afternoon, and how Henk simply put Peter's plan into action. He had cash for the occasion. Tens of thousands of American dollars because that currency was highly coveted... still was. He paid off the police... Jude was still in the building at that point, spinning her deceit. Money changed hands and Jude was served hot, sweet tea. Henk then paid off the local doctor acting as pathologist with the chief's help, and police officers began queueing up to offer Jude their condolences. That was how Henk managed to get back to the white house before her, because the police closed ranks to delay her.

'That was important,' he told Jos. 'I had to get Peter there before Jude returned. The warriors stopped her when she came, you see, she didn't see me, or what was left of her husband. If she'd seen me... or got there before me... if she'd been able to touch him or stop me taking him there. It all would have been for nothing. The laibon needed her excluded because she embodied evil, and the ritual had to be pure. The house had to be pure. And the storm! A private little storm that raged above the white house. The laibon was up on the roof shouting at the sky and the sky was yelling right back at him. And despite that, the Maasai warriors kept their fire burning. Even now... even with you sitting here with me now, like some strange matryoshka doll keeping my friend safe inside you, I still look back on that night as something incredible. I witnessed real magic that night, Jos... a power that reached out way beyond the boundaries of the natural order as we know it. And I didn't know for sure if it had worked until you turned up here tonight.'

Henk also paid off the head of Moshi District Council... a man who had to be paid twice due to his poor memory, paid handsomely both times not to interfere, and with the additional promises of annual, generous donations to the council for the duration of his tenure to ensure his memory loss didn't recur.

Jos had seen this man in her head, felt his firm handshake, seen his bright smile. Snake, she thought.

Henk had taken Peter's remains to the white house, arriving just as the Nyerere's were leaving. 'They knew nothing,' he told Jos. 'Of all those involved, the Nyerere's knew nothing then, and they know nothing now, beyond what they might suspect.'

'That ship already sailed,' Jos then explained.

'If anything had gone wrong back then…' Henk went on. 'Peter wanted them kept out of it. I felt bad lying to Beola about what I was doing there that night, but we were all breaking laws… we'd all agreed to it beforehand.'

'What happened to Peter's remains?'

'I don't know, Jos. The laibon needed his body to help bring his spirit home. I don't know what happened after that.'

Before taking their leave, Jos receded and allowed Peter to come to the fore and share a drink and a brief stroll down memory lane with his friend.

It was an emotional journey for them all.

*

On the drive home, Jos receded to the point that she was able to sleep.

So used to sharing her mind with Peter by then, their symbiosis was seamless. He was in complete control and tempted to just keep driving, to drive all night and keep on going. Maybe he and Jos could live like that for the duration of her life? Maybe he could stay safe inside her. A second chance. His life was stolen, ended too soon, and these sojourns into reality made him hungry for more. He wanted to see what the world had made of its self since his death. He wanted to live and love and travel. He wanted to swim in the oceans and cross every desert. He wanted to sit in theatres, stand in rock venues. He wanted to live!

Then Peter saw the laibon in the rear-view mirror.

He'd just passed through Moshi on the A23 heading west and was approaching the turn off to the south that would take him back to his white house prison. The road was quiet. Very little traffic. His glance at the rearview mirror was second nature, and the old man was smiling at him from the storage space behind the seats. Peter turned Jos' head, but of course the old man wasn't really there, just his image in the mirror.

Peter pulled over at the side of the road just short of the turning. Music and voices could be heard coming from various hotels and bars close by, but there was no one near. Getting out the jeep, he stood in the dark, wondering what to do, waiting for the next thing to happen, but not knowing what that thing would be.

Then he saw her.

She walked out from where she'd been hiding among the undergrowth, and Peter lowered the rear gate of the jeep, beckoned to her and, once she was lying low inside the limited rear space, he closed the gate again, got back into the jeep and resumed the journey home. All thoughts of escape banished from mind because Peter was focusing instead on something else entirely.

CHAPTER TWENTY-SIX

Jude woke well before dawn on Sunday morning, and immediately began last minute preparations for her trip.

Having a shower came first, and then she examined all her scars, finding them all healing nicely. She treated them all with a fresh application of the aloe gel, which was helping them to heal quickly, then used concealer and foundation to hide the worst of the scars on her neck. The rest would be hidden under the trousers and long sleeves she'd be travelling in, but she then applied a tanning moisturiser to her legs and arms for good measure. In six hours, she'd have a golden glow which would help reduce the unsightly mess when she was forced to wear less because of the heat.

Before dressing, Jude had breakfast.

It was while she was eating her cereal and sipping some cranberry juice that she remembered Imelda. It was after eight a.m. by then and she had less than two hours to get to the airport to check in for her first flight. Finishing up quickly, she loaded her dishes into the washer and started it up. She then went on an Imelda hunt. Not in her usual place on Jos' bed, or even under it. Imelda also wasn't in the wardrobe, which had stood open since before Jos left, half the contents hanging on the doors, or lying across the chair next to the window.

'Imelda?' Jude called. 'Immie,' she cooed. Wandering from room to room, she found nothing. She then decided to be methodical. Starting up in the gods, she cleared a room before closing the door behind her firmly. Once the top floor was done, she went back down to the first floor. Four bedrooms, two en suite bathrooms, a family bathroom, a dressing room, various cupboards, half open drawers, wardrobes, under beds, sofas, chairs, and her own chaise-longue. Nothing. Zip. Nada.

Back downstairs Jude checked that the cat flap was definitely locked, and then she tried to recall when she'd last seen Imelda. It was as she was lying on the landing floor, right after tripping over the cat and right before fat cat Gus jumped onto her head on his way downstairs and to his death in the boot room. Jude couldn't recall if she'd opened the cat flap since then.

Could Imelda be outside?

The clock in the dining room began to chime and Jude counted nine. 'Shit.' She raced back upstairs and began to get herself ready. Hair, makeup, dressed. It was almost ten a.m. when she came downstairs with her suitcase and her shoulder bag. She didn't even have time to deal with Joseph and there was also the little grave to be filled in. 'Oh, for Christ's sake, Imelda. I've spent too long looking for you, and now I haven't even got the time to deal with Joe.' Then she heard it! A cat's mew.

Turning around at the foot of the stairs, Jude saw Imelda sitting on the top step.

'Where on Earth have you been hiding? Oh well…' Jude sighed. 'I suppose it's only fitting. Imelda Marcos is still at large so I suppose I'll have to leave you be.' She went to the boot room and opened the cat flap. In the utility room, Jude kicked over the large sack of dry food so some of it spilled onto the floor. She stuck a little dish under the dripping tap in the sink, filling it with fresh water. Back in the hallway, she told Imelda, 'If you're still here when I get back maybe we can put all of this behind us.'

And with that Jude collected her things, went out through the boot room and got into her car.

*

Jos had also wakened up before dawn on Sunday morning.

Slightly hungover after all the wine drunk with Henk, but it had been a great night and she felt rested despite only having a few hours of sleep. Maybe she was finally adjusting to dealing with all the Peter-natural going on inside her head? Things certainly felt different in the sense contact with Peter was affecting her less and less. His pre-arrival lethargy was all but gone and switching between them when he was body snatching was seamless. Jos was able to choose whether or not to pay any attention to what Peter was saying and doing while controlling her body. She'd been able to sleep while he drove them home last night. But hadn't something happened just after they got back?

She couldn't quite recall right then.

As she showered Jos found herself singing 'Feed Me To The Lions' by Adam and The Ants. A song her dad used to sing to her when she was little. Was that why she was singing it? Was she thinking about her dad? Her lovely, calm and smiling Prince Charming dad who always knew what to do, how to fix something, how to make his little girl smile when all she wanted to do was cry. But no… it was something to do with last night. An idea, or perhaps a memory, flitted through her mind, and was gone before she could grasp it.

Back in the garden room Jos was dressing in her usual morning attire of shorts and a vest top when her memories of last night's journey's end crystallised in her mind in full and glorious colour. 'Oh fuck!' She dropped everything and ran down the internal stairs to the kitchen.

There was a big hunk of meat disguised as half a lamb sitting on the counter… oozing, on the counter. She remembered, or rather she remembered Peter impelling them into the freezer room in the very early hours of that same morning, taking the half carcass out, and then leaving it there to defrost. Beola would have kittens when she saw the mess. There was blood dripping down onto the floor. 'Fuck, fuck, fuck.' Jos stood in the kitchen torn between wanting to remove the body and clean up the mess. 'Why do you keep doing this to me, Peter?'

'Calm down.' Peter was by her side, having waited for her to wake up and remember. 'We need to take the meat downstairs.'

'We do?' Something else fluttered across her mind before she could quite grasp it, but Jos didn't have time to chase it right then, as she had evidence of foul play to clean up.

'Get a basin or something.' Peter suggested.

'A basin?' Jos was incredulous. 'The basin big enough for that hasn't been invented yet. Bloody hell, I always thought lambs were wee tiny things. That thing is the size of a Labrador.'

'Well, what then?'

'A bin bag!' Jos already knew where they were kept and also the cleaning things. Back at the table, gloved up and open bag to hand, all she needed was a zip up white forensics suit, a pair of wellies and safety goggles and she'd be good to go. A moan escaped her throat and Jos sagged visibly.

'What is it?' Peter wondered.

‘I hate raw meat.’ She made a face. ‘And you’re gonna be no bloody help!’

Somehow Jos got the half lamb into the bin bag without covering herself in blood. Just a few smears and drips here and there… mostly running down her legs, but she was erring on the side of brave, conscious that the sun was now shining brightly and Beola would be down any minute. Leaving the bagged-up meat on the floor by the door, Jos then got busy cleaning.

Peter pointed out any spots missed, though this seemed to irritate Jos. ‘Only trying to help.’

‘It would really help if you could tell me if Beola’s still asleep.’

‘She is,’ Peter said, without hesitation. ‘So is Kissi… and Ben too.’

‘Good.’ Jos got busy again. Having wiped up all the blood with paper towels, she was spritzing and wiping with some lemon fresh antibacterial multi-surface spray by then. Satisfied at last that Beola would never guess a frozen carcass had partially defrosted on her counter during the night, she binned the paper, shoving it all as deep into the bin as she dared, then covering it all over with some wilted salad leaves that were already in there. She put the spritz back in the caddy inside the cupboard, washed the gloves and added those too, then turned to Peter. ‘What now?’

‘Bring the bag and follow me.’

Jos had to heft that bag up and over one shoulder, until she looked like she might be off somewhere to deliver coal. It weighed around half a tonne. Easily as much as the water back pack of Friday morning. Peter just strolled along, looking back over his shoulder now and then, probably to make sure she was keeping up. ‘Couldn’t you have built a smaller house?’ she complained, tutting for good measure.

She had to put the bag down again to retrieve the key and open the door to the cellar. Shoving the bag inside with her foot she stepped onto the small landing herself and closed the door behind her.

‘Lock us in.’

Peter spoke from the bottom of the stairs, after presumably gliding effortlessly down there. ‘Why?’ Jos wondered.

‘Humour me.’

Jos did as she was asked, leaving the key in the lock. Then she had to heft the bag once more and hold onto the railing with her free hand in case she missed her flip-flopped footing and fell head first down the stairs. Imagine the questions as she lay sprawled and unconscious with her half lamb defrosting at the bottom. 'Not to mention the fact they'd have to break the door down to save me.'

'What?' Peter asked, confused.

'Nothing.' Jos was finally at the bottom and set her load on the floor. 'What now?'

Peter indicated the pile of boxes he was standing next to. 'I'm afraid you must move these.'

Muttering to herself about all the impositions she was having to put up with so early in the morning, Jos got on with it… inspired after moving the two top boxes, because there was a door behind the pile. Needless to say, the door was locked. 'Where's the key?'

'It should be at the top of the frame.'

Feeling with her fingers, Jos found it and opened the door.

'There's a light switch just inside.'

She found that too and switched on. 'Oh my god.' Jos was looking at a rough stairway carved in the rock, curving downward beneath an arched roof, strung with cobwebs and the odd lightbulb. 'Where does this go?'

'Come and see.'

Peter's voice came from somewhere ahead because he'd glided off again. 'I'm really gonna have to start calling him Caspar,' Jos muttered to herself, hefting the bin bag again. No rail to hold onto this time, and the steps were uneven and steep in places. She also had to duck to get under the cobwebs. Lucky she wasn't scared of spiders, but she wished she'd worn sensible footwear. She trailed her free hand along the rough wall to steady herself and made it down to the slightly wider passageway at the bottom unscathed.

Peter laughed when she got there. 'You might need another shower.' Despite all her ducking, Jos was covered in stringy bits of dusty cobweb. Most of it in her hair. 'Turn around.' When she did, he checked her for spiders. Saw none. 'Okay… follow me.'

‘What is this place?’ Jos set off along the passage that widened almost immediately. There were lots of clusters of little stalactites hanging from the ceiling in places, and little stalagmites offering plenty trip hazards directly below. ‘Are we going caving?’

‘I know it was on your list of things I’m not allowed to do while hitching a ride, but we’re in this together so I figured you wouldn’t mind.’

‘What are you up to, Peter? And how much longer do I have to carry this bag. The lamb is still part frozen. My back is numb.’

‘Not far now.’

Jos soon found herself inside a small oval shaped chamber with a high ceiling. The stalactites and stalagmites were bigger here, and water was dripping somewhere. She could also hear the distant sound of running water, and a low humming sound that seemed man made. Peter had crossed to the far side and gone into another passageway. When she got there the sound of water was louder, a small waterfall maybe. The humming was also louder. ‘What is that noise?’

‘The well,’ Peter told her. ‘We’re getting close to the pumping station.’ ‘Couldn’t we just have walked across the lawn?’

‘We’re not going that way.’ Peter had stopped to allow her to catch up because the passageway forked there. Indicating the narrower passage to the right, he said, ‘This way.’

‘There aren’t any lights that way,’ Jos noticed.

‘There is at the other end,’ Peter assured.

Jos followed reluctantly, feeling her way with one hand through the pitch dark that enfolded her almost immediately. She couldn’t even see Peter and was beginning to fear for her safety… recalling every single scene from The Descent movie and expecting some horrid translucent cave thing to rip her throat out any second. The cold against her back made her shiver and shudder. Her ears even started playing tricks on her and Jos was sure she could hear the throaty noises those crawler creatures made when they were hunting.

‘I feel your fear, Jos,’ Peter spoke from just ahead of her. ‘There’s nothing in here to be scared of. I promise.’

‘Where are you?’ she wailed. ‘I don’t like it.’

‘Just a few more steps…’ he urged. ‘There’s light coming in from above, a little way ahead.’

Peter hadn't lied, and Jos could soon make out his silhouette a few feet ahead of her. It was all she could do not to sob in relief. But she could still hear that noise, like a faint growling sound. 'What can I hear now?' she wondered.

'Don't freak out when you see her,' Peter advised.

Jos stopped dead, frozen in her flip flops. 'Who? What? What's happening, Peter?'

'It's all right.' Beckoning Jos forward, he waited until they were side by side, and then he moved forward again. 'I'd hold your hand, but you didn't bring that hat.'

Jos laughed despite her nerves.

The light was coming in from a narrow chimney above them. A small patch of sunlight that faded a few feet beyond itself. But there was more light up ahead, and more space. A sound of dripping water could also be heard… and that low throaty growl. Peter was moving towards it, and the source of the growl rose up from the floor to meet him.

When Jos saw what it was, she dropped the bin bag and backed away. 'She'll eat me.'

'She might…' Peter agreed. 'Unless you give her the meat. She's hungry, Jos. She's travelled a long way to get here.'

'But why?' Jos wailed. 'Why is she here?'

'Right now, she can smell the meat. Can you bring it closer?'

'You're good at moving books and shit around. Why don't you bring it closer?'

Sighing, Peter stood next to the lioness, hands on hips. He looked down at her, and she looked up at him. Then she sat down next to him, like a faithful dog. 'She won't hurt you, Jos. I promise.'

The lioness was looking at Jos by then, her head tilted to one side, the picture of cute. Her mouth opened, and she panted, her tongue hanging a little. She looked very relaxed, and Jos allowed curiosity to propel her forward, dragging the bag slowly behind her. The lioness closed her mouth and bowed her head then. Her gaze fixed on the bag. 'Do I have to take it out the bag?'

'We can't expect her to eat plastic.'

'I suppose…' Jos was only a few feet from the powerful looking animal and, without taking her eyes off that massive mouth, she pushed the bagged half lamb forward with her foot then, crouching down, she took the bottom of the bag in both hands and lifted it, tipping the meat out onto the floor of the chamber.

The lioness moved so fast, Jos took fright and ended up on her arse, clutching the bin bag which was dripping blood all over her feet by then. But the lioness wasn't interested in Jos at all. She simply grabbed the carcass in her jaws, turned tail and ambled past Peter, taking her meal away to a quiet corner to feed.

'Will it be okay?' Jos wondered, screwing up and twisting the bag so she could tie it up.

'She'll be fine now.'

'I mean the meat… it's still frozen in the middle.'

'She won't mind.'

'Beola might,' Jos realised. 'I hope we didn't just feed our Sunday roast to Lulu there.'

'Not Lulu, but they are definitely related. See her tail?'

Jos saw a long, smooth golden tail resting on the floor of the cave as its owner gnawed and crunched on meat and bone. 'No tail tuft.' 'So, she is definitely a direct descendent of Lulu's blood line.' Past and present were converging perfectly.

*

Wendell arrived early again, hoping there would be another pancake extravaganza going on in the white house kitchen. Unfortunately, not. There was nothing in there but the fresh citrus scent of recent cleaning, and another mildly metallic smell… especially near the side the kettle was on. A fresh kill kinda smell. Filling the kettle, he set it to boil and left the kitchen intending going across to the lodge to kick Ben out of bed if he wasn't already up.

As he was entering the foyer, he heard the unmistakable Scottish tones of Jos coming from somewhere nearby. Wendell had no idea there was a cellar under the white house. He'd noticed the door under the stairs but assumed it would be a cupboard. He reckoned Jos was in that cupboard, but she wasn't alone. She was with a man, their two voices easy to hear, but their words hard to decipher. When he heard a key going into a lock, he felt a little guilty standing there, as if he was spying. Too late, because the door was opening, and a very bedraggled and dirty Jos stepped out onto the pristine marble floor. 'G'day, Jos.'

'Wendell!' She clamped a hand over her mouth, laughing into it.

'Been exploring?'

Jos looked back over her shoulder, but Peter had done his disappearing act. 'Just the cellar,' she said. 'It's a bit dusty down there.'

'I can tell…' Sensing Jos was hiding something and thinking that something was her big blonde and elusive Uncle Peter, Wendell thumbed back over his shoulder, and told her, 'I'm just nipping over to the lodge to make sure Ben is up. The kettle's on if you fancy a cuppa.'

'Cheers,' Jos said, watching him leave, before she darted out through the French doors and up to the garden room via the roof garden. She went into the bathroom and cleaned herself up, picking chunks of congealed cobweb from her hair first, before brushing it through and putting it up. Then she used a flannel to wipe down her limbs and, finally, she swapped the dirty shorts and vest, for a clean set. Back in her flip flops, she made her way back downstairs and was in the kitchen making coffee and toast when Wendell returned with Ben.

*

At Edinburgh Airport, Jude drove into the long-term premium parking structure and handed over her keys in exchange for the receipt from the desk staff. It was then a quick walk from there to check-in and another short journey through priority security. Heading for the nearest Bureau de Change, she swapped a wad of sterling for a wad of US Dollars and then made her way to her gate.

Jude was soon on her way to Gatwick.

Once there, she collected her bag, and headed for the nearest Bureau de Change to swap her sterling for shillings as well as even more US Dollars. Then she found the dedicated first-class desks where they relieved Jude of her bag and checked her in before directing her to the first-class lounge. Staff there welcomed her with champagne and a delicious lunch. Just as well she had five hours before the overnight flight, because Jude needed a few hours in a private room to sleep all that off.

*

Ben and Wendell had stayed long enough for their own coffees and toast that morning but disappeared as soon as they'd finished. There was space for one more on the day trip to Lake Chala, but Jos thought she should spend the day at the white house repairing a few bridges between her and Beola.

When there was still no sign of her hosts after the guys left, she retrieved the cleaning caddy and took it up to the garden room where she cleaned the bathroom. Trying to be a good guest. Trying not to think about their other guest, down in the caves, perhaps still gnawing on her halffrozen lamb.

Having now seen the lioness with her own eyes, Jos was beginning to recall misty images of that same animal jumping down from the jeep last night. It was dark, and among trees which rose above her from a wooded slope. The lioness had wandered off up that slope, and Jos now assumed this was somewhere lower down the track which circled around the hill on its way up to the white house. She had absolutely no recollection of where the lioness had gotten into the jeep, however.

Eventually the sounds of life filtered up to Jos from below, and she went back down to the kitchen with the cleaning things. Kissi was sitting on the patio chatting to someone on his mobile, but he offered a cheery smile and a wave as Jos passed through and that made her feel better.

'Morning,' she told Beola.

'Good morning, my darling.' Beola eyed the caddy. 'Have you been cleaning in here too?'

'I spilt a little juice earlier,' Jos lied. 'I think I managed to clean it all up though.'

'I'm making chipsi mayai for breakfast, would you like some?'

'Sounds interesting.'

'French fries omelette,' Beola revealed.

'Really?' Jos laughed. But Beola was not having her on. She fried up a load of French fries straight from the freezer and, when they were golden brown, whisked up half a dozen eggs, seasoned with salt and pepper and poured it into the pan. As that was cooking, she chopped up a few green onions and chives and added those. Finally, she expertly tossed her omelette to cook it evenly on both sides, and then it was ready to serve with some fresh bread and chilli sauce.

'That was the best omelette ever!' Jos declared.

They had joined Kissi at the patio table to eat. He was feeling a lot better after a good night's sleep, and much relieved after his call. There had been no more sightings since the golf course yesterday afternoon. The lioness from the park was still AWOL, but that wasn't his problem for that day at least.

Jos almost felt guilty again, knowing that lioness had actually moved in, but she distracted herself by issuing a dinner invitation for that evening. Beola and Kissi both agreed with Ben that Mimosa was the place to go, and so it was agreed. Beola sent her son a text extending the invitation to him and Wendell and asked that they be on the porch by eight p.m. that night.

She ended that text with the words; no shorts, no flip flops.

A little later, Jos was given a crash course in using the ride on lawn mower and she was soon whizzing around the front lawn, doing U turns and three point turns and reversing around invisible corners. She enjoyed it so much she cut the grass around the lodge, and then whizzed around the back of the white house to cut the grass there.

It was while she was whizzing along the fence line that she was stung by a bee.

Beola had just realised what Jos was doing and had come out to put a stop to it, but Jos was already running for the safety of the house, with a hand clamped to her forehead. 'Oh dear,' Beola laughed a little. 'They don't like it. I wear the bee suit to cut the grass out there.'

'Oh no…' Jos was looking at the already impressive lump on her forehead, in the mirror. 'Sore,' she moaned. 'I am gonna look just great tonight.'

Beola laughed and laughed.

*

Mimosa was one of the best restaurants in Moshi.

It was also busy, but not so busy that the party of five who turned up unannounced couldn't be accommodated. They were offered a table inside, but they opted for a table in the garden instead. Most people did, because the mimosa trees that gave the restaurant its name were strung with thousands of colourful fairy lights, there were fire bowls along the pathways, and numerous water features added an aquatic tinkling to the general ambiance. The people inside were either looking for a quieter experience, or they just didn't want to be eaten alive by the mosquitoes that lurked in the shadows. Jos hadn't been bothered much by mossies, so was quite happy to sit outside in the magical looking garden, despite warnings from the waiter.

Jos, Wendell and the Nyerere's were all looking fine.

They'd assembled on the white house porch around eight p.m. in their evening finery. Jos arrived first wearing a pretty dress by Karen Millen and a pair of beaded heels. Her hair was neatly coiled around her crown and fixed in place with a set of three silver and green Scandinavian enamel butterflies that Jude had given her on her eighteenth birthday. Peter had popped in as she was holding an ice pack to her forehead in an effort to reduce the bee sting lump there and told her his mother had given them to Jude for her nineteenth birthday. Jos immediately felt bad, but Peter was glad his murdering bitch of a wife had passed them on to someone more deserving. So that was all right then. Jos finished her outfit off with a splash of make-up and a few silver bangles, swapped the big Fendi bag for a small, green satin one, bade Peter a nice evening, and skipped off downstairs looking forward to their night out.

Wendell arrived next, wearing black jeans with a fitted crimson shirt. His plaits were all gathered up into a short ponytail which hung from his crown and, when he sat on the chair nearest to Jos, she discovered that he smelled as good as he looked. He thought Jos was looking every bit as gorgeous… despite the little egg forming on her forehead and was almost disappointed when Ben rocked up before he and Jos had had time to exchange more than a few pleasantries.

Ben was looking very smart in dark blue dress trousers and a pristine white shirt.

'Whatever happens...' Wendell told his friend. 'You have got to go to

Mountain View tonight.'

'What's mountain view?' Jos wondered.

'Nightingale works there weekend nights,' Wendell revealed. 'And she hasn't ever seen this bloke looking so fine.'

'Who's driving?' Jos asked suddenly, realising that, without Peter, she was grounded.

Unless they could all pile on the ride on.

Beola arrived just then, looking stunning in a long pink dress with a beaded neckline and with dainty little sandals on her feet. 'Kissi will drive.' She also told Wendell to leave his car at the house. He could collect it later, or Ben could collect him in the morning.

Kissi arrived last, stepping out onto the porch in a rust-coloured linen suit worn with a bright blue shirt. He grinned at the whoops and whistles offered by the children and spun around on the spot for extra points.

At Mimosa, they enjoyed great service, wonderful food, good wine and perfect cocktails. Jos had a margarita or two for dessert. It was after eleven when the coffees arrived with little squares of deepest darkest chocolate. Jos ate all of those because no one else wanted theirs. Then she avoided doing battle with the men over who was picking up the tab.

Jos simply excused herself to the ladies and paid the bill on the way.

CHAPTER TWENTY-SEVEN

A timely wakeup call had brought Jude nicely round from her after lunch nap in the first-class lounge in Gatwick late on Sunday afternoon. She then had time for some more delicious refreshments as well as a quick freshen up, before she was on her way again.

Her first-class experience was as elegant and agreeable as that enjoyed by Jos less than a week previously. Champagne, top class dining, the famous goody bag. But Jude had been there and bought the T-shirt so many times in her past she took it all in her stride and, as soon as she'd had dinner, sealed herself inside her private unit, donned the eye mask and, for the first time in her flying history, slept like a baby for most of the rest of the flight.

A delicious breakfast was served just prior to coming into land, and then the captain's voice announced, 'Ladies and Gentlemen, on behalf of myself and my crew, I'd like to welcome you all to Nairobi.' The first leg of Jude's East African tour was underway.

Met in arrivals by a pleasant young man holding a board bearing her name, Jude handed over her bag and allowed herself to be escorted outside to where the hire car was waiting. A big black shiny Toyota Land Cruiser, luxury SUV. Her little bag would just slide around in the roomy rear, so Jude had the young man set it into the passenger seat foot well. She then paid close attention as he explained the details of the car. He had already entered her hotel destination into the satnav, so all she had to do was follow the instructions. She took the keys from him, tipped him generously with dollars and was soon on her way.

Nairobi was a sprawling city, a concrete jungle of ultra-modern buildings, peopled by locals, tourists and the two hundred odd thousands British expats who lived and worked there. The roads were chaotic with speeding buses, over-laden trucks and manic taxi drivers all jostling one another for every spare foot of the main highways. Jude was grateful to get off the outer ring road and into the leafy suburb of her five-star hotel and resort. The grounds were enormous, boasting a golf course as well as several lakes. It took her a full ten minutes to reach the main building from the gate house.

Once she was checked in, a porter escorted Jude to her suite of rooms overlooking a tranquil lake on one side, and the gardens surrounding one of the four swimming pools on the other. A welcome basket of fruit, chocolates, snacks and of course chilled Champagne awaited her. Would she like to reserve a table for lunch? Jude preferred to eat on her terrace and would contact room service when she was ready. The porter accepted her tip with grace and took his leave.

As soon as Jude had unpacked, she placed a call with the concierge.

'Good morning, this is Mrs Sinclair in the Kigwa Ridge suite. I wonder if you can help me. I'm here to visit my nephew. It's his birthday in a couple of days and I want to buy him a car. A little jeep of some sort. He works miles away from his parents' home and relies on his little moped to get around. I don't want anything too new or too fancy because he often travels on the dirt roads. A reliable four by four, I think. Do you know of anywhere I might purchase such a vehicle? For cash? I know this isn't really something I should be asking you to help me with, but my husband used to handle all that sort of thing.'

'And your husband has not accompanied you on this trip?'

'Oh no, I'm afraid he died.'

'Please accept my sincerest…'

'No need. He died long enough ago that I'm no longer grieving, but not long enough ago that I have become an independent woman. There are just so many things men are much better at. I had no idea until… well, you know.'

'It can be a complicated procedure, buying a used car in Kenya,' said the concierge.

'Oh dear… and I don't have a lot of time. Plenty of cash, but not much time.'

'Leave it with me, madam. I will make some enquiries.'

Smiling to herself, Jude thanked the concierge and hung up the phone. She then filled the copper tub, opened the champagne and relaxed in a deep bath.

No sooner was she out of the bath and dressed again in cool cotton than there was a knock at the door. A tall, slender man, dressed in a pristine charcoal grey suit was on the other side of the door. The word ‘concierge’ was printed in gold lettering on the black enamel badge pinned to his lapel.

If Jude wanted cocaine, or an escort, or a table at the most sought-after restaurant in Nairobi, then this man would get her these things and more, no questions asked, as long as she tipped him generously enough.

‘Mrs Sinclair? I do hope I’m not disturbing you,’ said the concierge.

‘Come in,’ Jude said. ‘Are you here about the car?’

‘Yes.’ The concierge walked into the middle of the sitting room and turned to his guest. ‘It just so happens that I have my own nephew. He works right here in the hotel. One of our chefs, as a matter of fact. He has a Jeep Wrangler. Its ten years old, but very reliable he assures me. He’s married now. An expectant father. He must get a bigger car for his expanding family. Less than seventy thousand miles on the clock. New tyres less than six months ago, a recent oil change…’

‘How much?’ Jude cut to the chase.

‘Ten thousand US dollars will buy you the car and the log book. It will then be up to your nephew to register the purchase with the NTSA. He’ll have two weeks.’

‘That sounds a little excessive,’ Jude mused, unwilling to allow the concierge to believe her a complete idiot. ‘However—’ She smiled brightly at him, holding his gaze. ‘As the price obviously includes your own finder’s fee.’

‘Of course.’ The concierge maintained his polite and impassive expression despite being duped. Already busy recalculating his percentage, as he asked, ‘When do you need the car?’

‘By tomorrow evening.’

‘I’m afraid we must be discreet.’

‘Of course,’ Jude smiled. ‘I need the jeep brought to Mtito Andie Railway Station.’

Blinking, the concierge said, ‘But that’s four hours away.’

‘Mmm…’ Jude nodded, still smiling sweetly. ‘My own nephew lives close to Tsavo. I can’t possibly expect him to ride his moped all the way to Nairobi, can I? I can leave my hire car at the station and deliver the jeep to him at home. He can then drive me back to the station a little later.'

'But my nephew must then get back to Nairobi.'

'Why don't you follow him down in your own car? You can then give him a lift back. Shall we say one thousand US for your trouble?'

'A perfect compromise, madam.' The concierge almost bowed, so impressed was he with this diminutive woman's blagging abilities. 'What time would you like to meet us as Mtito?'

'Shall we say seven p.m. tomorrow evening?'

'I'll ensure we are there on time.'

'Excellent.' Jude smiled brightly and moved towards the door which she then opened.

Expertly dismissed, the concierge took his leave.

'Now…' Jude wandered across the room to where the room service menu awaited on the desk. 'What shall I have for lunch?'

*

Jos' Monday afternoon was an informative one.

Henk had told her that, if she wanted to find out why Jude had reached a place where her only option was to murder her husband, then she would have to ask Peter. After spending most of the morning harvesting, cleaning and prepping vegetables with Beola for that evening's meal, she took herself up to the roof garden to do just that.

'Why did she do it, Peter?' Jos was still passing between the planters as she spoke. Pressing another ice pack to her forehead where an impressive lump had formed overnight. Sitting on their usual bench, she waited for him to join her. As soon as he had, she said, 'Tell me everything. I don't want to have to trawl through all your memories looking for bad stuff.' 'She's here,' Peter said.

Jos dropped her ice pack and jumped up from the bench, looking around frantically. 'Where? Where is she?'

'In Africa.'

Hands on her sternum, Jos patted herself calmer. 'Oh my god…' She sat down again. 'I just realised how freakin' scared I am.'

'Well done on not swearing.'

Jos tutted, picking up her ice pack and slapping it against her lump again. 'Tell me, Peter. I need to know how we all got here.'

'I wasn't aware there was that big a problem until Jude asked for a divorce. Of course, I was spending more time in the bush than here at the time… had been for months. She was bored. Jude was always bored by then, and I left her to it. I was having too much fun. Maasai men live separate lives from their women, they roam with their cattle, and they hunt, they sit around fires at night, drinking, smoking and generally having a great time. At least it felt like that for me. I had a bit of a shitty time growing up. I didn't really fit in until I went to America in 1967. I came back in May 1970 and was married to Jude by August. Don't get me wrong, I adored her! She was unlike any of the other women I knew. Fun and feisty and she didn't give a toss what other people thought. I think I fell in love with Jude the moment she walked into the room. I was certainly in love with her by the time I put her on a train back to Bristol. We had a fantastic life… we travelled, we loved, we learned. It was me and Jude against the world, and we won. Then life brought us here, and Africa changed us both. But me most of all.'

Africa was where Peter learned to put his money to work.

It started with a single well. The same well Jos had collected water from. Soon hundreds of people had access to good clean water. It was easy for him to make these small things happen, because he had resources, but he was also good at seeing things in their longer terms. Training local people to manage and maintain the wells would make them more selfsufficient. The Sinclair's had their own bees by then and knew how much honey a single hive could produce. A few rural communities already had their own hives, so there was soon a training course, a fund for equipment and clothing. After a few years, the new beekeepers were reinvesting a percentage of their profits so others could apply for start-up grants. A small collection of rural schools sprang up. Each school had a few hives, a plot of land for growing food, and facilities for raising livestock. They were able to feed the children and the staff, and they raised funds by selling excess produce. Years later, these funds were increased substantially by the alumni who were obliged to sponsor at least one new student. So successful were some of these alumni… doctors, teachers, lawyers nowadays, that they were able to sponsor a great many children who were then destined to follow in their footsteps. Scholarships that Peter set up to take young people through universities and medical schools were still in place, because the people who benefitted from them in the past, paid to see the next generation follow them into the future. People with good business ideas had access to grants as well as practical support to help them succeed. They, in turn, would reinvest some of their profits so others can do the same.

'It doesn't always work,' Peter admitted. 'But it does more often than not, simply because each project is built up around the people who will benefit from it, and then ran by them. All I ever did later on was iron out all the inevitable creases that couldn't be foreseen. Gary takes care of that now, and you're next. Everything I did is based here, but you can take the model to any country on Earth.'

'I love what I'm hearing, but none of it explains why Jude killed you.'

'My dad always said money was useless once you had enough of it. It's true. Oh, I had fun spending money when I was young. But I grew out of that after coming here, because the route to happiness changed for me. Making money useful became my greatest source of joy. To see that joy manifested in others, when things I'd taken for granted all my life were made available to people for whom even running water had been an unachievable goal. To see children laughing and playing, learning… and people all eating well, because of their own labours. Jude got as big a kick out of that as me, at first. But she wasn't content with just that and, perhaps because I neglected our own relationship, she began to resent it. She grew restless. She kept booking trips to Europe, and I kept on letting her down. She could have taken a trip on her own… visited you and your parents for example. But she wouldn't. She kept on at me to take her away from here, to stop spending so much money on others, and spend some time with her. Ironic really because a similar situation brought us here in the first place. But I didn't listen that time, Jos. I was completely immersed in my own happiness. I told myself she would get over it. We had the rest of our lives. We'd have kids, I'd settle more, invest my energies in my family.'

'Did you tell her that?'

'No. I don't really do arguments, and it seemed that every time we talked back then we ended up having a row. Jude would do all the shouting, and I would do all the walking away. Which made her worse. She could get a little scary when riled. She would throw things. She even kicked me out of our bed. I wasn't a good husband in the end. I was a coward. I even ran out on her on our wedding anniversary,' Peter admitted. 'I was dead two days later.'

'I've been on the receiving end of her vitriol.' So, Jos knew how that felt. 'But surely a divorce would have been the better option?'

'But she wouldn't have been nearly as well off.'

'But Jude is really well off. Her house, the car… she drives a top of the range Lexus. She never worries about money.'

'She has a fixed allowance… which, over the years, is probably more than she'd have gotten in a divorce settlement. The same as my mother's had since my father died. Jude hated that… she couldn't understand why Johnny left everything to me, and Astrid had to rely on what she referred to as a handout. But we didn't have children so Jude believed that, as she was my wife, everything would go to her upon my death.'

'So, she didn't know about the will.'

Peter smiled without humour, then said, 'No future is fixed until it becomes past, and I have pondered the wisdom of my secrecy over and over.'

'She'd have gotten herself into a rage about that too no doubt. Probably would've done you in anyway.'

'Thank you, Jos. That's very comforting.'

'Anytime.'

'She wanted to contest Gary's inheritance.'

'How do you know?'

'Gary told Beola at the time, Beola told me much later… when she got the chance. Jude made a lot of trouble for him back then. Late night calls, threatening letters. But she'd have forfeited her allowance the moment she stepped in that direction,' Peter revealed. 'I knew she'd try it on, so I prepared for that too. She would also have forfeited her allowance if she married again, or even lived with a man.'

'How utterly ruthless of you, Peter,' Jos was shocked.

'She burned me alive, remember. Had I known…' He faltered, remembering, staring into the distance as he recalled it all again so clearly. 'The pain was complete and utter. Every shred of me shrieked because of it. I couldn't get away and when I screamed… when I opened my mouth to give voice to the anguish, I took that burning agony inside of me.' Having spoken to the distance, Peter turned to face Jos and told her, 'If I'd known she was capable of doing me that level of harm, I'd have cut Jude off with a lot less.'

Jos sat quietly for a few moments.

She'd seen and heard it for herself; Peter's recollection of his death. The possibility that it hadn't happened like that had occurred to her from time to time. The idea that she may be being manipulated was a recurring theme. Mostly because Beola kept harping on about it like that. But if none of it had happened as Peter demonstrated, then there wouldn't be a warrant, and Jude wouldn't be in any hurry to come back to the white house. It was Henk who revealed the existence of the warrant, and Jude was coming. Jos knew that, because she had a rock in her gut and that was something she'd learned to associate with Jude. No one else had ever managed to make Jos feel so nervous, so inadequate. Having become so attuned to Jude's moods over the years, Jos had begun experiencing pre-emptive gut rocks, like an early warning alarm system.

But, this time, Jos wasn't worrying about what she'd done or said to upset Jude, or how long it would be before this particular dark mood would break and allow the tension to dissipate. This time she was worrying if they… her and the Nyerere's, would all come out of this alive. An animal was never more dangerous than when it was cornered, and they would corner Jude as surely as Peter had goaded her into coming in the first place.

'Don't be scared,' Peter told her. 'I won't let anything happen to you.'

'Can you protect us all?'

'I'd prefer it if no one else was here.'

Jos was horrified. 'No!' she told him. 'I can't... I'd let you down, I'd run away...'

'Then we need an ally.'

*

After lunch, Jude used the internet to discover the nearest garden centre and drove there to buy a sharp bladed trowel.

There was a shopping mall nearby, so she went there afterwards to do a little shopping.

She found the biggest, most expensive department store and visited a few of the cosmetic counters, before taking the escalator to lingerie. It had been a while since Jude had bothered looking for anything impractical in that direction, but she was planning to change that as soon as she was free. She could almost see herself, taking a boat trip out onto Lake Victoria with some other tourists, all busy spotting hippos or looking for crocodiles, and she would be dropping the bag containing the Glock into the deepest depths of those dangerous waters. After that, a few days at an expensive resort and perhaps she might shake off her second virginity; it had been so long since she'd last had sex it was a wonder she hadn't just healed up.

She also bought a wide brimmed hat against the sun, and a small, very heavy, sleeping cat of moulded blue glass, which would lend weight to the bag when the time came to drop it into the lake.

Back at the hotel, Jude settled down on a pool side lounger, drinking cosmopolitans and letting a rather handsome American man pick up the tab.

CHAPTER TWENTY-EIGHT

Peter was running out of time, so Jos took him out on Monday night.

There was to be a powwow the following evening, a discussion on what to do when Jude arrived. She was in Africa, and this was happening whether they liked it or not. They were all on their own, whether they liked that or not too; who in authority would take them seriously? Warrant or not, they had no proof Jude was coming, no proof of her crime, no witness beyond the testimony of a dead man. As far as Jos and Peter were concerned it was too late for that anyway. Even if they found the gun, the chances of it bearing any residual evidence of Jude's crime were next to zero. For them it was all about closing the circle.

They had their plan, and they would stick to it now, come what may.

As they reached the garages, Jos wondered, 'What about our guest?

Won't she be hungry?'

We can feed her again tomorrow.

'So, I can look forward to more fun with meat later tonight then?'

Would you prefer to go back to Beola now and ask her if it's okay to purloin another slab of meat out the freezer, because you have a lioness on a B&B deal in the basement?

Tutting and rolling her eyes, Jos let them into the garage and got into the driving seat. She then settled back into herself and let Peter take control.

As they were driving through the bush on the way north toward the A23, she wondered, *Will I be able to drive when I don't have you anymore?*

'Oh yes…' Peter laughed to himself. 'You were having quite the time on the mower.'

I've never been on one of those in my life and I made it move around quite efficiently I thought... until a bee told me off!

'At least your forehead seems to have subsided.'

*

Kilimanjaro Wonders Hotel wasn't busy that Monday night.

Ben and Wendell were set up at a desk in the reception and had spoken to less than ten people by nine thirty. The desk was used by travel reps during the day for general complaints and booking excursions, but the hotel allowed other tour operators to use it in the evenings for a small fee per booking achieved from among their guests. Red Earth Tours used the desk on Monday nights between eight and ten. Not the best night, or the best time slot, but they were just getting started with that hotel.

Ben kept looking at his watch.

'Got a date?' Wendell wondered. Watching his friend then grin from ear to ear. 'You dog!' he exclaimed. 'That explains the smell.' He laughed, remembering the last time his friend had smelled that good there was a very attractive Italian woman waiting in a suite at the Sunandah. 'Nightingale?'

'She called earlier, wondered if I'd like to meet for a drink after we're finished here.'

'So, Nightingale did the deed herself. Hats off to her, at least one of you…' Just then Wendell spied Jos sauntering into the hotel. No bag, no heels, no make-up. He nudged Ben, and together they watched her move through into the bar, sit on a stool and order. When the barmaid started pulling a draft beer, Wendell said, 'Thought she hated beer?' learned while they were all out the night before.

'I'm not sure that's Jos,' Ben told him distractedly.

'Of course, it's Jos! How many women…' Wendell stopped talking when he noticed Ben was looking at him as if he were an idiot. 'You mean…'

'Yeah.'

'Oh, this I have gotta see!' Wendell was on his feet. 'Let's pack up a few minutes early. Have a beer with me before meeting your lady.'

'But…'

'Tell you what… we leave everything out until ten but retire to the bar for some refreshments now. If anyone comes looking for us, I'll pop back across and do the business.'

‘Okay. But you’re buying.’

‘Deal.’ Wendell was already on his way to the bar. Sliding into the stool next door, he said, ‘G’day, Jos.’ And when she turned to face him, the expression on her face was so sarcastic, he wanted to laugh. Instead, he asked, ‘Fancy another beer?’

‘Let’s have a tequila instead.’ Gesturing to the barmaid, Peter asked for

two shots of her best tequila. He then increased the order to three when Ben arrived. When the tequilas arrived, he picked one up, raised Jos’ eye brows and widened her eyes until the boys did the same. ‘Cheers,’ he said, and then drank it down in one go.

Used to sipping margaritas, Jos then totally blew Peter’s cool by having a coughing fit.

While that was happening, a young couple approached the desk, so Wendell had to abandon play to deal with their enquiries, leaving Ben to deal with Jos. ‘Are you all right, Jos?’ he asked.

‘I’m fine,’ she told him. ‘Peter’s just having a little night out, but he’ll have to learn to accept my limitations when it comes to knocking back shots. Not to mention beer. My god, why do so many men drink that shit? It’s horrible!’ Then she started laughing because Peter was laughing inside her. Then she stopped because the barmaid was giving her funny looks. ‘Can we sit at a table, preferably in a dark corner?’

Ben guided her to the darkest looking table in the bar and, once they were seated, he said, ‘Look, Jos… I have to go soon. But Wendell can stay… I’ll ask him to. Just to… you know…’
‘Keep an eye on me?’ Peter wondered.

Ben heard the shift in tone, accent, felt the change in attitude. It was weird at the same time as being fascinating, and he found himself cursing the fact that Nightingale had chosen this night of all nights. ‘Jos,’ Ben corrected.

‘I’ll guard her with my life.’

‘But it isn’t your life, is it?’

‘Fair point. If it makes you feel better then I shall accept Wendell’s company.’

Meanwhile, Wendell had furnished the couple with flyers outlining all their options during their stay, bade them a good evening, and was hurriedly packing everything up. The hotel didn't store their stuff, so it all had to be taken out to the Land Rover.

It was just before ten by then and Ben would be late to meet Nightingale if he didn't get a move on, so he'd left the Peter Jos combo alone… sauntering back at the bar by then, to retrieve the half-drunk beer, so obviously Peter was still in control. Helping Wendell bag up their two roll up display stands, Ben asked, 'Will you hang around and keep an eye out?'

'Of course!' Wendell said. 'I won't let her… or should that be them… is it them?'

'The Peter and Jos combo. They just slip in and out of being each other. It's really strange. Her face, her voice, her whole demeanour shifts from Jos to Peter. I know him, I know it's him. I know her too. Anyone who doesn't know what's going on will probably think Jos has a split personality, or something. Please don't let her out of your sight, and don't let her talk to any strangers. My mama will kill me if anything happens to her.'

*

Richard Isherwood did not suffer from altitude sickness.

This fact remained undiscovered until the first time he climbed Kilimanjaro. Just to make sure it wasn't a fluke; Richard took the longer routes to the summit on the second and third climbs too. Since climb number four he'd opted for the fastest route and, after a little over twentyfour hours in his hotel, had set off last Wednesday morning for Machame Gate. He'd reached the summit on Saturday and was back at his hotel by that very afternoon.

He felt physically exhausted and, after sharing a few post dinner cold beers with his fellow climbers, had been in bed since nine p.m. trying to sleep, but in truth he was still too wired and so had come back down to the bar looking for anyone from his team to share another couple of pints and a bit of chit chat with.

But they had obviously moved on, so Richard simply made his way to the bar and ordered a cold beer. While he was waiting for it to arrive, he looked around and spotted Jos Ferguson. She was hard to miss. There were lots of pretenders to her crowning glory, lots of dye jobs and permanent waves, but few women on the planet had the incredible mane of deep orange hair as his fair Jos. The last time Richard saw her, she'd been that shrinking violet awaiting her friend back at the airport. Right then, she was seated alone in a booth, sipping a beer of her own and talking animatedly to herself.

Maybe she had one of those Bluetooth thingies?

'Fair Jos.' Richard made his way over, smiling. 'Fancy meeting you here.'

It took a split second for the switch to take place and then Jos' face lit up. 'Richard!'

'Are you alone?'

'Yes… no… well I am right now, but Wendell is here. You know him.' 'I do?'

'Red Earth Tours. Please…' She indicated. 'Sit. Tell me about your climb.'

'Just got back this afternoon.' Richard sat down opposite and was filling Jos in on his adventure when Wendell returned.

After the two men had greeted one another, Wendell decided to get a round in. 'Same again?' He asked Richard.

'Please.'

'What about you, Jos… another beer?'

She made a face, pushing the glass and its dregs away. 'Can I have wine please? Sauvignon if possible.' Once Wendell had retreated to the bar, she saw the look of puzzlement on Richard's face and realised Peter had been enjoying that beer when he'd arrived. 'Thought I'd give it a try,' she told him unconvincingly. 'It's not my thing.'

'I'm surprised it took you all the way to the bottom to decide you didn't

like it.'

'Well, you know…' Jos smiled sweetly, wishing Wendell would hurry back. Then she remembered. 'Did you cross the million-pound barrier?'

'Not yet,' Richard shrugged. 'But there's time. Some people don't like to even pledge until the deed is done.'

'I must arrange to make my own payment.' Wendell was coming back, and as he was sitting down, Jos said, 'Richard just climbed Kilimanjaro.'

'Again?'

Laughing Richard said, 'Nine times now.'

'While you were up in the clouds, we've had all sorts of excitement down here,' Wendell revealed. 'There are apparently half a dozen lions on the loose.'

'I heard about that on the way down… some guys on the way up had been delayed for twenty-four hours because Machame Gate was closed. A lion chased a woman outside a school very close to it, I think?'

'The last one was spotted on the golf course! Three fellas nearly tripped over her on the green.'

They talked about marauding lions for a time and had a laugh about the now infamous interview tussle between Julius Chokala and the Kilimanjaro News reporter. He was taking some time off to spend with his family, while she'd been head hunted to host an early evening chat show on Clouds, which was one of Tanzania's most popular TV channels. 'So?' Richard asked later. 'How did you two meet?'

'Remember the man who was coming to meet me at the airport?' Jos wondered. 'Well, that was Ben… Wendell was waiting in the car park.' She told Richard a bit about the trips they'd included her in since, sipping her second glass of wine by then, and feeling a distinct buzz kicking in as the wine met up with the tequila and the beer and decided to have a party. 'It's been really great. You were right. I love it here.'

'And has Africa changed you?' he wondered with a little laugh.

'It's tipped my life upside down and kicked me up the arse a few times.' Jos told him seriously. 'Turns out the uncle whose house I'm staying in… well my aunt murdered him. I've been living with a cold-blooded killer for nearly ten years, and I had no idea. Just goes to show…' She widened her eyes and raised her brows. '… you think you know someone.'

Richard was looking at Wendell for confirmation, and he shrugged. He had no idea what to say, so he said, 'Some evidence has come to light, I think.'

Snorting disdainfully, Jos said, 'If only we could find it. Excuse me…' Sliding to the end of the seat, she stood up a little unsteadily. Thankfully Peter could handle his alcohol a lot better and, in the time it took Jos to take a single, tentative step, he slipped in to her driving seat and crossed the floor confidently to the far side of the bar.

Wendell watched as Jos then walked straight into the gents, come back out again a couple of seconds later wearing a comical look, and then go into the ladies.

'Is Jos all right?' Richard asked.

Wendell nodded. 'She's just coming to terms, I think. It's all been a bit of a shock.'

'Murder?'

'Mate…' Whatever was on Richard's mind, Wendell didn't want to know. 'It's a complicated situation, and none of my business. I'm just here to make sure Jos gets home safe.'

Nodding to show he understood, Richard said, 'You're a good man, Wendell.'

*

After Richard took himself off to bed, Peter slipped back into the driving seat, and eyed his escort. 'Are you a good man, Wendi?'

'Don't call me that.'

'They called my mother a Nazi when I was at school,' Peter revealed. 'Which is funny, because her father was executed by them for his part in the Norwegian resistance. His name was Per. I'm named for him. My mother and grandmother escaped to Scotland the same night he was shot… only my grandmother didn't make it. My mother was all alone in the world, and my father refused to stay poor. Together they made me, and they made lots of money, but none of us were allowed in the club. They called me an oik at school — an uncouth, obnoxious person.'

'I didn't fit in either,' Wendell found himself revealing. 'Not black enough for the natives, not white at all. Everyone loves my mum because she's sweet and pretty, but those kids made my life miserable. They called me Wendi.'

'I'll bet Jos was bullied too.' Peter flicked at her hair. 'Gingers always are. I think it's probably a law.' After a few moments, he added, 'I've been aware of you for a long time, Wendell. You're a good friend to Ben, and Beola considers you to be a second son. You're part of the family.'

Wendell didn't really trust himself to speak. He was feeling rather emotional, and that wasn't what he'd expected when in a rush to get up close and personal with the Peter Jos combo. But Ben was right, they were completely different, and so completely real. Jos was the same as anytime he'd been in her company; funny and cheeky and a little bit nervous in her femininity. Peter was different. He spoke with Jos' mouth and voice, and he used her hands to gesticulate, but Peter was relaxed and insightful, he had an odd sounding English accent, and was masculine in every mannerism. He liked Peter. Wendell could feel his presence and hear his words, even if he couldn't actually see him. If he looked away, or down at the table between them, he felt exactly as if he really was speaking with an entirely separate individual.

'I need your help, Wendell.' Peter told him. 'Jos needs your help.'

'I'll do what I can…'

'No,' Peter stalled him with a hand. 'This isn't watching out for Jos here tonight or letting her tag along on a day trip. This isn't fixing a leaky tap for her.'

'What then?'

'How do you feel about breaking a few laws?' Peter then talked and Wendell listened.

Wendell paid attention the way Henk had fourteen years before, understanding what was at stake, and how Jos should be able to walk away, how the Nyerere's had to be protected. The way he spoke about Jos in particular, helped Wendell to understand how much Peter loved her, and how he would protect her above all else. Peter needed Jos. The world, he said, would be a much better place with Jos in it.

Jude was a different matter entirely.

CHAPTER TWENTY-NINE

Jude had returned to her suite a lot earlier than anticipated last night.

Her good looking American had proved to be rather good company over dinner and, perhaps inevitably, they ended up in his room a little later. Jude would never have taken him back to her place because she preferred to be able to leave when she chose… as opposed to having to wait on him to get the hell out. Not that Jude had gone to his room expecting to be leaving in less than an hour. My god, she'd spent three times that preparing… most of that being waxed to within an inch of her life at the hotel spa. And for what? Sex that made her feel like a virgin again, in the sense it was clumsy, uninspiring and over in seconds.

Wham bam, he didn't stay awake long enough to even say thank you ma'am!

On the up side Jude managed a full eight hours sleep, waking just before ten a.m. She had a coffee and began getting ready to leave. Using two of the envelopes found inside the desk in her suite, she transferred the tip for the concierge into one, and payment for the Jeep into the other. At noon she checked out and retired to the bar for an early lunch before setting off.

As she was leaving, her American accosted her in the middle of the busy reception area.

'Judy!'

Jude cringed, and turned to see him striding her way, waving wildly as if they were miles apart, wearing a big stupid grin. Yesterday that goofy smile had seemed so appealing. Right then, she just wanted to punch him. 'Jude,' she told him flatly. 'My name is Jude.'

'Are you leaving, honey? So soon? We had such a great night last night… I was kinda hoping for a rematch… if y'know what I mean.'

He actually winked, and Jude said, 'You have all the sexual prowess of a wet halibut, honey. Not on your life.' Blowing him a little kiss, she turned away and made for the doors, shooting a wink at the receptionist who was trying her best not to laugh.

*

At the white house Jos was in the caves with Peter.

Never in her life had she drunk as much as she and Peter combined, had put away in the Kilimanjaro Wonders Hotel bar last night. Even Peter, and his possibly hardened liver, had trouble walking back outside, and poor Wendell had no choice but to drive Jos home. She then vaguely remembered getting meat out of the freezer, sticking it in a bin bag and sending Wendell down to the cellar with it. The next thing she remembered was waking up just before dawn in textbook recovery position in the middle of the bed, fully dressed except for her trainers which were placed neatly together on the floor at the side of the bed. There was even a pillow tucked in behind her back to stop her rolling over onto it, and a large glass of water on the table de chevet. No way had Jos done any of that, so Wendell must have taken care of her unconscious arse before going home.

Peter had taken the next shift.

Sitting in the armchair by the window overlooking the roof garden, he'd watched over Jos all night. Completely independent from her then, and so as bright as a button and as smiley as a sickeningly smiley thing, when she eventually noticed him.

'You did this to me. Again!'

'We did it together, Jos. We make a good team.'

'Fuck off.' Getting to her feet very slowly, Jos began making her careful way to the bathroom, but ended up making a dash for it so she could throw up into the toilet. 'Oh my god…' she groaned, sitting on the floor afterwards. 'Why does it taste like bananas?'

'Dirty bananas,' Peter informed, from the doorway. 'Rum, Baileys, ice and a banana, all whizzed up in a blender. You loved them! You kept telling Wendell they were one of your five a day. We had three.' 'Why didn't you stop me?'

Shrugging, Peter pointed out, 'My last night out. Ever.'

Resigned, Jos reached for the door to push it closed. 'Bugger off. I need a shower.'

Feeling slightly better after that, she'd gone down to the cellar to fetch the meat. Any mess was, thankfully, non-existent. Jos then made her way down to the underground passageway, picking up Peter on the way.

Together they made their way along the darkened passage and into the dim light of the small chamber at the far end. Their friend was waiting, hungry again and, as she settled down to eat the fully defrosted, two kilos of minced beef, Jos sat down on a ledge nearby and watched.

'You and Wendell bonded last night,' she remembered. 'I can't believe you called him Wendi.'

'Like you haven't been tempted,' Peter smiled. 'Where do you think I got it from?'

'I like to imagine he lives in a yellow house with a red roof.' Jos returned his smile. 'He'll be okay though, won't he? I want everyone to walk away from this… especially Wendi. This has sod-all to do with him.'

'And if he didn't want to help, he wouldn't. Free will, Jos. We all have it. Some exercise it better than others, but it is up to us as individuals to determine what we are willing to do for others.'

'Okay, okay.' Having finished her snack, the lioness had made her way over to Jos where she nudged her with that massive head. 'What if she's still hungry? What if she eats me now?'

'She's just saying hello.' Jos didn't look convinced, so Peter told her, 'Just imagine she's a giant tabby cat. Tickle her behind an ear.'

Tentatively Jos reached out a hand, stroking the massive head. The lioness purred. 'Oh my god she's purring! I can feel the vibration.' Jos was delighted, and the thrill emboldened her. She caressed that head with both hands, feeling the depth of fur, the course outer hairs and the soft velvet close to the heat of her body. The lioness responded, pushing against Jos and she ran both hands down the length of the powerful back and, when the lioness lay down on the floor and rolled onto one side, Jos got down there with her, rubbing her soft white belly. She wanted to bury her face as well as her hands in there. To smell her, to cuddle her. When the front paws came up to her head, she flinched only very slightly. Feeling the weight as those big hairy paws batted her face, her hair, and gently held her head. The soft leather of the pads pressed against her cheek, and they were face to face. Jos could feel her breath, smell the metallic scent of the meat just eaten. She could also feel the stray tear that trickled down her cheek, because she felt overcome… stuck between joy in that moment and despair for what would come next. As if sensing the latter, the lioness licked that tear away with a decisive upward sweep of her rough tongue. Then, looking Jos in the eye, she snorted a little, raising her head in an upward nod.

Then she got up off the floor and went to sit by Peter.

'Tell me everything is going to be all right,' Jos told him.

*

After leaving the hotel, Jude took the A109 south from Nairobi, and reached Mtito Andei Railway Station at around six thirty p.m. She found a shaded parking space for the Land Cruiser, and then walked into the station where she sat down on the seat closest to the windows. They were a couple of minutes late. The Jeep Wrangler arrived first, closely followed by a beat-up looking Peugeot. Jude waited for them both to park up, and then she went out to meet them.

After some brief introductions, she lifted the bonnet, had the nephew get in, start and rev the engine. She then walked around the jeep, fingers finding small dings and scratches. She checked the tyres, oil, and fuel gage. Finally, she checked the log book details against the nephew's ID. He got a bit shirty then. 'You'd prefer that I come to the hotel if anything goes wrong?' she wondered.

'Nothing will go wrong,' he insisted. 'This is worth every cent of the eight grand you'll pay me now.'

Jude eyed the concierge, pleased to see him looking much more flustered than he'd ever allow himself to look in his pristine suit. 'Excuse me a moment.' She walked a short distance away, took out the fattest envelope and removed two thousand dollars. Tucking that into a zipped inner pocket in her bag, she removed the thin envelope and walked back to the men holding onto both. The fat one she handed to the nephew in exchange for the log book and keys. The other one she held out to the concierge. 'As agreed,' she told him. 'Thank you for all your help.'

They were both busy counting the money in their respective envelopes as Jude drove the jeep away. She didn't go far however, just a short distance south, where she waited for ten minutes before turning the jeep around and heading back towards the station.

After ascertaining both men as well as the beat-up Peugeot were gone, she parked next to her hire car and transferred all her belongings into the jeep before setting off for real.

Once again, she headed south, but this time Jude kept going. At nine p.m. she reached Voi, where she filled the tank, before turning west onto the A23 and heading for the border with Tanzania. Of course, there was the small matter of an outstanding warrant with her name on it. Who could forget a thing like that? So, she wouldn't be passing into Tanzania using the official border crossing.

Jude had other plans, and a detailed map of the region.

A few miles east of the border there was a fork in the road, and a short drive into the town of Taveta. There was a road from there that travelled south right along the border, but Jude opted for a second route that moved away from that border to a place called Kiwalwa. A junction close to a river there, pointed her in the right direction for the next leg, and she found that turning just after eleven p.m. on Tuesday night.

*

At seven thirty p.m. Jos was seated on the front porch staring into space.

She hadn't spent much time out there, and it was a cool, peaceful place to sit in the early evening. A nice place to avoid Beola, who'd had it in for her all day. She had wasted no time that morning pointing out that Jos shouldn't be allowing Peter to lead her so far astray. Peter was selfish and Jos was foolish. What if Wendell hadn't been there? What if Peter tried to drive? What if something worse happened?

And who would fetch the jeep?

Beola no doubt had several very valid points, but Jos didn't appreciate listening to them over and over, all day long, in slightly different formats. Knowing Beola's motivations lay in a past and unfulfilled attraction to Peter coupled with current envy of his close relationship to her, didn't make it easier for Jos to bear… mostly, because she was forced to keep that little nugget to herself.

Kissi had been around all day and, although Beola had kept her sniping little comments to times when her husband wasn't around to overhear, Jos knew the resulting fallout from any surprise bombshells on her part would undoubtedly attract his attention. She was, however, rapidly losing patience with trying to protect the woman who was attacking her. All because Peter wanted the Nyerere's protected from Jude.

Ben had inadvertently sparked the latest round of critique by arriving less than an hour previously in the abandoned jeep, with the news that Wendell was just popping home to collect a few things before returning to stay the night, and could he also have dinner?

'Why is Wendell staying the night?' Beola wanted to know.

Jos was minding her own business prepping a large salad but felt two sets of expectant eyes watching her. In for a penny, she thought and, turning around she said, 'Peter is sure Jude will arrive tomorrow. He thinks it's for the best if none of you are here when she arrives, and Wendell has agreed to be my moral support.'

'This is my home,' Beola spat. 'You don't get to tell me when to leave it.'

'Mama?' Ben was shocked.

'Whatever happened to… make yourself at home… my family are caretakers of this house, but it still belongs to Peter, to Jude… and it also belongs to you.'

'Jos!' Ben was even more shocked.

'I apologise for upsetting you, Ben. That was not my intention. But your mama has been speaking to me as if I'm a complete idiot all damn day.' Jos was looking directly at Beola by then, feeling rather satisfied to see the open-mouthed surprise gawping back at her. 'I'm sick of it, Beola. You've been off with me since Friday. Nothing specific, just little digs and comments designed to make me feel like the bad one. I know how this game works because I've been playing that shit with Jude for…'

'How dare you accuse me of…'

'Of being just like Jude?' Jos cut back in. 'Are you sure you're not just scapegoating me to make yourself feel better about something that is out of my control. You brought me here.'

'Peter brought you here.'

Putting on a mental pair of skates, Jos headed right for the edge. 'And now that the dynamic has shifted, you can't handle the fact I get all the attention now.'

Ben barely got started telling Jos off again, when Beola yelled at him to go back to the lodge until dinner was ready. As soon as he was gone, she turned on Jos again. 'How dare you!'

'I do dare,' Jos told her, a whole lot calmer, at least on the outside. Inside she was curled up in a ball on a bed somewhere and pulling the duvet over her head. 'I might only have been here a week, but I know everything there is to know about Peter now.' Pointing at her head, she added, 'His life, loves and experiences are all stored up here now. You can make your nasty little comments, feeling bitter because you think I stole him away. But if you think Jude won't come here… or won't harm you when she does, then you're fooling yourself, Beola. She knows as well as I do that you always had the hots for her husband.'

Beola was stunned, staring at Jos as if she'd been slapped.

Jos carried on, 'As far as I'm concerned Jude should be burned at the fucking stake for what she did to him, but Peter has his own ideas. He only needs me to fuel his influence in that direction, and I am wide eyed and wide awake in supporting him in this endeavour. That is not up for discussion. As for you staying or leaving. Peter's the one to be adamant that you, Ben and Kissi are protected. I'm just the messenger. If you have a problem with that…' Jos tossed the paring knife onto the counter. '… take it up with Peter.'

The porch seemed like the safest place after that, and Jos was still sitting there, still holding onto herself, when Wendell arrived.

'How was your head this morning?' he wondered.

Shuddering, Jos told him, 'Thank you for looking after me.'

'What was the meat for, Jos… you kept saying last night that it was for magic.'

'Yeah…' Jos had no idea how to proceed, so she just said, 'I was really drunk. Luckily, Peter remembered for us both, so I've cleaned it all up.'

'Don't tell me then.'

'If I promise to tell you everything tomorrow, will that do?'

'Reckon its good enough.'

'Good.' After a moment she asked, 'Are you sure about staying here tomorrow? You really don't have to.'

'How else will I find out about the magic meat?'

Jos laughed for the first time that day. 'But seriously… you are under no obligation to get involved in this shit at all. We could end up in real trouble.'

'Peter told me he managed to ensure his wife got free and clear after killing him. Something about a few bucks paid in the right places, and he has promised me that my liberty will not be interrupted. Someone called Henk…?'

'Of course…' Jos suddenly remembered the rehab centre conversation that took place just before heading back to the white house. It popped up from memory in its entirety. Peter and Henk hadn't just reminisced, they had laid the rescue plan groundwork too. Henk had funds enough to make sure that, if Jos and Wendell ended up in the hands of the police, he could make the charges disappear. Not murder this time, so easier perhaps. Once Jos was free, she would be able to reimburse the Dutchman. 'Henk made sure no charges were filed against Jude.'

'But why?'

'So, she would be in Edinburgh when I needed her. My parents were killed. I was fifteen. I needed Jude more than Peter needed her punished.'

'But how could he know that?'

'Maasai magic, Wendell.' Jos stood up and took his hand in both her own. He looked a little taken aback, wary even. Maybe he thought she was about to make a pass. The idea of kissing him right there and then occurred and made Jos' stomach do a few backflips. But now was not the time. 'Welcome to my world,' she told him firmly. 'It's a bit shit at the moment, but I'm confident now that, no matter what happens in the next twenty-four hours, me and you are gonna be fine.' Sagging a little, she let go his hand, and added, 'If only it was going to be as simple as it sounds.'

*

Heading west again, the town right on the border, was called Kitobo.

But Jude didn't reach Kitobo, because around seventy percent of the way there, having literally counted the miles on the odometer after turning onto the dirt road leading there, she had pulled in behind some road side shrubs and walked the route on foot using a hand torch until she found what she was looking for. But she couldn't see any decent landmarks to help her find the spot again when she returned in the jeep, so she spent a few minutes collecting enough stones to make a small pile on the opposite side of the track.

Back in the jeep, Jude drove back along the track, until she saw her small pile of stones, she then swung to the right and drove off the road and down the steep incline onto the flat bottom of the riverbed.

In rainy season this waterway would be flowing at full tilt with run off from the slopes of Mount Kilimanjaro. It cut across the north east corner of Tanzania and wound its way south and east into Kenya and beyond. Jude would follow it in the upstream direction and, at a steady speed of around twenty miles per hour, she should cross into Tanzania around two hours after setting off along this hazardous route. When the route cut into a small, forested area, she would know that she was close.

It was not a great journey.

Jude had to keep her headlights off most of the time, and the river bed was strewn with rocks and even boulders. The jeep lurched and bumped along, its undercarriage often grinding over bigger rocks, or its flanks scraping along boulders. Sometimes she didn't see the boulders at all until it was too late, and the resulting clash between stone and metal was attention seeking to say the least. It might have been less conspicuous just to drive through the official crossing with streamers and balloons and air horns blasting. But, if anyone was aware of her passing, Jude was never aware of them. And so, she kept on going, bumping and grinding her way to the border. Eventually, she became aware of deeper darkness closing in, and realised she'd reached the place where a long strip of forest straddled the water way.

She kept on going, risking her headlights in fits and starts; lighting up the way ahead, and then steering on memory. The water way was pinched between the trees, something not so apparent on her map. The sides were higher, and the going was much tougher in places. The little jeep struggled to traverse the landscape of large flat stones and huge rounded boulders. Sometimes Jude was roaring as loud as the engine, with the sheer effort of keeping moving. She had to keep going, so the jeep had to keep going.

There was no stopping her now.

Finally, she saw stars again, and knew the trees either side were thinning, receding. She was in Tanzania. Tired as well as relieved, Jude switched off the engine and set an alarm on her mobile.

It was one forty a.m.

CHAPTER THIRTY

'You should get some sleep,' Peter told Jos.

They were sitting in the garden in their usual place. Jos was shredding a wad of tissues with nervous hands. She'd raged and laughed and cried over the past few hours but, by then, she was just terrified. Peter had just told her that Jude was in Tanzania. He speculated that she'd crossed the border somewhere unofficial under cover of darkness. It was only a matter of hours now.

At least dinner was a lot less stressful than Jos feared, mostly because Peter came too.

Last night, once Wendell was sure Jos would be okay, but not sure if he should leave her alone, Peter had appeared out of thin air to tell him he would take it from there. So, when he did the same appearing act on the porch, just as Ben was walking up the steps, Wendell didn't bat an eyelash.

Ben, on the other hand, moved swiftly through open mouthed shock, to excited four-year-old, to jumping up and down wagging his hand and yelling, because he tried to touch Peter and got a shock. Literally.

'He did that to me too,' Jos told him with wide eyes. 'You should've seen my hair.'

Kissi came out then, to lie about dinner being ready.

He'd heard Beola shouting earlier and had been in the kitchen with her since. He'd asked her what was wrong, and she'd told him about her concerns surrounding Jos and how she was under Peter's influence, she didn't know what she was doing, she wasn't using brains she'd been born with. He'd heard little else recently, and enough was enough.

'You must think I am very stupid too,' he told his wife. 'Do you really believe that I am not aware that you and Peter were just a little bit close for my comfort when he was still living?' When Beola opened her mouth in protest, Kissi held up a hand. 'Do not treat me as badly as you have treated Jos. You are my wife Beola, my love, the mother of our son. My very soul belongs to you, and I know you have never betrayed me. Do you imagine that I have gone through the past thirty-eight years without looking with desire upon another woman? It's okay to look, okay to wonder.' She was melting before his eyes by then, her icy stare turning to tears, and he moved close so he could kiss them off her cheeks. Then he whispered into her ear, 'When I look at you, there are no other women. Only you.' Stepping back so he could look into her eyes. Kissi added, 'Our friend Peter may leave us for good very soon. Let's not waste these last few hours bickering about who saw him first.'

Sinking down onto the nearest chair, Beola covered her face with her hands, 'I am such a fool.'

'No one has ever called Beola Nyerere a fool, and we are not about to start now.'

'What must Jos think of me?'

Lifting her troubled face so he could smile down at her, Kissi suggested, 'That you are a jealous and unscrupulous woman?'

'She said I was just like Jude.'

'Then I am grateful you do not also have a gun!'

'How can you joke?' Beola wondered. 'I have treated you…'

'Always with the love and respect that I deserve.'

'I do not deserve you.'

'That is for me to decide.' Kissi encouraged Beola to her feet, and he hugged her and kissed her, and he held her face so he could look in eyes until he saw their little sparkles returning. He then sent her away to freshen up… a little rashly perhaps, because he then found himself in charge of dinner. Minced meat in a big lump in a bowl, tomato sauce, chopped onions, honey, mustard, garlic, and a mountain of chipped potatoes. That was when he decided it was time to fetch the children.

But Kissi forgot all about that when he saw his old friend. Peter Sinclair was right there, leaning back against the porch railing, legs crossed at the ankles, hands animated as he chatted to Ben, Jos and Wendell. He looked real, and yet he was dead. 'Peter…' Kissi barely whispered, moving towards him, a hand outstretched. Ben said something and pushed that hand aside. 'I… I…' Kissi's eyes filled with tears suddenly, his face crumpling. He'd just been strong for Beola but couldn't now be strong for himself. All the guilt of the past few days, knowing not only that it had been Jude, but how she'd succeeded too. It all felt so suddenly overwhelming, 'I am so very sorry, my friend.'

'Why?' Peter wondered gently; his face as troubled.

'I taught her how to shoot.'

'She missed,' Peter smiled. 'I think it was Girl Guiding that taught Jude to use a lighter. I'm definitely suing.'

When his papa moved further forward, his hand outstretched once more, Ben stopped him again. 'He's electric. It hurts. I'm still tingling all the way up my arm.'

'Jos' fault,' Peter said with an apologetic smile. 'I've become supercharged, because of her energy.'

'Just something else I'm to blame for,' Jos tried to sound light hearted, but she felt full of lead. She was waiting on Kissi to notice her, to shame her or shout at her.

'Jos!' Kissi gave her his best smile. 'Do you have any idea what we're having for dinner?'

'Homemade burgers and triple cooked chips.'

'Sounds wonderful.' Putting an arm around her shoulders, Kissi began steering Jos towards the kitchen. Over his shoulder, he mouthed, 'Triple cooked?' Then made a face, before adding, 'Come on people, sounds like we need to take turns cooking those chips.'

'Maybe Peter can zap them?' Ben looked around, but their ghost was no longer there.

Peter was already in the kitchen, ready to make everyone feel guilty about his inability to enjoy or even smell what was on offer, no matter how many times it was cooked. Jos put the real men to work mixing all the other ingredients into the mince so they could then make patties. The three of them interrogating Peter about his current circumstances as they worked.

'Of course, you are a ghost!' Ben told him at one point. 'Moving stuff around, making a mess, playing loud music…'

'Sounds more like a poltergeist,' Kissi thought.

'I am not a poltergeist. Or a ghost. I'm the same old Peter… just a little bit lacking in matter.'

Jos had just finished steaming all the chips ready for the first fry, when Beola arrived. She looked composed, but Jos could tell she'd been crying. She tried, unsuccessfully not to feel guilty about that, not to feel sick waiting on the next confrontation.

Beola could tell, and she wanted to let Jos know everything was okay, but then she noticed their other guest. 'Peter?'

'Don't worry, Bee…' He said. 'I'm not hungry. Though I would like to

try this new phenomenon of the triple cooked chip.'

Suddenly everyone wanted to know why the chips had to be cooked three times. 'Because they're bloody brilliant like that,' Jos told them all firmly. 'Have you finished making those burgers yet, they need to go into the oven.'

Burgers cooking in the oven was another new phenomenon.

'There's only eight,' Ben observed.

'That's all the minced beef there was.' Beola didn't understand it. 'I was sure I had more.'

Jos and Peter shared a look, then she distracted everyone by shaking up her steamed chips to make their surfaces fluffy, before starting to cook them for the second time.

Burger and chips took on a whole new dimension that evening. Jos received so many compliments… especially from Kissi and Beola who were definitely over-compensating, she was red faced with embarrassment. At one point, Peter disappeared from view and then immediately manifested inside Jos, just so he could try the now infamous triple cooked chips. She brought an end to it after a few mouthfuls… mostly because he was eating like a pig. 'Enough!' She spoke louder and more forcefully than intended, giving everyone a fright, and then she laughed at Peter's shocked face when he reappeared on the chair opposite her.

*

After dinner, and several rounds of beer and wine, they all got down to the business of impending Jude.

'I'd be a lot happier if none of you guys were here,' Peter told the Nyerere's. 'I know Jude will come. She knows I'm here, and I think she'll want to see me for herself. I don't know what she'll do when that happens, but I do know she's dangerous.'

'In an ideal world, she will come here, retrieve the gun and then leave,' Kissi said. 'Job done. But I suspect it won't be as simple.'

Beola refused point blank to leave the white house, but she had a wellreasoned argument to hand, 'I love this house and I want to keep it safe from harm,' she told them. 'I won't go anywhere near Jude, and I promise not to interfere, but I will not abandon this house.'

Ben was torn. 'I'd planned a day at the beach with Nightingale.' His

turn then to be embarrassed by all the comments and attention… though his flushed cheeks were a lot harder to see than the ones Jos had worn. 'I don't have to go… we can go next week.'

'You will go tomorrow,' Beola told him. 'I want grandchildren. Don't let me down.'

'Steady on,' Wendell told her. 'Pretty sure that sort of behaviour is frowned upon on the beaches of Tanzania.' Ben was mortified.

'While I don't particularly like knowing my wife will be here when a killer comes calling…' Kissi began. '… I feel a lot better knowing you will be here,' he spoke to Wendell, 'We've known one another these past three years and I know you will have Beola's back should she need that.' 'Absolutely,' Wendell told him.

'Then I will go to work as planned. If something happens… if we attract attention in ways I do not wish to go into now…. then we need to be where we are supposed to be. Go to the coast with Nightingale,' Kissi told his son. 'If you have any long-term plans with her, you cannot take part in something you will need to keep a secret from her for the rest of your life. Beola, my love, this is indeed your place and so you should be here. And Wendell… you will be here to spend some time with Jos… while keeping an eye upon my wife. Jos…' Kissi looked her in the eye, and said, 'None of us can protect you from what is coming. Are you prepared to make your stand with Peter knowing that?'

'I am.' She nodded once, determinedly.

'Then it's decided.' Kissi then stood up and went to the gun cabinet to collect the rifle and all the ammunition. No one staying in the white house the following day knew how to handle a gun… except Jude of course, and he wasn't about to leave her any options in that direction. He then stowed the rifle as well as all the ammunition in the locked box inside his jeep. He would take it all with him when he left home tomorrow for what could be a very long day indeed.

He then bade them all a good night and went upstairs with Beola.

'I feel like I'm letting you all down,' Ben said quietly once his parents were gone.

'When I first met you…' Jos told him. 'After the luggage trolley incident.' She laughed. 'I took your arm and I walked out of that airport feeling like I was immune to everything, from muggers to lightning strikes.

I was a frightened little mouse. One week on, I am a different person, Ben. Don't get me wrong, I am shittin' bricks at the thought of Jude rockin' up in this beautiful place, but Peter can't face her without me. He deserves his day.'

Ben and Wendell headed off to the lodge soon after that.

Jos went up to the garden with a large glass of wine, and the wad of tissues she'd been using to mop up her tears when she started blubbing. It was such a relief knowing Beola was no longer the enemy. Nothing had been said, but the atmosphere was back to how it had been during the first few days after her arrival. One less thing to worry about, because the thought of Jude heading their way was scaring the crap out of Jos. 'I'm far too afraid to sleep,' she told Peter in response to his suggestion that she try. 'I'll help,' he said. 'I need you to sleep because I need your strength.'

'Oh, all right.' Getting up, Jos went through the motions of her before bed routine and then lay on top of the bed without bothering to undress. Waiting. Worrying. Before long she felt Peter inside her mind, filling her thoughts with peace and tranquillity. She fought against him for a time, determined to stay awake so she could fret some more, but he won. After a short time, Jos relinquished her consciousness and slipped into sleep, carried away on a river of joy that took her into some happy little dreams.

*

Jude woke with a start.

‘Shit!’ Scrambling around she found her mobile and was set to toss it out the jeep window in her anger at its total failure to waken her, when she saw that the alarm had gone off. It was she who had failed. She’d slept through it and now it was nearly full daylight, and she could be seen. She had no choice but to get on with it. Digging into her bag she found a bottle of water and took a few swigs, then she keyed the ignition and resumed her journey along the last stretch of riverbed towards the Tanzanian side of the A23.

She saw a few boys herding goats on the way, but no one else. They pointed to her, laughing, as her jeep bounced and scraped its way on by. She ignored them and reached the road just before six a.m.

Two hours later than planned, but at least she’d slept and was fully alert again by the time she could see trucks passing by on the highway up ahead.

It wasn’t as bad as she feared though. Once Jude got close to the highway, she could see some kind of an outbuilding on her side, and it had a little access track leading down to it. The riverbed widened there too, and the sides were low, caved in in places and she was able to drive up and out of the waterway fairly easily. A few hundred yards across a dry field and she soon had all four tyres on the access track.

She stopped there for a few minutes, getting out of the jeep and ducking behind the building for a quick pee. Back in the jeep Jude waited for a gap in the traffic, which was light this early anyway, then drove towards the highway and stopped again just a few feet from it. She got out, taking her map with her. She made a show of spreading the map out on the bonnet and peering at it. Just a woman who had lost her way. No one passing by bothered to stop because no one was in the least bit interested.

It was as Jude was getting back into the jeep that she saw the state of it!

It was bashed and scraped; the headlights cracked but not broken. It looked like it had perhaps been squashed by mistake in a car crusher at a breakers yard, and then ironed out again as best they could. It also fitted right in. She might stick out like a big old sore thumb driving this wreck through the leafy streets of Edinburgh, but in dusty Tanzania it was just another beat up motor. She took a few minutes to pull the clumps of weed out from its bumpers and rocker panels… a dead giveaway that she'd been travelling off road. Then she got back in, started the engine which was running fine despite the damage to the bodywork, and headed west towards Himo.

*

Jos woke up just after seven a.m.

Still wearing the clothes from the night before, she stripped and showered, dressed again and was trotting down the internal stairs in time to see Beola and Kissi in a tight embrace in the foyer below. Part of Jos wished Kissi would toss Beola over his shoulder and take her away; that would mean one less thing to worry about when Jude showed up. But he didn't. He kissed Beola, holding her face in both hands and then he left. The sound of his jeep was soon fading as he drove away and left them all to it.

'Did you sleep?' Jos asked, when she reached the bottom.

Beola looked at her for a time before answering, 'A little.'

'Are you still angry with me?'

'I don't think I was ever angry with you.' Suddenly Beola was reaching for Jos, holding her tight and saying softly, 'Forgive me.'

*

In the kitchen Ben was munching toast and walking on air despite the weight that wanted to keep him down. When his mama came in with Jos, he got up and began fetching them coffee, juice, toast. 'Are you sure you don't want me to stay?' he asked his mama.

'I'd rather have a daughter-in-law,' Beola told him.

Ben looked at Jos, afraid suddenly, but she laughed, and so did he.

Wendell was last in, because he'd had to wait for Ben to finish up in the bathroom, before getting in there himself. 'G'day folks,' he said, looking at Jos mainly. Looking for signs of Peter, but she was one hundred percent Jos right then. 'How are you holding up?'

'I'm good,' she nodded, taking a mug of coffee from Ben before sitting down. 'I slept pretty well.'

'I hardly slept a wink,' he admitted, sitting next to her.

'Peter helped me,' Jos told him quietly. 'Are you still up for this?'

He nodded. 'No worries.'

'What are you two whispering about?' Ben wondered, delivering a round of toast and a tub of honey to the table.

'A bloke can indulge in a bit of harmless flirting, can't he?'

Ben accepted this answer at face value, but Beola sensed the schemes and plans. She kept her thoughts to herself though. Her son would be safe. Her husband would also be safe. She would not interfere, and so they would all be safe.

Wendell and Jos would have to look out for each other.

*

Jude passed straight through Himo and kept on until she reached Karamsingi.

She got there just before eight a.m. and stopped at a little store to buy fruit which she ate as she drove further along the road to the west side of town. There was a fuel station there and she stopped to refill the tank, buying a chocolate bar and some fruit juice to keep her going.

Next stop Moshi Urban.

*

Ben was gone by eight a.m., focusing on Nightingale and whatever the future may hold for them.

Beola was with her bees, preparing for the trials of the day ahead by focussing on hundreds of thousands of some of the most industrious creatures on the planet. She had to work quietly and calmly, moving from hive to hive. Her hands gentle and sure. Visiting, saying hello, making sure all was well inside each hive, before moving on to the next. It was meditative, healing.

Wendell was sitting on the white house porch alone, thinking about his mother and how, when this day was over, he would drink a few less beers a week and save just a little bit faster so he could fly her over to Tanzy for a visit. Thinking that he should call her tonight, when a Maasai elder walked out between the trees lining the top of the drive. He was accompanied by a single warrior. Wendell stood up, unsure how to greet them, and was just about to go fetch Jos, when she beat him to it.

She'd been standing in the garden with Peter.

There was electricity between them, static shocks if they got too close. Jos was functioning at a much higher level of awareness than usual. Her entire body flooded with adrenalin. Flight or fight, and she was totally wired. She'd plaited her hair tightly, one hanging down each side like a squaw in an effort to stop it taking off in the electrical storm that was building between her and Peter. They were side by side, looking out over the tree tops to the place his life had ended, when red coloured movements down below caught her eye. She turned and ran, taking the internal stairs two at a time and bursting through the front doors at full speed. Crossing the porch in two long strides, she then jumped down the steps in a single bound and ran out onto the lawn to meet them.

'Joseph!' She ran up to him, into him, hugging him, crying with relief because the cavalry had come. 'Thank you,' she told him. 'Thank you for being here.'

Joseph held her, stroking her back, soothing her, until she calmed.

When she relaxed, he held her away from him, and looked into her eyes. Then, smiling, he indicated his companion, 'This is Nalutuesha. He is Naserian's brother and so he is my brother. He is your brother too, little sister.'

Nalutuesha was the first Maasai warrior Jos had seen up close and personal without Peter inside her head, diluting the experience. He was beautiful. Tall and slender, with a great smile and sparkling eyes. Dressed in a bright red shuka worn as a kilt, with a bush knife tucked into the beaded belt around his hips. His bare chest was intricately adorned with beaded hoops and necklaces. His long hair, plaited and as intricately decorated. He wore numerous bracelets around both wrists and carried an eight-foot-long Turkana spear, its leaf shaped blade sheathed in leather. As she shook his hand, she fell in love with him just a little, and understood implicitly why Peter had wandered so far from home with these men. 'Won't you come in?' she asked. 'Are you hungry? Thirsty?' She introduced them to Wendell, and then they all went inside and into the kitchen.

Peter was there already and, after making as much of their greetings as was possible, he and Joseph went out to the patio for a little powwow.

'I fear that Jos believes I am here to defend her,' Joseph said.

'Jos knows exactly what is going on,' Peter assured. 'She just enjoys the moral support.'

'And our other friend?'

'Has agreed to help in the aftermath.'

'I would like to speak with him now.'

'Wendell?'

Joseph shook his head.

'This way…' Peter led Joseph back into the foyer via the French doors, told him where the key was and took it from there.

In the kitchen Jos was discovering she knew some Swahili.

'Ungependa chai?' She wondered of her visiting warrior.

Supposing his mouth, Nalutuesha replied in perfect English, 'I'd prefer to have coffee.'

Jos looked at Wendell and they both burst out laughing.

It was nine a.m.

*

Jude was driving through Moshi by then, heading west.

Ben was heading east.

When Ben turned off the A23 to drive northward towards where Nightingale lived with her parents, Jude passed behind him, still on the A23 heading west. She was beginning to feel nervous. She had no idea what or who would be waiting. Would they be expecting her? The last time she'd tried to get into the white house unescorted, she'd been barred by a whole battalion of Maasai warriors. Would Peter be there, a shimmering shadow of his former self? Would Jos be there, snuffling and blubbing like the selfish little piglet she was. What about Beola? Kissi?

Ben? Maybe they would all be there? If they were all there, what would she do? Jude hadn't really thought that far ahead. All she'd thought clearly about was getting hold of that bloody gun and dumping it into the lake. An endless parade of scenarios began to pass through Jude's mind, and she barely noticed that she'd slowed and turned off the main road to travel south towards the white house.

*

At twenty past nine, Peter appeared in the kitchen. 'She just crested the escarpment,' he told Jos. 'She'll be here very soon.' Getting up, Wendell said, 'I'll fetch Beola.' 'What will I do?' Jos wondered.

'Just stay with me,' Peter told her. 'Together now, no matter what.'

CHAPTER THIRTY-ONE

Jude couldn't see the white house at all as she approached the hill it stood upon.

The last time she'd driven that road it had been barely discernible to all but those who knew it was there. But now the trees had grown up around it, and the house was completely hidden. She wondered if the view still existed. The view from their bedroom, where Peter had loved to sit and look out across at the mountain. His favourite view.

Jude had seen it first, from their hotel room terrace, wrapped up in a shuka against the cold.

The land was flat all around, and she could see for miles then too, see there was no other traffic. The hill was soon all that she could see, and she just followed the track as it approached the base. Eventually the track forked, one continuing on past the hill, the other climbing almost immediately as it began winding itself around the hill, on its way up to the beautiful house her husband had built for her. The house he gave to another woman. Jude pictured herself scratching Beola's eyes out if she was up there waiting and the buzz gleaned from that little daydream bolstered her resolve a little.

She didn't follow the track for long.

There was a little flat area about a third of the way up, a natural layby. Driving into it, Jude pushed the jeep forward further than she needed to, pushing the front as far into the undergrowth as she could go. Pretty far as it turned out, because she had to climb over the seats into the storage space at the back and climb down from there. Having retrieved the trowel from her belongs first, Jude broke a few manageable sized branches from the surrounding trees and used them to hide the back of the jeep as best she could. She then began to climb up the slope towards the house.

Following much the same route the lioness took in the early hours of Sunday morning.

*

Beola was in the master bedroom, seated in Peter's chair.

She was able to see the top half of the mountain clearly, its summits swathed in a dome of cloud which meant bad weather was coming. She was alone in the white house because Wendell and Jos had gone to the lodge. Peter would be there too, she supposed. Beola refused to go. There had been a time when she refused to live in the white house, but that morning she refused to desert it. If Jude was to set foot inside that place then Beola would be there, watching.

*

Wendell and Jos were not watching anything much.

They were seated on Ben's sofa, side by side facing a TV that was off. Peter was seated on an armchair at one side, head down, delivering a running commentary in hushed tones. Jude's presence was an irritation to him. Her effect as tangible as that experienced with Jos, but at the other end of that spectrum entirely. Being around Jos felt good to him, her energy sunny and fresh, like a breeze blowing through the tree tops.

Every move Jude made took something good away. She was crawling across his landscape like an insect better suited to the depths of polluted earth. Her proximity a contamination, a disease infecting the paradise he'd created in life and protected in death.

*

Joseph and Nalutuesha were first to see Jude.

They heard her before they saw her, a brief glimpse as she passed on by close to the narrow cave mouth, climbing upward among the trees, carrying nothing but a small spade. The lioness shuddered and then tensed, every fibre of her being poised. Joseph blessed her with spells learned from his friend and mentor Laputo Edward Ngoyo and sent her on her way.

After a minute, he and Nalutuesha followed, moving as silently as the lioness stalked.

*

Having come up behind the lodge, Jude held her ground behind the tree line to watch, wait and listen for long minutes until she was sure no one was in there. After a time, she moved quickly and quietly forward until she was under the main bedroom window. Peeking in she saw signs of occupation, but no one was there then. Around the side, she peaked into the smaller of the two sitting room windows and saw nothing but an empty sofa and a blank TV. Nobody home. When she reached the front corner of the lodge she stopped again, hugging the wall and peeking around the corner, listening intently. Nothing, just the birds, the crickets, a monkey shrieking somewhere further off.

Nothing but the garages between her and the house.

Jude crossed the space between the lodge and the garage block as quickly as possible. Back to the rear wall of the garages she surveyed the front windows of the lodge, alert for any sign of movement inside. But there was nothing. Just blank windows. Silence. Moving along the rear wall towards the well housing end, she rounded that corner as carefully and quietly, crept along the side wall to the front corner of the building, and from there she could see the house. As beautiful and brilliant as it ever was. Jude's heart beat faster just to see it. How she loved that house. How she had missed it. A house worth killing for, if ever there was one.

Again, Jude stopped, listened, watched.

Again, there was nothing.

It had to be a trap.

*

At Peter's warning, Wendell and Jos had moved from the sitting room into the bathroom which had a small window set high up in the outer wall. Too high for anyone to see through without the aid of a ladder. Wendell sat down on the closed loo seat, quiet and patient and tracking Jude's progress simply by watching Jos and Peter.

They were side by side in front of him, close enough together to make the air between them crackle. Every so often electricity would arc between their arms, hands, legs. Tiny tendrils of lightening.

At first, Jos would flinch a little, but after the first few times she paid it no attention whatsoever. She was feeling what Peter was feeling by then. The closer Jude came, the more intensely Peter felt her effect, and so the more palpable his feelings of revulsion became for Jos. Jude was a stain upon their combined consciousness, spreading wider the closer she got.

They stood, heads bowed, united in their anticipation.

They faced the outer wall as Jude approached the back of the lodge, turning with her as she then made her way along the back of the building and then around the side. By the time she crossed to the garage they were facing the closed bathroom door. But Jos didn't open that door, until they knew Jude had put the garage block between them.

Back in the sitting room, Jos and Peter moved to the side window. From there they watched the lioness stalking in Jude's footsteps. And then, seconds after she passed beneath the side window, Joseph and Nalutuesha appeared, following the lioness.

*

From the corner of the garage block, Jude could see not only the house, but the bronze lioness lying on her plinth. A post Peter addition, and life had gone on without her. She could almost hear the Nyerere's living it up, laughing and loving in her house. She was tempted to take a closer look at the statue, sure it would be of Lulu… her little lion. Peter had claimed everything then, taken everything from her. But Jude was an unwelcome guest that day. That beautiful place, the beautiful home was denied to her now. Her beautiful life had blown up along with Peter, and for what? Jude had walked away from that one, but she'd never been free a moment since. Forced into seclusion, then forced to live with her pathetic niece. And now it was Jos who was here. Jos who somehow had Peter now too. It was as if Jos was assuming Jude's life and how she wished she'd bought a gun as well as a car. An idea occurred.

A new possibility began to take form inside Jude's mind.

Moving around the corner, she tried the door into the pump house, and it opened for her. Slipping inside, she closed the door and made her way to the door into the garages. She recognised her little jeep immediately, but it was the big Land Rover she was interested in. Red Earth Tours emblazoned on the sides, and maybe it belonged to Ben? A quick look in through the driver's side window told Jude everything she needed to know. The car wasn't even locked. 'Idiots.' She laughed to herself, going then to the big tool box at the back wall and digging around inside it as quietly as possible, until she found a crowbar. The crowbar made quick work of the lock on the gun box. Inside Jude found a Glock 28 and enough ammo to fully load it and pocket a few spares.

Lessons learned and all that.

*

The first indication Wendell had that something was wrong was the sound of despair that Jos made.

She sank to the floor, eyes closed. 'What do we do now?' 'The same,' Peter told her. 'Don't give up on me now, Jos.' 'What's wrong?' Wendell asked.

'Jude just took a gun from your Land Rover.'

Wendell felt like he'd just been punched in the gut. 'I'm so sorry…' he told Peter. 'I didn't think…' He told Jos, her head tilted back, face to the ceiling, but her eyes were closed. 'I thought I'd locked the garages.'

'You did. She got in there through the pump house.' Peter told him. 'And that is my fault.'

*

Armed and feeling much more dangerous, Jude retraced her steps to the side of the garage block and then headed diagonally across to the corner of the white house. From there she walked down the side of the building, looking in each window to check the rooms were empty before moving on to the next. She was beginning to feel like a cop in a movie; gun in hand, ready to shoot any and all who got in her way. She even checked behind her regularly, making sure no one could sneak up on her.

Feeling rather invincible, thanks to the gun.

At the rear of the house, she could see the colourful bee hives and the solar field beyond. Crossing the back wall at that side she looked around the corner to the kitchen garden and the patio beyond that. Everywhere was deserted, silent except for the usual wildlife sounds. Still, she took care crossing to the far side, glancing up at her garden hanging down.

That was where Jude needed to be.

*

Beola was still seated in Peter's chair, still looking out across the view, alone with her thoughts and her fears. She hadn't seen Jude enter or leave the garage via the pump room because from her angle that end of the garage block was hidden. She didn't expect to see Jude at all. More likely this was all an over-reaction. Jude wasn't stupid. She wouldn't risk everything coming here to dig up a long-lost gun after fourteen years, without any threat of paying for her crime. Jude would just sit tight in Edinburgh, and soon they would look back on this day and laugh.

Then she saw a lioness walk out from behind the far end of the garage block, she stopped momentarily, looking towards the side of the house, her tail swishing from side to side. Her long and smooth tail because there was no tail end tuft. As Beola continued to watch, she moved out and across the lawn towards the statue of Lulu.

The lioness then crouched down behind it, disappearing from sight.

Beola reached for her phone, realised she'd left it downstairs, stood up to go and get it, and then sat down again.

She didn't know what to do.

*

'Come on, Jos.' Peter urged her to stand up. 'I won't let her harm you.'

Her face crumpled into a mixture of fear and misery. There wasn't supposed to be another gun! Just an old, unloaded gun. What the fuck had she gotten herself into? What had Peter gotten her in to?

'Can you really protect her?' Wendell voiced similar concerns to those Jos was finding. 'Really and truly without any doubt whatsoever.'

'Not without any doubt,' Peter admitted. 'But I do have some power in this situation, and I will use all of it to protect Jos.'

*

Having glanced into the kitchen through the windows, Jude was on her way up to the roof garden. She didn't take the time to appreciate how beautiful it looked even after all the years between, because she needed to get to the garden room. She had to make sure no one was in there. It wasn't too difficult to cover the ground. Some of the plants were so big, Jude could stand up to her full diminutive height and walk behind them without being seen. She advanced quickly and was soon looking in the garden room window from her spot next to the bistro table and chairs. The room was full of Jos, although tidier than expected. Before getting what she'd come for, Jude ducked inside and made sure there was no one hiding in the bathroom.

Satisfied she was alone up there; Jude went to the bench where Peter and Jos always sat for their little chats. Kneeling on it at Jos' habitual end, she set the Glock down on the wide rim of the planter and then began pulling out the flowers by their roots. She hacked at them with the sharp blade of the trowel until they came loose. When enough of the earth was exposed, she began hacking at that too, scooping it up and tossing it aside. Hacking, scooping, tossing. Over and over, until she found what she was looking for.

The white house relinquished its second secret.

A milky white corner of plastic showed itself, and Jude used the trowel to dig carefully around it, revealing more and more, like an archaeologist exposing the bones of some ancient artefact. Every so often she would set the trowel down and tug on the bag.

Eventually it came free.

Holding it up in front of her face, Jude could see the shape of the old Glock through the opaque plastic bag she'd wrapped it up inside, before burying it up there minutes after returning home from the scene of her crime. It had been there ever since. Leaving the gun inside the bag, Jude brushed off any loose earth and then stuffed it into the roomy thigh pocket of her trousers. Abandoning the trowel, useless now, she retrieved the new and loaded Glock and went back into the garden room.

Now to spring that trap.

*

Beola was on her feet again, but that was as far as she got.

She was paralysed by indecision, knowing she should call her husband to tell him that his missing lioness was right outside, but knowing too that the animal was somehow connected to everything going on. Kissi said that only one lion was missing, but there had been maybe half a dozen sightings. Were there more out there, all closing in on the white house? As she stood there, looking down to where the lioness lay still, motionless and alert, more movement drew her eyes back to the garage block.

Joseph stepped out from the corner. He was the new laibon and he was looking up at Beola. He held her gaze for long seconds, and then he shook his head, deliberately and slowly. Finger to his lips in a gesture of quiet, he then used a flat hand to indicate she should sit back down.

She did so immediately.

*

Peter told Wendell to stay in the lodge, but Jos didn't look as confident as she had at the start of this. She looked drawn, and afraid. Wendell felt responsible and so he followed them outside.

Jude getting hold of another gun wasn't part of the plan, and now she was unpredictable and dangerous. Peter wanted to warn the two Maasai and caught up with them at the side of the garages farthest from the house.

'She's gone inside the house…' Peter's mind was recoiling from knowing that, from feeling that, and his white house was recoiling with him. Its habitual positive atmosphere was dissipating like breath being suck into a void. Fetid and corrupt air was leaching in to take its place. If he'd had a stomach, he'd have felt sick because of it. 'She has a gun now too.'

Jos was feeling the nausea for both of them. She was leaning against the wall, head down, sweat beading on her forehead. She felt faint as well as sick. She could no longer tell the difference between what she was sharing with Peter and the feeling Jude was inspiring inside her alone. The fear that she might die here today was growing arms as well as legs. Why not? Jude had already murdered Peter. Had they underestimated her, too busy enjoying all the fun times to understand that the past fourteen years had not lessened Jude's killer instincts? Jos wanted to run away, she wanted to run down the drive and out into the bush and keep on going.

'Focus, Jos.' And when she looked at him, Peter went on, 'We can only win this together.'

'And you have Maasai magic on your side,' Joseph told her, taking a hand and squeezing it.

*

Jude opened the door from the garden room out onto the gallery.

Sticking the gun out first, she followed with her head, looking and listening. There was nothing to see and nothing to hear. There wasn't any air either. Despite an abundance of open windows and doors, the air inside the house was static and stifling. She didn't remember it ever feeling like that. There was always a flower-scented breeze moving through the house. Must be something to do with the way Beola was keeping house these days.

As Jude moved out onto the gallery the air pressure became more defined, until she could feel the density of it shifting, pressing down on her. It felt almost too thick to breathe, and she wanted to get out of there, get back outside to where the air was clean and light and breathable. Suddenly the idea of hunting down Beola and Jos seemed less appealing, all Jude was concerned with was drawing enough air into her lungs to satisfy the oxygen needs of her body. She was also beginning to sweat, her clothing feeling tight and restrictive. Was she ill perhaps? Forgetting the need for stealth, Jude placed all her faith in her gun and advanced more quickly towards the top of the stairs.

Perhaps the air would be cooler down in the foyer?

CHAPTER THIRTY-TWO

Knowing exactly where Jude was on every step of her journey made intercepting her easy.

While she was still standing behind the garden room's inner door, clutching her new gun and working up the courage to open the door and step out onto the gallery, the two Maasai, Jos and Wendell all went around the back of the garage block and across to the corner of the white house.

There they split up.

Nalutuesha gave Jos a leg up and over the railing onto the porch where Peter was waiting, then he and Joseph returned to their observation point at the far corner of the garage block.

Wendell took off down the side of the house. He went not because he wanted to, but because he had promised Kissi that he would look after Beola, and Peter reminded him that Beola had no idea Jude had a gun.

Following in Jude's footsteps, Wendell went around to the back of the house, across the kitchen garden, and up the external steps to the roof garden. He followed her example up there too, ducking behind the plants as he made his low way down the length of the garden until he was able to look through the window into the garden room. Hesitating to do so, long enough to offer a small prayer to whoever might be listening, that Jude had moved on. The room was empty.

He went inside and quietly around to the other door which was standing ajar. He held his ground there, waiting for some indication that would let him know where Jude was now.

Meanwhile, as soon as Peter knew Jude would come down the stairs, he and Jos moved quickly along the porch towards the open front doors. Jos then opened the inner set of glass doors and then tucked herself behind him so they could advance through into the foyer.

Jos wished her shield was a lot more solid than the mere apparition of the man she was hiding behind. The electricity flowing between them was interesting, but she doubted it had any flair for providing a force field or a cloaking device.

It certainly wouldn't be bullet proof.

*

Jude was at the top of the main stairs under the big arched window when Peter walked in with Jos at his back. Everything about him screamed real. He was wearing the clothes he'd died in, and he also hadn't aged a moment since then. But Jude's mind reeled to see him looking so lifelike. He looked solid enough to touch. She imagined reaching for him, touching him. Memories rushed in, filling her head up with images and all the associated feelings of holding him, loving him. She really had loved him. Peter was possibly the only other human being Jude had ever loved.

Her heart lurched in her chest.

She was at the bottom of the stairs by then with no recollection of walking down there. As if she was drawn to him. Clutching the gun tighter, she drew strength from its power and maintained her calm demeanour. Still, it was hard for her to breathe. The air down there was no fresher. 'Come out, come out?' she sing-songed. 'I can see you, Jos… hiding behind my husband.'

'Murdering me ended our marriage, Jude.' Peter spoke softly, reasonably, and then he asked, 'Did you find your gun?'

*

As soon as he heard the voices downstairs Wendell left the garden room and headed for the door in the middle of the wide gallery which Peter had told him just minutes before, would open into the master bedroom.

As soon as he got there, he opened the door just enough to slip inside. Looking around, he saw the room was empty. 'Beola?' he whispered as loudly as he dared, turning to a second door as he heard the soft click made as someone opened it from the other side.

'Wendell?' Beola peeped around the bathroom door. 'Is it over?'

'Shhh…' He moved closer and told her. 'Jude has Ben's gun.'

Beola was horrified, afraid. But mostly she felt stupid to have doubted what Peter as well as Jos had been insisting upon for days. 'How could I have been so stupid?'

Wendell hushed her again. 'Seriously, Beola. Jude has no idea where

we are. We have to be very quiet, so it stays that way.'

'But Jos…'

'Shhh.' They'd been talking in whispers, but even that was making Wendell nervous, he'd take a charging rhino over a woman with a gun any day of the week. 'Let's just stay here and stay quiet.'

*

In the foyer, Peter knew his white house was the reason Jude was struggling to breathe properly. He was part of it, his In-between was part of it. He'd built it, bled for it, cried for it, and in a way, he'd also died for it. The white house was as repelled by Jude in exactly the same way as he was. It wanted her out. He wanted her out.

Jude had to get out so this could end.

Jos also noticed that Jude looked ill, like someone on the verge of an asthma attack or something similar. She kept putting her free hand up to her throat, and she was sweating. Her skin looked grey despite the glow from a few days in the sun.

'What's wrong with this place?' Jude looked around. 'There isn't any air in here.'

'You shouldn't be here.' Peter told her, allowing some of the malice he felt for her leak into his voice. 'Why don't you get out, Jude. Take your gun and go. You're not welcome here.'

'This is you!' she realised, waving her gun in his general direction. 'You're doing something to me.'

'Are you?' Jos wondered close to his ear. Closing her eyes, she explored her peter-natural senses to discover what was happening. 'The house…' she realised. 'I knew you were interchangeable.'

'What are you… whispering about?' Talking taxed Jude's oxygen resources and she had to keep heaving air into her lungs. 'I… can't… breathe.'

‘Get out,’ Peter demanded. ‘Get out of my home!’

Jude had been relaxing her grip on the gun by then, lowering it, but she wasn’t beaten yet. Lifting it up again to shoulder height, she stretched her arm right out behind it and pointed it purposefully at Jos who was standing side by side with Peter by then. Somehow Jude managed to hold it steady. Then she noticed the little sparks between them. Little threads of lightening and sparks blooming and fading like miniature fireworks in the narrow strip of space between them. Confused, she stepped back, bumped into the bottom step and stumbled a little before losing her balance completely and sitting down on that step heavily. ‘What… what’s that?’

‘Maasai magic,’ Peter winked. ‘We saw you coming, Jude, and we planned ahead. I’ve been here all along, waiting for Jos. She knows all about you now.’

Jude wanted to get up but didn’t trust her legs. Instead, she moved her thumb against the gun.

Jos heard a tiny little snick of sound, saw Jude’s finger tighten inside the trigger guard, and then all she could see was the black hole at the end of that gun, just waiting to suck her all the way into oblivion.

Time slowed right down.

No life flashed before her eyes, but multiple scenarios regarding what to do next, as well as the possible outcomes each action might lead to, swam across her mind, switching direction back and forth, like a huge shoal of glittering fish.

All in a nanosecond, and then Jos decided.

‘Stop!’ she shouted, stepping away from Peter as she did so and registering the surprise on Jude’s face. That was all she needed to continue, ‘Leave her alone!’ she cried, rushing towards Jude.

Towards the gun.

Peter’s face was a detailed picture of the shock, confusion and dismay he was feeling.

Jude was as confused but risked a laugh at Peter’s expense.

‘He’s manipulated me all along, Jude.’ Jos was crouching on the floor in front of her, holding her hand as well as the gun in both her own, keeping it pointed at her chest. ‘I’ve been trying to call you… over and over… I didn’t know where you were.’

'Mobile.' Jude was keeping it brief to save breath.

'You never answer that,' Jos reminded. 'I thought you were at home.'

'I am.'

'Yes,' Jos agreed vehemently. 'This is your home!' Turning to see Peter, she added, 'This beautiful house he built for you… and then he gave it to another woman! How could you?' she snarled at him. 'No wonder she hates you. I hate you!' Turning back to Jude, she told her aunt, 'I'm his heir. I have the will. I have it all, Jude. I'll take this house back. I'll make it yours again. You can come home. I'll use the money to make the past disappear for you. If you kill me it all stays with Gary, and he'll cut you off without a penny. Peter only left you with an allowance, so you'd be able to look after me. He didn't want you to have anything.'

Jude was confused. If she'd had the breath, she'd have challenged every word coming out of Jos' mouth, but she didn't dare and so she was forced to listen. 'Will,' she said. 'Show me.'

'I'll get it.' Jos scrambled to her feet and ran along to the library. Inside she went to the bookcase, found the little nub, pressed and released the secret drawer in the crown moulding. Grabbing the envelope, she hurried back to Jude. 'See…' Jos took the document out, showed her aunt the top page. 'All I have to do is show this to his lawyers and I get everything. We can share it, Jude. You've looked after me all these years… at your expense. I know he stopped you from marrying again… even living with someone. You've had to be alone. But not now… we can stop all that together. Please Jude.'

Jude had taken the document and was scanning the first few paragraphs. Jos was telling the truth. She would get everything. Everything Jude should have got. That was a knife twisting in her gut. Telling the truth too about Gary keeping the lot if Jos didn't inherit. It was there in black and white… no Jos, no allowance for Jude. Gary retained full control and could chose his own heir. 'Bastard,' she spat at Peter.

Peter was so completely shocked he was frozen in place. All the energy moving freely between him, and Jos was gone. It was all he could do to remain apparent. He wanted to dissipate, to retreat, to return to his Inbetween. But even that sanctuary would be broken if Jos abandoned him, and Jude returned to lay claim to the white house. He would be nothing. Everything he'd planned, all he'd prepared for was turning into nothing before his very eyes. Powerless, and silent, he stood there watching Jos dismantle everything they had built.

'Please, Jude.' Jos had Jude's hand and gun in her own two hands again. 'Don't do anything. We have to get out of here. He's killing you. His house is killing you. We have to get away before we can take it back.'

But Jude was actually beginning to find breathing was a little easier. It was as if Jos choosing sides had broken the spell Peter had over her. Jude handed Jos the will. 'Whatever you do, toots, don't lose that.'

Jos' stomach flipped over, and her heart dropped into her feet, but she didn't dare celebrate yet. 'Can we go now?' she pleaded. 'We have to get out of here.'

'Regroup,' Jude nodded. 'We'll take a trip to Bath and then come back.' But before getting to her feet, Jude gripped Jos' arm tightly. 'Promise me, Jos… promise me that I can have this house.'

'I promise, Jude. I will do whatever it takes to give the white house back to you.'

Satisfied, Jude got to her feet.

Jos took a step towards the front doors, but Jude didn't follow. She was looking past her towards Peter. 'Don't worry about him,' Jos assured. 'He's powerless.' She risked a look at him herself, as she added, 'Impotent.' Peter blinked.

'What about…' Jude looked around.

'There's no one else here,' Jos told her. 'He didn't want any witnesses. Come on…' she urged gently. 'I want to get out of here just as much as you do. I haven't been able to think straight since I got here. He's been messing with my head. They all have. I want to go home, Jude… please.'

Nodding, Jude began to move forward, still clutching her gun, but pointing it at Peter now.

Jos moved too, a bit faster than Jude, but not too fast. Nevertheless, the distance between them increased because Jude was nervous about passing Peter. Jos passed him then without as much as a glance, but she could tell he was turning to watch her. She kept looking back over her right shoulder to see Jude, but not him. She didn't want to look at Peter at all. Jude was still coming, moving as far to the side as she could to put as much space between her and Peter as possible.

Peter was watching Jude intently. Willing her to drop down dead at his feet, but she kept on breathing, kept on moving towards the front doors.

Jude was holding her breath as she passed him, letting it out again only once she'd cleared the glass doors. Jos was moving through the front doors by then, beckoning to Jude to hurry. 'What about your stuff, toots?'

Jos crossed the porch to the top of the steps. 'I can buy more stuff.'

Jude was so satisfied with this response she smiled. She moved faster then, and more confidently, stepping through the front doors and onto the porch.

When Jos saw her aunt turn back towards Peter, raising her hand to give him a little wave, she took one step towards her. She grabbed Jude's hair in both hands, twisted down to the left like she was turning a steering wheel, pivoted Jude around and pushed her as hard as she could down the porch steps.

Without waiting to see how or where Jude landed, Jos bolted back inside the white house, back to Peter, reaching out for him.

Peter was almost too stunned to react, and then Jos was grabbing hold of his hand.

A jolt of electricity coursed through her. Jos let go of the envelope containing the will, but she kept a tight hold on Peter's hand despite the nerve-jangling pains shooting up her arm. Immediately she heard her own voice screaming. 'Shut it all down.' Every door, every window.

Some closings were louder than others, some faster, so the overall noise was like rapid gunfire. Jude was on her knees at the bottom of the steps as it started, but she was on her feet by the time silence arrived. And that silence was complete and utter. Not an insect, a bird, or a far-off creature could be heard. Nothing, except the sound of Jude's rage which erupted from her lungs in garbled accusations and shouted threats. She waved the gun around as she yelled and cursed, raging up at the house, at the sky.

Then she stopped, sensing someone watching her.

When Jude turned around, she saw a lioness standing in the gap between the house and the garage block. Backing up almost without realising, she watched in horror as the cat crept forward just as slowly, low and intent, ears back, teeth bared slightly as her muzzle twitched. Turning Jude looked for an escape route behind her. But a second lioness came creeping around that corner of the house. Jude wondered what her chances might be if she made a run for the drive, but when she risked a look in that direction, a lioness was already watching her from the top.

Running back up the porch steps she tried to pull the front doors open but they were shut fast. 'Please…' She banged on the doors with one fist and one gun butt. 'Let me in!'

But the doors remained closed and impassive and when Jude turned to put her back against them, she saw there were five of them now. Five lionesses, united in lethal intent. 'Oh my god!' Her voice was barely a whisper. Eye to eye with each of them in turn, panicked to the point of near paralysis she watched them coming slowly closer, their muscular bodies rippling with all the power they contained. They had cornered her, and soon they would attack. Then she remembered the gun, and her paralysis was broken.

Pointing it at the lioness closest to her, Jude fired.

The lioness reacted to the noise, paused, but then kept on coming. Jude fired again, and again. Over and over, she fired wildly, and she also tried to take aim, her hands shaking with terror. Every bullet was useless. It was like trying to kill Peter all over again, but this time there was no combustible petrol to come to her rescue. When all the bullets were spent, she fumbled in her pocket for the spares. Hands shaking. Most of them ended up on the porch, rolling this way and that. The few left, she scrabbled to load and then fired them all in the subsequent few seconds.

By then, one lioness had reached the bottom of the steps.

Jude looked left and right; she saw no escape. She had to get into the house! She moved to her left, keeping the doors and then the wall against her back, reaching the first set of French doors and, when she turned to them to try to pull them open. 'Please…' she pleaded with the door. 'Please…' Banging on the glass. 'Please let me in. Please, please, please…' She begged, all the time watching the lionesses coming closer, watching her, gathering close to the porch.

But none of them made any move up on to it.

Jude was just beginning to wonder if all was not as it seemed when she saw yet another one. A sixth lioness came out from behind the bronze statue on the lawn. Without hesitation, she crossed the distance low and fast, her eyes fixed on Jude. This was the lioness who would kill her. Jude looked all around, looking for some hope, some escape. But there was no point in running. Every hunt finale Jude had ever seen crammed into her head. Chased, tripped, mauled and choked. Back then Jude had felt for the zebra, antelope, buffalo, but cheered the lionesses for their superior intellect, superior speed.

A killing machine was coming for her, and Jude's screams then were similar in volume pitch and intensity to those emanating from Peter when he was burning to death. Unlike her husband, Jude was able to keep on screaming. She screamed when she threw the useless gun aside, screamed when she picked up one of the wicker chairs. Adrenalin gave her the strength to lift it high into the air and smash it against the French doors at full force, roaring more than screaming then with the sheer effort. The glass should have broken. The wooden should have splintered. But the door held fast.

'Pleeeeeeease…' Jude pleaded. A look over her shoulder showed the lioness mid-flight, jumping up at the porch railing. Screaming again, she tried to batter her way in through the doors with fists and feet. It was as if all the glass in the white house had been replaced by Perspex and all the wood by steel.

No matter how hard she kicked, the doors merely shuddered.

The lioness paused for a split second on top of the railing to get her balance, and then she launched her two hundred and eighty pounds of weight onto Jude's back. The burden toppled her to the floor of the porch but because she was facing the French doors as she fell, she went down sideways.

The lioness also hit the floor on her side and had to scramble out from under the prey, get back up onto her feet, and pin the target down.

Despite literally feeling breath from the jaws of death against the skin of her face and neck, Jude struggled frantically to get away. As the lioness tried to pin her face down, Jude was trying to scramble out from under the immense weight. She felt large and wicked claws pierce and rend her arms, and she yelled louder and longer with the pain of it. The sounds coming from her throat were more like roars than screams by then, and it was hard to distinguish the sound of her own voice from that of the lioness bellowing rage into her ears. The combined noise was deafening, the heat of the fight cloying and the breath rank. Still Jude was fighting, frantic to get away. She kicked feebly at the lioness's rump with the heels of her boots and ripped nearly every single finger nail off trying to scramble out from under the might bearing down upon her. The weight was crushing her chest cavity and, once again, she was finding it harder and harder to draw breath. Her voice lost much of its power. No longer screaming and roaring, Jude grunted and gasped.

The lioness also quieted down.

Jude froze when she felt the heat of fetid animal breath blow against the left side of her face, her eyes drawn to see, and Jude found the lioness's eye waiting. Looking into that baleful orange eye, she realised this wasn't some chance misfortune. This was a weaponised animal sent by Peter to kill her. As soon as Jude made the connection, the lioness moved her head and clamped her jaws around the neck.

Six hundred and fifty pounds of pressure, per square inch.

Quick and clean.

CHAPTER THIRTY-THREE

Jos let go Peter's hand as soon as she was sure Jude was dead.

Her arm felt full of pins and needles, so she rubbed at it briskly. Her head felt full of horror for what they had done, and full of relief that it was over. She felt the house sighing relief all around her too, felt the atmosphere relax as the electrical charge between her and Peter diminished. That was when the front doors swung open.

Exchanging a quick look with Peter, they moved out onto the porch together.

Jude was lying next to the lioness. Her neck was horribly flattened, and there were smears of blood all around her, stark against the white boards. Her upper arms bore long, deep and bloody scars where she'd fought to escape the claws holding on to her, and even deeper holes in her neck where long canines had pierced the skin. Her head was turned towards the house, her mouth open like her eyes, her face frozen in an almost fatalistic expression. The lioness was sphinx like beside her, licking her lips a little, sniffing the air, panting from her recent exertions but otherwise perfectly calm. Jos moved forward, and the lioness turned to see her. Her head lifted in an upward nod, and Jos nodded back.

That was when Beola arrived with Wendell.

They'd remained in the master bedroom en suite for the duration. They'd heard raised voices a few times, so distant they had no idea who was shouting or what was being said. It had gone quiet for a time, and then doors and windows slammed shut all over the house. They heard Jude screaming and shouting outside at the front of the house. They heard her pleading, begging. That was when Beola got up from her seat on the edge of the bath and tried to pull the door open. It wouldn't budge.

When the gun fire started Beola stopped pulling at the door and started crying.

Wendell did his best to comfort her, but she was panicking too, and wouldn't be consoled. He just backed off and waited, listening, wondering. There was silence after the gunfire, a short break and then a few more shots.

The next thing they heard was the sound of Jude pleading again, screaming again. A moments silence, an almighty thud, and then she was screaming again. This time it was primal and spine chilling. It seemed to go on and on and even Wendell covered his ears against it.

When silence returned it was interrupted by a sound that Wendell could only describe as a sigh. It came from all around him, as if the white house itself had sighed. Curious, he went to the door, turned the handle, and it swung open without a sound.

Beola raced past him and was halfway down the stairs before he caught her up.

Stepping out onto the porch, they both stopped dead when they saw the gang of lionesses milling around on the lawn. Then they saw Jude's body and a sixth lioness. Wendell was about to ask why no one was concerned by the proximity of all these predators, when Joseph and Nalutuesha came trotting across the grass past the little pride playing on the lawn… one of them was standing on her back legs at the time, trying to swat a passing butterfly.

Wendell stared, trying to make sense of it all.

The warrior's spear blade glittered in the sun, because Nalutuesha had removed the leather sheaf in case he was called upon to defend his brother laibon from any threat posed by the woman, and now from the lioness who was no longer under the old laibon's control. But he found her to be docile and so squatted down beside her on the porch, keeping his spear within easy reach.

Joseph immediately set off to walk around the white house, casting spells and murmuring incantations as he went. More Maasai magic to purify the house and cleanse it of the sorrow and violence that had sullied it that day.

'Wendell.' Peter waited until he had his attention. 'Would you call Kissi now please?'

'You planned this,' Beola realised.

'If not Jude, then one of us,' Peter told her. 'She thought nothing of pointing a gun at Jos.'

Beola looked at Jos then, crouched down before the lioness, stroking her big soft head. Beola asked, 'What about all the others?'

All five of the lawn lionesses were milling around one another, head butting, nuzzling, rubbing up and down one another's flanks. Greeting one another, as cats love to do.

When a voice cried out, they all stopped and turned to see who it was.

Jos stood up and looked over towards the tree line opposite the house. The old laibon was standing a few feet from the trees. Her beckoning man, and he was waving to her, smiling. The five lionesses all trotted over to him, he greeted them all one by one and then, with a final wave, he turned and walked into the trees with his little friends. And they were little by then. Five domestic cats, all easily recognisable to Jos, and all trotting after him as if he had pockets full of tuna.

They had all soon disappeared among the shadows beneath the trees.

A noise escaped Jos and she looked to where her aunt still lay on the floor. 'Oh Jude…' she whispered. 'What did you do?'

*

Kissi wasn't far inside the park when he received Wendell's call. He was with a junior ranger at the time, a polite young man who barely commented when Kissi did a U turn and drove them to the nearest gate instead of up to one of the camping grounds where they were supposed to be heading that morning. Once there, Kissi left him in the Land Rover while he went inside the office and stole the keys for the safari jeep parked outside. The junior ranger then watched Kissi drive that jeep off at speed without protesting at all.

Of course, the jeep radio had other ideas and, within a few minutes of making his escape, Kissi was forced to pretend he was having radio trouble. He didn't care about the consequences. He only cared about getting back to the white house as quickly as possible and with a vehicle suitable for transporting a wild animal.

After Wendell had called Kissi, Peter told him. 'Jude's jeep is in the undergrowth close to the bottom of the track. Please bring it up here.' Once Wendell moved off in the direction of the drive, he turned Jos. 'Will you undress her?'

Having realised the lioness on the porch was no longer filled with the benevolent spirit of her beckoning man, Jos had been slowly extricating herself from the immediate scene, amazed that she still had both hands. But the lioness just seemed calm at best, confused at worst. Jos felt sorry for her. Glad too that the Maasai warrior was right there with his pointy spear in case the lioness decided she was hungry. Putting Jude between her and the lioness, Jos got on with undressing her. She was surprised, when Beola came to help. 'You don't have to.'

'I want to,' Beola said firmly. It had been her choice to stay, and she wouldn't walk away now. 'But first…' Bending down, she took a walking boot in each hand, and began pulling Jude towards the front doors. 'I'm not sure I trust our latest guest,' she said, eyeing the lioness. 'If she gets up from the floor, you are on your own.'

Together they stripped Jude down to her underwear, setting aside the still bagged Glock 1911, but then Beola insisted on going inside to fetch a sheet before they also removed that. 'The dead deserve whatever dignity the living can provide, no matter what they did in life,' she told Jos.

Jos was only able to appreciate such kindness when she saw the neatly waxed Brazilian landing strip Jude was hiding inside her workaday knickers. The look on Beola's face was priceless, and Jos almost laughed. She was feeling quite calm by then, relieved the initial threat was over, and not at all sorry for the way it had turned out. She could be the one lying dead just as easily. But she wasn't. She had taken Jude on, and this time she'd prevailed.

Now, all Jos had to do was make sure Jude disappeared without a trace, and then she would be able to look towards her future.

Once Jude was naked under the sheet, Jos beckoned to Nalutuesha. He came then with his bush knife and made quick work of cutting her hair off. That was hard to watch because it diminished Jude to the point of no return. Without her crowning glory she just looked small and pathetic, but it had to be done; it wouldn't do to have a mass of ginger curls blowing around in the breeze later. When the warrior was done, he tucked the pile of hair inside the pile of clothing, and then helped Jos and Beola wrap the body up tightly.

Wendell was back and parked a very bashed up looking jeep in front of the porch steps. He then collected Ben's Glock from the floor of the porch and went to the garages to fetch the Red Earth Tours Land Rover. The driver side door was open, a crow bar was on the driver's seat and the gun box lid was up, showing where the lock had been forced. Replacing the gun, he then went to the open toolbox, Wendell dumped the crow bar back in there and then rooted around for a few useful tools that he then used to bend and bash the metal around the broken lock back into shape. It wasn't perfect, but it would have to do for now.

Beola had taken the Glock 1911 inside for her husband to clean and replace in the gun cabinet later, and also fetched a black bin bag which she gave to Jos.

She'd also fetched a box of matches and a small container of lighter fluid. Lifting the bundle of Jude's clothing, hair and the boots, she went around to the side of the house to the corner closest to the solar field. There was a brazier there that they used for burning garden rubbish from time to time. It was already half full of dried sticks and leaves from the most recent clean up. Making a well in the middle of the sticks, she pushed Jude's things down into it. Dousing everything with a little fuel before tossing in a lit match. Beola was forced to lean back to avoid losing her own hair in the resulting WHOOMP. The flames receded immediately and began to burn steadily. When she was sure the fire was low and contained, Beola made her way back around to the front via the kitchen.

Jos had emptied the jeep by then, dumping everything she found into the bin bag. Every sweet wrapper, every bottle, every shred of paper. The only thing she left inside it was the log book she'd found in the glove box. She then grabbed Jude's bag and her little suitcase and returned to the porch.

Beola was also back on the porch, armed with a mop and bucket as well as a dustpan and brush. She immediately swept up both the dropped bullets as well as the spent casings, and then began mopping up the streaks and smears of blood from the white boards, exposing the damage done by claws and nails as she did.

Nothing a little filler and paint wouldn't take care of.

Wendell parked the Red Earth Tours Land Rover behind the now empty jeep, then he got into the jeep and drove it around and into the garages. He then closed the doors. When he got back to the others, he and Nalutuesha picked up the shrouded remains of Jude Sinclair and slid her under the seats, at the back of the Land Rover. Much easier spotted than a broken lock on a gun box. 'We're gonna need something black,' he told the sky.

Jos had emptied the bin bag and handbag out onto the porch by then. She went through everything carefully. She took house and Lexus keys, all the cash… almost eight thousand US Dollars and more than thirty thousand Kenyan Schillings. She also took the receipt for Jude's Lexus which was in the Premium Long Stay facility at Edinburgh Airport. She set aside the hire car receipt for a Toyota Land Cruiser due for collection this coming Sunday at Jomo Kenyatta International Airport, Nairobi. Showing the receipt to Peter, she said, 'Anyone's guess where that is.'

'The police will find it when it's listed missing,' he shrugged. 'It's probably still in Kenya and any investigation will be concentrated there. I doubt Jude told anyone she was coming here.'

'But she was a resident here.'

'If the police come here looking for Jude there must be no trace of her.' 'Even the devil needs an advocate, Peter,' Jos told him.

And Peter smiled, because Jos was looking at the bigger picture.

'Do you have anything black?' Wendell wondered of Beola. 'Fabric or something.' And when Beola looked confused, he nodded towards the Land

Rover. 'The white sheet sticks out like a sore thumb.'

'Maybe there's something in the cellar,' Peter suggested.

'I will look.'

As Beola headed off to do that, Jos called after her. 'We'll need an outfit for Nalutuesha too.' 'Why?' he wondered.

'You can't go into the park looking like that,' Jos pointed out. 'We're supposed to be low key.' Getting back to her job at hand, she added Jude's passport, the return ticket to Gatwick from Nairobi, and another ticket from Gatwick to Edinburgh to the unwanted pile. Make-up, perfume, hair clip, mobile phone, Ray Bans and other handbag detritus, all into the unwanted pile. Dumping the lot into the bin bag with the rubbish cleared out from the jeep, Jos collected up all the papers and cash and stood up. She looked to where the lioness was now lying on her side. Was she sleeping? Surreal. Jos shrugged, and then went inside. As she was entering the foyer, she saw the envelope containing Peter's last will and testament and picked it up. She then took it all upstairs to the garden room and stashed it in a drawer next to her bed.

Now for the suitcase.

Just a few changes of clothes, underwear. A little blue glass cat, still inside the shopping bag and a lot heavier than it appeared. A hat. A few toiletries. More cash. 'Jeezo.' Jos counted another ten grand in US Dollars. 'For a woman taking a short break in Kenya Jude had an awful lot of cash on her.'

'Money always talks.' Peter sat down on the porch steps close to where Jos was kneeling going through Jude's belongings. 'And it speaks every language too.'

'She could've hired a hit man with this lot.'

After a moment, Peter said, 'You had me fooled Jos.'

'Good,' she told him. 'By fooling you I also managed to fool Jude.'

'Risky.'

'She wanted this house back more than anything in the world,' Jos pointed out. 'That's why she wanted to believe I was going to give it to her.' Not to mention the fact Jude had no idea Jos had actually grown a backbone in the past week. 'I'm not so easily manipulated nowadays.' Eyeing Peter, she added, 'Unless it's you doing the manipulating of course.' He batted his lashes, and Jos smiled.

She took the money and the blue glass cat out of the suitcase, then shoved everything else from the unwanted pile into it. Beola had returned with a very dark blue curtain by then. She also had a pair of jeans and a Rolling Stones T-shirt.

Nalutuesha couldn't get the T-shirt on fast enough, but he was less enamoured with the jeans.

Beola collected up all his beaded finery, and then handed him a bandana.

'What is this for?' he wondered.

'Cover your hair.'

The warrior was horrified.

Jos went back into the suitcase, took out the wide brimmed Tilly hat, and stuck it on his head. 'How about that?'

'Can I also have sunglasses?'

Jos fished the Ray Bans out from the bin bag. 'Will these do?'

Nalutuesha would no doubt attract some inquisitive looks as he moved through the strange day from there on in, but he looked more rock'n'roll than Maasai, and that was the point. Jos took the case around to where Beola's little fire was still burning, and she began adding Jude's clothing a piece at a time. Even the Agent Provocateur and Guia La Bruna underwear… obviously meant to go with the ginger Brazilian! When she felt Peter appear next to her, she asked, 'What am I supposed to do with the bag, the case… I can't burn toiletries and make-up either.'

'Bury it.'

'Not today,' Jos sighed, then said, 'I suppose I can spread it around among my own things for the time being. It could as easily be mine.'

'Do it now then.'

By the time Jos was finished blending Jude's cosmetics in with her own, and stashing the small case containing her completely empty handbag on top of the armoire… wiped down inside as well as out, Kissi had arrived. By the time she got back downstairs, he, Joseph, Wendell and Nalutuesha were encouraging the still docile lioness to jump up and into the cage on the back of the Safari jeep.

'Is she drugged?' Kissi wondered.

'Probably as quietly stunned as the rest of us,' Jos said. She was just looking around for Beola, when she appeared carrying a big bowl of sloshing water.

'She should drink before you leave,' Beola handed Kissi the bowl. 'It's getting hot.'

Kissi looked to where he knew the mountain was. 'There will be a storm later.' He then pushed the bowl of water into the cage, and they all watched the lioness drink her fill. When she then settled down, Kissi removed the bowl, closed the cage and pulled the cover over it. He then got into the cab to radio it in.

He was sorry to have gone AWOL but had received a call from the rangers looking after the estate near his home. They were tracking a lioness and wondered if she might be the one missing from the park. Kissi had been so concerned for the safety of his family he'd hurried to meet these rangers and together they had successfully tracked and recaptured the animal. There was little doubt in his mind that she was the animal missing from the Mandara pride as she lacked any tail end tuft. Kissi was leaving immediately to drive back to the park with her.

When he got back out the cab, Jos asked, 'Who are the rangers around here?'

'Me and my son,' he winked. 'Unofficially, of course.'

Rolling her eyes, she said, 'Of course.'

'What happened, Jos?'

'Jude came, she stole Ben's gun from the…'

Kissi couldn't believe he'd been so stupid. 'I am such a fool!' he declared.

'For all the good that did Jude,' Jos pointed out. 'Death by lion. Trust me… she deserved it.'

Kissi would have to wait until later for the full story. Right then he had to get the animal back to the park. He headed off then, making for Mweka Gate which was closest to where the lioness' pride could often be spotted around Mandara Camp.

Wendell followed close behind with Nalutuesha in the back and Jos in the front. Joseph would stay with Beola and look after her as well as the warrior's weapons which his tourist persona was not allowed to carry into the park.

Peter would remain at the white house too, because Jos wanted to feel the unadulterated effects of disappearing Jude without a trace. The only way she could be sure her feelings and thoughts surrounding this deed were one hundred percent her own, was to separate herself from Peter and also shut down the part of her mind that harboured his memories and experiences. Achievable, because Jos was getting better and better at recognising where she ended, and he began. It would be easy to hide behind him for this part of their crime, but she wanted to be better than that. She wanted to take on the responsibility and own it, because that was what everyone else would have to do. Especially Wendell.

The Maasai lived by their own code of conduct, and they had been living with their connection to Peter and his revenge plans for many years. They were part of it, beginning, middle and end. The Nyerere's were protected as best could be achieved after Beola refused to leave the white house. She had remained, she'd witnessed, and she'd helped clean up at her own volition. It was now up to Beola how she dealt with it.

Wendell was as up to his neck in it as Jos was.

Their involvement was calculated, and their fore knowledge comprehensive. Maybe he'd allowed himself to be drawn in because he fancied Jos a little, or maybe he simply wanted to see Peter have his justice? It didn't matter. What mattered was the fact he would have to live with this day for the rest of his life and so Jos would live there with him. They would be each other's one person in the world they could confide in, and they'd already exchanged contact details.

When their convoy of two reached the A23, Kissi turned right, and Wendell left.

Forty minutes later, as they were approaching the Machame Gate, Wendell suddenly declared, 'Shit! I didn't bring cash.'

Jos dug into her shorts side pocket and produced an envelope stuffed with dollars. 'Take what you need.'

The gate staff were busy checking trekkers out as well as a large tourist party in. Wendell just caught a familiar eye and waved the cash. A short game drive, two passengers. No Ben today… he was out on a date. A storm was coming, maybe two hours and they would certainly take care. His radio was indeed fully charged. A quick form to fill in, and he was back in the Land Rover being waved through. Wendell just wanted to get on to the next bit then, but he was only able to do a top speed of around fifteen miles an hour. Any faster and the other drivers would suspect they knew something and might follow in the hope they would be led to a herd of elephant or even a pride of lions.

Jos tried to play the tourist, in the back by then with her rock'n'roll companion and taking photos. She took more photos of Nalutuesha than anything else because he was loving it;

sunglasses on, sunglasses off. Hat on, hat off. Hat back on in a hurry because his beaded hair might blow their cover.

When they emerged from the rainforest, they could see the brooding sky pressing down on the mountain top. As they began the climb up into the heathlands the messages came in over the radio; a general warning to everyone in the park that it was time. Time to seek shelter, or time to leave. As the first raindrops began to fall, Wendell stopped, and they all helped get the canvas sides on.

Then they set off again, still climbing. Twice they encountered other vehicles, and twice they were challenged on why they were not heading back down. Twice Wendell introduced Jos as a student meteorologist who was in the park to study weather patterns. Twice his explanation was accepted.

'If they ever ask questions we're buggered,' Jos told him.

'Just tell them you're doing your thesis on the eco-meteorological characteristics of the southern slopes of Mount Kilimanjaro. Spatial patterns of ambient air temperature play a major role.'

'They do?' 'They do.'

The rain soon got so heavy it was almost impossible to drive. The thunder and lightning were ear splitting and spectacular. If Joseph had been there, he'd have recognised this tempest, and known it would not travel far. This was the same kind of storm the old laibon summoned the night after Peter died; a storm to obscure, and to dissuade outsiders from what was going on within it.

All Jos and Wendell knew, was that they soon had that stretch of the mountain to themselves. To avoid any awkward questions later, Wendell placed a radio call to the rangers when he felt they were near their destination. They were above 3000m and would stay put until the storm passed or eased. The rangers accepted all of this at face value because Wendell was an experienced part of the scenery by then. They would pass this message along to Machame Gate and no one there would wonder where Red Earth Tours were, or what had happened to them. At least for the next few hours.

'Now I have to get out,' he told Jos and Nalutuesha. 'I'm gonna have to attract their attention.' Then he was gone, running low towards some rocks. Climbing up to the highest safe point he had a good look around for any signs of trekkers or vehicles. Seeing none, he did a few practise turns of a call that Ben was really good at and had been trying to teach Wendell. It nearly always worked when Ben did it, calling out a few predators for the tourists to get a better look at on those days when the drives didn't turn up any of the more celebrated creatures. No one thought they wanted to see a hyena, until Ben got to talking about his beloved dogs. He'd taught Wendell how to make a pretty good call for reinforcements and he began to do that then. A long low sound that ended in a much higher pitched whoop. Over and over, he whooped, pausing every few times to shake the rain from his hair and wipe it away from his eyes. He couldn't have got any wetter if he'd been standing under his shower, but he kept on whooping and eventually his efforts were rewarded.

A curious female arrived, closely followed by another.

As soon as they arrived, Wendell went back to the Land Rover and found Nalutuesha and Jos already at work.

Jos didn't think about what she was doing at all. She'd just waited until Nalutuesha told her it was time, and they'd jumped down from the Land Rover into the rain. Like Wendell, they took a few moments to look around and, seeing nothing and no one, they got to work. They manoeuvred Jude's wrapped body out from under the seats, and onto the floor between. They then removed the blue curtain.

That was when Wendell came back. 'Get in the front,' he told Jos, and when she opened her mouth to protest, he shouted at her, 'Now!' A little shocked, Jos did as she was told.

Wendell and Nalutuesha then carried the body towards the rocks he'd stood upon, and then around to where he'd seen the hyena arrive. There was no sign of them by then, but they wouldn't have gone far. They would be watching still. As the two men removed the shroud from Jude's body, Wendell hesitated, looking at her. He had barely glanced at her before when she was lying on the porch. Now she was there in front of him, damaged and broken. He was about to dump her body. Was this what he'd become? Covering up a crime? A murder. The fact that Jude had been the killer back then and had proved to be a dangerous woman that same morning was cold comfort. Looking at the warrior, he asked, 'Are we doing the right thing here?'

'Predator burial,' Nalutuesha told him. 'If that is good enough for my Maasai brothers and sisters, then it is good enough for this woman.' When she was exposed and soaked under the rain, he asked, 'Do you have a knife?' But Wendell was still staring down at the body, shaking his head slowly. 'Do you have a knife?' Nalutuesha shouted to get through to him.

Fumbling in a pocket, Wendell produced a Gerber with a small blade. 'Just this.'

Nalutuesha took it. 'Go back now, start the engine.' As soon as Wendell was on his way, he cut deep into the upper abdomen and made a downward cut. The dead do not bleed, so he pressed and kneaded the belly until the wound was oozing. He then smeared the blood over her skin. The rain washed it away as fast his hands could spread it, but the scent was spreading too. That done, he stood up and began to make the same whooping sounds of a hyena calling for reinforcements. Much better even than Ben, and they came quickly. He saw two dogs clearly, and knew there were others close by, because he heard their giggling voices communicating with each other.

Satisfied, the warrior headed back to the vehicle and jumped in.

Wendell moved off, but not too far. They had to make sure. Jos didn't want to see at all but made herself watch the start of it because this was her idea. As soon as the question of what to do with the body came up, she recalled Ben's gruesome tales of hyena and how they could disappear an adult zebra in less than half an hour. It seemed like a great idea at the time. But watching such an event… knowing the meal personally as it were, was almost as hard as listening to Jude's screams when she thought she was food for the lioness.

At first it was a single hyena, hesitant, curious, sniffing, stopping to look around. Her thick, spotted coat dripping in the pelting rain, her stubby tail wagging. Soon she was joined by another, and another. They greeted one another with yelps and nips. Jos was stuck between wishing they would get on with it, and horror of knowing that her Auntie Jude was about to be ripped apart by a pack of hyenas.

When they finally began to eat, Jos opened the door of the Land Rover to throw up. She had eaten nothing since a slice of toast early that morning and had nothing to give except the stomach cramping exertion of dry heaving, over and over.

Wendell had his head resting on the steering wheel, unable to look, unable to offer any comfort to Jos.

Nalutuesha watched for them all.

One became two, became four, became nine, became sixteen dogs. They snarled and snapped at one another, staking their claims and asserting the hierarchy. But they were soon also working together. They ripped into the body first, feasting fast on the organs and entrails, their snouts quickly becoming red and slimy. Then they pulled the body apart, tugging on the limbs until they were torn and shredded, consumed in great lumps. Bones were crushed between powerful jaws. Quick work was made too of the skull. In less than twenty minutes there was just a few lumps of bone and flesh being cleaned up by the late arrivals to the feast. Even the red mess was washing away in the rain. Satisfied, he told Wendell, 'We can go now.'

*

When Jos got back to the white house, she thought it was over. In her mind she was retreating to the sanctuary of the garden room where she would shower and then curl up on the bed to sleep. Peter could help her to do that at least. Then, when she'd regained some of the energy this day had sucked from her already, she would be strong enough to face the family.

But Joseph was waiting for her, and he had the third and final secret to reveal.

'Peter's bones are buried here,' he told her. 'To free him you must remove his bones and take them away from the estate.'

Jos sank down onto the floor of the porch, physically and mentally exhausted. 'Does it have to be now?'

'Yes,' Joseph told her. 'The circle must be made to close, so he as well as the old laibon can end their journeys.'

'But he was here…' Jos protested. 'The old man… he left with the little cats. I saw him.'

'He freed their spirits, then he made the storm upon the mountain for you. Now he must be allowed to end his journey once and for all. He cannot go until Peter is free. They are bonded too tightly.'

Wendell had been standing by, listening. He went to Jos then, reached a hand down to her. When she looked at him, he said, 'I'll help you.'

Accepting Wendell's hand as well as his offer, Jos got up onto her feet. She asked Joseph, 'Where are they?'

'Under the statue. But Jos… you must do this alone. You are bonded as tightly to the laibon as you are to Peter.' Taking her hand, he indicated where the scar was barely visible by then. 'You are bonded with him in blood. You must remove the bones yourself, and you must lay them to rest yourself.'

'You remember I can't drive, right?' Jos wondered.

'Wendell can drive you if he wishes,' Joseph conceded. He then looked to where Lulu lay looking up at the sky, then he led Jos across the lawn to the head end of the bronze statue. 'We must push,' he said.

Wendell joined them and then he, Jos and Joseph all pushed until the top of the plinth Lulu lay upon began to pivot on the single nipple that Ben had wondered about all those years ago. When they were done, Lulu lay across the bottom of the plinth, making it a T shape.

Jos looked inside, but all she saw was bare earth.

'You must dig.' Joseph said.

'Not yet.' And with that Jos turned and ran for the white house. 'Peter!' she cried. 'Peter!' She ran through the foyer, past Beola and Kissi and Ben who were all seated on the stairs. 'Peter!' She ran out onto the patio and up to the garden. He was waiting for her there. 'No…' she told him, sobbing by then. 'I don't want to lose you. I can't do this without you.'

'I don't want to go, Jos…' Peter felt as distressed, but he hid it well. 'I can't stay here forever. There's a danger in that, you see. If I don't let myself go when the magic is broken, then I might never be able to leave. I would remain here forever, I would become ancient, destructive, dark. That isn't me,' he paused, looking deep into Jos' green eyes. 'I love you, Jos, and I will forever be in your debt. Let me go.'

'I don't believe you. You don't want to go.'

'No, I don't,' he admitted. 'These last few days have been…' He searched for the right words and then laughed when he realised. 'It's been fun, Jos… who imagined being dead could be such fun.'

'Don't do this to me, Peter. I've been so unhappy for so long, and then I found you and you gave me back my life. I can't lose you. I can't do any of it without you.'

*

Jos was gone for a long time. The sun went down, and darkness rose up to surround the white house. A frugal meal was prepared and eaten. Voices spoke rarely and only in hushed tones. When she eventually came back downstairs, Jos was silent and red eyed, still wearing the clothes she'd had on all that day, still damp from the storm. She was carrying the sharp bladed trowel that Jude had left behind.

'Are you okay?' Wendell asked.

'No,' she told him softly. 'But I know it has to be done.' Without another word she went outside, walked across the front lawn and climbed inside the void previously covered by the plinth. Getting down onto her knees she began to dig. It didn't take long. It was a shallow grave, and Peter's bones were contained inside a tightly wrapped, black and red checked shuka. When she was done, she carried his still wrapped remains to the Red Earth Tours Land Rover, placed the bundle gently on the long back seat, and sat down with them. Joseph and Nalutuesha joined her.

Wendell got in the front and started the engine.

Beola, Kissi and Ben stood silently on the porch, and watched the Land Rover drive away.

Wendell followed Joseph's directions, taking the same route Peter had taken Jos less than a week previously. They went back to Joseph's village, and Jos carried Peter's bones to the same place the laibon had lain during the first few hours of his predator burial. His bones were scattered now, far and wide. No trace. Wendell went with her, using a torch to light her way. Looking for a fallen tree that was Joseph's designated landmark. When he found it, he spoke to Jos, told her they could stop now. He swept the torchlight across the ground before their feet. Nothing but tufts of grasses, stones and dirt.

An unremarkable patch of the Earth, where Jos gently laid down the bones of a remarkable man. Undoing the shroud to expose them and shocked to see the blackened, stained state of them. It was the site of this obvious abuse that sealed Jos off from any possible guilt revolving around the part she played in Jude's violent end.

There was nothing left to say, nothing else to do, and so Jos turned and walked silently back to the village with Wendell Cooper.

It was done.

FINALLY

On Monday morning, Jos disembarked at Heathrow at six thirty a.m. after another first-class night flight. There had been no Richard Isherwood to keep her company, no giggling, no quaffing champagne, no five-course dinner. She hadn't even looked at the goody bag. Had she slept? Maybe? She had lain in the dark, pretending to sleep her way through the entire flight and perhaps she had slept for some of the time. Her thoughts, her dreams, all seemed interchangeable these days. When breakfast was offered prior to landing she had fruit and coffee.

Knowing she wouldn't want to be bothered with her supersized suitcase, Jos had simply packed it full of her belongings and left it in the white house cellar beside Peter's things. Everything that had belonged to Jude that was combustible, Jos had burned before leaving. For the time being, she had only the essentials stowed inside the big Fendi bag so, while others went off to collect their luggage, she wrapped her pink and blue shuka around her shoulders and strolled on through customs and into arrivals.

There was Gary Preston as promised. A bearded man, wearing jeans and a Placebo tour T-shirt. She went right up to him. 'Hey, Gary. Thanks for meeting me this early.'

'Jos!' She'd caught him by surprise because her hair was plaited tight down her back and her red head was covered by a battered old Tilly hat, he was pretty sure had belonged to Peter. Taking her hand in both of his own, he smiled and said, 'I had to get up before going to bed. But it was worth it to meet you at last.' She smiled, but her green eyes were sad. 'No luggage?' 'Not today.'

'Hungry?' he wondered. 'I know a place we can have breakfast before heading in to Bath.'

The place was a greasy spoon café just off junction seventeen of the M4. Two hours had passed by then and, as soon as Jos caught the scent of the frying bacon, she discovered she was ravenous. Two of everything the full English had to offer, with giant mugs of steaming, instant coffee on the side. Heaven on a plate.

They talked about Peter as they ate, about how he and Gary had been pals from the day they met at nursery school, because Gary wet himself and Peter helped cover up this embarrassing mishap by filling a bowl with water from the little fish pond and throwing it all over Gary. Poor Peter had to sit on the naughty step for an hour after that, but no one ever found out his friend had wet himself.

'How much do you know about the way Peter did business?' Gary asked eventually.

'Everything,' Jos told him. 'We had a symbiotic thing going on in the white house. I knew about your embarrassing mishap. I also know you have a wife called Marnie and a son called Fraser. I even know Astrid's phone number. I'd like to meet her.'

'She's not the easiest person to get hold of.' 'I can wait,' Jos said.

Before setting off again, Jos remembered to switch her phone on. A message from Wendell giving her a row for leaving him that envelope stuffed with all Jude's dollars. "Use it to fly your mum over for that visit" she texted back. "I'll check (winking face)." Her first good deed.

*

George Trevelyan was the most senior partner in the law firm. He read Peter's most recent will over carefully and had another senior partner confirm with him that the document was valid. He then produced a document for Gary to sign. A statement that he understood he was signing all his assets over to Miss Ferguson, effective immediately. Gary signed it, in addition to the very similar statement he'd signed years ago, because the lawyers wanted it like that.

Satisfied that everything was legal and binding, Trevelyan said, 'May I congratulate you, Miss Ferguson? You are now a very wealthy young woman.' He then gave her the bullet points. Liquid assets amounting to two point seven billion pounds sterling. Fixed assets valued somewhere in the region of fifteen million. The estate in Wiltshire, properties in California and in the south of France. All furnishings, art works, and any and all personal belongings within were property of her estate. The property in Edinburgh, Scotland, another in Mollendal, Norway, and of course the estate in Moshi Urban, Tanzania, would remain the exclusive tenancies of Judith Sinclair, Astrid Sinclair and Beola and Kissiri Nyerere, respectively. At their deaths, each property would return to her estate. There were gold deposits valued at a further six million, and a stocks and shares portfolio which, at the close of business in the previous twenty-four hours, was valued at just over one hundred million pounds sterling. 'Please understand that these are all capital assets…' Trevelyan told Jos. '… belonging to the business. Peter's father, Jonathan Sinclair, set his estate up as a business for tax reasons. Peter carried on in this manner, and so too has Gary. We strongly advise you to continue in this manner, Miss Ferguson…'

'I'll explain everything,' Gary said. 'Once she's had a chance to digest the numbers.'

Jos understood those tax reasons inside out, but she hadn't seen the numbers coming. Peter may have known his net worth when he died, but he had no idea how much his fortune had grown since. Jos just sat there, stunned, trying to get her head around being a billionaire.

'Of course,' Trevelyan went on. 'We do hope you'll consider retaining our services, Miss Ferguson. We've been looking after the estate since nineteen fifty-eight…'

The lawyer droned on and on for what seemed like hours, and Jos had an endless parade of documents to sign. Banking details to submit. Contact details. Finally, the lawyer handed her a jiffy bag.

He said, 'There's fifty thousand in there to be getting along with. It'll take twenty-four to forty-eight hours to handle all the transfers of control.' Looking at his watch, he added, 'Shall we say midday on Wednesday. Everything will be finalised by then.'

Digging into her bag again, Jos took out a slip of paper with Richard Isherwood's money raising details. Handing it to the lawyer she said, 'This man is my friend. I checked on the way here and he needs just over thirtyfour thousand quid to fulfil a million. Would you please see to it that he reaches the million mark today?'

‘Of course.’

Second good deed.

When she and Gary stepped out into the cool September sunshine, Jos said, ‘Fuck me sideways, I’m a billionaire.’ Then she covered her mouth, laughing, before adding, ‘And I’m not allowed to swear.’

‘Peter always hated swearing,’ Gary laughed.

*

In a very nice wine bar by the river, Gary talked Jos through some of the other stuff she needed to know. ‘I was always a geek,’ he said. ‘And Peter was always into playing the stock markets. When the internet was invented, he knew how trading would start to work online and he asked me to write an algorithm that would do the trading for him. Fast forward a few decades and we had Method of Algorithmic Management of Money and Assets… MAMMA for short. Peter always referred to it as Mother and, for reasons known only to himself, when the time came to give Mother a voice, Peter insisted it was male. So, Mother still makes the money and I tried to keep spending it while waiting for you, but I haven’t spent much really. Mother now finds ways to hide the money. Switzerland, Samoa, Liechtenstein, Cayman Islands, British Virgin Islands, you have money all over the planet, Jos. It needs spending on the good stuff.’

‘For Peter,’ she toasted, and Gary clinked her glass. ‘Will you stay on?’ she wondered. ‘I don’t know the first thing about computers.’

‘I’d love to. Saves me trying to find another job,’ rolling his eyes, he added, ‘Not so easy at my age. Would you like to meet Mother today?’ He checked his watch. ‘We’d just about have time…’

‘Soon.’ Jos told him. ‘I really can’t think much beyond getting back to Edinburgh.’

*

It was windy and it was raining in Edinburgh.

Jos hadn't been sure whether or not she'd chance it, but the weather talked her into it. She took out the paperwork for Jude's Lexus and made her way to the premium long stay car park office. They simply glanced at the paperwork, had her sign another piece of paper and then the receptionist directed one of her colleagues to escort Mrs Sinclair to her car.

Jos thanked him and tipped him, and then she got in. It took her a few moments to engage the Peter Sinclair memorial part of her brain, but she was soon keying the ignition, and reversing the car out of the bay so she could follow the exit signs.

In less than an hour she was keying the remote on the dash to open the electronic gates and then she was entering The Grange house through the boot room. Inside the house, she called out for Imelda and Nicolae, the only two cats she'd not seen trotting off after the old laibon. The house was deathly silent, dark. Jos switched on lights and called again. Eventually she heard a mew and turned around to find old Imelda peeping out from behind the kitchen door.

'Imelda!' Jos knelt on the floor to greet her. 'I'm so glad to see you.'

The little cat was obviously pleased to see her too. 'Where's Nico, Immie?' Imelda led Jos to the utility room.

Jos could see the kibble strewn floor, the dish of water under the dripping tap. 'Bitch,' Jos said. But Imelda was sitting on the chest freezer and pawing at the lid. Jos opened it and a sob escaped her throat as she lifted frozen Joe out inside the carrier. 'Oh my God!' Jos was horrified. How could you, Jude?'

Imelda was fussing again, and Jos was almost afraid to follow her. The cat exited through the cat flap, and Jos opened the door, grabbing a torch as she went, and followed the cat into the garden. The folded table. The rocks. The pile of sodden dirt.

Removing the rocks, Jos lifted the table and peered inside. The smell was sweet and cloying, the maggots abundant. Crouched down on the earth next to Imelda Jos cried for all the little cats, for their sacrifice and their bravery. It was dark and wet and cold, and she couldn't deal with Jude's mass grave that night. Couldn't deal with frozen Joe either. It would all wait for tomorrow. She had to find Nico and make him and Imelda a slap-up dinner.

But old Nicolae was nowhere to be found.

It was unlikely he'd returned to a life on the streets, so Jos assumed he'd been sacrificed along with all the rest. She didn't understand why he was the only one who hadn't joined her in Africa to play his part in the conspiracy against Jude. Perhaps she would never know. Imelda was the lone survivor, sitting on the kitchen window sill, hungry for something more appetising than dry kibbles scavenged off the floor.

Jos found a whole trout in the kitchen freezer, which she wrapped in foil and stuck in the oven. While it was cooking, she stroked and groomed and made as much fuss of Imelda as she dared. The cat looked as thin as she was old, and Jos was almost afraid to hold her for fear of breaking her.

When the trout was done, Jos shredded it and dished some up. The little black and white cat purred loudly as she tucked in. Jos smiled a little, watching Imelda eat, thinking she should take her to the vet in the morning for a check-up. Once Imelda was curled up on the sofa with a fat belly full of trout, Jos made herself cheddar cheese on toast and savoured every single bite. Then she went to bed, taking Imelda with her so they could dream together. It was barely nine p.m. in Edinburgh, but it was eleven p.m. in Africa, and it had been a very long day.

When Jos wakened up next morning Imelda was still curled up beside her, but the little black and white cat was dead. Jos felt like her heart was breaking as she hugged the still warm cat, chastising herself for not calling the vet last night. But it was pointless fretting over what might have been. It was what it was, and she would just have to deal with it. Carrying Imelda down to the utility room, she fetched two towels. The first she wrapped Imelda inside. The second was for Joe.

In the garden she placed the little bundles inside the grave with their little friends. Hopefully, they could all be together somewhere beyond the dreadful place they now shared in this life.

After filling the grave in, Jos cleaned up and walked along to Morningside. It was a cold but sunny morning, the traffic bumper to bumper on the main road. She visited a little shop on Holy Corner where she bought a Rose of Sharon shrub. She also called in to a few of the other shops, buying fresh ingredients to prepare a meal.

Taking it all straight home, she planted the Rose of Sharon on top of the feline grave. A reminder of their presence and their sacrifice at Jude's bloody hands. Jos vowed always to remember their names, their colours, and all their little habits.

It was early afternoon by then, and she was hungry. But, before making her meal, Jos decided to act upon her latest decision. There was nothing left in Edinburgh now. She could go anywhere in the world but, for now, Jos wanted family around her. So, she picked up the phone and dialled. Waited.

When Beola answered, Jos asked, 'Can I come back to the white house?'

'Oh, my darling, of course you can. Just let me know when, and Ben and Wendell will bring you home.'

In the kitchen soon after, Jos prepared a lunch of fiskesuppe; a Norwegian cod and root vegetable chowder.

Just like Astrid used to make.

THE END

Turn the page for the first chapter of Making Sacrifices, a second novel by Bev Harris

CHAPTER ONE

Isaac Saddler pulled into the first available "permit holder's" space at the bottom of the walled rectangle of public gardens forming the centre of Gayfield Square. Surrounded on three sides by nineteenth century town houses and tall tenements, the mature elm, birch, and sycamore trees set within its low walls, easily matched even the tallest buildings in terms of height. The fourth side of the square bordered busy Elm Row at the very top of Leith Walk. This was the edge of the city centre. Bus lanes and taxi ranks. Shops, theatres, and cinemas. Museums and art galleries. Pubs, clubs, and restaurants. Everything central Edinburgh had to offer, within easy walking distance.

Isaac loved living at the bottom of what was really a rectangle but supposed Gayfield Rectangle just didn't have the same ring to it as Gayfield Square. It was just that little bit pulled back from the bustle, hidden behind all those lovely trees that not only blocked out the main road view, but also soundproofed against much of the traffic noise. There was also a police station. Built in the sixties, it stood out like a bit of a sore thumb amongst all that architectural grandeur, but the trees mostly hid it from Isaac's lofty views.

He was on his way up there by then, carrying his weekly shop up four flights of well-worn stone steps towards his top floor flat, blissfully unaware that the BBC was about to drop a bombshell onto his blond head.

A tall and attractive young man, Isaac was also quite a shy guy. A bit of a geek in historical terms and a talented artist, he was soft spoken, with a mild West Country accent, diluted by the fact he hadn't lived there in years. As soon as he was inside his flat, he kicked off the black leather flip flops he'd worn for his shopping trip, then went straight into the kitchen and began putting his groceries away.

The flat was on the large side, and full of light, thanks to its tall windows. Views across the treetops to the front, and all the way to the old observatory on the top of Calton Hill. The rear views were cut off by the tenements on East London Street. There was a lovely garden to the back of the building, but ground level was two floors below street level on that side, and Isaac hadn't ventured all the way down there since the day he moved in. That was two years ago, and right before he started his current job.

Employed as resident artist within The Scottish Heritage Centre, Isaac also had a first-class degree in ancient history, so the job suited him perfectly. Of course, he hoped to get a job that made full use of his qualifications eventually but was very happy working in the heritage centre surrounded by all the Scottish history he got to tinker with on a daily basis. It was a great place to work, the pay wasn't bad, and he had some wonderful colleagues… but more about that later.

Unassuming and mild-mannered maybe, but Isaac had a pretty big secret as well as a truly dodgy past. A previous life that had given rise to a whole universe of creativity inside his head. He often thought of this as his affair with insanity, and it was this brush with madness that was about to rise up and knock him sideways.

It was just an ordinary Saturday, mid-September. The sun was shining, Isaac had the whole weekend off, and was going to a barbeque later. First, he had chores to do. After stashing his shopping, he poured himself a cranberry juice and went into the sitting room where he switched on the TV mounted above the fireplace. He wasn't in the mood for music and, with nothing interesting on, he settled for the news. A *BBC News 24* anchor was introducing the latest update surrounding the discovery of a body in a car, in a field, somewhere near Nottingham. A suspected suicide, and relatives were yet to be informed. Sad, but wasn't everything newsworthy these days?

Leaving the room, Isaac went next door into his bedroom. Having stripped the bed before heading out for the groceries, he quickly remade it again before taking the washed bedding out the machine and stuffing it into the drier. This was all part of his usual Saturday morning ritual. He was back in the kitchen, head in the fridge, wondering what to have for lunch, when he heard the same news anchor say a very familiar name. Curious, Isaac headed back to the sitting room to discover whether his ears had deceived him.

A computer-generated face filled the TV screen… four faces actually, because the same face was repeated four times in a two up, two down grid. One had glossy black hair, the second was a flaming red head, the third was a blonde and the fourth a brunette. The sight stopped Isaac in his tracks, just inside the sitting room doorway. Mouth open. Brain stalled like his feet.

'When Taunton Constabulary mounted this last-ditch effort to identify the woman whose remains were discovered on Exmoor back in April, it's unlikely they expected to be inundated with names…' the anchor voiced in the background. '…but one name in particular is causing a storm on Twitter. Could this really be Vida, Queen of the Vidian Empire? She certainly looks very like her!' Cue an overlay image of Vida lifted from the book. 'Those of you who have read the illustrated novel… or perhaps simply looked at the pictures, will agree that the blonde version is a dead ringer for ultraviolent Vida.' The news anchor's face reappeared, and she smiled at her male colleague who was also now in shot. 'What do you think, Greg… are you a fan?'

'Not me, Betsy, but my sons certainly are.' Greg turned his one hundred watt smile to the camera. 'Not that their mother approves,' he joked. 'But what's a little mass murder between friends when you're a teenage boy with a crush on such a hot and homicidal maniac?'

Isaac was mortified, still open mouthed and still frozen in place as the bulletin panned out. His eyes told him he had indeed been looking at four Vidas. There was of course only one real Vida… she was the blonde one. He should know because he'd created her. The other three Vidas might have been wearing wigs. But his brain refused point blank to indulge such nonsense. It was ridiculous, his rational mind insisted.

A coincidence!

Lots of people had lookalikes.

A whole industry relied upon people who looked like celebrities to turn up at parties and entertain guests. *Vidian* had its own Twitter presence. It wasn't a conversational account. Isaac simply Tweeted things sent to him by his publisher: reviews, articles, and the odd fan photo shared from elsewhere on the net. Fans dressed up like Vida were common place. Some of them went to a lot of trouble and expense, so seeing a Vida lookalike was really nothing new. The dead woman was just someone else who, coincidentally, also looked like Vida.

Only, clearly… his rational mind reminded, the dead woman lived decades before he invented Vida, so surely it was his Vida who looked like the dead woman. Not forgetting… his rational mind was beginning to sound a little smug by then, Vida was born from nightmares, experienced by a man who grew up just a few miles from where the dead woman was found.

How's that for an in your face, class A coincidence?

'But it can't be anything to do with me,' Isaac reminded himself as well as the TV. 'I probably wasn't even born at the time she died. Tak reckons she was in the pool for anything up to forty years.'

Dr Takako Eavenson was one of those wonderful, heritage centre colleagues. Just another nail in the coffin full of coincidences, according to the voice of Isaac's rational mind.

'She's nothing to do with me,' he insisted. 'Vida is just a character in my book.'

Horrified… mostly by how pathetic his voice had just sounded, and yet unable to stop himself, Isaac went online as soon as the news shifted its spotlight elsewhere. He hadn't logged in for days but, when he logged in right then, he discovered more than three thousand notifications. The by then familiar grid of four Vidas was repeated time after time on the feed. Links to Taunton Constabulary were numerous. Missing Persons too. Comments went into the tens of thousands. Everyone wanted to know if Sabine had committed murder.

Sabine was Isaac Saddler's pen name.

Maybe Sabine was psychic? Maybe Sabine should show herself for once and answer some serious questions. Maybe the police should start looking for Sabine? Maybe the police should lock Sabine up and throw away the key! Burn the witch, chanted the usual feminist trolls, given a whole new dimension to their hate.

'Shit,' Isaac sighed, wondering if it was time to retire to an island in the middle of the Pacific.

When his phone began to ring, he knew who it would be. 'Hey, Graeme…' Skyward Independent Publishing was calling. 'I've just seen it on the news.'

‘What’s the story, Isaac?’ Graeme wondered. ‘Anything we need to know?’

‘I’m not a killer, if that’s what you’re implying. Or a dumper of bodies. That woman is nothing to do with me.’ His voice sounded so indignant this time; Isaac nearly laughed.

Graeme did laugh a little, then said, ‘The police could show up here looking for Sabine all the same. What do I tell them?’

‘Whatever you have to. I have nothing to hide.’

‘Except for the fact you’re a bloke.’

‘You told me to use a female name.’

‘Because the feminists would have slathered your bollocks in honey and left you outside a beehive, Isaac. And if the cops let this particular cat out the bag, then you may still find yourself in peril… if there’s anything left to cut off once the investigation is finished with you. Thank Christ for the silver lining.’

‘What silver lining?’

‘This is gonna sell a whole lot of *Vidian*,’ Graeme was a lot more excited by this prospect than he sounded.

Mostly because he was trying not to sound either greedy or disrespectful regarding the dead woman. But any publicity is good publicity, as the saying goes, and this was not simply raising the profile of the book’s main character, it was introducing her to a much wider audience. His usually uninspiring inbox was positively bulging that morning, and more than a few of the emails were from production company lackeys.

‘There might even be a movie,’ said Graeme.

‘Hopefully, they’ll let me watch it in prison, after I go down for a murder I didn’t commit.’

‘Chill out, Isaac. I know you didn’t murder anyone. All I’m really saying is… maybe you need to prepare yourself to be exposed?’

That was the last thing Isaac wanted.

Milton Keynes UK
Ingram Content Group UK Ltd.
UKHW020736101124
450942UK00010B/375

9 781068 514906